EDDA GAIA AND THE ORIGINS OF RAGNAROK

Ether Flows Book Two

RYAN DEBRUYN

ACKNOWLEDGMENTS

In memory of the wonderful fan I never got the pleasure to meet, Christopher 'Sulli' Sullivan.

&

In memory of Bev Miller the mother of the voice of Azrael, Steve Campbell.

PROLOGUE

Silver Spires – Gaia – Raguel

The Cathodiem Guild's city stretched out behind the podium and central square below. The stone towers almost seemed to be made of silver because of the light. Thus, the City's namesake, of the Silver Spires. Raguel approached the podium and looked down the flight of stairs into the gathered students in their white robes. He smiled, recalling standing in a similar space to where they stood now, looking up at the school teachers of Atlantean Academy. Many of those same teachers now wore Gold, White, or Black Robes behind him, tutors and leaders of this growing guild.

The initiates below him could earn the right to wear those same robes but for now, they were fresh, devoid of prejudices— empty vessels ready to be filled by the teachers still at the Atlantean Academy. Raguel's smile broadened. He loved seeing the transformations each member below would undergo. Some would be subtle, and others would be obvious. But each member would return changed. From semester to semester, the Atlantean Academy molded students. He just hoped that this batch would make Cathodiem proud. He pulled his well-creased single page of notes from his ceremonial silver robes' inner pocket and placed the paper on the podium. Raguel knew his speech. He'd done this many times since the guild's creation but, admittedly, that wasn't all that long ago. So he was pragmatic enough to ensure he had a reference. In case…

"Initiates," he began and allowed the stirrings of the crowd to still to silence below him. Ninety-eight pairs of eyes fixated on him. Hope, excitement, fear, and even fervor shone out from them. "I wish to congratulate this year's top one-hundred achievers. Some of you have taken a few years with our guild tutors to get to where you now stand. Others have taken considerably less time…"

He let that sentence hang in the air. The hard workers needed to be reminded of the talented. Not because they were inferior. No. To ensure that they realized that this was just the start of their journey. They'd clawed their way to the bottom of the mountain and now had to begin the true upward ascent. Raguel knew that struggle and hoped they would rise to it—as he had. There was one big difference between his time as a student and now. These young ones had an entire guild behind them. Raguel and the other strong council members behind him had accomplished that.

"With the filling of the moon, your first semester at the academy is approaching, and standing here means you've earned the right to represent Cathodiem. Take its honor with you into the Atlantean Academy's hallowed halls. Do your best during the exams and try to gain the sponsorship of an influential instructor.

"Regardless of your results in the exams, we expect you all to push hard and climb the ranks of students. Bring honor to our guild and strive at every opportunity to demonstrate your skills and those of Cathodiem.

"Keep in touch with your tutors and provide weekly reports of your experiences and lessons. You've all benefited from the lessons Cathodiem gained in this manner and now are the ones who pass more back to your fellow initiates. To our future students!

"Finally, and perhaps most importantly, keep your eyes open for powerful classes or recruits who may wish to join the ranks of Cathodiem. In the past, observant students have even gained the guild a few instructors."

He stepped back and congratulated himself on his segue as a gold-robed woman approached the dais. Dariel was vastly powerful and had once been an instructor within the academy. She was regarded as the most influential council member aside from the guild leader himself. Raguel studied her hard lines as he returned to his own spot. He'd listened to her speech numerous times since she joined and was always impressed by her brusque, no-nonsense delivery. This time though, he tuned it out. She began to describe the exact procedure that each person below would follow over the final few weeks with Cathodiem and before they moved to the school.

He couldn't help being distracted; his mind was elsewhere. This year was special for him in a way. His own daughter Jophiel would be returning to him and—spires willing—be attending the academy. Sometimes a very talented individual was picked from the initiates to perform a mission for the guild. His daughter had been one and while he was proud of that, he was also very happy to have her returning to him. Because of her birth, talent, and devotion to the guild, she had been married off in an alliance. With her guild training and skills, the council had thought that she would be able to gather information on the Tuatha De Danaan guild.

It even worked for a short period, until Ogma, her fiancé, had chosen to land on Tech Duinn! It was a prison planet, and none of their agents had successfully gotten a message off the surface. Or escaped. Raguel had railed against the council to send rescue and had even begun collecting his allies to undertake one himself. But then, just as suddenly as she had vanished, she had contacted the guild again. She was coming home, and Tech Duinn was changed?—destroyed?—out of control?

Her reports were quite strange—even conflicting—and the council eagerly awaited her return to sort out the confusion.

Still, two spots had been left for her and her powerful companion in this year's recruitment class. Raguel couldn't be prouder of his daughter.

The initiates began filing out of the square, and Raguel shook himself. He had missed Dariel dismissing them. The council members present gathered together and walked back into the Prime Tower. The tower itself contained penthouses for each council member. Dedicating two floors of space for each, and three for the guild master at the top. Right now the master was secluded above, working on a breakthrough, so Raguel didn't expect to see him at the meeting.

The building itself was made from white stone, and the tallest structure in the Silver Spires. Inside the building, each wall was painted with scenes ranging from wilderness beauty to that of past wars and heroes. The onyx floor tiles reflected the overhead LED lights and created a stunning contrast to the vivid artistic works.

The council entered the round lift at the center of the tower and the electronics of the lift chose a random meeting room within the building for them to use. This was a security measure Raguel had always felt was overkill, but admitted might be very necessary in the future. The meeting rooms all looked the same, with a large round and golden table in the center, and silver upholstered chairs surrounding it.

Once inside, they all walked over the black onyx tiles and seated themselves based on where Dariel chose to sit. The master's chair was always to her left, and the second vice president left the empty seat and sat to the left of it. Each council member now had a final chance to voice any concerns or change nominations. It rarely happened, but this year was anything but typical...

"Are we sure holding two spots for Jophiel and this vagrant, Azrael, is prudent?" Jerlil spat, his voice deep and tinged with annoyance. Raguel regarded the man coolly. One of Jerlil's branch family members had been excluded and he must owe that family something, because this was the fifth or sixth time

Raguel had heard this argument. Jerlil bringing it up again was redundant, as it had already run its course numerous times. However, his following words were new to Raguel. "With Magnus, the son of Thor, attending this year, we must ensure that our initiates are the very best."

Everyone seemed to sit back in their chairs simultaneously. The name of the most powerful man on the planet had that effect. Thor was even a former student of the headmaster himself! For his son to be attending the school this year—it was terrible news for the prestige of Cathodiem.

Into the shocked silence, Jerlil continued, "I understand holding a spot for Jophiel, as she already passed the exams years ago, but this Azrael isn't even a member of our guild. Allow Carliway to become a student this year instead. He has shown such great promise and has only just received his class. His promise could be as high as Magnus himself!"

Raguel closed his eyes before he rolled them. Jerlil was exaggerating, of course, but Raguel did agree that Azrael was a complete unknown. Still, Raguel was one of the few who also knew that Azrael was a Sovereign Son. Not to mention that Jophiel's reports claimed he was almost solely responsible for the events on Tech Duinn.

Even more shocking, the young man had also just received his class. Raguel cleared his throat and opened his eyes. Still, he couldn't reveal that information at this meeting, but he could give Jerlil hope. "Jophiel should arrive in a few days. I will meet with her and Azrael myself. If he refuses to accept the spot, Carliway shall have it—is that sufficient?"

CHAPTER ONE

A small marble slowly resolved out of the blackness of space. Numerous pinpricks of lights dotted the black canvas behind the growing marble. Azrael felt sweat drip off of his nose and tasted salt as he licked his lips. According to the freighter's itinerary, they would reach Gaia today.

The transport ship couldn't land on Gaia, of course. It was too cumbersome and would instead dock in an orbiting spaceport. Usually, that would have bothered Azrael, but luckily, they had held onto the pirate dropship and would be able to disembark once the freighter reached orbit.

The sphere grew and became shockingly blue with swirls of white. Azrael's eyes flicked over the orb, trying to discern the landmasses, but he couldn't find any. Perhaps there were tiny islands that his eyes couldn't determine from this distance, but the planet appeared to be entirely water from his current vantage.

There was so much water—how was this the most populated planet in the EtherVerse?

Azrael's head tilted as he regarded the growing planet. Not many hominid races lived in water. From his schooling, he could only recall perhaps ten that thrived in a pure water environment. Of course, those creatures weren't native to Gaia.

Right, 'Pangaea.' He had forgotten that Gaia was known for having one massive continent known as Pangaea. If the wispy white formations were clouds, then Azrael still couldn't see anything that looked like a continent. The orb grew ever larger until he was sure that he couldn't see any part of a large landmass.

The planet was relatively large, and the sheer quantity of water was baffling. How had humans become the champions of Gaia? You would think with this quantity of water something like mermen or kappas would have thrived. He continued to hold his sword stance as he considered the planet.

The ship began to circle the planet, and finally, Azrael's eyes found the telltale green of lush wilderness. He continued to study the landmass as more and more of it came into view through the training room's port window. Some cleared areas inside the vast sea of green became apparent. Azrael thought he noticed signs of cities, but not enough for him to believe this was the oldest known Planetary God.

The ship continued to round the planet. As it did, mountain ranges, lakes, rivers, and even metropolises became apparent. Azrael blinked. The landmass was quite easily the size of another Planetary God's entire surface. It was still growing too. He wondered just how big Pangaea was. His schooling claimed it covered nearly two-hundred million square miles, which was about a hundred times the size of the Sovereign Halls, where he had grown up.

Azrael hadn't believed it when he was told, but seeing this continent grow before his eyes, he was starting to. Sweat still dripped down his brow as he moved through kata. A quick internal check told him that the strange buzzing energy he had been feeling grow this entire trip was still there. Whenever he examined the buzzing area with Ether Manipulation, it felt like static; like a shock that numbed his mental feelers and returned a tasteless response. Technically, he was working out specifically to avoid thinking about the growing sensation, but studying the planet had been a good addition.

"Azrael," someone shouted from just over his left shoulder, causing him to jump and spin. Jophiel stood staring at him, her face flushed slightly red. He squinted at her, trying to figure out why she was breathing hard. "I have been calling your name for the last few minutes. Were you asleep on your feet?"

His eye twitched. How had she managed to sneak up on him? This was clear proof that his training was becoming lax. Not only had she snuck up on him, but he hadn't noticed her presence while she was talking to him. Unacceptable. He vowed to never let it happen again.

"Why are you breathing hard and red in the face?" he asked, trying to hide his embarrassment.

"I ran here to find you! We need to get onto the dropship and depart soon. We will be over the Silver Spires in five minutes..." She let the statement hang in the air.

Azrael raised an eyebrow, and her head sunk. She began mumbling, "Are you sure you want to land in El Dorado? In the Silver Spires, you will have the entire Cathodiem guild to help you grow. You will have the full support of the guild behind you—"

Azrael shook his head and interrupted. "I am sure that there are political situations on the planet we are yet unaware of. I think landing in Cathodiem territory could mean any number of things that I am yet unaware, and unprepared for. How long until we are over El Dorado?"

Jophi sighed and shook her head, giving up on the argument they'd discussed numerous times already. "Fifteen minutes. Bat is already at the dropship, running a final check of the systems. Do you have anything in your room that you need to pick up?"

She had clearly not given up on Azrael joining Cathodiem, even though Azrael had been adamant with her for most of the six-month trip. She was persistent, he would give her that, but he was stubborn. He flat out refused to put himself into a subservient position within a guild. The guilds were new and growing fast, but he felt a strong aversion to them. These were the same guilds that had ravished the Sovereign Empire and slaved him out on Tech Duinn. Not the exact same guild, but Azrael couldn't help lumping them all together.

He would take his revenge for his teacher who had died on that planet. He would find out what the guilds' goals were, and he wouldn't give anyone power over him again. If he could help it…

————

A few minutes later, Azrael climbed the gangway onto the dropship. It had cost him extra to transport the vehicle with them, but it would give him additional options once they landed on Gaia. Primarily, a way to leave again. After being trapped on Tech Duinn, he had a bit of a neurosis for an easy way offworld.

He could always sell the ship to recoup that cost once they landed. Still, he doubted he would. For now, he had four hundred crystals left, which was a small fortune. For approximately one hundred crystals a year, an individual or group could live lavishly. That number may increase on Gaia, because of its age and history, so he planned to spend sparingly at first. Once they joined the Adventuring House and got into a good routine, he would have a better idea of what their spending could be. He glanced at Bat, who was pushing buttons and nodding along to sounds that accompanied them.

"Do we have departure confirmation?" Azrael questioned.

"Not yet. I can contact them now and begin plotting a course to El Dorado," Bat squeaked hopefully.

Azrael blinked. Bat was extremely eager to pilot a ship and had been quite vocal about it. Unfortunately, the Batman race used specialized crafts with auditory feedback to help their blind pilots navigate. The pirate slaver dropship wasn't equipped with any of those. "I'm sorry, Bat. We have been over this. Once we are on the planet, we can look into having the modules for

Batmen installed on the ship. Right now, I will have to be the pilot. Jophi, have you informed Cathodiem where to pick you up?"

She stuck her tongue out at him, and he narrowed his eyes. Why would she feel the need to mock him? Sticking your tongue out at someone was a form of mockery, right? He took the strange action as an affirmative and went to sit down in the dropship's captain chair.

He clicked a button, and static greeted him for a moment as he fiddled the knob to the right channel. Once the static shifted to dead air, Azrael pushed the talk button and spoke clearly. "Cussing Parrot, requesting departure from frigate bay four," Azrael said, wincing momentarily at the name the pirates had given their ship.

"Initiating docking procedure and Hephaestus arm. Please stand by," a voice responded over the line. A moment later, the entire ship shook as a massive mechanical arm grabbed it with a vacuum gripper.

Azrael felt weightless as the arm moved them through a door that hissed shut behind them. The outer door opened, exposing the dropship's hull to the coldness of space. A literal chill swept over them, and Azrael clicked a few buttons to fire the engine. The chill was wafted through the cabin for a moment as the air kicked on. The heat from the engaged engines quickly warmed the space, banishing the cold. The Hephaestus arm turned, placing their dropship perpendicular to the freighter.

"Releasing in three, two, one. May the Ether travel with you," the voice said through the radio as the dropship rattled again, this time with the release from the ship. Azrael clicked on three buttons, engaging their own gravity system and pulsing their engines a few times to disengage from the freighter's momentum.

The final button was for tuning the radio again. He looked to Bat. "What is the channel for the port in El Dorado?"

Bat shrugged and pointed at a screen. The screen held four

numbers, which indicated the channel for El Dorado's landing port. Bat probably couldn't read the digital numbers from the flat screen—and he wanted to fly the ship! Azrael rolled his eyes and tuned the radio before looking at Jophi. "Coordinates?"

Jophi looked at her tablet and read. "Thirty-four degrees, thirty-three minutes, eleven seconds north, and eighteen degrees, two minutes, fifty-two seconds east. That's El Dorado. One more time, are you—ahh!"

Azrael punched the throttle and cut her off. He didn't need to listen to her spiel again.

———

"It's one crystal a week to keep your dropship in long term storage, and five crystals a week if you would like to keep it in an active port," a woman with black smears covering most of her body informed Azrael as he disembarked. "The active port will cut down on retrieval time when you need to use it, and comes with maintenance and cleaning."

Azrael brought a hand to his chest, looking around him. As soon as his feet touched down on the solid ground, the static thrum of the energy he had been feeling grow for six months vanished. Almost like it was sucked away through his toes. Had he missed a planet that much? If that was true, and he disliked space travel, it was a weakness that he didn't like. He made a mental note. He needed to work on being better during space travel in the future. He saw a transport slab under his ship and numerous people rushing around the landing zone in his perusal. The woman in front of him made a 'hurry up' gesture.

"And our luggage?" Azrael asked as he focused back on her.

"You can take it with you now, or if informed by the end of the day today, we will send it to a location within El Dorado," the greaser responded quickly, still obviously trying to speed up the transaction.

Azrael chose the long-term storage, and together the group walked out of the honeycomb-like landing port. Immediately outside of the building, Azrael was struck by golden sunlight reflecting off the sandstone bluffs surrounding him. He shaded his eyes and looked at Bat and Jophi.

Bat's ears flicked in many directions, but Jophi was staring to her right. Her mouth was set into a firm line, and she bit at her lip. Azrael followed her gaze to see a group of people standing around a small, sleek aircraft. A man in a silver suit stood near the front, and his smile was unmistakable even at this distance.

Azrael took another look at the surroundings and saw that El Dorado's metropolis was literally carved into the sandstone. He was currently at the bottom of two sheer cliffs. Down the center was a roadway that was bisected by a small river. On each side of the river, entrances pockmarked the walls—each with a sign for the type of shop or building it housed.

El Dorado, one of the only free cities remaining on Gaia...

"That's my father, Raguel," Jophi said, her voice not betraying any emotion. Azrael had already figured that out based on both individuals' shows of emotion; it was a needless thing to say. If it was meant to be a secret, they should have kept their feelings better hidden.

Azrael considered saying goodbye and making his way to the inn he saw a sign for, but a strange feeling in his stomach told him he should at least see Jophi off. This may be the last time he saw her. Together, Jophi, Bat, and Azrael walked over to the small group of people surrounding the vehicle.

"Jophiel, I am so glad you are safe and home again. Are these the two companions you told me about?" Raguel crowed, his voice overly excited. Azrael tensed at the mention of Jophi informing someone about him and Bat. While he knew she acted as a spy for the Cathodiem Guild when she was on Tech Duinn, he had hoped she would stop afterward. Still, Azrael had been very careful with what he revealed to her on the trip because of it.

Jophi showed a strained smile, glancing at Azrael and then back to her father. Her cheeks flushed slightly and she said, "Father, it is good to be home. This is Azrael and Bat. The two companions who helped me escape Tech Duinn. Without them, I would have likely died." Her cheeks grew redder as she seemed lost for words. Then she hurriedly added, "You didn't have to come to escort me yourself!"

"Nonsense. I needed to personally thank these two. I was preparing a trip to Tech Duinn myself when word came of your safe escape. I am far too grateful for their aid to not personally thank them," Raguel responded smoothly. The well-dressed man bowed to Azrael, and only Azrael. His eye twitched again seeing the underlying words Raguel hadn't said. Raguel continued, confirming Azrael's suspicions, "I just want to ensure that the offer has been extended for you to join our guild, young man."

Azrael forced himself not to groan and instead smiled respectfully. "Thank you for the offer. However, Bat and I would like to make a way for ourselves on Gaia and the EtherVerse. Perhaps in the future when we are stronger, we will discuss membership again."

Raguel smiled and shrugged more nonchalantly than a pet cat. "I feel like that might be sooner than you think. I won't keep you, but don't hesitate to contact us if you run into trouble. Jophi, we should be off. There are a lot of preparations to be made."

The confidence with which Raguel stated his proclamation made Azrael shiver. There was quite a bit in that quick statement left unsaid. Hopefully, Azrael wouldn't need to speak to the Cathodiem Guild ever again. Still, something in the man's voice told him there would be many surprises coming...

CHAPTER TWO

Azrael and Bat checked into the hotel that was visible from the port. It wasn't fancy or luxurious, but Azrael hadn't been able to find better than the one crystal a week price for a room with two beds. That price felt astronomical for what they were getting. Already, Azrael would be spending one-hundred and four crystals a year, and that didn't include food. Gaia was far more expensive than other planets, at least according to Azrael's previous schooling. Sharing a room with Bat and his snoring would be a trial, but perhaps if they made enough as adventurers, they could splurge an extra crystal a week for a room each.

The inn itself seemed to have been carved with a pickaxe, at the fastest speed possible. Azrael could even see the places the carver struck the wall, because the impact points were still jagged and chalky white. Clearly this hotel would be considered a hovel. Especially compared to the building they now stood in front of, after stowing their gear and changing.

They were in line at the Adventurer's Hall. The Hall was actually a five-story sandstone dome that was built over the river that bisected two walkways. Boats could pass under it, and likely could dock somewhere beneath, but Azrael couldn't see far enough into the darkness to confirm that. The dome had terraces on each of its five levels and large windows and doors looking out onto them. On the higher terraces, groups of well-dressed and pompous-looking individuals sat around tables eating food and drinking from extravagant chalices. On the lower terraces, armored men and women sat crunching on breads or greasy meats.

As Azrael's studies taught, the Adventurer's Hall had levels of prestige for its members. On the bottom were the working-class adventurers who likely ran dungeons every day and stayed on the lower floors. On the upper floors were likely the representatives of nobles or groups who went into dungeons for prolonged periods of time. This often earned more money but was much riskier as dungeons typically scaled up in difficulty the farther in one went.

Since Bat and Azrael had gotten in line, he had noticed that people were coming and going from the building without the line. What was the line they stood in for then?

Before he could ask a neighbor, someone came out wearing the Hall's yellow uniform and shouted, "All slots before eleven in the morning next Wodensday are booked."

Immediate groans from the line-up followed the announcement.

Azrael looked at Bat, who shrugged. The line quickly dispersed, so Azrael made his way to the desk at the front. Four tellers were cleaning up some equipment from a pop-up table. Azrael approached, and one of the four looked at him. "You can go to the main counter if you want to book a time for a dungeon. This table is only to book the early slots a week from today."

Azrael clicked his tongue. "Sorry, we aren't members of the Adventurer's Hall yet. Where would we go for that?"

The attendant looked over Azrael and Bat's clothing and likely Analyzed their levels as well. His face slowly morphed from curiosity to disdain. "It's five crystals per person to register, or you must be sponsored by a team. It's an additional fifty crystals to create a team. I wouldn't hold out hope of joining today," he said as he squinted at Azrael.

Azrael Analyzed the man in turn.

Gaston Fen
Journeyman-Clerk
Level 44
Health Points: 245 / 245
Skills: 14

Azrael put on a false smile and asked coolly, "What counter would we register to become adventurers, Gaston?"

Something in his tone forced the man's neck to hitch and his head to whip back around. The other clerks peeked at him, but they all ceremoniously dismissed him again. Azrael breathed out through his nose. He hadn't realized that people treating him this way would bother him. He mentally cataloged the clerks' names. Gaston smirked and pointed to a large mahogany counter across the room. The top of the counter was higher than Azrael's head…

Gaston was smirking as they walked away, and Azrael felt his body clench to contain his frustration. He couldn't understand why the clerks would treat him callously on his first day. Wouldn't it be better for the Adventuring Hall to have more members?

The person at the registration desk was more helpful, thankfully. Still, both Bat and Azrael had to crane their necks to look up at her. Despite her being a petite Elf, she was sitting on top of a raised chair and counter that came to Azrael's neck. She signed Azrael up as an adventurer, created a team, and then had Bat join the team to save them five crystals. It only took the better part of half an hour to get everything sorted. Her last question was clearly routine to her as she asked, "Is there anything else I can help you with?"

Bat whispered, "We should sign up for a dungeon if a spot exists."

Azrael nodded, having been thinking along the same lines. The woman heard Bat and gave both of them a strange look. "I can sign you up, certainly..." She shuffled some papers and looked at them again, opening her mouth before closing it. After a time, she stated, "Today, we have spots starting at one in the afternoon for the Labyrinth. Would you like me to sign you up?"

Azrael's interface read eight in the morning, and so he nodded slowly. Something was off about the interaction. The woman seemed to still want to say more, but she signed them up and handed them a writ for the reservation. She then asked again, "Is there anything else I can help you with today?"

They shook their heads and walked away. A few steps in, Azrael blinked as a thought crossed his mind.

Why was there a line-up to sign up for times next week if there were open times today?

He assuaged his inner turmoil considering that someone might have canceled the slot later that day. Adventuring teams did die from time to time, according to his lessons, or got injured. He immediately wanted to go back and ask the receptionist but saw Gaston take over the perch. His jaw clenched, and he resumed his walk out the door. They should get some maps and information on the dungeon anyway. Perhaps the people in the shop could answer the question about the oddity for him. He wasn't about to subject himself and Bat to Gaston again.

———

They arrived at the Northern Dungeon, also known as the Labyrinth, around eleven. The people in the shop had answered their questions to the best of their ability. They explained that after approximately ten in the morning, the chances of entering a dungeon as an adventurer dropped precipitously. They'd further explained that this phenomenon was due to guilds, lords, and other high-ranking individuals being able to line up in their own lines. Essentially, people with power were given priority. That meant that they likely weren't going to get in tonight, but Azrael had stubbornly wanted to see for himself.

He had wanted to know why adventurers were allowed to enter the dungeons at all, if the guilds and powerful people had control?

The surprising and comical answer was rather obvious, as well. The young nobles were often out drinking all night and rarely were awake before ten. After eleven was when the adventuring time slots and organization no longer seemed to matter. Azrael believed this was a new development for two reasons. First, the guilds were a relatively recent addition to the Etherverse. Second, his teachings at the Sovereign Halls had always claimed that the Adventurer's Hall held clout. For the guilds to amass power this quickly and completely overhaul existing systems was exactly what caused the collapse of the Sovereign Empire. For long-standing institutions to be crumbling likely meant the guilds were waging a type of war on the Adventurer's Hall as well.

Azrael wondered what had happened to the powerful adventuring groups that had given the Hall their power in the past. Had they been recruited by guilds? Died or been killed?

Regardless, the situation gave Azrael another reason to dislike the guilds and he stubbornly decided to spend the day waiting in the line for the dungeon. They may not get access to the depths, but he hoped to begin understanding some of the major powers on Gaia through observation.

"What are you doing here?" a Dwarf asked. Azrael knew they were called the Karacy, but everyone just referred to them as Dwarves. In fact, the entire team was made up of the small, burly Dwarves, and Azrael wondered why the question was asked. Maybe the Dwarf thought they were going to try to take their spot?

He chose to tell a bit of a white lie. "We signed up for the slot at one. We're an adventuring team from Karas. Just arrived on Gaia."

Jintel Stonehammer
Journeyman-War Cleric
Level 33
Health Points: 710 / 710
Skills: 12

Jintel likely would have stopped talking to them if he hadn't been the one to initiate it. "You won't get in today," the Dwarf stated, pointing at another line on the other side of the lane. "The all-powerful lords lined up early today. We might not even get in, and we are the eleven. Fragging guilds, and their young members."

"Why hasn't the Adventurer's Hall leaned on the guilds a bit?" Bat squeaked.

The Dwarf looked at him and smiled. "Haven't seen a Batman in a long while. Well met... Bat. Well, the guilds have all the power, don't they! All of the Adventurer's Hall's top members have long since joined a guild for the benefits provided. Gaia is particularly bad, but my guess is that all planets will eventually look like this. Guilds can just offer so much more than the Hall now."

Azrael tilted his head. "Why hasn't the Hall become a guild then?"

"Word is they are working on it, but the Adventuring Hall has always worked off of multiple inputs. Each world runs its own affairs. Last I heard, the appointment of a leader and a council has become ugly. That's why many of the top members left—"

Jintel cut off as the entire other line of ten people were admitted as a single party to the dungeon. Now that the other line was empty, Jintel looked excited. He even went as far as to forcefully mutter, "Alright, hurry up. Let the adventurers in!"

Azrael ran his tongue over his molars. That did explain the fall from power of the Adventurer's Hall. Typically, each planet's Hall was run by the strongest groups on that world. A change in the seniority would leave a great deal of bitterness and quite the power void.

Instead of continuing the conversation, Azrael kept his eyes on the other side of the road. It took a few hours before another group of lords arrived. A large blonde teenager strode up to the guard confidently. "Magnus, from Asgardian Guild. A future student of the academy and son of Thor. I would like to run the Labyrinth today."

A murmur from the adventuring line began. Azrael squinted and attempted to tune his ears to make out the snippets of conversation. "Thor's son... Strongest on Gaia... Magnus will probably be an apprentice of the headmaster, like his father..."

Eventually, he gave up and asked Jintel, "What has the crowd so worked up?"

"Thor is the highest leveled human currently on Gaia. He has two sons, Magnus and Mooi. Magnus is the youngest and is entering the academy after this moon fills. He is currently favored from this year's entrance exams to be chosen as a possible apprentice by the headmaster!"

The way Jintel said 'the headmaster' with near reverence made Azrael ask a follow-up, "And what is so special about the headmaster?"

"All the guilds want to recruit him. He has taught all the strongest students to ever go through the Atlantean Academy. Rumor has it his last student was Thor and he hasn't taken on an apprentice since. Many people claim he can even fly," Jintel answered before turning back to watch Magnus' group be ushered into the dungeon entrance.

"Are students of this academy given special treatment too?" Bat squeaked.

Jintel nodded his head as he continued watching the Asgardian group.

CHAPTER THREE

At around ten thirty, the line for the nobles began to fill. Based on what Azrael had seen, a new team was allowed entrance to the Labyrinth every thirty minutes.

"Troll bogey's, our group isn't going to get in this morning at this rate." Jintel spat.

Four groups had arrived on the adventuring side, seen the state of the line and left again. Even the ten thirty spots in front of Jintel's group hadn't been admitted. Azrael stayed in line for now. Not because he was hoping to get in, but because the interactions in the other line interested him. There was a clear hierarchy that was beginning to form.

"My name is Eiler Sovereign, and I am a member of the Sovereign Guild and a Sovereign Son," a dark-haired young man said as he approached the front. Azrael absentmindedly twisted the signet ring on his finger. The signet ring that still held the note from his father telling him the massive secret about the Sovereign heritage.

Eiler Sovereign
Apprentice-Sovereign

Level 21
Health Points: 160 / 160
Skills: 5

He couldn't see a ring on Eiler. That, combined with how utterly young the child looked, told him that Eiler had never been to the Sovereign Halls. The Hall was on a territory with maxed out growth benefits as well. If Eiler had been there, he wouldn't look like a twelve year old. Everyone knew that every Sovereign Son trained in the Halls—or used to. So, what game was Eiler playing at? He scrutinized his Analyzed information, hoping to prompt Perception and reveal the truth. It didn't, but Bat's Perception was much higher than his.

"What's his actual class and name, Bat?" Azrael whispered.

"Eiler Gall, and he's a Beast Hunter," Bat whispered back. After a moment Bat continued, "Do you plan to use your Sovereign Son status?"

Azrael shook his head and gave Bat a stern look. He should know better than to say that out loud where anyone might hear it.

Azrael looked around but didn't see anyone looking their way. This did give him a unique opportunity to see how a Sovereign Son was treated, and so he watched intently. Eiler definitely had his name written down by the guard. So, theoretically he would be given priority over the adventurers. Still, the looks the guilds and other nobles gave him weren't pretty.

The line almost closed ranks and forced Eiler to the back, which was far different than what had happened when other nobles or guild members gave their names and ranks. In all other cases, some sort of unspoken communication had occurred and a spot would open for the group where the nobles believed they should be. A few times, discussions had broken out and been resolved through some sort of magazine. Azrael had caught the title of the publication, '*Guilds of Gaia*,' and planned to pick it up later that day.

He assumed it had some sort of list contained within that

dictated the power of each guild in comparison to others. In some ways, it was fascinating to watch, but Azrael was currently only hanging out, waiting for a few outliers to arrive. The main question on his mind was where Atlantean Academy students fell on the hierarchy. Mostly because becoming a student seemed like a possibility to anyone of any rank. Or at least that was what the Sovereign Halls had taught. He was glad he had stayed, especially after Eiler's display. He hadn't even known to ask where the Sovereign Guild fell on that list.

I didn't even know my father created a guild...

A few more joined the noble's line before he finally got the answer to his question.

"Erica Gartz, Atlantean Academy student, sponsored by Assistant Dean Mordrid. No official guild membership status," a diminutive woman in white robes said shyly.

Erica Gartz
Journeyman-Priest
Level 14
Health Points: 330 / 330
Skills: 8

Azrael squinted as the people at the front of the line graciously gave their spot to Erica. The body language conveyed was not deference but kindness. His instincts told him that this wasn't specifically the student status of Erica. His gut was telling him that this was because she was a highly sought-after recruit for the guilds.

So, students of the academy could fall anywhere within the political hierarchy depending on their individual status. That also implied that students of the academy were somehow outside of the politics of Gaia. He filed that little tidbit aside for later.

He hadn't seen anyone from Cathodiem join the line and so didn't know where Jophi's guild ranked in the global scheme. He was eager to get his hands on the magazine the nobles kept referring to. If his guess about Erica was correct, students took on the status of the guilds actively trying to recruit them.

Azrael motioned to Bat and together they exited the line. "I want to get my hands on that magazine and discover what time the line-up starts at the Adventuring Hall. The groups, like Jintel's, look to be geared well, and are likely getting access to the dungeon more regularly. And based on the packs of the members, once they get into a Cardinal Dungeon they stay for a few days."

Bat nodded his head in quick motions that made his ears flap around. "I also overheard a few pieces of conversation that confirm your suspicions. The groups I overheard seemed to be planning on staying inside the dungeons for six days. Do you think they take a week off in between each run, though?"

Azrael shook his head. "My guess is that they have a member of the group stay outside and sign them up for the following week. Six days in the dungeon and then one day off before they have a timeslot again."

Bat nodded along with Azrael's logic. It was the way Azrael would do it. That or just give someone a certain percentage of your group's loot from the dungeon run. That would give people incentive at minimal risk to their lives. Not everyone was cut out to be dungeon divers.

———

Azrael and Bat were first in line the next morning. They had taken the initiative and arrived an hour early for the opening of the Adventurer's Hall. The previous night they had discovered it opened at five in the morning.

Azrael yawned. He probably shouldn't have stayed up all night studying the magazine of the Gaian recognized guilds. But he needed to know—his mind needed to find… targets. Targets was the wrong word in some ways. More like strategical advantages or possible paths for them to take on Gaia. For example, Bat and Azrael could join a minor guild and just show up early to run dungeons. In theory, that was an easy solution to the problem, but Azael had a feeling that there was some unspoken rule between the guilds and the Adventurer's Hall. Like a very tremulous handshake that kept the Adventurer's Hall from full blown rebelling against the guild controls.

To his surprise, the top five guilds listed in the magazine included Cathodiem, Tuatha De Danaan, and Asgard, with the latter first amongst them. He had to wonder how powerful the Tuatha were. It had to have been a pretty significant blow when Apep had consumed their planet, but they had only dropped to fifth in the overall rankings. The other two in the top five Azrael didn't know anything about, but assumed the Egyptians and Olympus were quite influential based on the company they were keeping.

Azrael grew more nervous as it grew closer to five in the morning and no other adventurers had shown up. When one finally did arrive at a quarter to the hour, he stopped dead in his tracks and stared at Azrael and Bat already in line.

The creature's look hardened until the Lizardfolk was glaring at them. The slitted eyes and constantly flicking tongue were eerie enough that Azrael used Analyze.

Arza Grarnok
Journeyman-Slitherer
Level 45
Health Points: 1,210 / 1,210
Skills: 14

"What do you two think you're doing?" Arza hissed at them.

Bat's ears folded in half and his shoulders shrank forward. Azrael didn't like seeing his friend cower and squared up to the verbal assailant. "Signing up to run the Western Delving dungeon. Is there a problem?"

"Asss long asss you don't take the earliessst ssspot for the Bluffsss, we don't have a problem. The Vipersss have firssst priority every Thorsssday!" Arza lisped dismissively.

Azrael immediately realized his mistake. Of course the adventurers would have a hierarchy of some sort. Them being first in line likely would cause problems for whichever group normally booked Thorsday morning for the Delving dungeon.

Still, everyone would likely just get bumped backward on spots until the eleven in the morning group got bumped out, right?

CHAPTER FOUR

Azrael looked over to Bat, who was eating an elephant ear pastry. Azrael shivered and looked away. It reminded him too much of Musth from the Arena Pit on Tech Duinn. He knew this was just a fried piece of dough with jam on it, but the name sent chills down his spine as he pictured the tortured red eyes of the beast.

Bat was also refusing to talk to him, because Azrael had woken him up at four thirty in the morning to get in line. They needed to be first to secure a spot in the Western Delving dungeon, though, for the following week. According to his information, it started with Apprentice-ranked mobs and only escalated to Journeyman at the eleventh level, after the boss on the tenth. Combine that with the safe zone on the fifth level and Azrael thought they could spend six days in the dungeon pretty easily.

Azrael finally looked back to the Lizardfolk. "We are going for the western dungeon," Azrael finally said a bit sheepishly. "I don't think that it's the bluffs."

"It isssn't! I will let the Radiant Rock Eater'sss represssentative deal with you," Arza lisped and then ignored them.

Azrael shook his head and waited as more and more early risers joined the line that was forming in front of the closed doors for the Hall. At around five to the hour, a very well-dressed Dwarf swaggered into the line. The Lizardfolk held up a hand and pointed at Azrael and Bat, indicating them to the individual. A frown instantly crossed onto the Dwarf's face and his walk changed to petulant.

As he approached, Azrael Analyzed him.

Rondo Stonefist
Journeyman-Blacksmith
Level 33
Health Points: 430 / 430
Skills: 12

"Are these two planning on changing the agreement, Arza?" Rondo said to the creepy snake person.

Arza flicked its tongue and nodded. Azrael scanned the line. There were at least ten other people present and waiting for a spot. With four dungeons and spots every thirty minutes starting at six, that meant there were thirty-two places for groups to take. Them taking one of them still left thirty-one.

"Listen, you two, I don't know who you are, but Analyze tells me that you aren't even Journeyman ranks. Perhaps you are here to sign up for another group?"

Azrael shook his head and said, "We are here to sign up for ourselves. We just want to gain some Etherience."

Rondo blinked and his eyes took on a look of pity. "Look, lads, I assume you are new to El Dorado. So I will give you the benefit here and explain this simply. Even if you get into the Delving Dungeon, you really will waste the spot. If you stop to rest anywhere before level fifteen, you will likely die."

"Is that a threat?" Azrael asked. He was confused because of the sympathy in the Dwarf's voice, but could still feel his ire rise due to the threatening message conveyed.

"Well, yes. In some ways, some adventurers, my group

included, will cause trouble. But I would be much more concerned about the lords and young guild members. If you don't have any powerful backers…"

Azrael felt his eyes harden. He still had a set of Ether Tech gear in his Ring of Holding, and his sword. He assumed part of the concern and lack of respect came from their ragged appearance. Still, he despised bullies or people who would try to stop others from gaining strength.

Rondo stepped back from his look and held up two hands. "Just the messenger, lad. Just the messenger—do what you want, but don't expect the Radiant Rock Eaters to take it lying down."

The doors opened and they were first in line. "The six in the morning spot for the Delving dungeon, please," Azrael stated, his voice monotone and cold even to his own ears.

If these people want to act like bullies, I will have no qualms with taking from them.

The line had filled up to about forty or fifty people just as the doors opened and Bat informed Azrael that there were quite a few grumbles about them in particular.

"You are all signed up, is there anything else I can do for you?" the clerk asked.

Thankfully it wasn't Gaston.

"Actually, can you check to see if there are any openings for the other days before ten in the morning?" Azrael asked sheepishly, it would be a long shot but there was a small chance that a group came out injured or died inside the dungeon. That would open up some slots for others who asked.

The clerk actually smiled, which caused goosebumps to form on Azrael's skin and Bat visibly shivered beside him. "There is a spot that just opened. The Cavills have returned with only a single member of their party alive. They had a spot today for seven thirty in the northern dungeon. Would you like me to register your group?"

The Labyrinth dungeon in the north was a really large unknown for Azrael. He hadn't particularly wanted to run it.

Labyrinths were particularly difficult because they had wandering mobs. This could mean that you ran into the highest-level creature right away—or that you never ran into anything. Still, with Bat's skills, that dungeon didn't pose as much of a threat to them.

"Please, mark us down," Azrael responded and looked over to Bat to find his friend's ears drooping open and closed. It was almost like he was sleeping on the spot. Azrael lightly punched his arm and Bat seemed to perk up when he realized they were going to be running a dungeon.

Azrael and Bat practically sprinted from the Adventurer's Hall after that. He hadn't planned on attempting a dungeon today, so now needed to pick up some supplies.

Bat trailed after him and called, "You sure this is a good idea, Azrael? These Cavills were practically wiped out. What if we run into the same creature?"

Azrael slowed down and let Bat draw even with him. "I think with your sonar ability, we will be able to avoid some of the issues. Plus, there are safe zones within the Labyrinth. The information we gathered on the dungeon says those safe zones are marked by small oases. If we are in trouble, we will try to find one. If we don't push ourselves now, we may not be able to overcome the grind and enter the Journeyman ranks."

"Well, what about Jophi? Couldn't we ask her to join?" Bat responded; his blue face was tinged with green. Azrael felt his chest muscles twitch and he wondered if his body was upset at him for not going through his sword katas today.

"She is in another city altogether right now. We have to be in line within the hour!" Azrael responded with some urgency. Azrael considered if they could pick up another fighter for the group, but with their limited time—he wouldn't trust anyone they managed to find. Better to roll the dice a bit. He had confidence that with Bat's skills they could escape danger, at the very least.

"She could probably make it back here with her resources, and even bring some Cathodiem members," Bat grumbled, allowing some of his annoyance with the early morning into his words.

"Bat, if we join a guild, then we inherit all the politics that come with it. We had this discussion when Jophi first made the offer," Azrael responded as they continued to walk through the streets. Bat folded his ears in half, a gesture Azrael recognized as closing his eyes. Azrael shook his head; he understood that Bat liked Jophi. Even he liked Jophi, and if she wasn't mired in the politics of a guild, she would already be here with them.

But Azrael needed to keep growing, to keep increasing his strength. Otherwise, he would likely be forced to join one of the same guilds that had invaded his home. Everything he had seen so far suggested that, on Gaia, the guilds were becoming a structure unto themselves. Each one functioning to protect its members, but also as a hive mind that directed its members to better the guild, not the individual.

Azrael felt his stomach churn whenever he thought on the changes he saw here in El Dorado. Was that same change happening across the entire EtherVerse? His jaw clenched as he fought to wrench his mind off that line of thinking. All he needed was power, right? With power, he could avoid the guilds and politics that came with them.

He needed power so he could destroy the Tuatha and any other guild that had participated in the attacks on the Sovereign Empire.

For now, all he could do was run dungeons and grind for levels. So, to maintain his independence from the guilds, and politics of Gaia, he would first need to learn the ins and outs of this place. The politics of Gaia were a puzzle that he could work within. The guilds were still something new to the Ether-Verse, and with the inherent corruption they seemed to already possess, he believed they wouldn't be more than a flash in the pan in the greater mosaic of history.

CHAPTER FIVE

Inside the shop, numerous wares sat on carved sandstone shelves. The items looked second-hand at best, but this was one of the only shops open at this early hour—at least on the way to the Labyrinth. Azrael scanned the interior of the building from the entryway before making his way to the back of the shop where tents and sleeping bags seemed to be displayed.

"Can I help you with anything?" an air-bleached merman asked from behind the counter. Azrael could hear splashes of water from below the counter whenever the merman moved. In response to the question, he shook his head and pointed to the camping gear, trying to ignore the man. Salesmen were pushy though, and the merman asked a follow up, "Which dungeon you headed into?"

"The Labyrinth dungeon today and the Delving dungeon next week," Bat responded. Azrael gave his friend a withering look and Bat's ears folded down.

"Sorry, Bat. Let's keep information to ourselves. Yeah?" Azrael whispered before glancing at the merman.

"Wow! Really, you two must be extremely strong... Wait, how are you two only Apprentice? Oh, you must be part of a guild, or an adventuring group?! I'm Nethune. It's a pleasure to have such esteemed guests in my shop," Nethune said, answering his own questions, which left Azrael a clear way out of the situation.

Azrael responded with a tight-lipped smile and a nod. After they reached the camping equipment, he pulled the cheapest tent, sleeping bags, and canteens off of the shelves. There was some flint nearby and he grabbed that as well as some dried meats, and a pre-prepped bag of trail rations. Once Bat and Azrael's arms were fully loaded, they approached the counter. Azrael could tell that Nethune was questioning why an influential lord or guild initiate would be purchasing such cheap supplies.

"We'll take this back-up set, and we also need ten Health Potions and Ether Draughts. Something appropriate for apprentice-rank fighters," Azrael stated flatly, hoping his lie about the back-ups would remove the suspicion from Nethune's eyes. It did.

"Ahh, of course, my lord. It's always wise to have a pair of backups. For the potions, do you think Mediocre rank will be sufficient?" Nethune responded, attempting to be as smarmy a salesman as he could.

Azrael just shrugged and put a single crystal on the counter. Nethune studied the crystal under Azrael's finger. After a moment, he said, "I will get you some change, sir."

Good. One of the only problems with allowing someone to think you had powerful backers was that they also assumed deep pockets. Azrael pocketed the two marks and single diamond chip the merchant placed on the counter as change and then made everything vanish into his ring. The look of disappointment on Nethune's face forced Azrael to hide his smile.

They were just turning to leave when the door flew open and banged against the wall. Rondo stepped into the space. He looked at Azrael and Bat, clearly here for them before turning to the merchant. "Morning, Nethune. I'm going to borrow your back room…"

He followed his order by raising an arm to block the swinging doorway, and motioning with his other arm to a second, much smaller, door Azrael didn't take note of when they entered.

Azrael rolled his eyes. "Move, Rondo, we don't have time for this. We have somewhere to be…"

Instead of moving to the back door, Azrael grabbed Bat and walked toward the man. Rondo's confidence seemed to flee his face and he opened and closed his mouth a few times. He dropped his arms in defeat and Azrael's shoulder brushed by him as they drew even.

"Listen, this is a mistake. If you don't relinquish that spot by the end of today, you'll be in trouble."

"How much do you get for signing up the Radiant Rock Eaters once a week?" Azrael countered.

"Two percent of their haul," Rondo said, tilting his head and looking at Azrael who was watching the Dwarf over his shoulder.

"So, perhaps we don't plan to listen to someone on another team's payroll," Azrael said before walking out of the door. He checked the system time and began jogging to make it to the Labyrinth for their time slot.

"You sure that was wise, Azrael?" Bat asked.

"We didn't have time to listen to him. We might get there with about five minutes to spare."

———

Azrael stood in the same adventurer's line they'd occupied yesterday as he studied the Dungeons of El Dorado Guide. They had purchased it yesterday, along with the Guilds of Gaia magazine. Bat and Azrael were at the front of the line waiting for the next entrance time. The book agreed with Azrael's earlier assumptions that the Labyrinth was considered the most dangerous of the four dungeons in El Dorado. It had a few powerful creatures that roamed the depths of the maze and were rarely seen on the peripheries.

He read a part to Bat out loud. "This dungeon offers the best chances for high level loot without high level encounters. Throughout the Labyrinth, chests form randomly. Groups can loot chests without slaying any mobs. The chests have a tiered system and as groups approach the center, there is a higher chance of finding higher tier chests. The tiers are ranked S, A, B, C, and D..."

Bat scratched at an ear. "Azrael. Doesn't that strike you as odd? If chests form, and people primarily stay on the periphery of the dungeon—won't there be a great deal of competition?"

A Naga guard slithered toward them and Azrael studied the creature. It was mostly purple scales and most closely resembled a snake with arms, while simultaneously being nothing like a snake. It only used the last four feet of its tail to move, and the rest of its body was in a perpetual forward lean as it drew even with them. Azrael smiled at the guard. "Good day. We are the seven a.m. group, signed up in the Adventurer's Hall this morning. What time slot are you up to?"

The Naga yawned, which revealed two very sharp canid teeth and square blocky ones everywhere else. The guard looked at the clipboard he held. "You're next and can go in immediately."

The people behind Azrael groaned. What had they been hoping for? That Azrael and Bat were just standing here? He felt his skin flush with excitement! It was their second day and they had already made it into a dungeon. After standing in line observing yesterday, this felt like a huge achievement.

They walked through the guard station and instantly saw the dungeon entrance. It was a huge triangle that jutted from the sandstone tiling of the street. The edges were stylized with images that ranged from a waterfall splashing onto a garden of plants, to a giant Minotaur tearing stick figures in half. He heard Bat gulp beside him as they stepped onto the first sand-stone step in front of them.

Azrael counted ninety-five steps before the stairs flattened out and became a hallway leading to another massive doorway. Two stone slabs with stylized carvings were closed at the end of the passage. Taking a deep breath, Azrael studied them. They looked extremely heavy, but the purchased information claimed touching the stone would open them to a random place in the dungeon's periphery. Did the Labyrinth spin or was this some kind of teleportation gate?

Azrael turned to look at Bat, who was facing him with his ears held fully open. They nodded to each other and touched the door. Blue light sprang up, confirming the teleportation gate and the doors whooshed open. Heavy air that smelled of damp earth assaulted Azrael's nose. They walked into the square room they had been deposited in, and heard a boom behind them as the doors to the Labyrinth closed.

Welcome to the "Labyrinth."
You have entered in a group of two, suggested group size 5-10.
Good luck.
Level: 44
Age: 280,284 Days
Best time: N/A
Clears: 7,134
Ether Concentration: High
To exit the dungeon, you must find exits or leave the way you came in.

He studied the space they were now standing in. The walls were the same sandstone of the city, but with a carving of two lines and crisscrossing x's right at the midpoint between the ten foot high ceiling and floor. Just about at Azrael's eye level, torches hung at regular intervals. These torches weren't on fire and instead contained an amber globe at the top of a carved stone handle. The orb flickered and danced like it contained fire, but Azrael knew it was an enchantment the dungeon was maintaining.

Azrael glanced back and studied the other side of the stylized doors that were still behind him. According to the information guide, this doorway would always remain an exit point for them and them only. Other exits would appear randomly throughout the Labyrinth as they conquered rooms or defeated boss mobs, but only they would see this particular one.

Bat turned his head in all directions, getting his bearings through what Azrael assumed was his sonar ability.

He smiled, feeling that electricity of excitement coursing through his blood—Azrael was finally going to make some progress again. It had been six long months of stagnating while traveling to Gaia.

Bat pointed through the wall to their right. "Over there are some humanoid creatures, which seem to be dungeon Goblins. They're as tall as your waist, with pointed ears. There is a massive chamber filled with groups of them, huts, and what I assume are fire pits." He pointed in the other direction. "And that way there are a great deal of traps that are triggered mechanically."

"Let's go to the chamber with the humanoids. Our goal is Etherience, not loot specifically. Should I wear the Ether Tech set or you?" Azrael responded as he pulled the gear from his ring.

Bat shook his head. "I can't tell what level they are from here. If they're strong, you will need the gear, but dungeon Goblins are rarely powerful. At which point, I would suggest I wear the armor and join you in combat, so I get more Etherience as well."

Azrael nodded. If they were Goblins, that would make sense. He stored the gear again and they crept toward the chamber, Bat directing which turns they needed to take.

Goblin Fighter

Apprentice-Snarler
Level 12
Health Points: 50 / 50
Skills: 3

They were low level Goblins, in groups of three to five. Bat put on the armor and Azrael waded into the creatures.

He used flowing sword forms to tear into them with his Sovereign Blade. Each group only attacked individually, even though their screeching and snarling attacks were loud enough to alert the whole room. This dungeon was using aggro rules, it would seem. Azrael was thrilled by that development. It meant that he could take breaks if his Ether pool got too low.

Speaking of Ether, he hadn't used his Soul Strike yet. He charged a single charge and unleashed it at a pack of the creatures from a distance. The entire group exploded like blood balloons and his skill continued on to wipe out three other groups. Each kill only awarded a small amount of Etherience—essentially a drop of water in an ocean, but it felt good to finally be making progress again.

Azrael poked his head into each hut as they passed and, finding them empty, kicked a burning log into the dried wood structure. The burning of the huts acted as a mark that they had already checked inside.

He also looted each corpse, but got nothing for his trouble. It was a bit discouraging, especially when they were halfway through the room and took a break. He clicked the summary option of his interface and looked at the prompts for his gains so far.

You and your group have killed 121 Goblinoids. This has gained you 3,004 Etherience.

101,321,402 Etherience remaining to level 24.

At this rate, it would be years for him to level. He checked on Bat in the Ether Tech suit of armor. His companion fought through another group of the Goblins. He used Analyze.

Bat
Apprentice-Sonar
Level 22
Health: 150 / 150
Skills: 5

Bat was likely very close to level twenty-three based on the huge windfall of Etherience they got from escaping Tech Duinn, and a strange quest called Releasing the Darkness. Azrael reopened that notification.

Congratulations. You have completed a quest.
God Quest
EtherVerse System Generated
Hidden Quest
Releasing the Darkness
You have helped give birth to an evolved form.
Congratulations, you have discovered a hidden truth
of the EtherVerse.
Rewards:
90,000,000 Etherience.

He closed the quest and shook his head. Whatever had happened in those last moments on Tech Duinn had created something Azrael didn't fully understand. From the massive gravity spike and the huge black spot forming in space, Azrael originally thought that they had destroyed the Planetary God. After reading the quest, it would seem they had created something else entirely.

He waded back into the Goblins, trying not to think about that particular mystery. Still, if he could somehow complete more quests of that scope, he would definitely gain in power. Yet, them escaping Tech Duinn even now seemed like a one in a million chance. So, instead he waded through low-level mobs and burned their huts to the ground, taking the slow and steady approach.

He killed the final creature and kicked a log into the hut. As soon as the fires caught on the hut, with a crackling intensity a notification popped up.

You have decimated the Goblin town within the Labyrinth Dungeon. The progenitor of the Goblin town has been informed of your trespasses!

Simultaneously, a chest rose in the center of the cavern. It was dark brown in color, with coppery metal making up its hinges and edges. According to Azrael's reading, this was a level D in rarity, which meant it wouldn't have extremely rare items inside. Azrael still approached it excitedly. Loot was loot.

"Wait, let me look over it first!" Bat shrieked. Azrael jumped, startled by the shriek of his friend. Then he waited as Bat's cheeks began to grow a darker blue. "It's, umm... all clear," Bat finished lamely.

Azrael laughed and patted him on the back. "I appreciate it, Bat. I wouldn't have opened it myself without checking, but I am glad you checked as well."

Inside the chest was a small, ragged money pouch containing five crystals, two scratched bottles of Weak Antidode, a mottled piece of fabric with tent poles, and one piece of enchanted gear.

Leather Boots of [Locked]
• These boots help the wearer move with improved speed but are graceless.
Enchantments: Locked

He was a bit torn seeing the locked status of the gear. Coming from Tech Duinn where the Tuatha had encouraged killing and raiding—by keeping all gear unlocked—this was slightly frustrating. On the other hand, this did mean that they were on a civilized world that didn't promote murder to steal other individuals' gear or wealth. They could get the gear unlocked when they returned to town, so he put the boots and crystals into his ring, but was forced to place the rest in a canvas bag and begin carrying it on his back.

Bat pointed back the way they had come and said, "A new passage opened up. I can't see far enough down the hallway to tell you where it goes, though. What was that progenitor thing about?"

Azrael shrugged. "No clue. Let's head down the new hallway—we know the other one is just traps, which net us no Etherience."

They walked down the hallway and Azrael scanned for traps even though he knew that Bat would see them far in advance of him. He had to increase his Perception skill somehow. Bat placed a hand on his shoulder a few steps later. "There is a T junction up ahead. One direction will lead to a single large Minotaur, and the other leads to a room filled with spiders."

Strangely Bat's voice came off more excited by the prospect of spiders than the Minotaur. Azrael felt his eyes narrow as he fought a shiver. Spiders were not a good thing! "Let's go toward the Minotaur..."

Bat frowned but directed them down the right passageway. The Minotaur wasn't in a room, but instead patrolled a hallway. Azrael managed to Analyze its back.

Lesser Minotaur
Journeyman-Hoof
Level 15
Health Points: 490 / 490
Skills: 8

CHAPTER SIX

Azrael considered the creature. Minotaurs were a strange monster, as they were also a sapient race. This phenomenon also existed with Goblins, Gremlins, Giants, Orcs, Nagas and a few other races. These races were often looked down upon by the rest of the EtherVerse for that reason.

Bat had done a poor job conveying the size of the creature in front of them. Thanks to that little mistake, Azrael didn't have the Ether Tech suit on. The Minotaur's bulk and size reminded him of the Fire Giant he had faced on Tech Duinn. That made Azrael doubt that his skill would be as effective against the monster's high inherent Ether. Add to that the problem of its attacks and Azrael not wearing the Ether Tech gear, and he was considering turning back for the spiders.

Bat flinched, which stopped Azrael's thoughts. His blue-skinned companion whispered, "It smelled us."

Damnit. In the future, I will need to have Bat be more specific about monster sizes...

The sound of crumbling stone reverberated down the hallway to Azrael as the Minotaur turned—its black horns dragging through the soft sandstone walls as it maneuvered its head to face them. Its nostrils flared violently as it continually scented the air. Its brown fur was clumped together and long. For a split-second, Azrael thought that the hair drooped over the creature's eyes, but then remembered a lesson from the Sovereign Halls that stated monsters classified as Minotaurs were blind. Unlike Bat, it didn't use its ears to direct it. No, it used its smell. Its two front hands slapped the ground as it got into a combination of a sprinter's pose and a bull's charge. Then it glowed blood red and plowed forward.

In response, Azrael stepped forward and released one of his stored skills from Soul Storage. "Release ten," he stated and felt the force blast outward and expand. The horns of the Minotaur began to screech as the ten reciprocating saws attempted to cut through them. One blade clearly landed on the snout as well— but in response, the bull head lowered, moving it onto the thick brow of its forehead.

Blood sprayed from that single strike, but Azrael's most powerful skill only stopped the charging creature and failed to cause significant damage. Still, that was better than being gored, as far as he was concerned.

"Do you have any attacks that might hurt this thing?" Azrael called to Bat.

Two mechanically gloved hands were raised into the air in response. The air in front of Bat firmed and grew heavy with Ether. The sound of multiple tuning forks began to emanate from right beside the Minotaur's head and quickly began to gain in decibels. Azrael covered his ears as the Minotaur added its roar to the din. Azrael's blades still assaulted it from the front, but its skin and hair began oscillating in wave-like patterns due to Bat's assault.

The sound disappeared but the effect continued, telling Azrael that it was now outside of his auditory range. His spirit blades only lasted for a few more seconds, but even after they dissipated, the monster shook and trembled. It shook its head, attempting to clear the sound and its mounting internal damage. Each shake of the head flung blood from the mouth and ears of the creature. Blood slowly painted the walls beside it, and it collapsed to the ground.

Azrael Analyzed the creature and found it dead. He looked at Bat. "Didn't know you had a sonic attack?!"

Bat lowered his hands and fell to his knees, the Ether Tech suit creaking. "It's my tier five skill. I need a stronger Ether pool to hold it longer. But it bypasses the skin and armor of opponents."

Azrael smiled broadly at Bat and looted the Minotaur.

Minotaur's Horns

Crafting Component

• These horns were once just bone but, due to the inherent Ether of the Minotaur, have hardened into a material harder than most metals.

He placed the item in his bag after showing it to his team-mate. Then checked his Etherience notification. Unfortunately, this creature didn't award them more than the Goblin room had. Azrael sighed and pointed down the hallway. "What's down this hallway?"

Bat tilted his head and said through the Ether Tech helm, "There is a false wall, right there. It leads to a chest. Then this hallway goes to a room filled with a pond, and many trees."

Azrael pulled out the guide book and flipped to this dungeon's section, wanting to confirm his thoughts. According to the information, any room with water and foliage down here was a safe zone. At least they knew where one was, for tonight. Azrael moved to the wall Bat had indicated and charged a single charge of Soul Strike.

He slashed his sword and the wall only withstood a few moments of the bombardment before it crumbled inward. Right on the other side was a chest that had gold filigree. Bat moved forward and studied it. "It's got no trap on the chest, but the roof will come down if you step on the stone in front of it. Open it from the side."

Azrael contemplated. Bat was an excellent dungeon delving companion. Together, they could theoretically do this for a living and continue to gain strength. It would be a slow slog, but if they added members to their group, they could surely attempt bosses and move faster!

He shook his head, dismissing the dream and returning to reality. He should figure out what type of loot this B-rated chest offered first, before dreaming of riches.

Health Elixir (Strong) x5
• **Returns 300 health over ten seconds.**

———

Ether Draught (Strong) x5
• **Returns 150 Ether over ten seconds.**

———

Ether-Imbued Robe of [Locked]
• **This robe's threading was imbued with Ether before it was woven. Each thread's inherent Ether is abnormally high, but it has lost some of its enchantment size due to this modification.**
Enchantments: [Locked]

———

10 Crystallized Ether

That was a very good haul. If he was to sell the gear and potions, he would make around two-hundred crystals—depending on the robe mostly. He wished that the robe had been a tunic or chest-piece, but was happy to have gotten loot with minimal effort. After Bat's latest display, he might be best geared toward becoming more of a ranged caster, anyway. So, the robe might actually be a piece of gear they kept—depending on the enchantments.

Azrael placed the smaller items in the ring and made a bundle of the robes before stuffing them into the backpack he had purchased for this trip. He slung it onto his back and, together with Bat, he walked to the oasis.

Entering the oasis was surreal. It quite literally looked like they walked from the mild darkness of an underground cave system, lit by torches, into the noonday sun. The multitude of greenery shimmered in the light and Azrael could make out a crystal-clear pond reflecting the strange illumination of some sort of gem in the center of the cavern as well. He looked up and saw that a massive diamond sat in the domed ceiling and shone with the ferocity of a star. On closer inspection, Azrael could tell that the light was whiter in color as opposed to the warm yellow of the Odin star.

The room was square with four entrances in the cardinal directions. Of course, below ground it was impossible to tell which direction was which. So, instead he assigned the direction they entered as south and shoved a stick into the ground to mark it.

For the next eight hours, they explored the other three passageways off of the oasis. The Minotaur was the highest-level monster they faced that day, and they only found one more D-ranked chest. Still, Azrael was unwilling to venture further away from the oasis. According to the dungeon guide, they were somewhat rare.

Azrael set up their tent and began cooking some rat steaks that they had obtained from a few rather large specimens. The oasis had plants of all types, including some that were extremely poisonous. He gathered some broccoli and spinach to accompany the rat meat, and didn't bother foraging for other plants that might be useful. He just couldn't recall how to safely harvest certain plants without accidentally poisoning himself.

"Bat, what would you think about joining the academy?" Azrael began a conversation. He wasn't sure himself of the endeavor, but Jophiel had claimed it was a very well-respected establishment that helped young people grow stronger. Not to mention the display he had seen with the student outside the dungeon.

As the meal sizzled over the flame, Bat spoke, "This is quite relaxing. What would the school offer you that would gain you Etherience faster than this?"

Azrael had been considering that exact question earlier in the day. He nodded his head to tell Bat he had heard the question and deliberated some more on it now.

Even if the academy had access to dungeons for students, they likely would take the loot to subsidize the schooling. Still, adventuring with two people was a bit risky, and the school would likely place them on a larger team. Again, that wasn't something exclusive to the school though.

He took a deep breath and looked up at the stalactites hanging from the cave roof. "I don't know, Bat. Something tells me that we would eventually run into trouble without some sort of backing. That if we don't have some sort of status on Gaia, then factions will have no fear—"

A scream cut him off mid-sentence and they both jumped to their feet. Azrael removed the makeshift grill from over the flames using two sticks.

"Was that a humanoid scream or a monster?" he asked Bat as he placed the mostly cooked meat onto a rock.

Bat put on the Ether Tech helmet. "That was definitely a humanoid. I can still hear the sound of combat. It sounds a lot like a battle between two groups and not a clash with the dungeon mobs."

Azrael recharged his Soul Storage with five stacks of Soul Strike as he breathed through his nose—attempting to remain calm.

I need to remember to recharge it with ten new stacks when I have the opportunity.

Should they get involved?

The simple answer was no. If they rushed into the conflict, they wouldn't know which side to take. It could also be a trap meant to lure people to the two groups that would then ambush individuals. Bat looked to him, seeming to be waiting on his decision. What should he do?

"We should eat," he whispered while motioning to their food. He didn't like the decision, part of him screaming that his choice was the wrong one, but he forced it down. It wasn't his place to mediate a conflict between teams. He wasn't a hero—he was just another delver. If the people came to the oasis and caused trouble, he would deal with it then. Similarly, if they came and needed aid.

Bat took off the helmet and sat back down, his ears twitching occasionally. Azrael assumed he was still listening to the combat taking place. After a time, his friend seemed to calm down and they both focused on eating. "I will take the first watch, as I meditate. Get some sleep."

Bat nodded and moved to the tent and sleeping bags inside. Azrael sat cross legged on the ground and focused on his Ether channels. He activated his Soul Cloak as well, to ensure he wouldn't be ambushed, and began circulating his Ether.

CHAPTER SEVEN

From the northern entrance, a group of three adventurers trudged into the oasis. Azrael could tell it wasn't a group from the nobility or guilds because of the state of equipment they were wearing. While the equipment itself was serviceable and likely of good, enchanted quality, it wasn't brand new. That was one thing he had clearly marked on all the groups that entered through the noble's line.

Adventurers didn't spend money when they didn't need to. They used the gear they had until it either broke or they found clear upgrades. Sometimes spending savings to buy those upgrades, but never spending on minor upgrades or side-grades.

Nobles, on the other hand, bought gear that matched. Meaning they cut quite the figure when they were walking around, but often one piece of equipment being replaced spawned their need to replace multiple pieces and spend more money. Perhaps this was because the nobles had access to enchanters that worked for the guilds? Could they purchase the gear, and have it enchanted personally for them?

Azrael warily watched the group enter and checked the

western entrance, which was the direction the sounds of fighting and screaming had come from. The adventurers gave a sleeping Bat and Azrael an appraising look from the other side of the pond. After a moment they approached the water's edge and faced their direction. The light from the diamond had slowly become pale white, like that of the moon, and in the low light, Azrael recognized a Vampire raise a hand in greeting. The group behind the Vampire came to a stop but didn't begin setting up their own camp. Azrael Analyzed the pale-skinned man to garner more information.

Vein Gough
Journeyman-Drainer
Level 41
Health Points: 310 / 310
Skills: 14

Vein didn't make any further moves, maintaining separation across the ten-foot pool at the center of the oasis.

"Would you mind if we shared your fire? It will save us some time in setting up camp and allow for some additional security for the night," Vein called over.

It was the polite approach, giving Vein an appearance of being non-threatening. But if Azrael was to guess, Vein was a type of mage class, which meant this distance was nothing to him.

Azrael looked to Bat, who had woken up thanks to the noise. The Batman shrugged. So, the decision was Azrael's.

"You can share our fire, but we would love to ask some questions," Azrael called back.

Vein nodded and his group unfroze before moving around the pond to set up their tents. Azrael and Bat had set their tent up behind them, and Vein's group set up its tents on the other side of the fire, which kept the groups separate but also together. Once they were finished, they joined Azrael and Bat at the firepit.

A female Vampire smiled at Bat as he emerged from his sleeping blankets and spoke as she set up the group's cooking tripod. "It is considered lucky to share a fire with the Batmen. Well met, I am named Rosary. What are your names?"

After the introductions, Azrael knew that the three were all Vampires. There was of course Vein, who was a tall whip-thin male Vampire with dark features; Rosary, a well-muscled female Vampire, with silver hair and auburn eyes that seemed to glow in the firelight; and lastly Shroud, who was so pale, his skin seemed see-through. The last member of the Vampires' group had a shaved head and seemed to have no hair anywhere on his body. Even his eyebrows were gone, which made Azrael's hand shoot up to study his own. Shroud's unwillingness to meet eyes told Azrael that he didn't want to talk, so Azrael left off asking about his peculiar appearance.

"What questions do you two have that you felt needed to be announced?" Vein chuckled over the pot he hung from the newly setup tripod.

Azrael forced a chuckle himself. "Mostly about adventuring on Gaia. This is our first run of a dungeon, and we have a slot booked for the Delving dungeon next week. Still, we seemed to piss people off by taking an early spot. Does your group know of any way to adventure without politics?"

Rosary's face went straight as she started cutting up roots and vegetables. Shroud glanced up briefly as he added the water, his eyes wide with either shock or fear. When Vein responded, his voice didn't carry the amusement it had a moment before. "I'm afraid you likely took an adventuring group's timeslot. What time did you sign up for?"

Bat's ears vibrated beside Azrael as a cold silence descended onto the circle. "We signed up for the earliest time available. Won't it just push everyone back?"

Vein licked his sharp canine teeth and took a deep breath. Beside him, Shroud pulled the pot off the tripod and Rosary grimaced. She sighed heavily through her nose and bowed to them both. "It appears I spoke too soon. This meeting is far from lucky. We will move our camp and set up our own fire."

A chill ran down Azrael's spine. He looked to Vein and pleaded, "Please explain before you leave."

Vein gave them a pitying look and closed his eyes. "Because you are new to the planet, I will give you what explanation I can. The guilds are squeezing the adventurers hard. The pressure is building in the city, and a hierarchy of sorts has formed amongst the remaining adventuring groups. The most powerful groups take the earliest slots and run the dungeons once a week. They even have representatives that sign up for them, so they get the same time slots. That time is theirs, and while they likely can sign up for a different time, they usually won't because every other time slot is occupied by another established adventuring group.

"At first, groups were signing up for the times they wanted and ignoring this hierarchy. Until the powerful groups began hiring mercenaries from the guilds to ensure that people weren't stupid enough to take their spots," Vein explained.

Azrael closed his eyes, and berated himself. Of course, that was why all the representatives felt safe showing up in line a few minutes before the doors opened. Adventurers would likely line up all night and sleep in the streets if it was a first come situation.

I should have seen that!

"Do you think there is anything we can do?" Bat squeaked.

Rosary and Shroud looked up from taking down their tent. It was Vein who answered though. "Pray that the group you usurped for that spot doesn't have mercenaries on retainer. You also have a chance because you are in the Labyrinth. Most guild teams leave at night and come back tomorrow. In addition, they can't know what safe zone you are staying in...

"Still, first thing tomorrow, get out of this dungeon and remove your names from that time slot. The group likely was entering the dungeon when you took their spot, and you can hope they aren't yet aware of the problem."

After his quick explanation, Vein turned and helped the other two Vampires move the rest of their camp to the far side of the dungeon oasis.

Imbecile. You should have taken more time to understand the dynamics here before signing up for a spot. And you had to go and pick the earliest time!

Azrael had assumed the groups would all push each other back and that they would only have to deal with a weak group that got ousted from the 10:30 or 11:00 am time slot. To find out that it would be a powerful adventuring group sent shivers down Azrael's spine.

"Bat, what do you say we try to get back out of the dungeon tonight?" Azrael whispered, thinking about the screams they had heard earlier.

Bat nodded but his mouth was set in a frown. "Didn't the information we read have a warning about nighttime?"

Azrael pulled out the guide from his Ring of Holding. He had scanned it quickly earlier in the day, but his sinking stomach told him that Bat was right even before he found the passage. "You're right. At night, the Labyrinth has a much higher chance to encounter boss level creatures. By the Halls, what should we do?"

Bat stayed silent, clearly understanding that the final bit was a rhetorical question. Azrael weighed the options out. On one hand, boss monsters were a possibility. A higher chance of running into them wasn't a guarantee—especially with Bat guiding them. Still, there was an outside chance that no mercenaries were coming to deal with them either.

Was it worth risking their lives for the chance that mercenaries had been hired? Those same mercenaries would also have to discover that they were in the Labyrinth. Then find them inside of it. That first part wouldn't be hard, though, because the Adventurer's Hall likely didn't hide information about its members. Not to mention Bat's slip of the tongue to the store clerk...

Azrael stood and started to pace.

It all boils down to a group of mercenaries hired to kill us, versus a spawn in a dungeon that may kill us.

"Let's pack up the tent and get out of here," Azrael said with a nod.

He wasn't happy with his decision, but it was made.

CHAPTER EIGHT

"Bat, I think it's best if I take the armor," Azrael suggested as they packed up the campsite. Bat nodded before getting back to folding up the tent. The armor was inside the tent on the floor, anyway. Azrael stepped into the lower half before raising the Ether Tech chest guard and helmet.

Azrael had been packing up the cooking instruments and utensils they used, and got back to that task while wearing the armor. Once he finished, he did a once-over of the campsite and turned to Bat again. "Alright, do you think you can lead us back to our entrance?"

Throughout the entire rushed packing job, the Vampire adventuring group remained silent as they watched and cooked their meal. Azrael could almost feel their pity for him and Bat wafting across the pond and it caused his jaw to clench.

"It's that way," Bat answered as he pointed through the south entrance. They walked back into the hallways that led to the Minotaur's room.

A few minutes passed before Bat hissed, "There is a group of six coming down the hallway. They are near the Goblin's village, and we can't make it back to our door without meeting them."

Azrael cursed their luck. There was a good chance that it was just another group attempting to find an oasis. "Bat, is there anything that would mark them as hostile?" Azrael asked hurriedly.

Bat nodded. "One of the voices sounds nearly identical to one of the voices I could distinguish during the noise at dinner," Bat whispered and hung his head.

Azrael stopped and looked back the way they had come. He was fairly certain that the disturbance during dinner was an adventuring group fighting with another one. Should they avoid this group?

Yes, they definitely needed to, but was there some way to avoid them and still get back to the entrance they knew?

"We should head back to the oasis, and out a different path," Azrael decided. He wished there was a way to hide and have them pass by but other than the trap hallway, Azrael didn't know of any.

They backtracked through the oasis and out the entrance that was to the left. The Vampires pointedly ignored them as they passed through, this time not even glancing in their direction. Goosebumps broke out on Azrael's skin. If that group behind them was actually after them, the Vampires wouldn't hesitate to betray them, it seemed.

"The group behind us has picked up our track or scent and is increasing its pace to us," Bat whispered, adding a whole new level of stress to the escape.

"If we are lucky, they are just hostile to all other groups and those damn Vampires will take care of them or slow them down," Azrael called over his shoulder, then added, "You take the lead here in case they catch up. Watch for traps."

Azrael pulled back to let Bat into the lead. Until that point, they had been moving side by side and Azrael figured Bat would have a better chance in front while he guarded their rear.

"Stop," Bat called. Instead of pointing out a trap, he turned back the way they had come. His blue face began going pale as he stuttered, "They are—are asking ab—about us."

By the edge of the Sovereign Crescent.

"Alright, change of plans. Start heading toward the center of the Labyrinth," Azrael stated in an urgent whisper.

Bat nodded and began jogging forward. Bat's speed was slow to Azrael, but he needed to remain behind the Batman and be their first line of defense. At each junction of paths, Bat would hesitate and then take whatever path he must have decided was safer. They hadn't seen a mob yet, so Azrael was sure that they were avoiding roaming creatures.

Unfortunately, a team tracking them would get that same benefit without the hesitation at each turn. What they needed was something that Bat could see but the pursuers couldn't. "Bat, you need to find a trapped hallway. You can navigate them, and I will follow. Our pursuers may have to stop to disarm them or may even tread upon it," Azrael called to the blue figure in front of him.

In response, Bat stopped and turned back toward the pathway that he had just dismissed. Azrael felt his heart stutter and increase in tempo. They couldn't afford the backtrack, but also didn't have a choice. Bat whizzed by and whispered, "They are catching up; this is the fastest route to traps."

Azrael hoped his decision was the right one and began following precisely where Bat chose to step. His companion wouldn't have time to turn around and explain things to Azrael. Azrael called, "I'm following you precisely, don't stop," to convey that exact sentiment.

They ran on and Bat began jumping between steps. Azrael found it easy to mimic the Batman with his higher Agility and Strength but even more so with the armor. After a hundred yards of sporadic movement, Bat began jogging in the center of the hallway. Azrael turned and released a single charged Soul Strike as a thrust back the way they had come. The phantasmal blade stayed in the center of the hallway and didn't make contact with any of the walls but pulled with it a wind that swept the sand behind it, covering their trail.

It won't be perfect, but it's the best I can do.

He turned and caught back up to Bat in a few long strides. They reached a four-way split and Bat hesitated. The hesitation stretched for a split second longer than normal and Azrael called, "What's the problem?"

"Monsters in every direction," Bat squeaked.

"Head to the one you feel is weakest," Azrael responded, not wanting to stay stopped with a group of mercenaries closing in.

Bat nodded and jogged straight ahead. Azrael pulled out the piece of fabric from the first chest and dragged it behind them, realizing that he probably should have been doing this right from the start. The trapped area had clearly accentuated the need to cover their footprints. Azrael jogged to keep up with Bat for another half mile before they entered into a square room filled with spiders on webs. What was it about spiders and the Batman?

How does he think spiders are the weakest enemy?

Aracula
Journeyman-Arachnid
Level 8
Health Points: 380 / 380
Skills: 7

Azrael took up the lead position and plotted a course through the webs to the exit. The path he chose only passed through two of the five-foot-long spiders and Azrael hoped that cutting through others' webs wouldn't immediately aggro them.

His first slash of his sword didn't immediately aggro the spider that was perched fifty feet away. Still, the vibrations the slash made did make the spider move and begin to turn. They needed to be fast.

"Bat, stay close," Azrael called as he slashed his way through more and more webs.

Azrael arrived at the next spider within ten seconds of entering the room and entered Headsman's Bloodletting. Using this form, he dropped his blade from full extension above his head onto the abdomen of the arachnoid. He charged the blade twice with Soul Strike but left it coating the edge. The abdomen split under his assault but then his blade caught as the spider darkened in color. Azrael pulled the sword out in a reverse thrust and then dove as the spider leaped at him. Bat's sonic attack crashed into the creature and the hardened black skin began to vibrate on the creature's body. Azrael used Ploughman's Field on the quivering, grounded arachnid and split it in two horizontally.

The spider from the last web was slowly making its way to the hole they had carved through the web. Azrael hurriedly cut through the final web in front and they continued on. They ran into another spider and used the combined attack again to make quick work of it. In perhaps a minute, they exited the other side of the room and Azrael peeked over his shoulder. There was a clear path for the group behind to follow. The only upside was that the spiders on those destroyed webs were at the holes and fixing them.

A tall figure stood at the entrance with his bow drawn but held his arrow. He had no easy line of fire at Azrael and Bat. Azrael used Analyze.

Fandral
Journeyman-Tracker
Level 21
Health Points: 790 / 790
Skills: 10

Fandral glowed red for a moment and then called over his shoulder, "I have marked them, but they have fought through a room filled with spiders." Turning back, Fandral grinned at Azrael. "You can't get away now."

Bat and Azrael began running again, and took a few more turns before Bat said, "They have finished with the spiders. There is a group fighting a large monster ahead of us. What should we do?"

Azrael realized that they wouldn't be able to lose the mercenaries behind them. Their best chance was to hope that the group in front was fighting a boss. Exits always opened after defeating a boss—according to the information on the Labyrinth dungeon.

"To the group fighting in front of us, Bat," Azrael said.

They took off and, before long, Azrael himself could hear the sound of combat. The whomps of spells hitting something solid, mixed with the clangs, cracks, and shouts of a team in the heat of a fight.

Bat and Azrael rounded a corner and watched on as a group of Dwarves whittled away at a huge stone statue. The statue looked human and was made of sandstone. The *artist* that created it had given it a robe and two sandals along with a stone harp. Every so often, the creature would reach up and begin plucking the strings, but a white circle would flash into place on the creature's head. The circle shrank rapidly before becoming a white headband that seemed to be squeezing the stone forehead. This seemed to cut off the music, and the golem would resume trying to stomp the Dwarves into the ground.

Azrael motioned along the wall to Bat, and they slunk sideways, hugging the sandstone wall around the chamber, as the fight continued. Azrael could tell they had been noticed but the fight was too intense for the members to deal with them, at least for now. The white headband snapped, and the creature moved to strum again, but a huge creaking crack interrupted it this time. The entire left side of the statue crumpled away, and it collapsed to the ground with a reverberating boom. From the way the statue's knee shattered, it was clear that the group had been targeting it almost exclusively.

Once the group had easy access to the head of the statue, the fight didn't last much longer. As soon as the head crumbled, the mage and two archers of the ten-person group turned and pointed weapons at Azrael and Bat. Azrael held up his hands, and Bat followed his actions.

"What are you doing sneaking around when we are fighting?" the most heavily armored of the group asked as he clanked toward them.

"Well, we are trying to escape a group of mercenaries that are trying to kill us," Azrael said sheepishly. He decided that the truth was the best way to deal with this situation.

Azrael had noticed the exit to the Labyrinth form, but, *of course*, it was on the other side of the room.

CHAPTER NINE

"Whose spot were you stupid enough to steal?" the leader asked as he clanked closer, his voice stern.

Tortak Lodestone
Journeyman-Boulder
Level 43
Health Points: 3,210 / 3,450
Skills: 14

Azrael addressed the heavily armored Tortak, seeing that the rest of this particular group was clearly deferring to him. "The Radiant Rock Eaters," Azrael said simply. The entire group was Dwarves, and they were all facing them now. Azraek caught a few of the members blink before looking at each other.

Tortak continued to advance as the semi-circle closed around Azrael and Bat. "Why would you take the Radiant Rock Eaters' spot?" the tank asked angrily.

Azrael began to open his mouth, but Tortak held up a hand. "Not you. I want to hear from the cowering Batman, there," Tortak ordered brusquely.

Bat's ears quivered, but he managed to stand up straight despite his body shivering. "We only ar-arrived on world yesterday and be-believed that the teams would just push each other back by one time slot. Ending with the el-eleven o-o-o'clock slot getting bumped or choosing a different d-d-dungeon," Bat squeaked.

Azrael realized why Tortak had chosen to hear Bat's answer and not his when the Batman began stuttering. It is nearly impossible to lie when being as nervous as Bat appeared. Unlike Tortak, Azrael knew that his companion was far more capable than he seemed. Regardless, Azrael would have told the group the same thing, and probably have been far less convincing in his delivery.

"And now—" Tortak began but was cut off by the arrival of the hunter Fandral, who slid into the room and looked around. Tortak pointed at the hunter and called, "Hold for a moment, mercenary, these two have my party's protection."

He turned back to Bat. "And now that you two know the consequences, what were you going to do?" Tortak finished what he attempted to say earlier.

Fandral coughed to interrupt Bat's response. "I apologize, Tortak, but this is a contract from the Radiant Rock Eaters' representative and not your Stone Axes. We cannot ignore our contract, even with your group's status."

The other five humans of the hunter's group of mercenaries arrived on the tail of his words. To Azrael's surprise, the Stone Axes turned to face the group and formed a defensive wall between them and the mercenaries. Tortak growled deep in his throat. "Lady Silfa, does this imbecile speak for you and your team?"

"Well met, good Dwarves. I'm afraid we took a contract—" Silfa began but was cut off by a roar.

"To kill children! Is that the state of Gaia, now?" Tortak howled with evident disgust. "That Batman is fourteen, according to my perception, and while that young man with the cold eyes looks older, he is only eight. Does the mercenary's guild now slaughter initiates of the system?"

The vacant stares and dropped jaws from the mercenaries told everyone present that they hadn't known. Tortak saw his opportunity and pointed to Silfa. "So, it's that you didn't do enough research before storming after them. Let me finish asking my questions, and then maybe—just maybe—you will see that the guild's bloody tactics have already worked."

He pointed to Bat and made a spinning motion with his wrist. Bat coughed and blurted, "We ar-r-re trying t-t-t-to get out and rem-m-m-moove ourselves from the sp-p-p-pot."

Tortak held up both hands and then looked pointedly at Silfa. "Your contract no doubt states you get paid in full as long as the spot is returned to the Rock Eaters, no?"

Silfa nodded but pointed to Azrael and Bat. "I have heard the intention and will honor Tortak's protection. But I will escort you out of the dungeon and to the Adventuring Hall in the morning to ensure the completion of this job. Agreed?" Silfa asserted as she looked between Azrael and Tortak.

Azrael nodded, seeing that he had no option and fighting now would be meaningless. Even looking at Tortak, he noticed the man lowering his head in resignation—this was the best the man could do. They had been intending to relinquish the spot anyway, so it was easy to nod to Silfa.

The two groups nodded at each other and Fandral came forward to place a hand on Bat's shoulder. Another member who was heavily armored in gear similar to Tortak did the same for Azrael. He Analyzed the man in turn.

Volstagg
Journeyman-Axbrother
Level 19
Health Points: 2,300 / 2,300
Skills: 9

Just as they passed by the central dais, a strange shudder crawled up Azrael's neck. Bat's head jerked toward him when it happened, but his companion didn't speak. His ears folded in half multiple times though, almost as if Bat was blinking rapidly.

Soon they were walking back down the exit hallway and up the sandstone stairs to re-enter the city of El Dorado.

Just like that, their very first dungeon run on Gaia ended.

Azrael looked at the group of mercenaries who were paid to hunt down people in El Dorado. It would seem that to be truly safe on Gaia, one needed to join a guild or the academy. Otherwise, they would likely end up riddled with arrows, or on the end of Silfa's rapier.

They traveled back to a different inn than the one Azrael and Bat were staying in. They didn't stop at the front desk, but moved to the lift and rode it up. Getting off on the top floor, they entered a monstrous suite that was comprised of several joined rooms. No one had spoken during the walk through town, but Silfa finally broke that silence. "You two will stay in that room. First thing tomorrow, we will escort you to the Adventurer's Hall, understand?" she stated. Her last question was clearly rhetorical. Just as they prepared to turn away, she continued, "Fandral, hand them the guild initiate contracts. Let's give them the opportunity to join us…"

"We aren't really looking for guild memb—" Azrael began.

"Read the contract over," Silfa cut in, her voice a hard-edged whisper.

Azrael felt goosebumps rise on his skin and he looked to Bat. Silfa turned away and entered one of the adjoining rooms, which cut off any further discussion.

Bat and Azrael moved to the windowless bedroom and each took a bed. Azrael was exhausted after a day of adventuring and a night of running for his life. He scanned the contract that Fandral had handed them on their way by. It was a contract to join the Asgardian guild, which was rated the top guild on the planet. It only took Azrael flipping the page one time before he was ready to rip the paper into confetti and light it afire.

The contract gave the initiate an advance on their room and board against their guild stipend. The problem was that initiates didn't get paid and would thus need to move up in the organization before they began working down whatever debt they had built. If the initiate left the guild, they were expected to pay the debt off plus twenty-five percent, which was considered a discount for guild members. The real terrifying part was that the guild was able to remove an initiate within the first year if they didn't meet expectations. So, not only was the contract slave labor, but you could also be removed from the guild and owe them retroactively for living and eating their food.

"Have you read this contract?" Azrael asked Bat, his voice offended.

"Not really. While I can make it out based on the ink imprints on the paper, it would take me a while to work my way through it because it isn't the tactile writing I'm used to. I take it from your tone that it isn't something we will be signing?"

"Definitely not—" Azrael began while shaking his head.

To his surprise, the door opened, cutting him off. Volstagg came in and handed a cup to Azrael and Bat.

"Drink it!" the man ordered, sternly. The timing of his entrance might have just been coincidence but Azrael had a suspicion that he had been listening outside the door.

Bat opened his mouth, wanting to say something, but Volstagg's eyes transferred to the Batman which seemed to change Bat's mind. Bat quickly drank the contents of the cup, but Azrael wasn't as timid.

"Why would I drink this?" he asked, his voice raised slightly in anger.

"Because if you don't, I have permission to end your existence… or torture you until you do. Your choice. Still, the liquid will just put you to sleep and make sure you don't try to escape in the night," Volstagg responded, with a sick kind of smile coming over his face.

Azrael considered resisting Volstagg, but the man's higher level and his friends outside meant that the chances of Azrael's success would be slim. A glance at Bat showed his friend's ears drooped and steady breathing. He tried to Analyze the cup, but it didn't tell him what the liquid inside was. After a few more minutes of hesitation, he followed Bat's lead and drank the liquid.

Azrael was determined to fight the liquid and stay awake. Unfortunately, his interface chose that moment to notify him of a debuff.

Sleeping Aid
You have consumed a high dose of powdered Sleep Root. This will cause you to sleep for a minimum of four hours.
Time remaining 3 hours 57 minutes and 33 seconds.

His eyes quickly grew heavy, and he had just enough brain power remaining to recognize a second debuff begin floating onto his interface, but not enough to read it.

CHAPTER TEN

A sharp pain in his heart woke Azrael up, and he groaned while his hand flew to his chest. Bat caught his hand and seemed to hold a finger to his mouth in a 'quiet or they'll hear you' action.

"Good, you two are awake, let's go!" Volstagg's gruff voice accompanied the creak of the door opening. Today, the man wasn't wearing his armor and Azrael examined him. He was round in the belly but had massive arms, long brown hair, and a massive beard that still obscured half of his face. How had the helmet managed to hide that thing? His hair seemed to hang halfway down his torso, from both his beard and his head.

From the minimal sun entering the window, it had to be extremely early. Azrael wondered why Bat had been kneeling over him at this hour, and what had caused his chest to hurt like that. It still felt tender. Not on the surface, but a deeper ache, seeming to come from his heart. It reminded Azrael of the way his teachers described heartburn. Just to be sure, he checked his status information but found nothing amiss. Wasn't there a second debuff yesterday?

He stood up and made his way to Volstagg at the door. The smile the man wore seemed off, but thanks to Volstagg's large stomach, Azrael just assumed the man was thinking about breakfast. They were forced to wait as Silfa's group of mercenaries got ready to go. Azrael took the opportunity and looked around. The rooms of the inn were clearly lived in, and there were signs of minor wealth accrued in the furniture and décor. Whoever Silfa was, she and her group were paid well for their work of hunting down thieves of spots.

A few moments later, they were escorted down to the Adventurer's Hall. Despite the line, the mercenaries frog marched them right to the front of the line. The smug looks that the representatives of other groups gave them made Bat shiver, but Azrael's eyes just twitched continuously.

He wanted to cut throats; these cowards were allowing the guilds to regulate them, and it infuriated him. Maybe a part of it was embarrassment as well. It was one thing to make a mistake, but to have these pompous windbags attempt to lord it over him? The dichotomy of cowards attempting to act superior infuriated him in a way he hadn't felt since he was a student at the Sovereign Halls.

Funnily enough, thinking about school calmed him down some. If he was in Silfa's position, he would have done the same thing. Parade the catch to the front of the line—make sure everyone saw it. This was some of the best free publicity she could get from the situation. Clearly, she hadn't killed the two young men, but she had completed her task.

The people at the front of the line ushered Silfa to go ahead and she, in turn, gave Azrael a small nudge to get moving. Shaking his head, Azrael opened the door to see the smug face of Gaston wearing an infuriating smile. "Hello, gentlemen. Something tells me you aren't in line today to take an early spot. What can I do for you?"

Azrael clenched his teeth but forced his lips to part in a smile. He raised an eyebrow. "Hmm, I guess you can remove us from the earliest spot next Freyaday for the Delving dungeon. *And* please check if there are any open spots for times this week that are earlier than eleven," Azrael added in his best disdainful voice. The people that had let them walk to the front of the line groaned and began to act unruly.

Silfa grabbed him by the nape of the neck. "Trust me, kid. You have bigger problems on your plate."

Gaston's smile widened. "I see this one needs some lessons in manners, Lady Silfa."

Silfa's hand tightened on Azrael's neck and the glare she gave Gaston could have frozen more seasoned men.

"Remove them from the list. You two don't say another word!" Silfa ordered further and some color returned to Gaston's face, but he didn't speak again. Azrael ground his teeth, frustrated with the way this was going. He had no chance of getting out of it, though, and thus was forced to bear it.

Once that was completed, Silfa dragged Azrael outside, and Volstagg towed Bat. There was a small cheer from the adventuring group representatives and Azrael couldn't hold in his sigh. These idiots had lost almost all of their power to the guilds but were cheering those same guilds for maintaining a hierarchy within themselves, because it let them hold onto that little power that remained. The political clout of the guilds in this transition was astonishing, and it only made him more determined to defeat them.

They were marched a block away and pulled into an alley before they were allowed to stop. "You believe you are pretty clever, but that little bit of snark back there just reinforces my decision from last night," Silfa intoned. Her lack of emotion instantly forced Azrael into a state of hyper-awareness. That was a tone he had heard from professors at the Sovereign Hall right before they brigged a student.

"Both of you have a week. At the end of that time, the Heartworm that we fed you last night will puncture your heart's walls and kill you. If you come to us and join our guild, we will give you a medicine that will place the Heartworm in a dormant state. If you choose to try to find another way out of this, you will die. Only the top guilds on the planet have the cure for this particular parasitic monster." Silfa fiddled with her armbands as she explained. Azrael's hand had risen to his chest as she talked. Was that what the pain from this morning was? Was this parasite so strong that it didn't show up in his status?

"The Asgardian's would force you to sign up today, but all the guilds that employ this method have agreed that there must be time for a choice. In case a guild is unknowingly encroaching on another guild's recruit. Regardless of what guild you choose, you will no longer be able to cause problems. Oh, one more thing," Silfa added the final sentence as light exploded from her hand. The light seemed to have substance, almost like that of smoke, and it quickly settled onto Azrael and Bat.

You have been Muted.
Speaking of anything that Silfa and her group has done within the last twenty-four hours will be near to impossible.
Last for 7 days.

Silfa and her cronies didn't even bother to stick around after that. Instead, Azrael looked up and they were already walking away down the street. His eyes widened and he looked to Bat. "I'm sorry I got us into this…"

To Azrael's surprise, Bat smiled. "Don't worry—" Bat made a pained face and fell to his knees. "—it seems I can't talk about it." Bat panted on the ground and Azrael worried the worm creature was hurting his companion. "Please just trust me, we are safe," Bat finished after a moment.

Azrael blinked at the Batman and then asked, "What do we do now, then?"

"We should probably get off this planet before anyone discovers what I—" Bat cut off with a scream again.

Azrael growled in response. "The pain you are in suggests otherwise, Bat!"

"I am being targeted by the spell we are both suffering from. Not the creature that witch of a woman inflicted upon us," Bat said. Azrael could tell he was avoiding talking about the specifics. So the Mute skill was what was causing the Batman pain.

"How can you guarantee that the first problem is taken care of?"

"I was able to attack the creature with a sonic attack. Those things are quite dead…"

Azrael felt a malicious smile cross his face. Bat managed to kill the Heartworms already. That was incredible, and lucky, but Azrael felt something inside him balk at the suggestion for leaving the planet. The guilds on Gaia were just a slightly more civilized version of the Tuatha on Tech Duinn. Maybe each one of these top guilds had a prison planet where they were keeping prisoners from wars.

So, no, if they were safe from this Heartworm, there was still one final option left. One option that would allow them to be outside of Gaian politics, protect them, and still give him the opportunity to take revenge on these guilds. Was the way the Tuatha de Danaan and the Asgardians the way guilds treated everyone?

Such barbaric recruitment methods reminded him so much of Tech Duinn and their treatment of him that he was even more sure of his need to avoid the guilds and take revenge.

———

It was just after noon, Bat and Azrael were back at the starport, waiting impatiently for the Cussing Pirate to be removed from long term storage and brought out to them. The shops had opened at ten and Azrael discovered that the last day to sign up for the academy, as a non-sponsored student, was today. At least, according to the nervous Nethune. The terrified shopkeeper had clearly been the one to reveal the information about them entering the Labyrinth, and he had been very forthcoming in answering their questions because of it. Not many were admitted through this process, but this was the last chance to enter the school without guild or noble sponsorship.

Azrael wanted more than anything to have entry to the school without having to rely on any of the guilds of Gaia, especially after the display he'd seen this morning. The offer from Raguel would remain a back-up plan for them. They would only take it if they couldn't gain some sort of standing on their own. Azrael's contemplations were interrupted by Bat.

"I forgot to talk to you about what happened last night," Bat squeaked, seeming almost excited but also agitated. Azrael could understand his worry. That Muted debuff might have caused him intense pain, but it would seem he wasn't talking about Silfa.

Azrael's responding look must have been strange because Bat held up a hand to forestall an interruption. "I didn't think it would be safe to tell you when, umm... anyway," Bat began explaining himself.

"Bat, get to the point, please." Azrael chuckled, having experienced Bat's apologetic nature for the last six months of travel.

"Oh right—sorry. When we were leaving the dungeon, something happened. Remember that strand of darkness that I told you about after Tech Duinn? Well, as we walked out of the Labyrinth, it flashed brightly and seemed to shrink," Bat explained, trying to make hand gestures to illustrate what he meant.

Azrael thought the words were clear enough, but that didn't really tell him anything. "And? Do you have any idea what it was? I thought you told me it was going away," Azrael said, feeling his heart begin to drum on his ribcage as his nerves amped up. Bat had told him the strand was shrinking daily for a long while now, and Azrael didn't understand if the flash of light was a good or bad thing.

The shrinking part was definitely good, right?

Bat shook his head while shrugging. "No clue. You didn't feel anything?" Bat asked, seeming genuinely curious.

Azrael remembered the strange shudder that had run over his body the previous night. He pushed his palm into his eye and rubbed it around, trying to consider if that gave them more information or just complicated the entire issue. "Did it happen as we passed the dais?" Azrael asked in a whisper.

Of course, Bat had no problem hearing it. "I'm sure it was nothing." Bat said, clearly reading Azrael's body language.

The problem was it was too late to un-ring the bell. He would now need to worry about this strange line of connection again; could it do more than give him a shudder? Could it take control of his body or influence him in some way?

The ship came rolling out from a large door, and Azrael pointed at it. "Alright, let's get going. If we can get signed up today, we may be able to sign up for some dungeons in the meantime."

Bat pursed his lips and shook his head. "It's all about gaining more Etherience with you, isn't it?"

To try to take his mind off of the situation, he thought back on the two pieces of gear that they identified in the shop earlier today.

Ether-Imbued Robe
• This robe's threading was imbued with Ether before it was woven. Each thread's inherent Ether is abnormally high, but it has lost some of its enchantment size due to this modification.

Enchantments: Inherent Ether Protection (+50%), Intelligence III (+6)

———

Leather Boots of Agility
• These boots help the wearer move with improved speed but are graceless.

Enchantments: Inherent Ether Protection (+10%), Agility II (+3)

The pieces of gear were actually worth something, but Azrael held onto them both for now. Currently, he was wearing the boots and Bat wore the robe. Perhaps in time, they could build the Batman as a mage of some sort. The display he had used on the Minotaur and spiders certainly showed a lean in that direction. The deft handling of the Heartworm inside of their bodies made that even more clear. That would have taken some very precise magic usage.

———

Bat and Azrael approached the coordinates for the academy, and Azrael studied what could be seen of the campus from the sky. There was a massive white city behind the school that, from the air, shone brightly enough that he couldn't look at it for long. He wondered if it was part of the school or something else entirely. The school grounds were lush greenery with numerous paved walkways that connected buildings. Each building was a speck from the air, but Azrael could tell that each one served a different purpose. It appeared some were for sleeping and others specifically designed for outdoor lessons. Then there were others that he couldn't distinguish the use of from the air.

"Cussing Parrot, requesting landing and day dock for Atlantean Academy pier," Azrael called through the radio.

"State your business and sponsor," a voice crackled back.

"We're here to sign up for the academy, and heard that today was the last day of non-sponsored admissions."

"You are cleared for landing on helipad one-hundred, at the far end of the compound. Someone will meet you there to confirm your story."

Azrael looked to Bat, who could only shrug. Neither of them knew how they could convince someone that they were here to apply, but Azrael steered the ship to the now-highlighted direction on the ship's interface. Turned out that the one-hundredth pad was the literal last one in line. The Cussing Parrot passed by nearly fifty empty pads to get to the assigned one.

At first Azrael felt confused at the illogical procedure, but the ships he did see began to explain the situation to him. The

Cussing Pirate was not a new ship by any stretch of the imagination. He might call it ten years old, if not closer to fifteen, but it was well maintained and functional. The ships they saw on the helipads were something completely different.

Each ship was the epitome of luxury. If it wasn't brand new, it was fully stocked. Comparing the Cussing Parrot to any one of these ships was like comparing Mark's rusty transport frigate back on Tech Duinn to Raguel's luxury intercity car. Each one of the ships seemed to preen in the sunlight of the day, and Azrael immediately realized that they were about to try to climb a mountain carrying boulders, as a thunderstorm blew down the face.

Azrael chose not to mention this to Bat. Better not to get his companion flustered before they arrived.

Once he landed the ship and disengaged the engines, they lowered the plank to exit their 'ratty' ship. Three figures stood beside their landing pad with arms crossed. Each of the individuals wore black from head to toe and carried some sort of rod that reminded Azrael of the enchanted rods of the prison transport that had electrocuted him. He shivered at the memory but continued walking toward them.

"Hello, gentlemen. Are you here to escort us to the registration?" Azrael asked, choosing to try to take control of the situation before they put on any airs.

One of the men chuckled. "No, we are here to ensure you haven't already taken the entrance interviews in the past two years, and to send you on your way if you have," the security personnel stated disdainfully.

"I'm Azrael, and this is Bat. No last names for either of us. I can assure you we have never taken the entrance interviews before," Azrael responded coolly, trying to hide his worry. Interviews? He had thought today would just be writing his name down and perhaps paying a fee.

The same man who had done the talking held up a hand and clicked his radio to repeat Azrael's words. Azrael was glad that his skill was hiding his actual last name. He definitely didn't know how people would respond if they found out he was a Sovereign. Azrael took the opportunity to Analyze the lead guard.

Gustaf Rademacher
Master-Gargoyle
Level 62
Health Points: 13,230 / 13,230
Skills: 28

Azrael Analyzed the other two guards and felt his heart stop. These were security guards? They were all master-ranked and high leveled as well. He instantly felt his assessment of the school climb into the stratosphere. The Sovereign Halls had some master-ranked teachers certainly, but guards? No way.

The radio gargled back, and Gustaf closed his eyes for a moment before breathing out through his nose. "You two are cleared to take the interview, but will come back immediately once you're finished. There will be no loitering on academy property, do you understand?" Gustaf grumped at them and attempted to turn away.

Azrael cleared his throat. "Sorry, Gustaf, this is our first time on campus. Could you provide us with an escort to the interviews? I am sure it would help prevent loitering."

Gustaf's eyes widened and his straight face morphed into a sneer. Still, he pointed at one of the two guards accompanying him and snapped his fingers before leaving.

Well, they certainly think we don't belong here. I wonder why they take interviews in the first place then? Azrael thought as they were led away from the Cussing Pirate at a near jog.

CHAPTER ELEVEN

The guard walked with Bat and Azrael jogging behind him for nearly fifteen minutes. The academy grounds were monstrously large. As Azrael had flown the ship toward the port coordinates, they had been faced with a green expanse of grass, lined with cobblestone pathways and dotted with large marble buildings of varying designs. From the air, they hadn't looked as impressive, but from the pathways they were marvels of architecture. They were behemoths in size, and Azrael couldn't help but wonder what each one was used for specifically. There were so many buildings on campus that he doubted he could have classes in all of them even if he was here for five years.

Off in the distance Azrael began to see water, but even more surprising to him were the four tall white towers that seemed to materialize out of the fog and clouds. He pointed at them and realized that no one was paying him any attention, so he asked, "What are those four towers that surround the huge fifth one?"

The guard shook his head and muttered, "Podunk bumpkins," before turning to Azrael. "That is Atlantis. The capital of

Gaia, the home of the Council of Ancient Wisdom. The hub for the Atlantean Net."

Azrael shook his head. "Great, and the towers?" he asked condescendingly.

The guard's jaw clenched but he did answer. "The heavenly tower and the four cardinal towers."

Azrael blinked, and then felt his heart accelerate. Those were the legendary Pentaclimbs? The five towers that had only been conquered by the universe's strongest fighters. He stopped walking and stared at the central tower; the monolith his father Erebus was fabled to have conquered.

That was, of course, all part of the massive lie, because if Erebus had successfully beaten the four outer towers, he would have successfully locked his class to his bloodline. He may have defeated one or two of the towers, though, because theoretically that would lock others out of his classes through the ranks, but it was hard to say for certain.

It's really tough for me to tell what the truth is, from the propaganda he intentionally created.

Bat squeaked, "Azrael, he is going to leave you behind."

Azrael snapped out of his awe-stunned state. He was forced to sprint a bit to catch up as the guard approached a building. At the front door, the guard motioned to the double oak doors and smiled with only his lips.

Azrael returned the odd smile with a mirror image and walked into the building. He realized that status played a huge role on Gaia, and that he appeared to be a dewy-eyed hopeful from a small world. He now wondered how this whole situation would be playing out if he revealed his last name.

Bat and he walked down a hallway. Azrael distinctly heard the squeak of his leather soles on the polished tiles as they passed doorways on either side. The only reason he didn't check any of the doors was that he could distinctly make out a large oak table with a bored Satyr sitting at it. The table imposed itself at the end of their current hall. It was at the top of two steps and had two doors behind it. Azrael assumed that was their intended destination or, if nothing else, this man would know where to go.

The scuff of their boots alerted the Satyr before they arrived, and the half-goat man sat up straight, his face seeming to change with each step. At first, a wide excited smile broke on his hairy face, but was quickly followed by a squint of the eyes. The Satyr ran his tongue along his teeth as his head tilted and his smile shrank. He had clearly Analyzed them and wasn't sure how to proceed. Azrael Analyzed the man in turn.

Calum Tallhoof
Journeyman-Clerk
Level 47
Health Points: 440 / 440
Skills: 15

"Can I help you two?" Calum asked, his voice carrying genuine curiosity.

Azrael looked to Bat and said, "Hello, sir, we are here to attempt to enroll at the Atlantean Academy. We were escorted here and told this is where the entrance interview is to take place. Is that correct?"

Calum seemed to grow excited again, and he began shuffling papers as he mumbled, "I don't think there was an appointment." He reached a page and tapped it before exclaiming, "Not a scheduled interview! Oh, what fun. Could you please fill out these forms? I will go gather the teachers for an impromptu meeting."

Calum handed them two sheets and then clacked into the room behind him after swinging open the doors. Bat tried to get the Satyr's attention, but he was gone too quickly. Azrael immediately saw the problem; this was a printed sheet and Bat, while possessing some very unique skills, couldn't read it. Azrael chuckled. "Don't worry, Bat, I will fill mine out and then help you with yours."

The form was straightforward, and just asked questions for

place of origin, level, Etherience, name, age, and more. But for Azrael, those things were almost all things he didn't want to share. He filled it out as best he could without revealing his secrets. After his own, Bat's was much more straightforward, and Azrael only had to avoid the subject of Tech Duinn. Hiding Tech Duinn might be pointless, since Raguel and Jophi knew about it, but guilds likely would try to control information like that from others, or at least Azrael hoped so. All the other guilds seemed to keep very tight reins on its members, if the Heartworm was any indication.

Since the two were left outside of the room for a rather long period, Azrael decided to go through a few subdued martial katas, since he hadn't had the chance to perform them yesterday or today, thanks to Silfa and the dungeon. Bat began following him through the movements as best he could. The Batman had begun doing this on the freighter.

Azrael was always tempted to correct his companion but chose not to. Bat was never going to be a frontline fighter, and Azrael doubted that Bat wanted the type of strict direction Azrael had been given.

And that was the only type of instruction Azrael knew…

***

The few katas morphed into all of his martial forms followed by a few sword forms. Azrael only had a single practice sword, but lent Bat his sword sheath, which he never used since his blade was able to become a formless blob that clung to his body.

Finally, after more than an hour, the Satyr came out of the room. Calum looked vastly different than an hour earlier. Instead of a groomed hairstyle and beard, Calum sported a flustered mad scientist appearance. His hair stood up in two spikes on both sides of his polished horns, his beard was similarly frizzy, and his brow was covered in sweat.

Despite all that, Calum smiled. "You can go in now, enough of the teachers have been gathered to conduct the interview," he said sheepishly.

Both Azrael and Bat moved to step forward, but Calum held up a hand. "One at a time. Can't have one person answering all the questions," he amended.

Azrael looked to Bat, and his friend raised a hand indicating the door to Azrael. Clearly, Bat would like him to go first, and Azrael wondered if his friend would try to cheat with his insane hearing ability. The thought made him mentally shrug as he walked to the double doors—that wouldn't affect his results in the slightest.

Use the talents you have, he thought as he controlled his breathing and entered the room.

The room he entered was cavernous, and he could tell by the slightly stale air that it wasn't used frequently. The flooring had changed from stone to dark carpet, and there was a raised stage with a large, rounded table set on it. Three people were sitting at the table, each one in different attire and looking slightly surprised to be there. Azrael approached the beam of light that clearly indicated where the interviewee was supposed to stand and stepped into place.

The three teachers each trained their eyes on Azrael and then, without asking questions, began making notes on something in front of them. He rolled his eyes; Analyze, while helpful, could also be a strange skill. Each one of the teachers now knew a certain amount about him based on their level in the skill. He just hoped their skill wouldn't be able to penetrate his Obfuscate skill.

He Analyzed them in turn, but was surprised when no information appeared in his system heads-up display. *What in the name of the eight?*

"Ahh, sorry. Let me explain. All teachers at the Atlantean Academy wear a brooch that prevents Analyze," a voice said from behind the table. Azrael blinked and stood on his toes in an attempt to get a view of the speaker. The other teachers all turned their gazes to the sound as well, but their body language told Azrael something unexpected was going on.

One of the three had their mouth hanging open, while

another was blinking repeatedly. Only one at the table seemed to have a poker face in place, but even he couldn't look away from whatever was offstage. Azrael followed the teacher's heads, and soon enough a white-haired man approached the table.

He pulled out the chair at the direct center and sat before continuing, "I will apologize for my teachers. It is very rare that prospective students who have no guild affiliation appear before us, nowadays. Even more rare that the applicant has never applied before.

"My name is Merlin," the gray-haired man said. Then Merlin pointed toward the one wing of the table and coughed. The man he indicated was a beefy individual who wore no shirt and had hands that could easily encompass all of Azrael's head inside a single palm. His skin was dark like onyx and his hair was closely cropped and curly. "This is Maat, and he is one of our teachers for physical skills here at the academy.

"And the lady on the other side of the table is Keerthilata. She is our teacher of history and politics," Merlin continued as he pointed to a brown-skinned woman with long black hair that seemed to reflect the light. She had been the one who couldn't keep her mouth from hanging open at Merlin's arrival.

Merlin began to indicate the final member of the group but was interrupted by the man with the poker face. "My name is Karn, and I am the archery teacher at the academy. I also can teach beginners small blades," he finished before smiling at Azrael.

Azrael nodded to each of them, unsure if it was polite to introduce himself in response. He looked to Merlin who seemed to read his thoughts, as he made a hand gesture that signified Azrael to go ahead. "Ahem. I am Azrael. I just arrived on Gaia a few days ago, and wish to enroll in the Atlantean Academy for further learning."

CHAPTER TWELVE

Karn knocked his knuckles on the table, which got Azrael's attention. "Enough of the pleasantries. Let us begin. My first question, where have you studied before this?" Karn questioned, his voice rhythmic.

"Sir," Azrael said to buy himself a moment of time. He realized his mistake a split second too late on his introduction. "I have been trained by a master since I was able to walk. Master Janus, of Gaia, was how he introduced himself to me," Azrael responded, using a half truth. Janus was one of his sword trainers and had been a very recent hire of the Sovereign Halls. According to the man, he had trained here at the academy in the past.

Something on the right wing of the table creaked, and Azrael noticed Maat was leaning forward in his chair. His bulk was now resting more on the table, which was bowing under the impressive bulk.

It was Keerthilata that spoke, though. "Janus is barely passable as a master. If he was to apply at the Atlantean Academy as such, he would likely be hired as a guard. If that is the only teaching you have had, I am afraid you won't fit in here."

Azrael's eye twitched. Janus hadn't exactly been his teacher, more of a sparring partner and teacher's assistant. Still, Azrael didn't want to reveal too much. Telling them any of his true teacher's names would risk the chance of them knowing the person's status or location. Either way, he didn't like Keerthilata's tone.

"I thought this interview was to ask questions to discover a student's learning?" Azrael said while making eye contact with the woman.

She sniffed and shook her head, before rifling through her papers. "As you wish. What are the three superpowers of the EtherVerse?" she asked condescendingly.

This question was mildly amusing, but also terribly disturbing in equal measures. The school had already shrunk the list of superpowers, or perhaps the Sovereign Empire had never been included on Gaia, and only in the doctrine of the Empire itself. Azrael took a breath and began, "Teacher. The Gains, Martians, and Coalition of Dragons."

Keerthilata nodded, but fired the next few questions like it was arrows from a quiver. "What is the most dangerous monster type historically? What is Arbuckle, and where can I find it?"

Azrael swallowed the saliva in his mouth. Those weren't questions that he knew rote answers for. He licked his lips and volunteered, "Arbuckle is the most compatible metal with enchanting. It is extremely rare and, as far as I know, no one knows of a connection with its mined locations." Keerthilata didn't nod but she was still looking at him, so he continued, "The most dangerous monster? If I answer based on sheer power, one of the World Dragons, but if I answer historically, it would be the Goblins."

"Explain your logic," Keerthilata said.

"Well, the Goblins of Griore Nine were able to enslave other monster races and capture numerous territories. By the time the Griorians asked for help, the Goblins were so deeply entrenched on their world that they were forced to abandon the planet altogether. To date, Goblins are the only monster that has successfully conquered a planet, as far as I know."

She nodded and pointed to Karn. "It seems you have some learning behind your claim. It says here on this sheet that you are only eight years old. Explain.," the man monotoned into the stale air.

"Teacher. Explain my age, sir?" Azrael asked, and heard a chuckle escape Maat.

"Explain how you look eighteen, and claim your age is only eight," Karn clarified, his voice still showing no hint of emotion.

"Teacher. I was born in a Territory. Others told me it had its growth perk maxed. From my understanding, the perk made my physical age that of an eighteen-year-old in eight years," Azrael stated the answer all children of the Sovereign Hall knew.

"And do you have any proof of your age?" Karn continued.

Maat slammed his fist on the table. "Your Analyze reveals the same information. Why do you ask this?"

Karn turned to the other teacher. "My Analyze does reveal that he is eight years old, but it also tells me that part of his sheet is changed. My Perception isn't high enough to see through those sections," Karn answered.

Merlin raised a hand and waved it back and forth. "I can assure you that the hidden information is of no concern to this interview. He is the age he claims," the strange teacher called, his voice filled with excitement. Azrael felt his heart fall; of course there would be people powerful enough to see through his Obfuscation skill. What was Merlin's role at the school?

Azrael realized the man had never told him. The other three teachers nodded and accepted Merlin's claim, which made Azrael consider the man more. Who had this kind of clout at a school? The only logical conclusion was that this was one of the headmasters.

Would it be rude of me to ask? Probably.

Merlin didn't say anything more. He just sat there eyeing

Azrael with a gigantic grin on his face and a bright twinkle in his eyes. Was the man cracked?

"What are the three considerations of combat for a ranged fighter?" Karn asked, bringing the interview back on track.

Considerations were taught to ranged damage dealers as something to continually be mindful of. Each one of the considerations that were taught needed to be accounted for at all times or the fighter could suddenly find himself in a very unfavorable position. One problem; he had been taught four considerations to always be mindful of.

"Teacher. Distance, environment, and cover. May I add line of sight to that list?" Azrael answered and expounded.

"No, you may not. Line of sight is included in distance," Karn retorted with no inflection, before he pointed down the line.

Merlin was next, but the man waved his hand and Maat leaned farther forward, causing the table to creak ominously. "What is the most important kata?"

This was actually a question that had multiple answers depending on who you asked. Azrael felt that Maat would be a martial expert and could tailor his answer to meet the man's specialty but decided against it. "Teacher. The kata that teaches the user the importance of constant effort and hard work."

Maat actually bellowed a hearty laugh at his answer. "Cheeky. What stat is the most important to an ax wielder?"

Azrael shrugged. "Teacher. Strength certainly would be the universal answer to that question, since an ax is meant for damage and not accuracy or speed. But an argument could be made that you need great Stamina to wield a battle-ax for any length of time."

Maat's face went stoic. "Who said that you were wielding a large ax? *Meine* student. Do not make an assumption and ask follow-up questions," Maat growled down at Azrael.

The man had just called him a student, did that mean he would get in?

Merlin coughed politely and Azrael turned to him. "What

do you know of Soul?" Merlin's question elicited utter silence. Azrael could almost feel the pressure in the room increase, like some unknown force was squeezing his body.

"Teacher. I know the etymon of the word. Is that your question?"

"Not to worry. How would you create a container to hold something that you can't see?" Merlin asked for a follow up.

Again, Azrael felt the room's silence fall upon him. Was the man trying to trip him up? "Teacher. If I knew where the thing was, I could set a trap for it," Azrael ventured.

"No, not like this. What if every trap you created failed to hold this substance? What if this substance contained the properties of water, smoke and air?"

Azrael blinked. What was this line of questioning? "Teacher, do any laws of physics apply to this substance? Does it follow any patterns?"

"Yes. They do and it does!" Merlin crowed into the room as he clapped delightedly. Before Azrael could venture another guess, Merlin continued, "I think we can all agree that this potential student has surprised us. I call for a vote. All those in favor of sending Azrael... to the entrance exams, raise your hands," Merlin said over the creaking of Maat leaning back in his chair.

Three hands rose into the air. All but Keerthilata's. She wore a vivid frown as she studied Merlin.

"You may now leave, Azrael. Please send your *friend* Bat in," Merlin cooed excitedly.

Friend? Why had Merlin said it with such emphasis?

Azrael scratched his head as he walked back to the exit of the room. What in the world was that all about? The first bit had made sense, the teachers were asking questions to test his knowledge—just like Dara and Verimy once had. The questions from Merlin were nonsensical at best. Azrael opened the doors and found Bat and Calum waiting for him.

Calum shot out of his seat and ushered Azrael out of the doorway while simultaneously motioning for Bat to enter.

Azrael opened his mouth to speak, but Calum shushed him. "No speaking between interviews. They should have told you that, but I am guessing that they have forgotten the procedure," Calum admonished.

Azrael settled for a thumbs up, and mouthing 'good luck,' to Bat. Once the doors closed Azrael asked, "What are the entrance exams?"

Calum flinched. "Wait, you were accepted! That's fantastic news. Well, the entrance exams start tomorrow, which is why this is the last day of interviews," Calum exclaimed and began ruffling through sheets on his desk again. "Ahh, here they are," he mumbled as he handed a piece of paper to Azrael.

The sheet was broken into three sections, each with a headline: Written, Combat, and Delving. Under each heading, it gave a few words of outline for what the test would entail. Written asserted that the prospective student should study math, history, tactics and logic. Combat suggested some sparring practice for preparation, and lastly, Delving would take place within the academy dungeons. The individuals participating would be broken into their prospective roles and then be rated based on performance.

He glanced at Calum and held up the sheet. "This all takes place tomorrow?" Azrael asked.

"No, no. It takes place over three days. Students can't advance to the next round without sufficiently passing the round before."

Azrael nodded his head before studying the page again. The first paragraph outlined the three-day schedule and the start times for the tests. He felt his cheeks flush when he read this section. It would probably be best to read through carefully before asking questions in haste—at least from now on. He didn't want to make a bad impression.

"Will I be able to land at the helipad in the morning? We currently have a room booked in El Dorado," he asked after seeing the final paragraph, which claimed rooms would be made available for prospective students if they were needed.

"Let's wait for Mister Bat to finish up, but I would think it might be better to stay on site. The next three days are dreadful for traffic and parking," Calum claimed.

Azrael nodded his head, but was cut off by Bat's exit from the double doors. Bat's body language told the story, but his next words confirmed it. "I didn't get accepted," Bat whispered. Calum went and patted Bat on the back as Azrael watched.

He found it to be a strange gesture. What would that ineffectual back patting do for the Batman? He wanted to get back to the conversation that Calum and he had been discussing before Bat exited, but something told him that would be rude. For now, he just stood there silently as Calum interacted with Bat.

Would Bat get protection as a student if he stayed with me?

After a great deal of muttered platitudes and awkward physical gestures that Azrael was slightly confused by, Bat finally seemed like himself. Azrael was about to jump in and ask Calum to continue their earlier discussion but a strange pop sounded from above Calum's desk, and two scrolls fell onto the table. Calum jumped and rushed over. "Oh? It seems these scrolls are for you two…"

As soon as a scroll was passed to Azrael he felt a surge of cool energy that gave him goosebumps.

Your Muted debuff has been dispelled.

Clearly, someone inside had noticed the debuff and, once combined with the scroll, he suspected they realized the reason. Merlin had the highest levels of Perception or Analyze for him to have seen through Azrael's Obfuscate and everyone else to have accepted it. Right?

He looked over to Bat with a raised eyebrow, and Calum, while clearly surprised by the Dispel scrolls and their activation, didn't comment. He just gave them concise instructions on where to go to find sleeping rooms, before rushing back into the interview hall.

CHAPTER THIRTEEN

The next morning, Azrael walked into the cafeteria just as the sun began rising over the water to the east. He shuddered at the familiar sight of metal tables surrounded by benches. The room reminded him so much of the champion mess hall in the Pit arena on Tech Duinn. Azrael had the same goosebumps the previous night when they arrived at these dorms.

He was here alone this morning because Bat had refused to answer his door despite Azrael knocking for fifteen minutes. He made a note of this for the future—it would seem that Bat wouldn't get out of bed early in the morning unless Azrael physically removed him from it.

Regardless, it wasn't like Bat had anything to do today, and Azrael really did think that the cafeteria had affected the Batman more than it had him the previous night. He couldn't be sure of that, but they hadn't spoken a word to each other and gone straight to bed.

Today, Azrael was awake three hours before the start of the written exam. The nutrition teacher at the Sovereign Halls had always claimed that it takes approximately three hours for the brain to be fully functional after a full night's rest.

I'm still not sure where she got that piece of wisdom, but I always aced tests following it so I will keep doing it.

The usual buffet style serving of the cafeteria was currently not in production. So Azrael approached and asked the chef for a plate. The man cracked his back and stood up smiling. "Any preferences?" he asked.

Oliver Greer
Master-Hash Slinger
Level 61
Health Points: 4,500 / 4,500
Skills: 32

Once Oliver stood up, Azrael admired his portly appearance. Oliver wore a stained white apron, along with a long-sleeved black shirt and long black pants. Everything on the bottom half of the outfit hung loosely, where in contrast the top half all clung to the figure of the man. The apron hugged his impressive belly and muscular arms, showing off their impressive contrasting dimensions.

Azrael couldn't help but match the smirk, and responded, "I know nothing of good food, chef. I think I will leave it up to you."

Oliver chuckled and patted his round belly. "Don't you worry, sir. As you can see, my experiments have all been successful."

The chef started cracking eggs with one hand and mixing with the other. Somehow, he was separating the whites of the eggs and the yolks despite only using a single hand. Azrael checked out the man in the Ether spectrum and felt his mouth fall open. Things were happening all over the kitchen as the man worked on the main bowl. It looked like Oliver was surrounded by tentacles that all completed tasks as he simultaneously worked with his two hands. This was Azrael's first time seeing a non-power class operate in this spectrum and he was beyond impressed.

This man's skills on a battlefield would be no joke either!

As if he was watching a perfectly orchestrated dance, flour, butter, cream, milk, pepper, and salt were all added to the bowl as Oliver stirred. Two ceramic dishes zoomed from a shelf and were quickly filled with the mixture before entering the oven. Oliver threw the bowl into an industrial sink and moved to the fridge as a pan floated onto the stove top.

Two thick slices of back bacon flew from the open fridge into the pan, with a sizzle. Oliver exited the fridge holding bell peppers of three colors, an onion, and mushrooms. He began dicing the vegetables into perfect shapes as another pan zoomed toward the stove. This pan didn't set down but instead had a dollop of bacon fat dripped into it from the other pan before it zoomed back to the chef.

Azrael couldn't even follow the movements of everything happening, because somehow Oliver was finished chopping the vegetables and was scraping them into this pan. He carried this pan back to the stove top and began moving it back and forth over the heat. The sizzle of the bacon was joined by the popping of the vegetables as they all mixed together with a succulent aroma. Azrael wiped the side of his mouth as he felt a small bit of drool escape. He also swallowed the copious amount of the stuff in his mouth.

The bacon was flipped by an Ether tentacle and Oliver asked, "Are you a prospective student taking the exams?"

Azrael nodded, not trusting opening his mouth, which was filling back up with saliva.

Oliver smiled. "Most of the students nowadays seem to come from the guilds or noble houses. This dorm truly hasn't seen more than forty students a semester, when a decade ago it used to be full to the brim."

Azrael tilted his head but had his question answered by Oliver, who must have anticipated it. "All the students stay in the sponsored villas or dormitories that their guilds or families established through donations. It's a shame. I used to love making holiday buffets."

He pulled out two perfect souffles from the oven and applied salt and pepper to the vegetables before placing everything onto a large plate. The plate was loaded onto a tray and cutlery joined it before Oliver added, "I truly hope you make it through. It would be an honor to cook for another student this semester."

Somehow in the span of Oliver's cooking, Azrael had relaxed. Standing with his hands on the food tray, he realized that the tension in his shoulders was gone. He hadn't even realized he was wound so tightly, but the absence of tightness was quite obvious, now.

Azrael pointed upward, intending to indicate the higher levels. "A Batman will be down here later. I know he only thinks about food and would love a personalized meal. Both of us are a bit squeamish in mess halls, I think," Azrael said, hoping that a meal like the one he had just received might help do for Bat what it had just done for him.

Oliver's eyebrows raised and his smirk turned into a true smile. "I feel there is a story I will want to hear in the future, but you need to eat before the food gets cold. And I need to go get some food fit for a Batman. I have never cooked for one of the blind folk before," Oliver exclaimed and practically skipped from the kitchen.

———

Azrael studied the thousands of potential students that stood in front of a rather monstrous stadium. It put the Pit Arena to shame. Of course, this was probably not a dungeon—Azrael hoped. Instead, from the letter Calum had handed him, this was the location of the written exam.

Based on the time in Azrael's interface, it was fifteen minutes from the start of the test. People were milling about on the green lawn in front of a large, coliseum-like building. No armor or weapons were on display, but a great deal of wealth was still evident. While Azrael wore brown slacks and an off-white shirt, the other men all wore suits of finely woven material. Some even had embroidered patterns that looked like they were done with actual gold and silver. The suits ranged from casual jackets to three-piece tuxedos. The women wore suits or gorgeous dresses of elegant designs. If anything, the women had more embroidery and designs in even fancier patterns. But to a one, each person, no matter the race, looked like they had woken up extremely early to put on make-up and do their hair.

Of the people on the lawn, Azrael estimated that ninety percent were human.

A magnified voice interrupted his slow assessment of the people on the lawn. All of the prospective students stood up as soon as they heard the electric hum begin. "The doors are opening. Please make your way to an empty desk within the stadium grounds. There are enough desks for everyone, so there is no need to push or rush. The test will not begin until all participants are seated."

Azrael shivered, recalling the announcer in the coliseum on Tech Duinn. Why was everything at the Atlantean Academy so similar to the Pit? He followed along as the throng of young adults entered through multiple doors around the stadium-like structure. The doors' sizing ranged from small to elephantine, but it seemed that the other side of the doors all led to the same place—

Welcome to "Academy Coliseum."
All groups have been disbanded. Dungeon currently inactive.
Good luck on the exam.
Level: Adjustable
Age: Ancient
Best time: Expand to see scenario leaderboards.
Clears: 10,000+
Ether Concentration: High

Azrael felt his chest tighten, and an irrational need to run came over him. He turned left and ran into the neighbor on that side. Right was likewise blocked. He jumped up into the space above the crowd and started to run across the shoulders. Something grabbed his foot and he toppled to the stone floor.

Azrael had time to glance at his assailant and found a large muscular man with long blond hair stomping toward him. Under the large teenager's heavily furrowed brow he glared at Azrael and even pointed a meaty finger his way. "Watch who you step on, rat," the muscular-teenager stated before he kicked Azrael in the stomach; hard. The kick was powerful and must have had the familiar teenager's weight behind it, because it slid Azrael back a few feet. It also knocked the air out of his lungs, but thankfully the intense pain removed some of his earlier mania.

Azrael Analyzed his attacker. It was the same kid that he'd seen in El Dorado, albeit much better dressed, and put together.

Magnus Thorson
Journeyman-Thunderclap
Level 14
Health Points: 1,450 / 1,450
Skills: 8

Azrael had exited the dungeon thanks to the kick, and the pain plus the safety allowed his brain to begin thinking rationally. He glared at the back of Magnus. The son of Thor had his hair finely woven into a complex braid, and he wore extremely expensive-looking clothing as he stormed further into the stadium. Other people were walking around Azrael on the ground, and some whispered to each other about what had just happened. Ignoring the gossipers, he stood and dusted himself off, while collecting himself further.

Even if this is a dungeon like the Pit, you've survived it. You will face hundreds more challenges—do not back down.

The final thought clinched it, and Azrael walked back through the doors to the same popup message. He needed the safety from the guilds that being a student of the academy would provide. This academy may have a new chance at failure around every corner, but it also had great opportunities. Not to mention, this was the best place to learn more about the guilds and discover the best path to revenge. The best path to returning the EtherVerse to the way it used to be—before the guild's arrival.

Azrael felt the edge of his mouth turn up into a smirk as he heard some of his neighbors' comments on the grass stains and state of his clothing. Others had underestimated him in the past, and now there was a giant black hole in space, thanks to their dismissal. Okay, admittedly, he had help from numerous sources on that one, but the sentiment still held.

The hallway crowd flowed down and moved through a strange doorway that didn't seem to fit with the design. If Azrael were to guess, this should have been a wall, and most people would take the branching side passages up into the spectator section. He studied the square opening that revealed stairs that led down. Both the stairs and the opening were rough cut, seeming to be in complete contrast to the rest of the dungeon's prolific design.

The bottom of the stairs opened up onto a wooden floor that also seemed out of place. Small grains of sand still dusted the top of the wood planks, and the wall beside the entrance had a worn surface with a dark stain demarcating the normal fill level of the sand. This floor was almost two feet below the stain.

In the center of the stadium floor were row upon row, column upon column, of single seat desks. Azrael noticed that the prospective students entering from all sides in the arena sat at the first desk they came to, which left a protective ring of filled desks around empty desks in the center. Having seen this, Azrael couldn't help himself and moved through the desks to make his way to the relatively clear center.

He sat down and looked around himself. After his most recent epiphany, the familiarity of the arena made him comfortable. Could any other prospective student say they had fought on the sands of an arena in life-or-death combat? Of those who could, would any of them be able to claim they had fought against other sapient races to live?

Just like it always had been for Azrael, the nerves of the morning vanished now that the time for action was drawing near. He had trained his whole life against others who wanted to be better than him.

This was just a bigger pond.

CHAPTER FOURTEEN

The test was of the escalation variety. Azrael completed the first section in record time and was now reading and re-reading a question to ensure comprehension before moving on to the answers. These were always his least favorite types of questions to work through because they could be answered in numerous ways, but one of the multiple choices always fit best.

The clack of bones rattled by his shoulder and he chuckled. The dungeon and proctors of the exam chose to use dungeon mobs to monitor the students. For some reason, they settled on animated skeletons that walked the rows at random intervals. The level of fear some prospective students exhibited when the skeletons had begun their patrols still amused Azrael.

The announcer had warned them that it was coming, so he hadn't even flinched. Still, the paper and pencils that the bones passed out would have put him at ease as well. Undead monsters usually attacked with rusty weapons, not paper and pen.

Azrael continued to check the boxes on the computerized tablet that worked like an answer sheet. The screen of the tablet only had boxes labeled with the multiple-choice options, and all the tests were paper. At first, he wondered why the entire test wasn't just on the tablet but then had gotten to the math questions and saw the area to work out answers, and the tablet had a button to convert to a calculator. He assumed this was a process that had been perfected over many years for convenience, because flipping screens on a single tablet would likely infuriate most participants. Him included.

He blew air through his nose when he heard a student bang his head into the table. This was also a common occurrence and, in the silence, only interrupted by clattering bones, every noise was amplified. Azrael couldn't help but find the whole situation amusing. This was a simple pass or fail written test. Hadn't these people learned to fill out what you could and not stress over the things you couldn't?

Perhaps they were coddled by teachers in the past?

The test booklet was thick enough to be called a short story, which told Azrael the academy wasn't expecting perfect scores. Someone still might succeed and ace the written exam, but the passing grade would be low enough that a large group could pass, yet high enough that it shaved down the number of applicants.

He continued to work through the reading comprehension section as people of all races despaired around him.

———

The tablet flashed as he clicked complete, inputting his final multiple choice selection onto its surface. Prospective students had begun filing out of the stadium about an hour ago. Some likely giving up and guessing on all the final questions, and some having truly finished before Azrael. None of that bothered him. The final quarter of the test had been a brutal section filled with absurd math, fallible logic, and obscure history questions. He had thought he knew ten to twenty percent of the answers and been forced to guess on most of the others.

He cracked his neck and stood up, leaving the tablet and

booklet on the desk with his pencil, before navigating through the desks to the nearest exit. A perusal of the stadium floor told him that he was one of the last students remaining. Perhaps a hundred others were spread out and scratching at their heads. A clock counted down from forty-three minutes on the jumbotron above. He shrugged and walked out to join the majority of the others on the grass and stone outside. His interface read three fourteen in the afternoon, and he wanted some food. Maybe the chef would still be working the dormitory kitchen?

People were congregating near a large screen to the right of the entrance though, so Azrael moved to see what was drawing all the attention. "Results will be posted at the conclusion of the test," scrolled across the display on a constant loop. Why would people wait here for everyone to finish? It was definitely time for food.

"The next test isn't until tomorrow, what's the rush to find out if they made it through?" Azrael muttered and turned to leave.

"Oh look, the pauper doesn't understand why people want to get their results and go home. Does he even have a home?" a mocking voice called out of the crowd.

Azrael blinked. Was that directed at him? He slowed his exit and glanced over his shoulder to see Magnus glaring at him. "Did anyone see the fear on his face earlier today when we entered? He probably can't even read!" Magnus shouted over the silencing din. Magnus' spectacle only drew a few laughs but everyone's eyes.

What type of insult was that? How could you interact or understand the system if you couldn't read?

Azrael scratched his head before shaking it and continuing to walk away. "I'll bet a run in the Asgardian Rainbow dungeon that this quaking coward doesn't make it through the first exam. Any wagers?" Magnus called as he saw the first reaction he got. This time more laughter and mutters rose when no one jumped up to take that bet.

Azrael was extremely confused about the reasoning behind

Magnus' showboating but stopped and turned. A run in any dungeon, and a Territorial Cardinal Dungeon at that, was worth quite a bit. But a run in the infamous Rainbow dungeon! That was an egg of a totally different color. Wasn't it the strongest dungeon on Gaia, not including the Pentaclimbs?

Azrael raised his hand. "Am I allowed to take that bet?"

Magnus guffawed but his eyes narrowed. Clearly, he hadn't been expecting someone to take the wager. "What do you have that could be worth a dungeon run? No one wants the rags you're wearing. Scram, rat, actual Gaians are talking."

Azrael blinked and felt a small heat suffuse his neck and cheeks. He pushed that feeling down and considered; he had quite a few things that would be worth a wager. His old sword, crystals, or the Ether Tech suit. Two of which he wouldn't be willing to part with…

Calmly looking at Magnus, Azrael confidently asked, "What price in crystals would you deem a fair wager?"

"Paw. Like you have anything worth two-hundred and fifty crystals. That's the lowest fee that our guild charges outsiders to run the Rainbow. Even then, it's only by appointment," he responded, his tone haughty, almost impetuous.

Azrael smiled widely before reaching behind his back and pulling out the purse of nearly four-hundred crystals from his ring. He displayed it to Magnus from the ten feet that separated them, then opened it and showed a nearby Elven maiden the contents. The Elf licked her lips and turned to Magnus, who raised an eyebrow. In response, she raised both hands as if to say I am not involved but nodded her head. Azrael smirked and made a motion to return the bag behind his back—but summoned it into the ring.

"Shall we wager? I would think that the son of the highest-leveled member could get on the schedule for his own guild's dungeon. Or was your earlier wager just words?" Azrael asked, he tried to return a small amount of the haughtiness that Magnus displayed earlier.

Magnus looked around and realized that he couldn't turn

down the wager after his boasting. He nodded his assent and this time Azrael didn't let his fake smile reach his eyes. As he stared at Magnus, he called, "Good, I am assuming a thousand witnesses is enough to ensure I am paid when I win."

Azrael turned and walked toward the dorm again. This response drew a round of subdued chuckles, but the glares Magnus and his cronies distributed silenced those rather quickly.

———

"You can't antagonize powerful people, Azrael," Bat scolded Azrael as they sat at a metal table in the center of the mess hall.

"I didn't. He made a bet, and I took it. What am I supposed to do? Cower because his father is powerful?" Azrael retorted and took a bite of his chicken rigatoni pasta. He felt warmth spread down from the back of his neck as the creamy sauce and salty flavors intermingled on his tongue. This was easily the best food he had ever eaten.

To his surprise, a few lone students sat at other tables and ate plates of food as well. They all sat as far as physically possible from Azrael, most giving him quick glances before turning away again. That alone should have told him how serious of a problem he might have just caused. Yet, it was the people who were consuming the fantastic tasting food at the speed of light that really made him consider the problem again.

Each person who sat nearby had a plate fixed by a very happy Oliver, and if the man cooked their food as well as what Azrael was eating, that sort of neglect and speed signified an intense need to be away from him before something went wrong. Azrael glanced at Bat's food. His *friend* was eating something called 'black pudding,' which looked like a sausage to Azrael but was far darker and more pungent smelling than anything he had eaten before.

The sausage itself looked appetizing but the leaf filled with insects and topped with moldy cheese looked absolutely horrendous. Each bite the Batman took crunched! Azrael shuddered and went back to ignoring his companion's meal.

"Yes. That's exactly what you are supposed to do," Bat said, exasperation tinting his voice. "Did you not see what happened when we took the spot of a dungeon team? Think, Azrael. Silfa and her party were just low level enforcers of the Asgardian guild. What sort of power would the son of its most powerful member command?!"

Bat was practically screaming, and Azrael caught the students across the cafeteria nodding along with what the Batman was saying. He glanced at the time in his interface instead of answering. Two minutes to four. Well, the results would be up in a few minutes and it was too late now.

"Honestly, I am quite sure I passed this written test, Bat, so I figured a dungeon run we actually get to complete might be worth it. I don't see how he will be upset if he loses when he suggested the bet."

"Have you had no social interactions growing up at all? Azrael, Magnus wasn't making that bet to win something. He was trying to humiliate you, and instead you have turned it on him."

Azrael nodded his head as his lips pursed; that had been his intention after all. He just hadn't considered the fallout of his actions. His head nod stopped, and he felt his neck list to the side. "But then if we win, will he not honor the bet?" Azrael asked.

"You're not getting this! With all those witnesses, he can't ignore the bet. If you win, he will honor it, but likely try to kill you for it!" Bat hissed at him.

"Ahh, nothing lost then. It seems like he and his guild would've tried to kill me either way," Azrael said with a shrug.

"Why would he have tried to kill you either way?"

"I stepped on his head or maybe shoulder, and he seems to dislike people that aren't born into wealth. At least, that's my first assessment of the situation," Azrael stated, his voice eerily calm.

Bat buried his face in his hands. "You really know how to make *friends*, Azrael…"

CHAPTER FIFTEEN

Azrael didn't have to return to the stadium to discover the results of the first exam. Approximately twenty buzzing students streamed into the cafeteria and headed straight toward where Bat and he sat. The leader of the group of teenagers threw his hands in the air and exclaimed, "You finished first overall on the written portion of the exam! How did you manage it? Did you cheat?"

The leader wore brocading blue velvet that had somehow been sewn into a suit, and his lackeys were all similarly colorful. Each member of the impromptu fashion parade was human and seemed to have varying levels of confidence in what was taking place. Some looked uncomfortable to be in the cafeteria, but whether that was because of the leader's recent accusation or that they felt above such an establishment, Azrael didn't know.

He furrowed his brow and asked, "Why would you think I cheated?"

"You had so much confidence that you would pass. Why else would you be willing to take Magnus' bet? You must have been sure you would win, or have a death wish," another student, this one in orange, called out from right behind the leader.

Azrael glanced to Bat, who everyone was ignoring. The Batman's ears were spread wide as he shifted his attention between the students.

Without a proper explanation or aid from Bat, Azrael tried to figure out why he was being accused of cheating. "What was considered a passing grade?"

"Fifty-five percent," the first student said. That number suggested a high passing rate to Azrael, which would be counter to the accusation.

"How many people moved through to the next round?" he followed up.

"One hundred and ninety-eight of three thousand and eighteen," one of the students called from the throng.

Now that figure made a bit more sense with the current accusation. Less than ten percent of the students had moved on. Azrael had made the assumption that the first test would cut the group down to about half, but in fact it decimated the prospective students. Still, for him to be confident of passing would be entirely based on his teachings and understanding. Why then would they be accusing him of cheating?

"Maybe I am missing something, but why do you think I have cheated?"

"You scored an eighty-two percent, which set a new record for the academy. The last record was seventy-five percent. The closest student to you in this grouping was seventy—look, you have already passed, so, just tell us how you cheated. We can't enter this year through the guilds anymore because we chose to try to stand out to sponsors. We need a leg up for next semester's test." The whole picture snapped into place with the group leader's words. These people failed and were likely upset because of it.

The score wasn't too huge of a surprise to Azrael. He had been confident in approximately seventy percent of his answers, and highly sure of another five. Since he had been forced to guess at approximately twenty-five percent of questions, and they each had four possible answers, his score was in line with his expectations. Perhaps a little on the high side since he had effectively gotten slightly more than twenty-five percent of the guesses correct. But how did you explain that to a bunch of coddled nobles?

From the morphing looks on some of the students' faces, they were on the verge of violence as well. Would he have to kill them?

Oliver shouted from behind the cafeteria kitchen counter, "You lot going to order some food, or are you here to pester the prospective students?" The threat in his voice was accentuated by the sound of a knife sharpening itself in mid-air behind him. Azrael had seen his trick before and held back a smile when he saw the twenty students flinch and pale.

"This *prospective* student cheat—ahhhh," the leader of the mob began but cut off in a screech when the knife swished through a watermelon and embedded itself deeply into a wooden cutting board.

"I'm sorry, I didn't hear the response to my question," Oliver called over.

The leader took off and, like colorful birds in flight, the rest of the group began stumbling over themselves in their haste to escape. The looks of anger and violence were replaced with fear and confusion.

Azrael stood up and waved at Oliver. "Chef, I will see you for dinner," he called as he motioned for Bat to follow him upstairs. This seemed to all stem from his appearance. Perhaps it was time to get some new clothes and stop looking so ratty.

———

The next morning, Azrael was back at the stadium. He showed up at eight fifty and was instantly glad he did. There was a schedule for the exams this morning. Each student had a five-minute window scheduled for the combat assessment. Azrael seemed to be first and, based on the eighty-two beside his name and the descending numbers below him, the test was ordered off the scores from the previous day.

The test was still in the Atlantean Academy Coliseum dungeon, and while there were a few students in the area, it was a far cry from the thousands that gathered on the grass yesterday. Azrael continued reading down the list.

Magnus' score was tenth overall and a small flush ran over Azrael's arms and shoulders when he saw that. There was a second blessing in the Asgardian's score—Azrael wasn't currently standing shoulder to shoulder with the young-man. Not only would that have been awkward, thanks to the bet, but also because of the wealth gap. Azrael had purchased some nicer clothes the previous night, but they would look like Magnus' hand-me-downs at best.

Azrael could have afforded more expensive clothes, but he had a finite number of resources, currently. He also had no place to keep spare sets of clothing or get them cleaned and repaired. The list could go on. At the very least, he needed to have an income source before he began to spend the crystals in his ring.

The doors to the stadium opened and Calum stepped out. "Azrael, Prateek, and Fenton, please come in. Go down the stairs and enter the sands. The instructors there will give you the rest of their instructions," the Satyr said with a neutral expression.

As Azrael walked by, he thought a corner of Calum's mouth twitched up, but he couldn't be sure.

Prateek and Fenton held themselves back a bit on the walk, which made Azrael enter onto the replaced sand of the Coliseum floor first. The feel of the shifting grains beneath his feet reminded him of the Pit again, but today—with his resolve set —the reminder forced a grim smile onto his face. He had fought life or death battles upon similar sands, and now they were well acquainted. He had been tortured at the hands of a sadistic Orc and Bearkin.

Belittled, stripped of humanity, and thought of as expendable. What was Magnus or any other student in the face of that?

Four instructors stood near a metal gate which glowed a soft blue. Azrael recognized it as a protection enchantment that would keep the four professors and the waiting students safe from whatever happened to be on the other side.

Azrael didn't recognize any of the teachers from his interview and his Analyze failed to trigger again. He turned to one of the following students and tried using the skill on him instead.

Prateek Khatri
Journeyman-Physician
Level 11
Health Points: 350 / 350
Skills: 8

His Analyze was still working, so this must be the bracelets or brooches that blocked the skill. The second surprise Azrael faced was that the prospective student was a healer class. His brown skin and dark features combined with the insignia on his robe marked him as a member of the Hindu Guild, but he would definitely be a good contact to have for the future. Healers were hard to find and would often have entire groups built around them.

A half-Orc instructor with light green skin and tribal markings stepped forward. His ears were pointy, and the canine teeth were elongated, but the distinguishing factor between him and a full Orc was his slimmer build. Most full Orcs were broadchested, shorter, and built like tanks. Half-Orcs were tall and lean in comparison.

The half-Orc stated, "Azrael, please state your role within a group and don any equipment that will aid you in combat."

Even this half-Orc has nicer clothes than me. Is Gaia just a far richer planet for everyone who lives here?

He cut off his wandering thoughts by scolding himself. He should have thought to come equipped in his gear and with his sword extracted. Doing so would have stopped him from revealing his Ring of Holding, but spatial rings and bags of holding wouldn't be too uncommon for wealthy guilds and the students of the Atlantean Academy. He shrugged and dumped his Ether Tech equipment onto the sand before climbing into it. He held onto the helmet, waiting to place it on his head.

"I am built for solo fighting, which would place me in a utility role. I can act as damage from range or in close and, with my armor, I could likely act as an offtank if necessary."

One of the other teachers, a short human who could be a Halfling, wrote on a clipboard as Azrael dictated, and he assumed the professor was marking down his words.

A second brawny Beastkin instructor walked around Azrael and knocked on the back plate of the Martian suit of armor. "Ether Tech?" the androgynous figure asked in a distinctly feminine voice. Azrael studied *her* again and nodded.

She returned to her spot in front of the gates and the half-Orc spoke again. "Since you are a damage dealer, once you enter, you will face Maat in a full suit of armor. You shall attack with your strongest skill on his shield. After the initial attack, a mana potion will be made available to you if you need it. Maat will then spar with you for a full minute. Your goal is to showcase your skills, or how you chain attacks together. Do not worry about Maat's safety. Understood?"

CHAPTER SIXTEEN

Azrael nodded but couldn't help but worry about Maat. How could a man withstand the strongest charged attacks of all the students? He wasn't arrogant enough to believe his would be the strongest attack today, but he certainly believed that his Soul Storage and full Ether dump wouldn't be easy to withstand.

The half-Orc opened the gate for him to walk through. As he entered, he heard the half-Orc say, "Prateek Khatri, please state your role within a group and—"

The gate closed behind him and cut off the sound just like it had in the arena on Tech Duinn. In front of him on the sand was the huge form of a man in thick plate armor. Not just any man though, no. The behemoth Maat stood in front of him with a tower shield that looked like it weighed as much or more than the Cussing Parrot. Azrael pulled his sword from storage and asked, "Ready?"

Maat raised and lowered the shield on the sand, which was affirmation enough. In response, Azrael charged his sword with nine stacks of Soul Strike. He couldn't afford to bottom out his pool of Ether and collapse in front of a teacher during a test. Still, he had two stored ten stacks of Soul Strike within Soul

Storage as well. He had never tried to simultaneously release both stored attacks but was about to. He just hoped his attack wouldn't cut the professor and trigger Bloodletter.

Using every ounce of strength he possessed, and the added mechanical power of his armor, he charged in and attacked from a high position. He entered the finishing strike for Headman's Bloodletting, crunching his abdomen, then bending his elbows to bring the hilt closer to his body and speed up the blade. Just before contact, he mentally shouted, *<Release ten. Release ten,>* using a slightly new mental trick to unleash the skills. No point announcing your intention to the entire world.

A boom like a starship cannon firing went off from inches away, and the power of the blast actually reversed Azrael's momentum, flinging him back onto his butt. Maat fared worse as the sand exploded off the ground all around his shield and his feet slid across the sand. The base of the initial boom changed to the wail of nearly thirty saws on metal. A shining light of white shone through the sand for a split second before it was replaced with pure silence.

The change from deafening decibels to overwhelming silence made Azrael blink, before the moment was broken with an elastic *boing.* Azrael looked up to find the top of the dome straining to contain a spread-out version of his Soul Strike. Not just any spread out version, but twenty-nine stacks of it. The elastic blue of the barrier bulged in so many areas that Azrael felt his mouth drop open. With the sound of cracking glass, the barrier shattered, releasing the skill into the sky and harmlessly away from everyone.

When the sand finally settled, Azrael turned to see Maat studying a discarded shield. The four foot thick piece of equipment was nearly split in half. The big tank touched it with his toe and watched the metal fold along the gouged center. He pulled off his helmet and scratched his head.

"Good thing I prepared," he said as he turned to Azrael. "Do you need an Ether potion before the minute sparring session?"

That was it? The reaction of nearly splitting the man in two was to move on? Azrael worried that his display wasn't as impressive as it had seemed to him. He nodded as he stood back up and a blond-haired, robe-wearing teenager rushed over with a tray filled with potions.

Azrael hadn't noticed anyone else in the space, but now saw an open door off to the side. Attendants must have been waiting just off the sands. Azrael Analyzed the bottles and discovered he would need two to recover his missing one hundred and eighty points of Ether. He drank both and watched the young man run off the sands before closing the door behind him. The enchantment had gone back up sometime during the aftermath of his released skill, just phasing back into place as if it had never been destroyed.

Maat was now waiting, back in his original position and this time he was holding a thick Katzbulger sword. This type of sword went by many names but was a thick, square piece of metal with a hilt that was used commonly by tanks. Unlike a normal sword, its end was rounded to a flat top and its edges, while sharp, weren't meant for cutting deeply—more splitting or gouging. This sword was more similar to an axe than its hand and a half sword cousin Azrael used. The thickness of the blade made breaks far less frequent and the weight of it added to severity of damage tanks could inflict.

It wasn't a sparring weapon, and Azrael felt his eyebrows raise in response. "Are you going to use the Katzbulger sword for sparring?"

Maat didn't respond but got into his ready position and Azrael clicked his cheek. Whatever. It was the big man's problem, not his. Azrael entered Dancing Dragonfly, realizing his advantage in this fight would be speed. He charged his blade with a single stack of Soul Strike and lunged forward in a modified fencer's thrust. Instead of intercepting the blade with the Katzbulger, Maat brought its vambrace up to deflect the point of Azrael's sword high.

Azrael flexed his forearm and reversed the upward

momentum as his feet came together. The tip of the blade descended from just above his opponent's shoulder. It stepped out of the path of the quick downward slash, and Azrael stepped right while torquing his oblique muscles to follow his prey. Finally, the Katzbulger moved and caught the horizontal attack on its edge.

He released his single charged Soul Strike before sending the blade into his storage ring and followed through his body motion, now weaponless. At the other side, he crunched his opposite oblique and resummoned the blade from storage. The one downside to this method was that he couldn't store the blade if he still had the skill imbued on it, but releasing the strike did keep the tank busy. His sword approached and the vambrace caught its edge as Maat held off Azrael's single charged Soul Strike with one arm on his other flank.

Just like the form's name, Azrael jumped and dropkicked his prey in the chest with both of his Ether Tech boots. The mechanically assisted dropkick staggered his opponent, and Azrael rolled back over his shoulders and regained his feet as he continued to attack by charging back in. His opponent just caught its balance as Azrael, now in Wind's Etching, spun into a low slash aimed at the ankle.

His blade whiffed through the air as his opponent lifted its front foot and avoided the blow, Azrael lifted his non-pivot leg and brought it up into a half pike as he extended his bottom leg and leaped. Simultaneously, he allowed the spinning slash's momentum to carry on and drew in his elbows to accelerate the strike. In a heartbeat, he struck at Maat's head from the same side as his leg strike. The vambrace came up to block and Azrael dismissed the blade and brought his other leg together to return to Dancing Dragonfly. This kick connected double boots with the helmet of his opponent and staggered it even more.

Azrael back rolled again and pulled his sword back out at the bottom of the motion. He charged, then released a double stacked version of Soul Strike in an upward slash from Trelus Lilly. The skill exploded out and Maat barely got its Katzbulger in a cross guard in front of it. Azrael pushed off and recharged his blade with a single charge of his Soul Strike and entered Dante's Needle, fully extending into a fencer's lunge. He released his skill and watched as the blow slammed into Maat's stomach armor.

The man glowed yellow, and it shouted, "Deflect."

All of Azrael's skills flew into the walls above and behind the tank, but Azrael wasn't done. He entered into a low stance for Glas Wen.

His opponent held up a hand. "That's enough. Make your way out of the stadium through that door," it said as it pointed to a door opposite, where the blond-haired youth had entered from. It took Azrael a moment to remember this was a spar, and to return Maat's name to the teacher across from him.

Azrael blinked and checked the timer in the stadium. They had only sparred for twenty-eight seconds. He thought he had a minute. As he stored his sword and armor, the same blond kid entered the arena. Azrael heard him say, "You okay, Instructor Maat? We have a new shield standing by. Did you need further changes to equipment?"

Azrael looked at Maat's stomach and saw only scratches from his attack.

"Just the shield, Gregory," Maat responded.

Azrael walked out the indicated door, but turned a final time to assess his opponent. The man was outstanding at defense, having easily survived all of Azrael's attacks with a single skill. Still, Azrael was pleased to see Maat doubled over and breathing hard as the door closed behind him.

———

Azrael sat eating a second breakfast with Bat half an hour later when the ground shook in the cafeteria. At the same time, white light, brighter or closer than the sun, lit up an entire wall of windows. Then thunder rolled over the room in a booming echo reminiscent of a storm. Azrael jumped up and ran to the window. The morning was slightly cloudy, but they were all white cumulostratus clouds and far away, not black and stormy or nearby.

That wasn't a lightning strike? Bat had stayed seated but was quivering slightly as Azrael looked over. For just a moment, Azrael was confused, but then he remembered who was taking the combat exam right around now.

Magnus Thorson...

CHAPTER SEVENTEEN

Azrael sat at the table; he moved the food around on his plate with a fork as he considered the results that were posted. Azrael had passed the combat exam, but only scored twenty-first over-all. Twenty people were superior to him in combat, and that irked him greatly. His earlier assumption that he wouldn't rank first in this exam rang false in his head now. His gut told him that he was definitely physically upset by the outcome.

And of course, Magnus Thorson ended up ranked first...

He realized that this test wasn't exactly fair to him, since he was still in the apprentice ranks, but for some reason that didn't let him completely dismiss the feeling. At the Sovereign Halls, he had experienced this feeling before and had possessed a similar excuse with the students that were older than him. Still, he had needed to be the best then, and that fire inside him was demanding the same now.

What about the students that are in their second or third years? Are you going to beat them too? He countered his feeling of inadequacy. Then he recalled his saying from the Halls. "Each challenge conquered is a step on the journey to power," he mumbled to himself.

"What is that from?" Bat asked exuberantly, clearly wanting to change the subject and buoy Azrael's sour mood.

"Just a saying that Verimy taught me," he responded and watched the Batman's blue face fall. Clearly his companion hadn't thought that this question would lead to Verimy. Azrael shrugged. Everyone died and Verimy had sacrificed so they could escape Tech Duinn. Azrael didn't find the memory of the man to be distasteful, the way Bat did.

"Did you hear that the Labyrinth in El Dorado increased in power? A few adventuring groups that ran it died recently, and it sparked an investigation," a prospective student at a nearby table exclaimed loudly to his tablemates. The students, while still avoiding Azrael, were more numerous and thus forced slightly closer to him and Bat.

The cafeteria had become more and more popular in the last two days, growing in guests as more prospective students chose to stay the night instead of flying in and out each day. Currently, there were more than thirty people sitting at various tables consuming Oliver's personalized meals and discussing exams, weather, and world news. This particular line of conversation drew Azrael and Bat's highly sensitive ears.

"Really? That's excellent news. The Labyrinth was already a high-level dungeon, but if it got even stronger, I bet our Canaanite guild puts it back on the training regimen," a woman at the same table stated excitedly. She continued after a brief pause. "I know our guild dungeons have become pretty monotonous, seeing as we only have the single Territory."

Azrael felt his eyebrow raise. He had never considered that as a problem that could exist. He trained himself every day through the same routines for almost seven years, and they found a dungeon too monotonous? He shook his head and considered his katas and meditation from today; when was the last time he felt improvements?

The Ether Channels and Manipulation were relatively stagnant, and even the feeling of coagulating power from the freighter trip to Gaia was gone. Still, he searched every day for small improvements; for understanding of a tiny piece of the greater whole. How could these spoiled nobles find a dungeon —where concrete gains could be seen, felt, and experienced —boring?

"Yeah, you're right. Maybe we can run it on our breaks if we become students? Supposedly, there is an armored Rhino that has never been seen before. It is worth quite a bit to armorers and weaponsmiths. The horn can make some excellent weapons, and the plates some pretty high-end protective gear," the first student responded to the woman.

Azrael shook his head and stood up in disgust. These Gaian natives didn't even realize the opportunities they were squandering—if he had a dungeon, he would farm it until his level gains stagnated. But here were Journeyman imbeciles who wanted to run something new, even if it was more dangerous.

"Let's go, Bat," Azrael said as he picked up his tray and turned to leave. Still, something about Bat's posture made Azrael stop and turn back around. Had the Batman gone paler again? Was he still worried about bringing up Verimy?

The Batman shook himself and stood up, forcing a smile across his lips. "You're right. You should get some rest for whatever the Delving test will be tomorrow," Bat said ruefully. "Sorry about that, I couldn't help but picture that Rhino you fought on —" Bat looked around seeming to remember the prospective students around them. He shrugged. "—you know where. Anyway, I am not sure I ever want to run the Labyrinth again, if things like that are in there."

The thought hadn't occurred to Azrael. He did recall the armored Rhino he had faced on Tech Duinn, now. The thing wasn't all that strong, and he had beaten it by himself. He immediately disagreed with Bat's conclusion from the situation, though. If he could get access to the Labyrinth in the future, he was going to take it.

———

The next morning, the screen outside of the stadium featured thirty groups of five. Azrael did the quick math and realized that meant there were one hundred and fifty participants, which didn't make sense. Two days ago, only one hundred and ninety-eight had passed the first exam. Certainly more of those had to have failed the second, right?

He looked over the groups and started scanning the names to find his own. Before he arrived at his name, he came across a name that had a star beside it. At the bottom of the screen, a legend with two items on it explained the star and the plus sign that he had yet to find. "A star indicates a senior student whose role is tanking; a plus sign indicates a senior student whose role is healing."

Suddenly the extra thirty to fifty students made a great deal of sense. If there were twenty-four groups made from only first year applicants, then they needed twenty-four of both tanks and healers for good group composition. The need for thirty or more additional students to make up the slack meant that this intake only had less than eighteen of the rare tank and healer classes still in the exam.

Actually, upon counting, only five tanks and thirteen healers. So, exactly eighteen.

Of the rare classes, healers were still far more abundant than tanks. To be a tank took something that a lot of people just didn't have. Tanks were the first line, the damage sponge, and what Azrael's teachers often referred to as the gluttons. They were only really valuable inside of dungeons, as well. In war, healers and tanks often were used far differently. Healers, for instance, were hidden away on back lines, in triage tents—to ensure they weren't targeted directly by the enemies. In the rare cases healers were brought to the battle lines, they would have a tank assigned as their protection.

He kept scanning and found that he was in a group composed entirely of first years. He already crossed paths with his assigned healer, Prateek, but the tank was named Oslow and he hadn't noticed a student with that name in any of the top ranking spots listed for the last two tests. Additionally, despite Analyzing most students he passed, Azrael couldn't recall an Oslow. Luckily, Prateek was easy to pick out in the crowd and Azrael made his way over to the tall, skinny, dark-skinned man.

Prateek noticed his approach and turned to face Azrael. "Hello Azrael, it is an honor to be making the acquaintance. Let me introduce Oslow," Prateek said in a nasally sing-song voice that highlighted English as the man's second language.

Azrael looked to where the healer was indicating and felt his stomach fall. A whip-thin child wearing his big brothers' clothes was standing half-hidden behind Prateek's back. He Analyzed the pale, blushing kid.

Oslow Aimo
Journeyman-Haltija
Level 14
Skills: 8

He wasn't sure what to make of the skinny and scared-looking Oslow. If anything, this unimposing, nervous child looked scared to meet Azrael's eyes. How could he meet a monster's attack?

It's not like you have a choice. The team is assigned, and all you need to do is showcase your skills.

That brought up a question; would they be judged as a team or individually in this final test? Azrael turned to address Prateek. "Any idea how they are going to run this test?"

"From the words told to me by Vishnu, they will give multiple challenges. We must go as far as possible and be judged by our success," Prateek responded.

"From what Ukko told me, we will each be judged individually on our roles in the group but also as a whole. Failure at early challenges usually results in the whole team's failure, because no one had time to demonstrate their skills," Oslow whispered from behind Prateek's back.

Azrael glanced at the small tank and sighed when Oslow

leaned further behind Prateek. Was the boy scared of him? Or was this another by-product of angering Magnus?

"Alright, let's try to collect our other teammates and discuss tactics," Azrael said as he glanced around the area. He noticed that students were holding up hands with fingers splayed in strange patterns. He pointed to the nearest one, assuming the individual was indicating his group number, but unsure what the thumb and pinky displayed indicated. "Does anyone know how the hand symbols work?"

Prateek blinked before nodding exuberantly. He then held up his hand with only his pointer finger held down. Based on their group number Azrael began to understand the system, but was reinforced by Prateek explaining, "This is thirteen, the thumb, in this position, indicates ten, if a finger between is down. The five, and fifteen are indicated with an adjustment of the thumb angle, and two hands are used for sixes to nines. Once you get into the twenties and above there are further thumb positions, but we don't need to get into those today."

Azrael nodded and said, "You two stay here and indicate our group number. I will take a walk around and see if I can find anyone looking for number thirteen."

CHAPTER EIGHTEEN

"Ahh, group thirteen. See, I told you it was probably easy to find the cause of the terrible smell of rat," Magnus said from twenty feet away.

"Why would you be looking for group thirteen?" Azrael asked, having already seen that Magnus was in group twenty earlier. By the look of the scene setting up, he was coming over to insult Azrael some more. Or make another bet…

"I had to try to help your final two members find where they belonged. They were practically in tears when they saw they were paired up with the weakest member in the exam. It almost seems like a sure failure for anyone on the team." Magnus made a derogatory gesture by making his fingers form the letter A. It was a stupid insult that pointed out someone's Apprentice rank, but today despite the childishness of the taunt it drew quite a bit of laughter.

Azrael frowned deeply as the two members came out from behind Magnus and silently joined Oslow and Prateek.

The final two members of group thirteen were a Centaur berserker who used a two-handed axe, and a half-Orc hunter who used a laser rifle. Azrael saw that he truthfully was the only

Apprentice rank on the team with the two additions, but he didn't let it bother him. Instead, he tried the tack Bat suggested yesterday. "Thank you for guiding them here, Magnus. I wonder why I couldn't find them during my walk earlier."

"As I said, they were rather distraught and needed a bit of a pep talk. Sorry, you two, I realize that failing today isn't what you hoped for after passing the first two exams, but I'm afraid the teachers won't listen to me about destroying the reputation of the school by letting this commoner in. Come see any recruiter from Asgard after the exam and I'm sure we can let you join our guild."

This can't be good. Azrael thought as he looked between the two members and Magnus. The latter walked away and the other two began talking to each other while ignoring the group. Azrael stayed silent for a long while as he tried to overhear what the two were saying. He immediately wished Bat was here, as the Batman would have definitely been able to tell him.

Oslo and Prateek talking about strategy broke him out of his dark thoughts and he turned to listen.

"Well, you see, the group should give me a chance to hit and evade an attack from each enemy before beginning to damage it. My class has no direct taunt skill, but comes with a passive aggravation skill that enrages the mobs if I evade an attack from them. This pairs really well with my spirit form, which allows attacks to phase through me," Oslow explained in a low whisper.

"How do you plan to gather enemies if there are more than one?" Azrael asked, truly curious about how the unique class Oslow used worked.

Oslow's head fell as he mumbled, "I carry a few flame flasks and grenades to gain some damage on all of the creatures at once, but I must ask that you give me just a few moments to gain aggro from the mobs."

Azrael watched as the Centaur and the half-Orc rolled their eyes. Were they minions of Magnus? Prateek continued to regard Oslow with a serious expression and Azrael felt himself begin to worry. They had twenty minutes before they were scheduled to enter the stadium and he was dealing with a shy tank and two possible saboteurs.

"That sounds really good, actually. I assume this means you don't need a lot of healing?" Azrael said, attempting to highlight the benefit of this style of tanking and perhaps bring the Centaur and half-Orc around.

At Oslow's nod, Azrael continued, "Alright, well that means me or the berserker can pick up anything that you don't manage to gather. Prateek, can you keep an eye on us if we have a mob's attention?"

Prateek's lips seemed to twitch upward as he nodded. The Centaur and the half-Orc nodded along with the healer and Azrael held back a sigh. Maybe they weren't Magnus' minions after all?

Azrael truthfully didn't wish to tank at all. His Ether Tech gear was particularly bad for taking attacks. It wasn't like high stamina players that could take a beating and receive healing. His armor would take damage and need repair afterward—repairs that he didn't think would be cheap, or possibly even available.

Still, he was starting to understand the complications of this next part of the exam. The berserker, hunter, healer, and tank would need to work in concert to advance deep into the challenges. Right now, the issue for the group dynamic was Oslow appearing weak and being a unique class to boot. Azrael would need to somehow instill confidence in Oslow from the others. It could work as long as the two additions weren't already against him.

That would take pointing out the tank's advantages, which he just had, but also a good performance by the tank in early stages. Hopefully the first few rounds of the exam would further solidify the boy's skills.

———

The third and final test also took place in the Coliseum dungeon, this time without any changes to its usual functioning. The dividing barrier between stands and sand was up and both students who had already run the test as well as teachers watched his group perform. They were on the sixth wave of mobs, and were already struggling. At first, the mobs had been easy to defeat, but they were slowly growing stronger. Azrael's initial worry about the two final members of the group that Magnus had brought to them had proved to be valid.

To call this exam a disaster would be an understatement. They were only on the sixth encounter and already the half-Orc was screaming, "You need to get aggro on this ghoul, I can't do effective damage if it gets too close! Learn how to play your role, tanks don't dodge!"

The berserker was no better, as he continued to charge into the groups before Oslow even got to them. He wasn't sure yet if this was sabotaging the group intentionally, or just two people acting in their own best interest. Azrael shook his head. As far as he could tell Oslow held the attention of anything that got close enough to take a swipe at him. Prateek was keeping the group alive, but the accumulated sweat on his brown skin wasn't a good sign.

Azrael continued to dispatch the enemies near Oslow using nothing but his sword. His goal was to conserve Ether in case the two members turned on him, but with the chaos around him, it was proving to be difficult. It felt like two members of the group were working in concert, and perhaps a third would be if the others weren't taking damage and needing healing. Had Azrael said the wrong thing earlier, and somehow given the two imbeciles permission? Or had Magnus paid them to?

No, they were going to act this way from the start. That was probably the reason they didn't offer much during the planning sessions.

The two hadn't even introduced themselves, and Azrael was only aware of their names and classes from his Analyze skill. He continued to lop off a ghoul head using the form Fan Opens as he desperately considered options. "How are you doing on Ether reserves, Oslow? Prateek?" Azrael asked.

Oslow's eyes flicked up as a ghoul claw phased through his head. "I am still sitting at ninety percent," the tank claimed.

Prateek was standing behind their backs and called, "Dropping from forty-five percent..."

Azrael assessed his situation. He had full Ether, but of more concern was the damage he had taken on his Ether Tech armor. It had taken a bit of work to understand how to fight alongside the phasing tank. Being too close would make Azrael the unintended target of strikes as they passed through the tank. Standing too far would make counter attacks slow, but now he stood behind the dodging tank and struck at each enemy as it stumbled from the missed attacks it made.

In some ways, Azrael standing behind Oslow helped gain the initial attention of the mobs. Unfortunately, the two imbeciles currently running around the sand of the stadium didn't even attempt to fit themselves into the group. No, they were just attempting to show off powerful skills or sabotaging the group intentionally.

Should I do the same, and just worry about myself passing? Something about that doesn't feel right, though. His final deduction of that being too similar to the second exam rang true. A good group would have easily cleared past this challenge already. This exam must be about group composition or leadership...

Theoretically, their group could probably all be sitting with over ninety-percent Ether pools, because of the tiny amounts of damage Oslow took from enemies. Instead, Prateek was burning through Ether healing the two idiots...

"Oslow, we need to get rid of the deadweight, but if we just stop altogether, they will suspect something and react accordingly," Azrael said as he watched the Centaur rear up and pummel a ghoul with its hooves as the ghoul's claws simultaneously opened up cuts on its underside. "Got any ideas?" Azrael finished, hoping that the timid tank wouldn't give away the plan.

To his surprise, Oslow nodded and said, "We need to finish off this batch and then let them peel their targets during the next phase. Only if it's a blank encounter will my skill work."

Azrael nodded and pushed off with mechanically assisted speed to arrive at Prateek's side. "During the next encounter, do not heal the two others anymore. We won't make it past the ninth encounter at this rate, and I think that would be considered an exam failure," Azrael whispered.

"Are you sure we can pass if we don't have those two?" Prateek whispered back.

"I think they might be working for Magnus to intentionally fail us. I think we're better off taking our chances without them." Azrael weaved back to his position behind Oslow, and continued his attacks.

Within five minutes, the ghouls were all dispatched, and the Centaur and half-Orc returned to the center of the stadium's sand. "You picked a tank class and avoided all the damage. You are useless to groups, and should give up on the academy," the berserker neighed through huge, blocky teeth.

Azrael felt his jaw clench and he closed his eyes, trying to hide the eye roll that followed. Hopefully, the next encounter would finish the two imbeciles off, or if they weren't working with Magnus, entice them to stick to their roles.

The next monster exited the gates on the circumference of the stadium sands. It wasn't a group as Azrael would have hoped for. No, this was a huge ape, with white fur and startling blue eyes. The fangs that protruded from the mouth almost seemed to be made out of glass—wait, Azrael had heard of this creature before…

Frost Gorilla
Journeyman-Beast
Level 31
Health Points: 990 / 990
Skills: 12
Boss

"Ignore what I said," Azrael called to Oslow, but the tank was already glowing orange, and both the Centaur and half-Orc's attacks were streaming toward the Frost Gorilla.

Well, they were probably about to pull all the aggro of the boss. I was hoping they might survive the encounter and be cowed into working as a team...but this, this is certain death.

Oslow flashed orange and grit his teeth together. "I'm sorry, it was too late. Both of their attacks will seem more powerful to the Gorilla."

Prateek jogged over. "Are you sure about this? I know that they will get ported out instead of dying, but they might just be bad group members and not Magnus' lackeys?" Prateek asked, his voice slightly higher than normal.

Azrael, who had wanted to stop the hasty plan at least until after they finished the boss, was forced to shrug. "Unfortunately, it's too late," he said as a huge fist coated in ice crashed onto the sand where the Centaur had stood a moment before. The force of the blow sent the Centaur careening ass over tea kettle into the sand.

The half-Orc, being a ranged fighter, had time to turn and run toward them when it realized Oslow hadn't moved to engage the boss creature. "What are you doing? You need us for our damage, you can't just—"

The bulk of the white gorilla landed atop the fleeing hunter. Then the gorilla began pounding the area under it with the massive, ice-enhanced fists. The hunter ported out of the arena as the berserker climbed to its feet behind the boss.

"Alright, Oslow, Prateek, I think we made our point," Azrael said hastily as he swallowed nervous saliva. He hadn't intended it to be a lesson quite so vivid, but unfortunately that's how life worked. There weren't any easy lessons.

Oslow shot forward and his saber bit into the fur and black skin of the beast. Azrael let a few pounding strikes phase through the tank before he too shot forward, going as far as to charge his sword with his Soul Blade skill. Since this was a boss, there was no point holding back.

He moved to the back of the creature before performing an Ether Tech-assisted leap and slashing downward in the form of Parting the Mists. His blade and the skill's reciprocating saw chewed through the boss and red blood sprayed out of the gash. Oslow proved his worth in that moment. Despite the clear damage Azrael just dealt, the beast continued to target the tank.

Azrael laid into it, linking Parting the Mists with Asura's Rise, followed by Bull's Rush. His Ether dropped slowly as he continually recharged the blade. Within a few minutes, the gorilla crumpled to the sand, breathing heavily.

Azrael assessed the group as the gorilla struggled to push itself back to its feet. The berserker Centaur had stayed clear of the combat, its health bar dangerously low. Now though, the imbecile chose to charge in and attempt a killing blow of the boss. One of the legs of the Centaur was hobbled earlier in the fight and the charge was clumsy because of it. Azrael shook his head, realizing even now the berserker was attempting to show-case its skills above the group's. It would appear they had just been grouped with two idiots and not Magnus' lackeys.

Azrael pointed. "You can heal him but make it something slow. Maybe an over-time effect?" he said to Prateek as he buried his own sword into the ribs of the gorilla, killing it.

———

The Centaur was eliminated from the exam four rounds later when it charged into a group of gnolls and began spinning in a circle, cleaving all the enemies before Oslow even closed the distance. Whirlwind, or some variation of the skill. Azrael shook his head; had the imbecile made an arbitrary decision that beating the tenth round meant a pass? Azrael just shrugged and told Prateek not to heal the berserker.

From that fight on, the encounters were slow going but Prateek's Ether continued to recover and was nearly back to sixty percent. Azrael's own was climbing back above ninety percent, but the real problem was that Oslow's had dropped below fifty. Since the exam didn't allow use of elixirs, Azrael was attempting to figure out a strategy to allow Oslow to regenerate some of his Ether.

Unfortunately, Oslow's tanking wasn't traditional, and his phasing ability created a constant drain on his resources. This left Azrael with few options. A group of four demon wolves careened out of the paddock and began charging at the group's position for the twelfth round. Azrael began his Fan Opens techniques as soon as Oslow gained the threat of all four creatures. Oslow groaned as a paw laced in demon fire slid through his form.

Azrael was jerked out of his thoughts by the sound. What had just happened? Prateek glowed with golden light and Oslow straightened back up as the light transferred to him. "Demon fire works in both planes, I can't fully avoid the damage," Oslow shouted.

Already charging his blade with his Soul Strike skill, Azrael began moving out from behind the tank. This fight needed to end quickly, he just hoped that the kid wasn't aware of this weakness before the fight. Otherwise, he should have told the group sooner. Azrael released two stacks of his Soul Strike at the four wolves, purposefully avoiding Oslow, who would likely take damage from the Soul component in his attacks, even if he was phased. Azrael continued moving to their backs.

Once in position, he loaded a Soul Strike onto his blade and began moving through the Threshing Wheat sword form. Each horizontal slash transferred his weight from his back foot to his front before he reversed the motion, creating something like an elongated figure eight with his sword. When the mounting damage killed a wolf, Azrael stepped forward onto its corpse and continued his attack. Within thirty seconds, the fight was finished, but Azrael was now also down below sixty percent Ether.

He spun on Oslow. "Do you have any way to regenerate Ether?" Azrael asked hurriedly.

Oslow shook his head. Before this fight, Azrael had been

considering an attempted solo of the next boss they ran into, but now with low Ether, he doubted he could pull off that strategy. Prateek was sweating again as well, which likely meant he had also dropped his Ether in the last fight.

The only option left was to attempt to cripple the next wave and earn a respite. For the thirteenth wave, a hulking Troll stepped out of the paddock and Azrael swallowed. This was not a foe that leant itself to Azrael's final desperate strategy. Monster Trolls, like this one, were known for terrifying regenerative abilities. He analyzed the creature as it roared across the sand.

Forest Troll
Journeyman-Champion
Level 44
Health Points: 1,510 / 1,510
Skills: 14
Boss

Azrael felt his heart sink for a moment, before he remembered the words of his tactics teacher. *"Always have a goal. When you win a battle, what message must be sent to future enemies? When you are forced to retreat, what small victories can be gained? When death comes, how do you wish to greet it?"*

The look on Oslow and Prateek's face probably mirrored Azrael's own from a moment before. He took a deep breath and plastered a bloodthirsty smile onto his face. "Hey, the worst that can happen to us here is phasing out of the stadium. What do we have to lose? Let's try to take this boss down with us, right?"

Oslow swallowed hard enough that Azrael could hear it.

Prateek's shadow bobbed its head, which was enough of a mood change for Azrael.

CHAPTER NINETEEN

Azrael's sword cut through the thick flesh of the Forest Troll as soon as Oslow dodged the first strike. Azrael chose not to imbue his blade with Soul Strike to give Oslow a few more moments to garner sufficient anger from the creature. But watching the six-foot cut close and heal in front of his eyes made Azrael want to curse.

He continued to slash at the beast, refusing to attempt any thrusting attacks, in case the wound healed around his sword. The health of the Troll dropped by ten points on each slash but shot back up by five to eight each second. Azrael, at best, could score two hits in a second, which was leaving the mounting damage far too low. The worst part was that neither the Troll nor Azrael had used a skill yet.

Shoot, I jinxed it, Azrael thought as vines shot from the ground and attempted to wrap Oslow up.

The vines phased through the tank but Oslow shouted, "This is going to sap my Ether faster!"

Of course it was. No point holding back anymore. Azrael charged his blade and began moving through the Saber's Fangs, a form that utilized steps or jumps during attacks to increase slashing length. Each cut grew from six feet to ten, and the damage Azrael was inflicting increased.

Oslow moved from the vines, obviously attempting to find a place where they wouldn't be occupying the same space as his phased form. Unfortunately, the vines followed their target and now Oslow abandoned attacks with his own sword.

Some sort of grass began growing out of the sand and attempted to wrap Azrael in its stalks. His mechanically assisted legs pulled themselves out of the grip and he increased his movement to ensure that only a few stalks had hold of his armor at any one time. This reduced his slashing length and damage, but he couldn't allow the restricting skill to take full hold.

"Help!" Prateek's sing-song voice shouted over the relative silence of the battle.

Azrael spared a glance and saw that two small Treants were rising from the ground near the healer. Normally, the offtank, Azrael, would be in charge of gathering any additional mobs and bringing them back to the damage dealers. However, Azrael was the only damage dealer, and if he took the time to gather the mobs, the Troll would likely recover fully.

"Try your best to avoid them," Azrael shouted back, unwilling to stop stacking damage.

"Are you serious? We should have kept the other two alive!" Prateek yelled as he began rushing toward Oslow.

Azrael took a deep breath. They wouldn't have made it this far if Prateek had continued to waste his Ether on the two imbeciles in the group, but of course once something started going wrong, fingers began to point. Should Azrael have just let the team fail and refused to get involved? He wouldn't know if he had made the right decision until after the test.

He continued linking his attacks together but removed a hand from his sword. Holding it forward he mentally commanded, *<Release ten!>* His hand had been pointing up toward the larger Troll's ass and back. As it exploded out of his palm, it expanded and ten closely packed reciprocating blades ripped into the Troll. The regeneration and tough skin of the Troll fought back against the massive damage of Azrael's most powerful skill, but once the blades reached the heart of the creature, it would likely die.

Green blood fell to the sand, but the wounds started to heal in the wake of the skill.

This thing's regeneration is insane! It's even clearing my Bloodletter skill as soon as it's up!

The blades exploded out of the front of the Troll, but it continued to fight with Oslow in front of him. Azrael Analyzed it again.

Forest Troll
Journeyman-Champion
Level 44
Health Points: 645 / 1,510
Skills: 14
Boss

Even as Azrael watched, its health jumped up higher. He began swinging his blade again to counteract the regeneration. Should he use his second stored skill as well?

A flash of light caused Azrael to blink and peer around the green calf. Oslow was gone. Whether the tank had run out of Ether or made a sloppy decision, Azrael couldn't tell, but the vines that had been targeting the tank instantly began attempting to creep toward him.

The Troll needed a split second to recover from its last attack on Oslow but instead of targeting Azrael, like the vines, it leaped toward Prateek. The healer had time to open his eyes wide as he sprinted away from the two Treants that followed him. Azrael had assumed he would gain the attention of the Troll but now was staring at further problems. He couldn't release his skill, or he might connect with Prateek accidentally.

This fight had taken a terrible turn.

Azrael chased after the back of the Troll with everything he had and was able to close the gap that had opened in the split second of surprise. He resumed his attacks on the creature's calves, hoping to pull its attention back to himself. The cuts and slashes Azrael made did change the creature's mind about attacking Prateek, but unfortunately it was too late.

Prateek flashed out of the stadium as well. In response to the charging Troll, the healer seemed to have changed directions and run right into the Treants. Azrael felt himself suck in a deep breath as he watched the Treants change their target to him as well. Now he had the creeping vines behind him, the turning Troll, and the Treants all focused on him.

He expelled his breath and leaped into the air, attempting to gain a height that he could release his final stored Soul Strike on a downward angle. He needed it to hit the Troll and the Treants simultaneously. And for that, he needed the distance for it to spread out. He gained the height he estimated he would require and mentally commanded, *<Release ten,>* again.

The phantasmal blades began spraying green blood and even forced the Troll to a knee as the pressure of the blade against the tough skin fought the Troll down; almost like a new form of gravity. Then to Azrael's relief, the resistance and healing ended all at once, the blades suddenly careening right through the Troll like it was paper and blasting out the back of its body. The two Treants that charged in were mowed down like weeds and Azrael landed, watching the sand spray up from the continued force of his stored skill.

The vines behind him withered and died, turning into dust. He had completed the thirteenth challenge and the second boss. Hopefully, Oslow and Prateek would be given credit for that as well. Eight porcupines waddled out of the paddock next, and Azrael had time to dive behind the bulk of the Troll before their quills flew toward him.

The quills missed, but three tracked him enough that they tore through the green corpse, rotating like drill bits. Each quill arrow crossed the sand and dug into the walls. These creatures likely had more skills that they could call upon, and Azrael only had twenty percent Ether remaining.

He glanced around the corpse's shoulders and saw the porcupines instantly fire more drilling projectiles in his direction. As he dodged, his heart pounded against his ribcage. Had some of the porcupines been setting up as mortars? Five thuds echoed over the sand to match with his thudding heart.

Ba-thump, ba-thump.

He kicked off the sand hard and lunged away from the cover of the corpse. An explosion rocked the sands behind him, and he heard liquid splatter onto the back of his armor. He couldn't afford to let the armor be severely damaged in this fight and likely this was a losing endeavor, anyway. He breathed out his breath and shouted, "I give up."

The phrase had been highlighted in the instructions they had received. Between one step and the next he was suddenly no longer sprinting on sand. His foot clanked down onto stones and he joined his other foot to it and leaned back onto his heels. Unfortunately, due to the slick stone and his built-up momentum, he couldn't stop that easily.

He bailed onto his back and directed his feet at the quickly approaching wall. His Ether Tech suit scraped over the stones and the servos whined as his feet hit the vertical stones hard. A few cracks even spiderwebbed out from the impact point, but he managed to arrest his slide and turn over. He found eight sets of eyes regarding him. Some were sullen, while others looked openly hostile.

The fact that they weren't pouncing on him told him the story. Each one was unsure if they had passed or failed this exam and didn't want to start a fight if they had succeeded. He felt rage from the Centaur and half-Orc directed solely at him, and he wondered if Prateek and Oslow had ratted him out the instant they were ported out.

Azrael got to his feet and chose to leave his armor on.

Hopefully, none of these imbeciles would attack him in earnest if the results were unfavorable.

Bat's right, I sure am good at making friends…

CHAPTER TWENTY

Many people were sitting at tables spread out through the cafeteria. It seemed everyone had discovered the quality of food
Oliver served. That or the fact that this place served food at all,
while they waited for results. Many of the high-ranking nobles
weren't present; Azrael heard they chose to bide their time in an
upscale restaurant located across the bridge in Atlantis.

*After this is over, I need to go look around Atlantis myself. The greatest
city ever built, huh?*

He could see the members of his group spread throughout
the dining area, and Bat sat across from him. Azrael already
conveyed the events of the day to the Batman. Bat at first
appeared confident in Azrael's success, but now sat twitching in
apparent worry.

"You really think Magnus might have paid off those two?"

"Bat, it's fine. Even if he did, and I failed because of it, we
will just go to another planet to avoid the Asgardians and other
guilds," Azrael stated, but his own nerves rode close to the
surface.

Bat shook his head and his ears went wide. As Bat spoke, he
indicated the room at large. "Everyone is talking about how far

they made it in the test. It seems you guys were above average, but your group members in particular are pretty upset with you. They sound like they want to kill you right now."

Azrael smiled, which made Bat jump and shiver. Bat and he still enjoyed a table entirely to themselves because of the other students' fear of Magnus. Would his teammates attack him if they failed? The Centaur and Dwarf weren't a big loss but if he was honest, Oslow and Prateek would be. Not because of their skills, but because of their rare classes. The other two imbeciles could burn to death a few feet from him in a dungeon and he wouldn't piss on them.

A wave of euphoria washed over Azrael and the room exploded in gasps and startled shouts. A blinking exclamation point alerted Azrael to notifications, and based on the feeling he just had, he had gained multiple levels.

He opened the first notification.

Congratulations! You have reached level 24, 25, and 26.
Excess Etherience has been banked. Stasis entered.

The first notification sped up his heart rate significantly. He felt his palms begin to sweat. There was an extra level in his Apprentice class. Most Apprentices ranked up at level twenty-five. Anyone who saw him at twenty-six would know immediately how rare his class actually was. He needed to get out of the cafeteria right now. As quickly as he could without arousing suspicion, he stood and walked to the back stairwell, which led up to his and Bat's rooms. Bat followed him and as soon as they got to the hallway Azrael whispered, "Did anyone notice?"

Bat shook his head. "I only noticed after you stood up to leave suddenly. You don't often leave a plate half-filled with food. I think the others were too engrossed in their own notifications. Is the extra level that big of a deal?"

"The Asgardians already tried to bully us into their guild. If they knew I possessed a rare class, what do you think they would do?"

Bat's ears went wide. Azrael was just glad no one had noticed; he didn't need to add another reason for people to be interested in him. To gain the amount of Etherience he had in one go likely meant he passed the tests and was now a student, but he needed to scan his other notifications from the safety of his room.

Once he was seated in his unadorned, white-walled quarters, he pulled up the other notifications.

Congratulations! You have completed a quest.
Multiplier Quest
Atlantean Academy Entrance Exams
Pass the Exams
Written Exam
You have finished the written examination and finished first overall.
Reward: 100,000,000 Etherience
Combat Exam
You have finished the combat examination and finished twenty-first overall.
Reward: 21,000,000 Etherience
Delving Exam
You have finished the Delving examination and been given an overall grade of B- for your leadership and skills.
Rewards:
Etherience Multiplier x6.
726,000,000 Etherience (21,125 Etherience diverted to Etherience Bank).
FFA place has been reserved for you as a first-year student in the Atlantean Academy.
Bonus Reward: The mentor Merlin has chosen you as a prospective student.

Merlin, that strange professor who asked the odd questions. He dismissed that part for now and immediately opened up his character sheet. What skill was awaiting him in the sixth tier?

Azrael Finch (Sovereign) Level 26 (*Rank up?*)
Class: Apprentice-Revenant
Class Skills: Soul Strike (V), Soul Cloak (V), Soul
Storage (V), Bloodletter (V), Call of the Soul (III)
Health Points = 290/290 Points
Ether Pool = 170/170 Points
You have 0 stat points and 3 skill points to distribute.
Stamina – 29
Strength – 33
Agility – 42
Dexterity – 42
Intelligence – 19
Wisdom – 18
Charisma – 18
Luck – 12
Skills:
Analyze – Strong 11
Butcher – Moderate 21
Combatant – Strong 35
Enchanting – Weak 5
Endurance – Strong 21
Ether Channels – Moderate 12
Ether Manipulation – Moderate 14
Essence Conversion – Weak 3
Martial Arts – Strong 46
Mediation – Moderate 18
Obfuscate – Strong 15
Sneak – Moderate 4
Stone Cutting – Moderate 11
Swordsmanship – Greater 45
Tracking – Weak 12

___

Tier 5 Skills

Call of the Soul
● **All Soul abilities will increase in potency by 50% per talent point. You have gained a specialization: Soul Revenant Class.**

> **Skill gained at 5/5, "Soul Superiority."**
> **<5>/5**
> **Each skill will be updated per talent point.**

Call of Blood
● **All Blood abilities will increase in potency by 10% per talent point.**

> **Skill gained at 5/5, "Unknown."**
> **0/5**
> **Each skill will be updated per talent point.**

The fog of war rolled back, and his breath caught. He had dreamt of this skill since he was a child. Since he learned of his last name and been trained as a Sovereign Son. He eagerly placed his point into the only option available on the sixth tier.
Tier 6 Skill

Soul Blade
● **Create and summon a blade connected to your soul. This blade will be able to gain levels and paths of specialization.**

> **Skill gained at 1/1, "Soul Blade."**
> **<1>/1**

Bat made a squeak and stated, "You just became a Soul Revenant. Did you just specialize?"

Azrael had felt the wave of heat rush through him but thought it had come from the unveiling of his Soul Blade skill. Now he reread the Soul Superiority and realized that this class granted him a specialization in Soul. Would that have meant he could have specialized in Blood as well?

Not that it mattered. To specialize in the Apprentice ranks was not unheard of but it was definitely rare.

"Yeah, I guess I did. That's not all. I got an actual Soul Blade, too. I'm going to summon it now and then advance my class. I can't be sitting at level twenty-six or people will get suspicious," Azrael said hurriedly.

Once they arrived on Gaia, Azrael began Obfuscating his sword as a common item, hiding its name. Sovereign Sword was a bit of a give-away about his past. If people could discern the enchantments, he might have become a target for thievery at best, but the name of the sword invited far larger political problems.

Bat's ears audibly flapped open and closed in response to Azrael's announcement, but he remained silent as Azrael began casting his new spell.

Blue light began to coalesce in front of Azrael, almost seeming to be a ball of water because of its thickness. Waves rolled over the surface of the energy as it elongated and changed. To Azrael's shock, it seemed to be demanding something. He could feel the tug on his hand and followed the sensation to his ring finger and the storage ring it held.

Did it want the Sovereign Sword? It was the only thing he could think of that was inside his storage ring. He pulled it out.

Would you like to offer the Sovereign Sword as a catalyst for the creation of your Soul Blade? This may increase the starting level of your Soul Blade.
<Yes> | No

———

Sovereign Sword
This sword is a near-perfect replica of the Sword of the Sovereign King.
Ether Pool: Large
Current Ether Pool: 130/130
Enchantments: Stats X (+3), Ether Edge V

His guess proved to be correct, and he hesitantly accepted the offer. It may have been wise to have kept it as a back-up, for desperate times, but a higher-leveled Soul Blade was just too tempting.

The blue Ether pool greedily consumed the blade, seeming to turn it into a blue dust that only deepened the shade of the floating bubble. The liquid-like Ether began to grow brighter, to the point that Azrael was forced to close his eyes. Then even that wasn't enough shielding, and he hid his face in the crook of his elbow. He activated his Ether Channels and Manipulation and watched the flows grow ever more complex. The weaving inside the ball was so beautiful it reminded Azrael of millions of tiny snowflakes, each pattern unique and intricate. It was safe to say that without the system's help, he never would have learned a skill like this.

Something dark black to his Ether sense grew in the center of the oblong-patterned bubble. Then all of the pattern sucked inward and stuck itself onto the black shape, which clearly looked like a glowing sword now. Something cold dropped onto Azrael's lap and startled his eyes open.

A smoking blade rested there in a black scabbard. The hilt was stylized in a pattern Azrael instantly recognized as a bird. It took him a few moments to realize that it was meant to be a raven. The pommel was gripped in artistic talons and held a clear crystal, and the guard was meant to look like spread wings. He bared the blade, exposing the long fuller that ran down the center of the piece. The blade itself was dark but still metallic in coloring and the edge looked sharp enough to cut silk.

His intense scrutiny activated his Analyze.

Raven Tide – Soul Blade
Level 3
0 / 150 Ether Pool
The Strength of Arms III
+6 Strength as long as the Blade has Ether from its pool to draw on. Unlock higher levels of your Soul Blade for more.
The Strength of Body III
+3 Stamina as long as the Blade has Ether from its pool to draw on. Unlock higher levels of your Soul Blade for more.

In some ways, it was a let-down. His other blade offered better enchantments, but it wouldn't have ever grown. He immediately Obfuscated the blade, removing the name and replacing it with "Sword of the Bear," a common name for a weapon that held these two enchantments. That done, he sheathed the blade and looked to Bat, who was standing open-mouthed.

"Did you see the complexities of the Ether weave?" Bat asked. His question was clearly rhetorical.

Azrael chuckled and nodded. "I did. There is no copying that skill. Alright, time for me to rank up. Make sure no one disturbs me, okay?" Azrael responded jovially. His spirit felt buoyant. He finally had a Soul Blade and was advancing to the Journeyman rank. Coming to the academy was proving to be the right decision, even though his hand had been forced at the time.

When he mentally clicked rank up, another surprise awaited him.

Ranking up to Journeyman could take up to two weeks, are you prepared for the process?
<Yes> | No

He didn't accept right away. Instead, he looked to Bat, and said, "This says ranking up could take two weeks? I know that your body goes into a form of stasis according to my lessons, but don't classes start here in seven days?"

Bat nodded and scratched his ear. "That's what I heard in the cafeteria, but you have to rank-up, and teachers would have to understand, right?" Bat asked, his voice gaining confidence as he continued.

His companion's logic made a great deal of sense, but to be sure Azrael instructed, "Go find Merlin. He is my mentor, according to the quest completion notice. He should be able to inform others of my situation. When you are doing that, I will accept the rank-up, so he doesn't see my level. Good?"

Bat nodded and so Azrael clicked the accept button. His world instantly went black.

CHAPTER TWENTY-ONE

Azrael blinked; his world lit back up with a strange, multi-hued luminescence. He looked to the source of the light and found a vaulted cavern ceiling with a multi-faceted gem inlaid right at the peak. The stone was a dull gray and muted some of the rays, but also reflected them downward into the large circular room he stood in. The entirety of the room was illuminated, but only the area around Azrael received direct light.

The gem itself gave off different colors of light based on the ring of the facets of the gem. The center shone white, and the next ring had a tiny hue of green added, after that came a sky blue, but strangely the other, larger rings were completely black. Azrael looked around him to see billowing white clouds that resembled human silhouettes. Directly around him were five stacked rows of the things, resembling an army of close-pressed bodies encircling him. Behind that in the greenish light were two rows of the closely packed cloud-humans, and then in the blue area stood one row of slightly spread-out figures. Azrael shivered.

"Are you done staring?" a nasally voice called from near the floor of the cavern. The words came off irritated, and Azrael jumped, causing the shiver to raise goosebumps all over his skin.

He scanned the area from which the voice emanated and found a tiny gray-skinned creature. Its limbs were spidery and seemed too long for its emaciated body. It wore only a brown leather loincloth. What in the world was this thing doing here? Was it a Gremlin?

"Now the imbecile is going to stare at Nyx. Truly, Apprentices are the worst to deal with. Any halfwit can make it to Journeyman, it seems. Do-you-know-where-you-are?" The angry creature, whose name was likely Nyx, exaggerated each word.

Azrael raised an eyebrow in response. Was it even worth saying something to this spiteful parasite? Since he had no idea where he was, he chose to cave and responded, "I have no idea where I am, but if you continue to speak to me like a man who took a blow to the head, I will ignore you. I assume this place has to do with ranking up?"

Nyx smiled, revealing teeth that seemed too large for its head. Were they sharp? It was tough to tell since Azrael only caught a glimpse. "Very well, but since I was only treating you like a noob, then you shouldn't have any issues, correct?" Nyx stated and continued before Azrael could interject. "To answer your question, this is the Cavern of Choice, and it has everything to do with ranking up." Nyx began cackling and Azrael closed his eyes to pray for patience.

It would seem this was some sort of guide, but Azrael hated people with this sort of superiority complex. They were exhausting to deal with. "Please stick to just answering the questions I ask. What is the Cavern of Choices?" Azrael stated, hoping that if this spiteful Gremlin was a guide, it would have to obey him.

A sparkle flashed across Nyx's eyes before it replied, "Not a problem, inept master. The Cavern of Choices is a spirit realm that highlights your options for advancement." Nyx casually waved a spindly hand around the room, indicating all the ranks of cloudy figures, but then stopped and interlaced his fingers, acting like an obedient servant.

Azrael felt his teeth begin to grind as his pulse rocketed up and beat in his eardrums. "No more attitude," Azrael grit out from his tight jaw before taking a deep breath and asking, "Do I just walk around and assess my options?"

"If the Apprentice approaches a figure, the fog of war will roll back and reveal the option underneath," Nyx stated flatly, not seeming to show attitude but also distinctly offering it with his lack of emotion.

Whatever, just leave the ornery Gremlin to deal with itself. Who put the creature here anyway?

Azrael approached the nearest human-shaped cloud and saw the fog roll off the shoulders of a somewhat transparent version of himself. This version held a bow and wore black leather armor. He tilted his head and watched this version of himself do the same. His scrutiny triggered Analyze, which gave him the information he needed.

Journeyman Soul Hunter (Common)
+1 Dexterity per level
+1 Agility per level
+1 Strength per level

Azrael nodded, seeing the increase of stats per level from his Revenant class. This common option was already an upgrade. He started to theorize what the layers meant when the next fog of war rolled back in the white lit area and revealed another common class, this one a Sniper class. The next two rows also proved to be common classes and variants of a hunter. Did that mean the rings were highlighting the class rarity?

Azrael didn't bother theorizing and instead approached the first row of the two in the green-hued area. On his approach, the cloud evaporated, and he was studying himself again, this time in a suit of Ether Tech gear very similar to that of the

Martian one in his Ring of Holding. He instinctively looked at his finger and found the ring gone. He felt a surge of heat rush over his shoulders, and he began to sweat. "Nyx, what happened to all my gear that I was wearing in the real world?" he asked the Gremlin as he looked down to find himself in the same style of loincloth the angry creature wore.

"Stu—ahem. Apprentice, you cannot take items with you into the Cavern of Choices. Unless you chose a particularly dangerous place to go into stasis, you will still have them when you wake up," Nyx stated flatly but wiggled his eyebrows, insinuating that Azrael probably did choose to enter the rank up somewhere unsafe.

Azrael shook his head and grit his teeth. At least he still had everything. Bat would ensure that no one disturbed him, but being in a loincloth left him feeling particularly exposed.

He Analyzed the version of himself in front of him.

Journeyman Soul Commando (Uncommon)
+1 Dexterity per level
+1 Agility per level
+1 Strength per level
A Commando gains the class skill Vanguard which, if equipped with Ether Tech gear, boosts the Stamina stat by 50%.

Azrael saw the addition of the Vanguard skill and checked the next in line to see if that was normal for uncommon classes. It was, which made Azrael smile and move to the blue-tinted area. Since these were spread out differently, he had to walk about ten steps before he came to the first clouded figure.

The smoke slid to the ground and pooled there, revealing himself holding a carved staff and wearing a great deal of animal fur.

Journeyman Soul Druid (Rare)

+1 Stamina per level
+1 Strength per level
+1 Intelligence per level
+1 Wisdom per level
A Druid gains access to the Shapeshifter skill. Choose one animal form and shift into it or out of it four times a day. Other forms may be available in the skill tree.

That was a very interesting class and would build the stats he hadn't gained from his Apprentice Revenant. That being said, by the equipment, it looked like the class may be more of a spellcaster, and he wasn't sure it would pair well with his up-close fighting skills of the Revenant tree. He would just have to keep checking.

He glanced at the nearest row in the next section. It looked a bit like a gray thundercloud because the light wasn't hitting it. He did his best to estimate how many options existed in each section. If there were one hundred rare classes in his current row, there were maybe twenty of the next grouping, and only perhaps four in each cardinal direction of darker black clouds behind those.

He approached the nearest gray cloud and, to his surprise, saw the fog begin to peel back slightly.

"Those classes are not available. I don't know why you would tempt yourself," Nyx called into the cavern.

Azrael shrugged; he wanted to know what exactly he was missing out on. The fog didn't fully pull off this version of himself and he found himself looking at his own calm face wearing white robes. Behind his back, the hint of wings protruded from shoulder blades.

Journeyman Soul Seraphim (Epic)
All Etherience requirements for levels are 90% lower.
+1 Strength per level
+1 Stamina per level

+1 Dexterity per level
+1 Agility per level
A Seraphim can gain access to the Grace skill. One time per day, the Seraphim can completely restore his or her Ether.
Locked

Okay, so that skill alone was insanely powerful, but Azrael didn't miss the wording change. It was a skill inside of the tree of the Seraphim class, and could be top tier, or possibly not even become uncovered, depending on the direction someone took. Yet due to the Etherience requirement reduction, he would still rank it well above the Druid class.

He moved to the nearest figure in the darkest area, truly hesitant to uncover a class he had no chance to take. Especially if he would find a skill powerful enough to put the other classes to shame.

The dark storm cloud only pulled back enough to reveal Azrael's face looking back at him. The eyes reflected a confidence and power he couldn't ignore, but unfortunately that was it for clues. His Analyze triggered.

Journeyman Soul Chimera Knight (Legendary)
Different roles based on Chimera tamed.
All Etherience requirements for levels are 60% higher.
+1 Strength per level
+1 Stamina per level
+1 Dexterity per level
+1 Agility per level
A Chimera Knight can tame an intelligent Chimera. The Knight can take on one squire at a time. The squire gains the class Apprentice Chimera Knight (Squire role), based on performance the individual may be able to access the Journeyman Chimera Knight class.
Locked

The class was strange. Was the Etherience rate disadvantage for a chance to tame a Chimera? Azrael knew that Chimeras were the nightmares of Gaia; depending on what variant you faced, you might have to deal with a creature that could fly, poison you, and was as large as Musth. That was just insane.

Still, the ability to train others as Squires. Was this where my father got his Sovereign Sons idea?

To have the ability to train a Legendary Class army, and perhaps even lock this class to your bloodline one day, was a power that anyone would dream of. Considering that each Knight would be able to take a squire, it would be slow going at first, but in time as more individuals were knighted into the class, the growth of such an army would become immense. With a class like this, Azrael could theoretically create an empire far stronger than the Sovereign Empire, which had been based on the lie of an Ancestral class that didn't exist.

It was very difficult to turn around and return to the illuminated rare classes, but he did so. Nyx chuckled, which he failed to hide as a cough. Azrael felt his cheeks heat, but he ignored the Gremlin, not wanting to give it the satisfaction.

––––––

What felt like hours later, Azrael uncovered his Revenant class.

Journeyman Soul Revenant (Tech Duinn Rare)
+1 Stamina per level
+1 Strength per level
+1 Agility per level
+1 Dexterity per level
A Revenant gains access to the Mag Mell skill. One time per day, the Revenant and his party can enter the Mag Mell spirit realm; inside this realm, the Revenant is safe from all external harm and gains recovery bonuses. Revenant must enter back into the true plane in the same place they left it.

Truly a very powerful skill to gain. In theory, Azrael could escape imminent death once a day, or use it to sleep while inside dungeons, creating a safe zone anywhere. So far this was the most powerful skill he had found amongst the thirty or so other classes he had revealed. Still, he was determined to look through every option available before making a final decision.

Nyx had been silent the entire time, and Azrael was beginning to grow frustrated with the lack of help from the Gremlin. Wasn't it supposed to be a guide?

"Nyx, is this the most efficient way to compare the classes? This is going to take me forever," Azrael complained.

A sigh came and Nyx stated flatly, "Finally, the apprentice asks. There are many options for viewing your available choices. The manual option is what you are currently using. You can also use the automated option, which will pick your class for you, or the system assistance to compile all available choices and scroll through them on a screen."

Azrael's heart thumped a maddening rhythm into his ears. Everything from his shoulders up felt like it was on fire and his fists balled as he shook with rage. He could have just been looking through a compiled screen!

Should I try to strangle Nyx?

"Being stingy as always, Nyx," a deep voice boomed into the cavern, seeming to come from everywhere.

Azrael looked up and then down to the addressed Gremlin. Nyx was snarling at the roof, its fists balled as Azrael's still were. "You pile of beetle dung! You know you aren't supposed to interrupt during these trials," Nyx shouted, his head still directed upward. The Gremlin was practically spitting due to the clear anger Azrael could see reflected in every limb.

"I wouldn't have to interfere if you offered the boy all of his options," the booming voice retorted, sounding slightly amused. "Perhaps you didn't notice his skills? No, that couldn't be it, Guide Nyx is all seeing and all powerful, right? So, then why are some of his options unavailable?"

Nyx snarled and yelled at the roof, "You mother-cauliflower!

I will make your next rank up as painful as possible! Damn heliotrope."

Azrael felt his mouth drop open. Ever since the swearing filter was added to the system, the use of profanities was nearly non-existent. This likely meant that Nyx was either extremely old or indignant in his anger. Azrael initiated the report function on his system, out of habit, but caught himself before sending. This wasn't a fellow student at the Sovereign Halls that was swearing to try to be cool. This creature could very well be an all-powerful, almost godlike existence—better not to mess with him.

Nyx continued snarling at the ceiling but waved a hand in Azrael's direction.

Cavern of Choices
Scroll down or think next to continue browsing.
Use tabs to increase the rarity of classes.
Click on the class for a more in-depth description.
Ranks:
[Common] / Uncommon / Rare / Epic / ~~Legendary~~ /
~~Godlike~~
Displaying 10 items of 500
Custom Journeyman Class Option
Journeyman Soul Actor
Journeyman Soul Adept
Journeyman Soul Archer
Journeyman Soul Bat
Journeyman Soul Berserker
Journeyman Soul Butcher
Journeyman Soul Champion
Journeyman Soul Combatant
Journeyman Soul Dart
Displaying Page 1 of 50
2, 3, 4,...
Next | Previous

As soon as the screen popped up, he changed his mind and browsed back to report Nyx. The angry little creature had been keeping Epic-ranked classes from him!

CHAPTER TWENTY-TWO

Azrael opened the Epic class options and found three waiting for him. He turned to Nyx, and asked, "Why are there three Epic classes unlocked now when they weren't there before?"

Nyx's eyes detached from the ceiling and fixed on Azrael. They held all the suppressed destructive force of a volcano. The Gremlin sucked in air through its nostrils and then began to grow larger. At first, it was barely noticeable, but when the creature approached half of Azrael's own size, Azrael felt his throat constrict and swallowed a lump of saliva that formed. In moments, the Gremlin was a head taller than him, and more muscular than an Orc.

Nyx pointed a finger, and hissed, "You must ask the proper questions in the Cavern of Choices. Having outside help, while not forbidden, is a very poor decision!"

The tone caused Azrael's eyes to widen and his mouth to fall open; Nyx was very clearly upset by whatever had just happened. Azrael looked up to the ceiling and tilted his head; outside help? Who could have given it to him?

His first thought was Bat, but the deep voice couldn't have been the Batman. His next thought went to Merlin because that was who Bat had been on his way to inform. That did seem more plausible, but why would the instructor help him, and how would he have the clout to do so? His final thought was Ogma, due to the deep voice, but again the same problems as Merlin arose. His father then?

Yeah, that's the most unlikely option yet!

He scanned back to Nyx to find the Gremlin reverting back to its normal size. Nyx cleared its throat and said, "You clearly didn't set up this help beforehand. I will have to contain my displeasure to the offending party. To answer your question— this is a test of sorts. If you aren't aware of your worth, why should you be rewarded? As for why they are available now, well, your benefactor forced them open using a very powerful method."

Azrael blinked at him and frowned. How was an Apprentice rank supposed to be aware of the functions of the Cavern of Choices? He better make sure to ask the right questions from now on. "Is there anything else I should be made aware of before choosing?"

Nyx smiled menacingly, its teeth still seeming enlarged from the earlier anger. "Oh, a great many things, young Apprentice —a great many things."

Azrael smiled back, realizing the game that was being played. If he hadn't been given the help from outside, he may never have come to realize it, but he now had some information to use. Some threads to pluck at, in hopes of unravelling the tapestry that Nyx hid. "Alright, why am I eligible for these three Epic classes then?"

Nyx's smile faded and he nodded before replying, "Now that is a good question. You have a skill that is highly beneficial to Gaia. Due to that, your extended life would be preferential to early death. These three classes are exclusive to Gaia's rank up system and could be considered an incentive to stick around on her surface to gain even more—cough—rewards."

His eyes squinted at Nyx before Azrael asked, "Can you tell me the specific skill I possess?"

Nyx shook his head, a smirk playing onto its face.

Azrael scratched the nape of his neck before asking another question. "Are there any drawbacks to taking a higher-ranked class?"

Nyx smirk morphed into a sneer before it shrieked, "Of course there are!"

Raising an eyebrow, Azrael made a motion with his hand, indicating he wanted more information. Nyx drew in a deep breath, seeming to take in more air than his 'tiny' body should hold. After a long pause, he exhaled and said, "The higher-ranked the class, the longer your body may take to change. Each rank also carries with it a higher chance of failure and a more difficult confirmation."

"And what is this confirmation?"

"A red quest that will be assigned to you at some point. In some cases, two quests," Nyx retorted hotly.

"And where are these Godly class options?"

"You don't have access to them, and they are hiding somewhere in the blackness. Even now you will only see the name of the class and no information on the tabs."

Azrael switched to the tab in question and confirmed the Gremlin's words. There was a class called Journeyman Soul Gaiad, but the information for it was non-existent. Azrael scanned the four Legendary classes as well: Chimera Knight, Warmancer, Moon Druid, and Storm Sorcerer.

He went back to the Epic ranks and smiled at the Seraphim option. He was already aware of its possible strength in the Grace skill, but Demon and Necrocast were options he hadn't uncovered in the manual walk.

Journeyman Soul Necrocast (Epic)
All Etherience requirements for levels are 10% lower.
+2 Intelligence
+2 Wisdom per level
A Necrocast gains access to the Soul Consume skill.
This produces a resource known as Soul Points. The

EDDA GAIA AND THE ORIGINS OF RAGNAROK

Necrocast consumes Soul Points to unleash devastation on a battlefield.

———

Journeyman Soul Demon (Epic)
All Etherience requirements for levels are 90% higher.
+1 Intelligence
+1 Wisdom
+1 Strength per level
+1 Stamina per level
A Demon gains access to the Abyssal skill. One time per day, the Demon can completely restore his or her Health.

There were some interesting options to choose from. Seraphim could gain a skill that returned full Ether, whereas Demon would definitely gain a skill that returned full Health. Based on Azrael's fighting style, that would likely be preferable in most situations. He also liked the stats the class would award per level. This would, in theory, make him more balanced as he continued to gain strength. The one downside was that Etherience hinderance.

He scanned over the Necrocast but dismissed it rather quickly. It clashed with his Apprentice class and would likely be more of a mage or necromancer in style. It didn't mean he wasn't tempted and curious, he just had to make a decision to solidify the power he already had. While it wasn't unheard of to change from a melee fighter to range—or the opposite—it was somewhat rare to go into the mage classes from there. Most who did so found themselves ineffective at Master or Epic ranks, according to his lessons in the Sovereign Halls at least.

Then again, would the ones who were successful share the information?

Azrael sat down where he was and began to truly consider the options before him. Seraphim would be a great choice for faster leveling and if he could uncover the Grace spell, that added some unique options down the road. Then there was Demon which gained him a boon right away and balanced his future development. He truly did like that option except for the higher Etherience.

Finally, just to be sure, he dug into the Necrocast again. Theoretically, this class could be heavy into summoning, or large casting spells. He turned to Nyx. "Can you tell me anything more about Necrocast?" he asked hopefully.

"I can give you a class description. A Necrocast uses powerful spells to devastate opposing armies. It specializes in death magic and can also summon undead to a lesser degree," Nyx responded quickly.

Closing his eyes for a moment, Azrael considered before shrugging. He had been on the fence before that, but the description made it seem like the Necrocast leaned heavily toward spells and not summons. After that, he was able to dismiss it.

If it was between Seraphim and Demon, he had to lean toward the Demon class. It was more suited for his current skill set. He also thought it gave him a skill right away, instead of hiding it in his skill tree. Just to confirm, he asked Nyx another question. "To be sure, Seraphim doesn't get the Grace skill on class confirmation, but Demon does get the Abyssal skill?"

A corner of the Gremlin's mouth quirked up. "That is correct," he responded with a nod of his head.

Azrael got the impression that Nyx actually liked being asked questions. Strange, considering his earlier attitude. Maybe the Gremlin was trying to be mysterious to draw out questions?

Shaking his head, Azrael dismissed that and moved on. Demon seemed like the choice for him. "What are the downsides to each of these classes, Nyx?"

Nyx broke into a toothy grin. "I am glad you asked, Azrael. Seraphim is tied to saving lives and its red quests will lean in that direction. Demon, on the other hand, is connected to inflicting pain and death. Its quests will extend in a very different direction. As for the downside of skills and the like, you can only discover that for yourself."

Death fit Azrael far better than becoming a healer or savior. He chose Demon and was ushered into darkness by a rather smug-looking Nyx. His heart stuttered from the look. What had he forgotten?

CHAPTER TWENTY-THREE

Azrael could hear someone shuffling around his room and tried to open his eyes but found he couldn't. "It's good your heart rate is back to normal. There was a time I thought it was going to explode," the squeaky voice of Bat said into the silence of the room.

To his horror, Azrael couldn't respond. He tried to open his mouth but couldn't even manage that. What was wrong with him?

Intense pain wracked his body, and the blackness came again.

———

The noise of shuffling feet and the feel of a wet, cold compress on his forehead woke Azrael to consciousness the second time. This time he was able to open his eyes, but his vision was anything but clear. Darkness contrasted by a bright light swam in front of him. A bluish shape moved toward him in a rush. "Azrael, are you awake? Classes start tomorrow and I haven't been able to find Merlin again to convey the news, I need—"

Bat managed to squeak before the pain overrode his sense of hearing.

Azrael managed to groan before he faded back into unconsciousness.

———

"I can't tell you how much longer, and I know this room isn't officially assigned to us, but I can't move him during his rank up!" Bat shrieked before the percussive sound of a door closing reached Azrael's ears. "Go talk to Merlin if you have a problem with this," Bat finished, sounding exasperated.

Azrael opened his mouth and croaked, "Water." A weight lifted from his chest when his mouth worked and formed the word. A noise of something moving over the floorboards reached Azrael's ears and a heartbeat later, water dripped into his mouth. He hadn't opened his eyes yet, but that was mostly because the light that he could see through his eyelids already upset them.

After a moment, Bat informed, "Going to drip more water in now, okay?" That question was followed by a small, cold spoon on Azrael's cracked lips. Then the refreshing drizzle of cold water onto his tongue. He forced himself not to cough or gag as he let the liquid roll down his throat. It wasn't the most comfortable feeling in the world, but his body desperately needed liquid; he felt like a dried husk.

After numerous spoonfuls of water, Azrael attempted to speak. "Ho—errghh." Water dripped into his mouth, causing him to choke and begin to cough.

"I am sorry, I thought you were opening your mouth for more water," Bat exclaimed. A rough towel wiped the spittle off of Azrael's face after the episode.

"How long have I been out?" Azrael croaked out, his throat rawer after the coughing. His eyes were even watering from the coughing bout. He opened them though, and the world swam in his blurry vision.

Trying not to pass out, he focused on Bat's response to try to ignore the vertigo. "Well, it has been about eight days since you entered stasis. Only six to seven days since you exited stasis, and received your new class—does that really say Demon?" Bat responded, sounding nervous.

Azrael groaned as his vision resolved itself. Bat didn't only sound nervous, he looked like a wreck. His ears were drooping, and his complexion was closer to gray than blue. Had Bat spent the entire eight days by his side? "You really need some solid food, Azrael," Bat continued. "I have tried my best to get broth into you, but your body definitely needs more."

"Wait, Bat, didn't classes start a few days ago?" Azrael asked as he lifted his arm and studied his shrunken wrist.

"You've only missed a single day of classes. The first day was Freyaday, and the weekend didn't have any classes. Right now, it's nearing midnight on Voskresenie, and tomorrow, Mōnandæg, will be the second day of classes. They also want you to move into the villa reserved for the prospective students of your mentor."

Azrael groaned, and weakly levered his body into a sitting position. He definitely needed to take care of the food now. He looked to his debuff bar to discover he was a few hours away from permanently losing stats. It seemed that Bat had truly saved his future development by being such a stalwart friend. He would have to do something for the Batman in the future.

That will teach me to not ask enough questions of Nyx.

He spotted a roast chicken on a side table and couldn't take his eyes off of it, to the point that it actually caused Bat to chuckle and bring it over. Azrael scarfed down the food with prodigious amounts of water for the next fifteen minutes. It seemed to help, and increased the debuff timer to permanent stat loss to a few days. He still needed lots more food before he would be out of the proverbial woods, but he doubted Oliver was in the kitchen.

"Wait, is someone in the kitchen, or is there food out for students late at night, Bat?" Azrael asked, remembering the lesson he had just learned—always better to ask and not assume.

Bat nodded but then opened his ears wide. "I would adjust your class with Obfuscate before we head down there," Bat said sheepishly. "I don't think I will be the only one who is bothered by that name."

Azrael nodded his head and used his master class skill to adjust the class back to Revenant. He also had a large number of notifications to sort through, some of which looked to be level ups. Regardless, he could sort through them as he ate.

With Bat's help, Azrael made his way down the stairs to the cafeteria, where he found a great deal of snacks laid out on the buffet table. Nothing was fresh, but it was food. Bat slid Azrael onto a bench and then went and heaped two full plates of varying snacks for him. The Batman returned and both of them began to pick away at the delicious snacks that Oliver must set out every night.

Why did Azrael have to move out of a place like this?

Still, that was a problem for a later date. It was time to go through his notifications.

Congratulations! You have successfully ranked up and become a Journeyman Soul Demon.

———

Congratulations! You have reached Level 3. 2,625 Etherience remaining until Level 4.

———

**Azrael Finch (Sovereign) Level 3
Class: Journeyman-Soul Revenant (Demon)
Class Skills: Soul Strike (V), Soul Cloak (V), Soul Storage (V), Bloodletter (V), Call of the Soul (V), Soul Blade (I)**

Health Points = 310/310 Points
Ether Pool = 190/190 Points
You have 8 stat points and 3 skill points to distribute.
Stamina – 32
Strength – 36
Agility – 42
Dexterity – 42
Intelligence – 22
Wisdom – 21
Charisma – 18
Luck – 12
Skills:
Analyze – Strong 11
Butcher – Moderate 21
Combatant – Strong 35
Enchanting – Weak 5
Endurance – Strong 21
Ether Channels – Moderate 12
Ether Manipulation – Moderate 14
Essence Conversion – Weak 3
Martial Arts – Strong 46
Mediation – Moderate 18
Obfuscate – Strong 15
Sneak – Moderate 4
Stone Cutting – Moderate 11
Swordsmanship – Greater 45
Tracking – Weak 12

———

You have a new quest.
Demon of Gaia
Red Quest
Class Confirmation Quest
Collect a Soul
To gain access to your Abyssal skill, you must collect

**an appropriate level soul. Failure to do so will result in
loss of your class and randomization into a different
class.**
Time limit: 8 days
Best of luck!
Rewards:
Etherience
Journeyman Demon Class Confirmation
Abyssal Skill

Azrael had been expecting a quest, but a quest to kill someone and take their soul seemed a little dark. Then again, he had chosen the Demon class. Wait, it had not specifically said a human soul was required. It definitely seemed like that might be the case, but perhaps an animal or mob in a dungeon would suffice.

Probably best to try those options first. He wasn't against killing a sapient being, but he would try a creature first. He didn't doubt that there would be other requirements of this class in the future. He looked away from his notifications to ask Bat a question to find the Batman face down on the table, snoring softly. No wonder he had been left alone to study his notifications.

He couldn't help the smile that crossed his lips. Bat had been a truly great companion ever since the day Azrael had saved his life. Perhaps he should reconsider why the Sovereign Halls told him to never make friends. Why had the Sovereign Hall taught that?

He opened up his Skill page for his new class, truly curious what would be available.

Tier 1 Skills
Ring of Fire
**Creates a storm of fire around the Demon. The storm
will move with the Demon, creating devastating
damage and a fiery shield against many attacks.**

Damage dealt is based on your wisdom and your opponent's wisdom. Costs fifty Ether to initialize and one Ether per second after.
Skill gained at 5/5, "Ring of Fire."
0/5

———

Ether Burn
Viciously burn Ether from your opponent's pool. Each point of Ether burnt will do half a point of damage to your opponent. Base cost of twenty Ether per cast, but can vary based on comparative Ether levels. Ether burnt is based on your and your opponent's Intelligence.
Skill gained at 5/5, "Ether Burn."
0/5

Both of those skills seemed fantastic. One would be ideal against melee fighters who didn't invest into the Intelligence stat. Take himself for example, if he was hit with Ether Burn and lost most of his skills, he would just be left with his sword and martial techniques. The Ring of Fire skill would make him a terror in large-scale combat, but probably wasn't as effective in single combat. The Ether cost was just too large to be maintainable for long periods of time. In large battles, he wondered if the fire would impair his opponent's visibility at all or if the additional medium change for ballistics would make him harder to target? Since he already had Soul Cloak, though, Ring of Fire seemed like a poor choice.

He couldn't receive either of the skills yet, and so held onto his skill points. His free stat points were a different story. While his new skills needed Intelligence or Wisdom, he desperately needed to reach breakthroughs on Agility and Dexterity. It was likely time to go find some casual equipment for himself that would force that issue. For now, he placed four points into both

Agility and Dexterity, bringing them both to forty-two and leaving one point to spare.

Finished with the notifications, he glanced at Bat. Azrael decided to let the Batman catch up on sleep; he could still use lots of food and needed to look through his class schedule. Bat had a stack of papers beside his plates and Azrael assumed that his companion was planning to talk to him about them all. One was a brown envelope with Azrael's name on it.

He started with it.

Azrael,

It was a pleasure to meet you during your interview. I have chosen you as one of my prospective student apprentices from amongst the first years. The job of a mentor would be to guide the student along his journey. Of course, that means you are enrolled in my class.

You also should move into the villa. I do apologize, but since you don't have any other offers from other teachers, it's your only choice. All my other prospective student apprentices have other teachers' interests, so you will be the only resident. Feel free to take Bat with you or invite other students to liven the place up. Bat can be hired as your personal attendant thanks to your position as a prospective student of mine.

All the best,

Headmaster Merlin

What? Merlin was the headmaster? Magnus was favored to be the apprentice of the headmaster, wasn't he? Azrael couldn't help the self-satisfied smile that broke out onto his face.

I bet Magnus is one of the prospective students as well, and he likely has another sponsoring teacher. If not many other sponsoring teachers… What would happen if I got Merlin's favor over him?

CHAPTER TWENTY-FOUR

Azrael stood at the back of his first lecture hall, looking down five stories of tiered seating. Students sat in small clusters spread out all over the five sections of seating, separated by concrete stairs that led down to the front of the classroom. No one stood in front of the chalkboards, projector screens, or the holographic table; at least not yet. Azrael moved to an empty section of seats and sat. He didn't see any students with manual writing instruments, and so opened the system note-taking feature.

The note-taking feature was something he had never been able to use before at the Sovereign Halls. All the sons and daughters in his class were younger than eight years old and needed to take handwritten notes. Still, the teachers had informed them that once they gained system access, this was a far superior method. All he needed to do was think about what notes he wanted to take, and they would appear.

In theory, Azrael could record the entire lecture if he was so inclined, but that would just make extra work for him later on when he transcribed the important parts.

The class today was called The Responsibilities of Immortals and was a mandatory class for first years at the Atlantean

Academy. Since it was in the theology department, Azrael was not looking forward to this lecture in the slightest. Someone sat next to him and his shoulders drooped as he sighed and turned toward them.

Come on, I chose this area to avoid—

Beside him sat Jophiel, dressed in a white dress. Behind her, a group of students followed, also wearing white clothing from head to toe. The other students left a small but noticeable separation as they began to sit. They also were eyeing Azrael suspiciously. He noted all this but kept staring at Jophiel. What was she doing here?

"What are you doing here?" he blurted before he could think better of it.

Jophi smiled at him and shrugged. "I was accepted a long time ago, but unfortunately couldn't attend." She looked around meaningfully and continued, "For guild reasons." Azrael caught the hint and looked around at the students behind her, all dressed the same. Were these all students from the Cathodiem guild?

More and more of them were filling out seats in this section and a quick head count told Azrael they numbered close to forty. A small few of the others he could remember from the entrance exams, but Jophi hadn't been a part of those. Was she saying she had passed them before but then got sent to spy on the Tuatha De Danann guild? Or perhaps the only reason some of the other guild students took the exams was in hopes of being sponsored?

He would ask her later if he could get her alone. "Well, I guess it's nice that I know at least a single—"

"Already ingratiating yourself with Cathodiem? Don't think just because you are staying in Merlin villa that you actually have him as a mentor. Everyone knows the last apprentice he took on was my father and you are still trash!" The angry voice of Magnus interrupted Azrael and caused his head to jerk to the nearest stairwell. He followed the stairwell up, twisting in his seat to find a large group of first years all in green clothing with gold embroidery. It was extremely ostentatious, maybe even garish. However, between the Cathodiem white and silver and these students, he now knew that guild students would be dressed extravagantly.

He also now knew that the entrance exams weren't the only way for first years to gain access. Many of the Cathodiem and Asgardian students he could see definitely hadn't attended. So they must be attending by guild sponsorship.

In five years, the changes to the top academy in the EtherVerse have come this far. That seems to bode poorly for my plans…

At the head of the group of richly dressed students stood a red-faced, blond-haired youth. He was glaring daggers at Azrael and Jophiel. Azrael felt his jaw begin to clench, but then he recalled that Magnus had been the favorite prospective student to mentor with Merlin, the headmaster. The thunderclouds that rolled around in his blue irises made it abysmally clear why he had come to pick a fight today. Magnus was actually threatened by Azrael, and he needed a victory in front of his posse…

Azrael put on his best smile and directed it at the students behind Thor's son. "Is his daddy upset that his old teacher didn't find his son worthy right away?" Azrael crooned at the group of sycophants who crowded around to watch the spectacle.

Magnus' face darkened and his eyes widened comically, at least to Azrael. The gasps from behind Azrael told him he might have chosen too direct a tack in this particular battle of wits. If even the Cathodiem students found his words offensive, then he probably should have dialed it back a bit. Guess this wasn't the Sovereign Halls where such directness was encouraged.

"You dare to insult a member of the ruling family of Asgard?" Magnus sputtered. "Look at you, a level three Journeyman with no backers—" A cough from behind Azrael made Magnus sputter and change his next words. "—from any *significant* power. Without access to dungeons and resources, you will likely be expelled before the semester ends. Do you truly think that Merlin will pick you over me?"

The smile that came over Azrael could have been criminal. "Good thing I have access to your Rainbow dungeon then, right?" he asked meaningfully. A few people around the room who knew the story chuckled and then explained to those around them what Azrael had implied.

Magnus breathed in a lungful of air before storming away, clearly no longer wishing to pursue his current tactic. As soon as the group of students departed, Azrael frowned, though. Expelled? "I'm confused, why would they expel me?" he asked as he turned back to Jophi. "Thanks for your support, but I could have handled him," he added.

Jophi made a face, pulling her lips back from her teeth in a gesture that clearly wasn't a smile. Azrael took it to mean she wanted to tell him something she didn't think he would like to hear. "First off, the Rainbow dungeon is the most powerful Cardinal dungeon on Gaia, so don't use it to provoke Magnus again. Secondly, you shouldn't provoke him in the first place; his family wields a monstrous amount of power. He could truly remove access to a great deal of future opportunities for you," Jophi scolded.

"As for the expulsion, that would happen if you don't meet the goals set out by your student advisor. In your case, it would be your prospective mentor who sets those goals. Hasn't he explained all of this to you?"

Azrael shrugged, before saying, "Actually, I was ranking up for the last week. I missed the first day of classes and haven't seen Merlin at all, yet." He kept his suspicions about Merlin being his supporter in the Cave of Choices to himself.

"Congratulations on your ascension. Also on your possible sponsorship by Merlin. That is quite… unexpected. Truthfully, because of Merlin's tentative support, you likely won't need to worry too much about Magnus, but you can still be expelled if you don't meet your prospective mentor's criteria by the end of semester. Usually, students need to have achieved an eighty percent average in all courses to move on to their second year. But thanks to your sponsorship, more will be expected from you."

"Can you give me an example?" Azrael asked, truly curious.

"Well, the obvious ones are your grades in class, but the less obvious ones will be specific skills or levels that they expect you to achieve. Each semester follows a pattern of a week of classes and a week of grind time. The off time is used to run dungeons, and work on those other goals," she responded, a smile beginning to hint at the corner of her lips as she finished.

"That's why I came to see you today actually. I was wondering if you wanted to join me for dungeon runs?" Jophi asked, her mood seeming almost bubbly.

Azrael was thinking about a response when the teacher arrived and called for silence. Azrael shrugged to Jophi and whispered, "Let's chat about it after class."

She nodded and they both faced front as the rest of the students got into seats and quieted down. Once the teacher had relative quiet from the class, he began. "My name is Darwin Fage and welcome to my class on The Responsibilities of Immortals. I expect people to be open-minded in this class and explore their inner thoughts and morals. Since the system extends our lives for such a long time, we must understand ourselves to a deeper extent. Only in this way can we find our groundings and live our most meaningful life. By the end of this class, you will hopefully be able to understand what drives you."

Azrael assumed that this speech was meant to be impressive, but he found it to be very preachy. The teacher began to prepare for the lesson and Azrael listened to him drone with half his mind, taking notes for things that sounded important. The rest of his mind considered what Jophi had just suggested. Should he join her team?

Would that not be the same as joining her guild?

———

During the class, they were separated into random partners to discuss the questions posed by the teacher. The randomness was supposed to 'add a degree of difficulty' to the discussions that followed. Instead, most of the students, like Azrael, chose to share very little of themselves in the new environment.

When the bell tolled to end the three-hour lecture, Azrael immediately walked up the stairs to head for lunch. He still needed to move into his new villa and wanted a full stomach before he ventured into those waters. Not that he had anything to move... but he definitely wanted a final meal, in case the villa wasn't stocked.

Azrael felt that the place was going to be far too extravagant for him. He also wanted one more meal cooked by Oliver. Something about a meal prepared for him was a luxury he didn't want to lose. Still, if the chance for Merlin sponsoring him existed, he shouldn't do anything to upset the strange man.

Something in the corner of his vision caught his attention, and he jerked his head sideways to find Jophiel exchanging a paper with a nondescript man in green clothing. Azrael watched the exchange and changed directions after exiting on the bottom floor behind the green tunic that bobbed through the crowd.

He followed the man out into the hallways on the first floor and waited for an opportunity. Just as the green tunic passed through a group of students, Azrael bumped into him, making it appear to be the jostling of the crowd. He mumbled, "Oh, sorry about that," as their shoulders collided and went to steady the man. He looked at the man's face up close and still found him to be rather nondescript, but Azrael marked the face for later.

Green tunic brushed him off and continued on his way, and Azrael retreated to a window. What had Jophi passed him?

Contact and offer made. Answer to come later.

It was a small slip of paper, only meant to carry small amounts of information onto a handler, but Azrael sighed all the same.

A pain in his chest started, and he felt his mouth turn down into a frown. Simultaneously, his blood seemed to raise a few degrees in temperature. Was he angry? Then what was the pain? Regardless, it was going to be difficult to interact with Jophi now, and by extension the Cathodiem guild. They were already back to playing games. Had they not learned from the last experience of sending Jophiel to the Tuatha?

Why couldn't she be more like Bat…? At least with him, I am relatively sure he won't ever give away my secrets…

CHAPTER TWENTY-FIVE

Vines crept up the walls of the house in front of him, snaking through the siding and even through the tiled roof. The pathway leading to the front door was completely overgrown by tall weeds and stalks of dried grass. Azrael scratched his head as Bat asked, "Are you sure this is the right place?"

"This is where the professor we asked said to go, but truthfully after all the admiration I can't believe it's correct. How long has it been since someone stayed here?" Azrael said, unable to hide his dismay. "Well, maybe the inside is better?"

The house and its surroundings looked like they were a few years from being fully reclaimed by nature.

Together, Azrael and Bat navigated the long weeds and made their way to the front door. The menacing face of a lion dominated the knocker, but the dust and rusting hinges told Azrael, again, this device wasn't in use. He tried the door, only to find it bolted.

"Did Merlin give you a key?" Bat asked.

Azrael shook his head and Bat placed his hand on the door. The entire thing began to vibrate and as Azrael watched, the knocker fell to the rotting wood of the deck. The sound of metal chiming was joined by a great deal of the same from inside the house and the door itself. Bat removed his hand and the door popped open.

"What did you just do?" Azrael asked, his voice excited. Could Bat force open all doors?

"All the metal was completely rusted through. Vibrating the door crumbled it to dust," Bat explained with a shrug, ruining Azrael's dreams of getting through any door in the future. He had hoped Bat possessed some sort of lockpicking skill.

Azrael opened the door and wrinkled his nose as a wave of stale air assaulted it. What was going on? How were they supposed to live here?

The entryway was small and would have been cozy if the furniture was still standing, but the wicker bench and coat rack had long since crumpled to the floor. The cushions were so filled with dust that no amount of beating would remove it. Azrael sneezed, and looked at the floor, seeing his two shoes sitting down in an inch of dust. No wonder students chose to stay elsewhere even if Merlin's sponsorship was a possibility…

There was also another brown envelope sitting in the dust on the floor. It was addressed to him, and clearly had been slid under the door through the dust, leaving a dust pile on one side and trail leading to it.

Azrael picked it up and beat the dust off the envelope against his hand. He sneezed again.

Azrael,

First, let me welcome you to my villa. Hopefully, you will be here a long time and be able to fix it up. This villa is rather special and is repaired and cleaned by use of Ether Channels and Ether Manipulation, two skills I know you have. I have repaired one bedroom with two beds and the kitchen, along with its adjoining chef's room, but the rest of the house and its exterior is up to you.

All the best,

Merlin

He closed his eyes and tried to control his breathing as he passed the note to Bat. He only had a few more hours before class, but now not only would he need to be taking classes but fixing up this dump of a villa. Azrael rubbed his forehead and eyes before nodding and resolving himself to get to work. He hadn't meditated much the last few days and, in some ways, Merlin was helping him keep up good habits.

Bat asked, "Do you think I can help?"

Azrael shrugged, and said, "Let's give it a try after we check out the kitchen and the two rooms."

The bedrooms were dust free, at least, but far from in perfect repair. One contained two beds with mattresses that might have been new ten years before Azrael was born but now looked like some sort of lumpy sack thrown haphazardly on top of some rather questionable framing. The flooring looked ready to give a splinter to anyone who was stupid enough to walk barefoot on it, and the metal that held everything together seemed to be just shy of rusting.

I would like to repeat my earlier thought. Why would anyone choose to live here? Was it Magnus' influence that stopped other teachers from sponsoring me?

The kitchen was fully stocked but looked like something pulled out of a decommissioned space station pub. Dents and food stains were apparent on each pot or pan, and Azrael worried that would hinder them from finding a chef. The kitchen contained another note saying that they could hire one, and Merlin would pay the man or woman's salary up to five crystals a month, plus living arrangements and food. The room off the kitchen was the second room that was repaired by Merlin and it only had a single small, lumpy bed. The room was clearly intended for a chef, and Azrael groaned, thinking of sharing the upstairs bedroom with Bat until they could figure out how to repair a second one.

He left Bat in a second moldy-looking bedroom with the instructions to try to fix it.

Bat is going to try to figure out how the Ether Channeling and Ether Manipulation can be used to fix it. But I should definitely try to find a chef.

Azrael shook his head and continued his hurried walk toward the coliseum building for Combat Preparedness class. A figure wearing flowing blue graduation robes moved along another stone path to his left. The blue-robed man was also mid-twirl of some dance with an unheard beat. A spin from the blue-robed man brought the face of Merlin into view. Eyes wide, Azrael adjusted his course and began to jog to catch up to his prospective mentor.

"Merlin, wait!" Azrael called as he jogged over.

In response, Merlin waved as if in choreographed steps, but continued to dance in the direction he was heading. Azrael caught up to him rather easily since the man's dancing wasn't a particularly effective way to move around. Once he was beside his mentor, Azrael asked, "Shouldn't we sit down and talk about the criteria I need to meet to continue to enroll here?"

My first question should have been what in the nine halls is he doing.

Merlin didn't falter as he answered, "Have you found the vessel yet?"

Azrael blinked, instantly remembering the odd questions on the entrance exam. "The container to hold something I can't see?"

Merlin clapped his hands excitedly. "I knew I wasn't wrong to choose you. You're clever!"

Azrael froze. Had that been condescending? Merlin gained a few steps of separation during Azrael's brief pause, and he took a few hurried ones to catch back up. "Is that a question I must answer to remain here?"

Merlin laughed. "Of course not. That question took me years to discover. How could you learn it in a semester?" The man continued to move in rhythm to some unheard song. Was it classical?

"Well then, aren't there supposed to be criteria for me staying on as a student and avoiding expulsion?"

"Ahh, yes. Let us say, if you can pass your courses—say with a C average. And shall we add completely fixing the villa to that list? That should be more than enough for a first semester student."

Azrael felt his muscles all tighten in unison as he stopped walking again. "A C-average?" he sputtered. Did Merlin think he was daft?

He took a few deep breaths to calm down, but when he glanced back up, he found his mentor sprinting away. For a brief second, he considered charging after the man, but the speed of Merlin suggested Azrael couldn't catch him.

Is he running away from me? And how in the Hall is he moving so fast in robes?

The bells that signaled the start of combat class began to sound. "By the Nine Halls," Azrael muttered. He was late.

———

Arriving late to his first combat class gained him a frown from Maat. Considering that the man had been one of the first to accept Azrael into the academy made him feel the teacher's disapproval even more. Still, he arrived before any sparring began, and the lesson today was in katas and how to utilize them to improve your forms. Something Azrael hoped he was ahead of the class on.

"As I say. A kata can be a series of movements, or it can be purposeful. Do you understand difference?" Maat exclaimed toward the forty students standing in rank and file.

Was that a question?

Maat caught Azrael nodding his head and called, "Does Azrael have an answer to the question?"

Oh, so it was a question. Overcoming his surprise, Azrael stuttered, "You can practice with intention, or you can move through the motions. One is a workout, the other is training." Those words were his sword master's favorite whenever a student wasn't going through the actions with enough drive.

Maat smiled. "Yes. This is it. Train against a fictitious opponent, move weapon to block a strike, defeat shadow foes, but stay in forms. This is essence of kata training," Maat stated to the class.

Magnus, who Azrael had failed to notice at the front of the class, sneered at Azrael and then elbowed his neighbor. The student who was dressed nearly identically to Magnus, in a fancy blue shirt, and brown britches asked, "Why not just spar with a real opponent then?"

Had the imbecile never been in a combat class before? That was the question the teacher wanted someone to ask because—

"Of course. Come spar, Asgardian. Let me show, why you first learn form, then you try in combat," Maat responded. His voice carried no arrogance, only a confidence Azrael respected.

Magnus' crony smiled menacingly.

The student pulled a warhammer from thin air; a testament to the Asgardians' wealth that a student owned a storage device. He twirled the monstrous thing around in the air and it began to crackle with lightning. Was this imbecile planning to use skills during a spar?

That was particularly frowned upon in martial circles.

The other students backed away and cleared a space for Maat and the Asgardian student to duel. "Just tell me when you are ready to begin, old man!" the particularly dense student growled at Maat.

Maat shrugged and held both of his empty hands up before forming fists and getting into a martial stance Azrael recognized. It was Earth's Embrace. Azrael felt a smile tug at the corner of his mouth. This wasn't going to be pretty. Azrael had suffered numerous times under this particular martial form. It was extremely hard to deal with and overpoweringly effective against opponents who used long or heavy weapons. As long as you could get inside of their range.

Magnus' crony growled and lifted his massive warhammer up into the sky. "Taste my liege's lightning—ahhhh!"

The Asgardian didn't even have time to move the hammer a fraction more. Maat pushed off with his toes and closed the ten-foot gap between himself and his opponent in the blink of an eye. Then the very large man was wrapped around his opponent's arms like he was a blanket the student had spent all night tangling around himself.

Thump. The hammer fell to the ground and the student began to shriek. Maat was applying a bit of pressure to the shoulder joints, which was causing the Asgardian's chest to arch forward. Azrael grimaced, remembering his own painful experiences with this particular hold. With the chest expanded like that, you couldn't breathe easily. Everything in your body would tell the individual they were drowning. Shrieking was truly the only response a student could have.

As the student continued to scream, Azrael realized Magnus was glaring not at the teacher and his friend, but at him.

Why glare at me? I only answered the teacher's first question.

CHAPTER TWENTY-SIX

Maat let go of the student after he admitted his defeat. The teacher stood up and brushed the dirt off of his clothes. "This is why you learn forms. Student Kelan was attacking in a motion, but knew no opponent like me. How should he react?"

Jophi's voice floated out of the crowd of students. "He should have ingrained a reaction in his body, so he would stand a chance of victory."

Azrael leaned out of line to see the slim form of Jophi standing in the same row as him, closer to the front. No wonder he hadn't noticed her earlier. Her answer was good, and Azrael leaned back into place to hear Maat's response. "Yes. Brain is muscle, so all muscle can act as brain. Teach muscles to react without need to think and you succeed.

"Today work on this martial kata," Maat finished and then went through forms very similar to Prowling Tiger. A few differences existed in the kata Maat showed, and Azrael noticed them. "This form is called Crouching Tiger," Maat added after the final sweeping punch.

The class dispersed and each student found an open area to move through the kata. The similarity in the name and the movements furrowed Azrael's brow. Were these a derivative? Had they both been a form taught by a teacher and then changed by students, who later became teachers?

He began to feel a headache coming on, and turned his mind over to the exercise. He repeated the kata first with Crouching Tiger, and then on his second time through adjusting to the forms he knew in Prowling Tiger. He realized that the forms taught to him at the Sovereign Halls were slightly slower from position to position. The hands, elbows, knees, or feet taking a slightly more abstract route from the finish to the next position.

Azrael would not have noticed the small errors in Prowling Tiger if he hadn't just performed the Crouching version. As he moved through the forms and envisioned an opponent, he tried to find imperfections elsewhere in the forms. If the Sovereign Halls version was a seven out of ten for its nearness to the original perfect form, perhaps this Atlantean Hall version was only an eight. Azrael slowed down his motions, examining each step, each strike, each muscle movement.

There are still other connections that are sloppy. Are they only sloppy for me or all practitioners?

He felt goosebumps raise on his arms as he eliminated more of these perceived problems with the form. Slowly, he sped back up his training, feeling the fit of each strike. Could this be done with the sword?

"Some still look like rag doll kid plays with, but all improved. Good!" Maat shouted from the head of the class, startling Azrael out of his contemplation. "Class is finish. I hand out quest for homework. Complete nine variation of martial kata and choose one kata for prefer weapon. Practice makes muscles brain. You can be leaving," Maat finished.

It took a few more moments for Azrael to fully come back to himself. Time had passed far faster than he had thought. Class was already over, and there hadn't been any spars? Strange. The Sovereign Halls had pitted them against each other on day one. Even though most students were at the pulling hair and scratching stage.

His mouth turned down and the sweat on his body chilled as he watched two people begin approaching him. One was Jophi, which admittedly wouldn't have brought on his mood change. It was Magnus and his cronies' approach that clenched Azrael's jaw. Now what?

"It does not matter how hard you work, urchin, I will ensure that you don't get on any dungeon teams," Magnus stated, with a large grin plastered on his face. "When you didn't show up for class on Friday, we all thought you had figured out that you didn't fit in."

Azrael took a deep breath in through his nose and held up a hand in Jophi's direction. The woman was turning red with anger, and her mouth was just opening to respond. Azrael didn't need her to fight his battles. He sighed theatrically before responding. "Magnus, I realize that you rely on the strength of those around you to complete dungeons, but before I was accepted, I was running dungeons by myself." Okay, admittedly a bit of a lie, but Magnus wouldn't know that.

Magnus' smile morphed into something sickly. The son of Thor spat, "I am strong enough to run dungeons on my own as well. The people with me lean on my power!" The crony beside him bobbed his head, agreeing with the sentiment.

"Right, and daddy never ran you through any of the tougher dungeons that your clan holds?" Azrael pushed his needling a little farther.

He watched with satisfaction as Magnus' face paled. Azrael was aware that the act of power-levelling was a common practice, but the way Magnus had responded left him no direction to save face now. Azrael would take a round of a speed dungeon run from Thor if it was offered, but he didn't have to admit that here and now.

Magnus sputtered and balled his fists as Jophi came up beside Azrael, smirking. Magnus' crony responded for the struggling Asgardian, "Our guild will ensure you don't have an opportunity to enter a single dungeon, even if you want to run them solo!" The intervention of the man forced Azrael to Analyze the imbecile, as he himself fought to keep his face calm. This was a serious problem, if it was true.

Kuhl Boar
Journeyman-Executioner
Level 9
Health Points: 310 / 310
Skills: 9

"Are you telling me you haven't heard of the bet Magnus made with me at the entry exams?"

Kuhl looked at Magnus who had gone quite red in the face.

Azrael, seeing his chance, continued, "Oh, he didn't tell you that I have access to the Rainbow dungeon thanks to a bet he lost?"

Magnus turned a few shades redder, changing from flushed to tomato. Kuhl sputtered for a bit looking between Magnus and Azrael. Finally Magnus shouted, "That doesn't change the fact that you are a weak, worthless little rat, who won't make it through this semester. Did you want to do a double or nothing?"

"No, thank you, I was planning on running the Rainbow dungeon before the semester ends…"

"If you run it now, you won't—" Kuhl began but was punched in the shoulder rather hard by Magnus. They exchanged a look with each other after that 'subtle' exchange and both of them turned in unison to storm from the manmade combat arena.

Azrael shook his head as they went, he already assumed he needed to get stronger before running the most powerful dungeon on Gaia.

He clicked his tongue and turned to address Jophi. "Did you come over to ask me to join Cathodiem again?" he asked pointedly, making it clear with his tone that she would get a solid no to the question. Especially after he caught her spying on him.

Jophi smiled and shook her head. "No, I came over to ask to join your dungeon team, if you will have me. My father is slightly upset with me and has taken away my access to the guild dungeons until I *improve myself*," she said, her voice making an impression of a stern father toward the end.

He studied her as he considered. Azrael assumed that she was in trouble for the note that he had stolen. So, in some ways he probably owed her a bit of help, but on the other hand, she was likely getting close to him to gather more information. He shrugged off the problem. Technically, he didn't have a team yet and she was a very strong member. If she was going to spy on him, he could get some help out of the equation. "It would just be me, you, and Bat, I'm afraid."

Jophi shrugged in turn and they began walking as they chatted. "That's okay. Did you fight alongside a tank or healer from your class in the exams?"

He remembered Prateek and Oslow. "Yes, I did. I'm not sure they will be *enthusiastic* to join my team again. I kind of let two of our members die to save Ether for our healer."

Jophi laughed. "They will likely join you. If for no other reason than because you are Merlin's prospective apprentice. As much as Kuhl and Magnus threaten, most guilds will give deference to you, or recruitment runs in their Territory dungeons in hopes of one day recruiting you," Jophi said nonchalantly. Azrael raised an eyebrow and Jophi blushed as she realized the implications from her own guild.

Together they walked and chatted about how to recruit the two other members. He was acting a bit guarded with her now, and saw a few long, studying looks from Jophi during the conversation that likely confirmed she knew it as well. Unfortunately, with confirmation of her acting as the Cathodiem spy again, they couldn't go back to the easy camaraderie they had shared on the freighter.

Bat and Azrael walked into a large, square building that smelled of antiseptics and Ether Technology. This was the healer's campus and supposedly where he might find Prateek and Oslow. According to a few other first years he asked, they liked to eat at the cafeteria together. The hallways were white, and each room was occupied with either a class or patients in bed with long-term illnesses. These illnesses were often in the form of curses, diseases, or parasites. Each room with a patient had a label on the door, which told Azrael this as he walked by.

According to rumor, this was the only such building on the entire continent, and healers would often stop in and attempt to heal the people within. While most curses, diseases, and parasites could be healed by a skill or spell, some refused to go away, and had no timer until dissipation. Those people often arrived here in hopes that a powerful enough healer may one day stop in and be able to remove the affliction.

The cafeteria was different from the one in the bottom of the student dormitory for unaligned and unsponsored students. Each table sat a maximum of four students on seats that swiveled to allow access and turn back to the surface in front. Each table often sat one or two people with notes spread out in front of them as they absentmindedly ate from a tray. Both Bat and Azrael got themselves some rather standard-looking food, and walked the large space until Azrael recognized Prateek, sitting with Oslow.

He approached them and sat down when they nodded to his unspoken request to join them. Not wanting to jump right into the question, Azrael took a bite of his food. The mashed potatoes tasted like they were made from the same dehydrated powder Jophi, Bat, and he were forced to eat on the freighter. He frowned at the plate before pushing it slightly away with a sigh. Maybe after, he would go to the unaligned student dorm and get a plate from Oliver.

"How have your first few classes gone? And why haven't I

seen either of you in any of my classes?" Azrael asked to break the ice.

"We have specialized classes as healers and tanks," Oslow said around a mouthful of food. "We have some together, later in the week, to work on formations, but most of them are individually tailored to our roles."

"I guess I was also surprised to find you both in this cafeteria. Didn't you both get apprenticed by a different teacher?" Azrael asked for a follow-up.

"The food in Maat's compound for tanks is more about quantity, and I'm not exactly looking to bulk up," Oslow responded sheepishly as he scratched his neck nervously. The kid just confirmed what Azrael had heard. Maat was the teacher that sponsored any tanks who made it through the entrance exams.

The tone of Oslow's voice allowed a knot in his stomach to unwind. There was no anger or resentment he could detect. Prateek was squinting his eyes at them but it didn't appear hostile, more curious. Azrael motioned to Bat. "This is my friend Bat. Bat, this is Oslow and Prateek, the two who helped me pass my exam," Azrael introduced everyone.

Both Oslow and Prateek were now squinting at him. *Too far?* He shrugged and gave up the pretense. "I am very glad you two passed as well, and apologize for how close it was. However, I came over here to ask if you two wanted to form a real dungeon raiding team with me?"

Prateek's squinting stopped, and he looked to Oslow. Both of their faces morphed into a rather unpleasant smile. "What split do you propose?" Prateek asked, still looking at Oslow.

Oslow nodded. "Yeah, our class on Friday was about making sure people value us and the types of deals we should expect. What's the size of the party?" he asked as he turned back to Azrael. The subtle exchange between the two wasn't missed by Azrael. He guessed that because of Oslow's rather unique style of tanking, they had limited choices when it came to group invites.

"I was thinking of a five-person group. Another student named Jophiel will be the fourth, and Bat here will be the fifth," Azrael answered.

Prateek frowned and squinted at Bat. "I know Jophiel, but is he a student here?"

Bat shook his head and Oslow pounced. "Then he will have to take his cut from you, Azrael. I can agree to a seventy-thirty split. Thirty percent to you and Jophiel and seventy percent to us."

Azrael smirked back. That was a bad starting point for negotiations, and they seemed to be thinking that it would be a four-man team based on the figure. "I propose we keep it to the standard sixty-forty. Not only are you getting Jophiel, a member of Cathodiem in high standing, but the prospective apprentice of Merlin."

"Still, since Bat here isn't a student, and we don't know his capabilities, it seems like you and Jophiel would be receiving twenty percent each in that case. How can you ensure that we won't have to carry the group and don't deserve the additional five percent each?" Prateek interjected.

Azrael chuckled; they had overplayed their hand. "Look, guys, this wasn't my idea to ask you. It was Jophiel's. I'm positive that some members of the adventuring guild would be happy to work for a fifty-fifty split. So, that's my new offer. We split it fifty-fifty or you two can wait for other students to ask."

Oslow's face fell, and he looked to Prateek, hoping the healer had an answer or counteroffer. Prateek scratched his head. "Did we push it too far?" he asked sheepishly.

Azrael nodded. "Sorry, guys, you are only first years, and from the start you should have known that sixty-forty was the best you were going to get. My guess is that you don't have any other offers, Oslow, and if Prateek is sitting with you, he's probably committed to stick by your side," Azrael responded with a wink. "Plus, I have a ship that can take us to El Dorado, Saturday morning. Meet at the villa?"

Both of them nodded and they spoke of mundane things as

they ate their meals. Azrael couldn't help but smile; he had a real dungeon party now. Perhaps they could even challenge the Rainbow dungeon together. If they were strong enough.

———

"I tried to meditate on the front porch, and as you can see it helped a bit. But I swear we are missing something," Bat exclaimed. "The house is willing to take the Ether I channel toward it, but I get the sense it wants something else."

Azrael scratched his head. *Could it be?* "Alright, let me give it a try," he said to Bat before sitting down and beginning his own meditation. Jophi also sat down beside him. She had met him on his walk over, attempting to make their meeting a coincidence but failing miserably. She clearly had been waiting for him.

He put those thoughts out of his mind as he began to sink into himself and circulate his Ether. Again, he had been lax on his maintenance, and the first thing he did was fix some of the blockages and pooling he found. Once he manipulated his Ether Channels and had them flowing freely, he checked his central ocean. It was again circulating like a whirlpool that ended in nothing. In the past, he made the mistake of touching the bottom of this Ether whirlpool with his mind and accidentally passed out. Today he didn't dare, not in front of Jophi and Bat.

He manipulated a strand of Ether from the whirlpool and ever so slowly reached it toward the rotting deck he sat upon. As soon as the strand exited his body, it snapped back into his pool and stung his mind. It was similar to feeling the lash of an elastic band on a wrist but inside his head, which made it far less comfortable. He shook his head to dissipate the pain before trying again. This time he succeeded.

As soon as the strand touched the deck, he felt a strange pull on his Ether pool. He could feel his Ether draining down the thin strand and into the deck. It was currently a trickle that was far less than his regeneration. So he widened the channel until his regeneration and his expenditure matched. Then he studied the dissipation of the Ether as it entered the deck. The rotting wood greedily drank the Ether, and as it did, Azrael could see individual splinters of the wood slowly revitalize.

Based on the speed, it will take an entire semester to repair this deck alone! Azrael exclaimed inside his own mind. He felt around at the junction between his channel and the deck. What Bat had said didn't fully make sense to him. Azrael felt the hunger of the wood, the *thirst* it had suffered under. Why did Bat say it wanted something else?

Azrael left the connection and half emerged from his meditative state. "Bat, what do you mean when you say it wants something else?"

Bat, who also was channeling nearby, took a moment to pull himself into a half meditation and answer. "Touch a splinter as it repairs. The wood is desperate for Ether, but once it is repaired, it is still unquenched. It's like the kitchen or bedroom Merlin did. It only revitalizes itself to a point, but clearly can go further."

Azrael felt his head jerk back in surprise. That was a very in-depth response. He nodded and went back into his full meditation. With a mental exercise, he touched one of the tiny splinters that had been repaired by his Ether. It no longer consumed any of the Ether from the channel, but it pulled on the strand still. Bat was right, it was like it was looking for something. Azrael mentally scratched his head—he wondered. The *Essence* he converted immediately fell into the soil; or so he assumed.

The only time he hadn't felt that way was out in space.

Could he pull the tiny strands of Ether at the bottom of his whirlpool and link them to the deck? Was that what it wanted?

Mentally, he retracted the current channel back to his pool and then moved his *hand* to a place nearer the bottom of the whirlpool. He took a choppy breath and then touched it. He slowly extended it toward the wood, but the turbulence inside the strand made extending it difficult. When it exited his palm into the outside air, it recoiled like a ballistic from a gun.

A spike of pain shot into his skull and he heard a startled, high-pitched gasp as he fell to the rotting wood.

Admittedly, that could have been Bat or Jophi, he managed to think before his world went black.

CHAPTER TWENTY-SEVEN

Azrael woke up with his head in someone's lap as they stroked his hair. He had a damp rag on his forehead, which also covered his eyes. He moved his hand to uncover his face as he opened his eyes. To his relief, the person he looked up at was Jophi. She wore a small smile on her face and stroked his hair again.

He jolted up, the sensation startling him.

The top of his head clipped Jophi's chin, and he felt his heart leap into his throat. By the Halls, he had reacted without thinking. No one had ever stroked his hair before. Why was it fine when he couldn't see the person though?

He turned around; his stomach felt like it was in literal knots. Jophi was holding her chin and her lip was bleeding. "By the Halls, I didn't mean to hurt you," Azrael pleaded. He held out the wet rag in his hand. Jophi blinked at him in surprise, her eyes sparkling with unshed tears.

By the Nine, I hurt her, Azrael thought as he sat near her ineffectually. He wondered what he could do to help. He reached out and lowered his hand helplessly as she rubbed her chin.

"I'm fine, Azrael. Don't worry about it," she said hurriedly.

"Just an accident. What happened to you?" she asked as she brought a bloody finger in front of her eye to look at.

Azrael rubbed his forehead sheepishly. Could he explain it? Should he? He moved the hand to his temple and scratched. Not yet. "I am not sure. The pull of the deck caused my channel to snap back into my pool. It was very unpleasant," he lied as convincingly as he could manage. He had already been hot under the collar before he responded, so that might help.

Bat exited the villa, and exclaimed, "Good, you're awake! What happened?"

Azrael groaned, and explained again.

———

That night, the three of them moved through the katas two of them had been assigned as homework. Azrael went through the final of the assigned nine martial katas with the same intention as his earlier practice. The darkness descending outside the window of the villa's workout room made him rush more than he had in class with the Tiger forms. He didn't want to be up all night—not with more classes the following day. The workout dojo floor creaked with each movement, highlighting its advanced state of disrepair.

As he moved, he quickly picked out flaws in his movements and corrected them. It was very helpful to have directions to a variation of the form to help identify areas of inefficiency. Still, he would need to keep practicing to identify others.

All that was left was his sword form. He picked Glas Wen, because it was a sword form he practiced often at the Sovereign Halls. The name was the same as the form he already knew as well, so he wondered how different the motions could or would be. As it turned out, they were nearly identical. The Glas Wen forms as indicated by the book instructions had one huge variation, though. Where the Sovereign Hall taught an upward slash, the Atlantean Academy taught a diagonal upward thrust that formed a straight line with the back leg.

Azrael tried both. The diagonal upward thrust felt odd since he had practiced the slash so often. He tried to picture a use for the final motion. What kind of opponent would a thrust like this be useful against? An upward slash was more versatile in Azrael's mind, as he could easily picture a humanoid opponent at ground level. After some thought, he came to a bit of a conclusion. The function of the upward thrust may be useful against mounted or larger foes. The connection between the fourth strike in Glas Wen and the diagonal upward thrust flowed much better in actuality than the slashing strike he had learned at the Sovereign Hall. The thrust also lent itself better to getting his blade back in place for the sixth strike, a step through horizontal chop meant more to push the opponent than cut.

This wasn't as clear cut of a distinction, but as he worked his forms and the sky continued to darken, he attempted to better fit the upward slash with the forms before and after it. Perhaps there was a lesson he could learn here.

Congratulations! You have learned a new skill, Innovator.
Current Rank: Apprentice-Innovator Level 1.
Innovator
Through experimentation and testing, you have managed to create something that is new or an improved version of something else. This skill increases the chance that your innovation will be useful by 1% per level.

Azrael couldn't help but chuckle as he came out of the trance he often practiced katas in. That skill was mostly useless, but it did tell him he was on the right track with improving the katas.

To his surprise, he found himself alone in the training room. A quick glance at the time told him it was approaching midnight. He moved to take a quick shower and changed into some bed clothes before entering the room Bat and he normally shared.

Bat wasn't snoring, which was a blessing, but Azrael wasn't sure he would have cared even if the Batman was. He gave a brief consideration to Jophi and her trip back to her own dormitory before he practically crashed into his foam mattress and instantly fell asleep.

———

The next morning, his internal clock woke him up with the rise of the sun. Verimy and Dara had long since instilled in him the necessity of being an early riser, and he wasn't going to break that habit. He got out of bed and changed into one of his best repaired sets of clothes. Unfortunately, even these looked ratty when they were compared to Magnus' and other students of the academy. He sighed and turned back around to exit the room, attempting to move silently, as not to wake Bat.

He froze mid-step as the dawn light coming through the window highlighted long brown hair and pale white shoulders sticking out from the sheets where Bat's blue head should have been. Azrael had just gotten changed, and he was ninety-nine percent sure that was Jophiel. He rushed out of the room, closing the door behind him as his heart reverberated against his ribcage.

What in the Nine?

Where was Bat?

He moved to the kitchen as his body slowly came down from the adrenaline surge that finding Jophiel in his room had brought on. He took eggs and bacon out of the chiller and pulled two pans to place over the gas range. A new question dawned on him. Should he prepare breakfast for Jophi? While he was at it, should he prepare something for Bat? Was Bat even at the house?

A loud snort that morphed into a snore led Azrael to a room just off the kitchen. Bat had complained that the small single bed in this room wasn't fit to sleep on when Azrael had suggested he sleep in here earlier. The room itself was sparsely furnished and very small. It was clearly meant to house a servant or chef, and Azrael had to wonder why Bat would give up his larger bed for Jophi. *He must really like her…* From under the ratty covers in the room, a blue head sporting long ears was peeking out.

Bat's snoring had cut off as Azrael opened the door, and Bat groaned loudly before mumbling, "Another five minutes, please."

Azrael chuckled and apologized to his drowsy companion. Guess that answered where Bat had slept. How had he missed whatever led to these sleeping arrangements last night?

The fact Bat was awake decided it, and he began prepping eggs, bacon, and toast for three. If Jophiel was going to be sleeping here, she would have to get on his timeline. A quick image of her bare shoulder made him flush. And perhaps they should prioritize another room to repair instead of testing the repair methods on the deck.

A scant fifteen minutes later, he knocked on his own door and called, "Jophi, breakfast is ready."

Some rustling inside the room could be heard and Jophi answered a moment later, "Okay, be down in a moment." For some reason, Azrael flushed again and quickly moved back to the kitchen to fill his own plate.

He was sitting at the island on one of the high bar stools when Jophi entered. She was still in a top that had thin straps and bared her shoulders. She smiled at Azrael and made her way over to a kaffee pot. Azrael smiled back and held up his mug in a salute. He hadn't had kaffee in a long time and was relishing in the hit of caffeine each glorious sip contained. He also didn't blush this time despite Jophi's 'pajamas.' Clearly, his sleep-addled mind had been acting strangely.

After taking a cup of the dark black kaffee, she moved to the bacon plate and took the entirety of the contents to a seat opposite Azrael. She ignored the eggs entirely and began crunching into the bacon with a certain gleefulness Azrael found refreshing. He did raise a hand and say, "Bat hasn't had any yet, so you know."

Jophi laughed and responded loudly, "If he is still sleeping, he won't get any, either!"

The sound of someone hurriedly getting out of bed and dressing came from the chef's quarters and Azrael joined Jophi in her laughter.

"Any reason you stayed the night here?" Azrael asked after his amusement was back under control.

"Well, I am mentored by the spell control professor, Madame Marjoree. Her place is *wayyy* across campus. We worked on homework pretty late, and Bat offered."

Azrael licked his lips and tilted his head. He had known she had a mentor, but hadn't known the specifics. "Is her villa or house as bad as this?" Azrael asked and pointed around.

"No, she has an entire dorm though, with lots of students. She picks about ten full apprentices per year, from what I can tell. It's really crowded over there, and here it's just the two of you…"

Bat stormed out of the room and hurriedly plucked a few pieces of bacon from the rapidly emptying plate in front of Jophi. He placed them on a new plate and split the eggs before putting the egg serving dish in front of Jophi and sitting down as well.

"Morning Bat," Azrael said exaggeratedly.

Bat made a shape with his mouth that clearly indicated he wasn't happy with the hour but didn't respond. This only caused Jophi and Azrael to laugh harder.

Azrael turned back to Jophi and stated, "I am glad Bat offered, but maybe we should make another room here a priority in case it happens again."

Jophi smiled and shrugged. "Doesn't bother me to share, but you're right. You probably want a real chef too. While I enjoy bacon and eggs just as much as the next girl, I think some diversity of meals will help this place feel more like a home."

Bat nodded eagerly. "Any chance we can get Oliver? He was a great chef," the Batman exclaimed squeakily, his voice slightly higher this early in the morning.

Shrugging, Azrael responded, "Unfortunately, when I went to the dorm cafeteria, he wasn't there anymore. So, we would have to find him first."

"He knew just the right way to make buttered insects..." Bat crooned.

Azrael ignored his friend and looked over to Jophi. "How long will it take to walk across campus to our first class this morning?"

"Class Synergies is at nine, and it should be a pretty quick fifteen-minute walk. Thinking of getting some meditation in this morning?"

Azrael nodded to her and put his plate into the dishwasher before heading to the second floor and one of the disused bedrooms. He felt like there was something he was missing in his Ether spiral. Some more practice would definitely help him understand it.

He sat down and entered meditation, starting with a deep breath in and an exhale that took away the tightness in his chest. He moved on to each body part, breathing out the stiff- ness and caged energies of inaction. Distantly, he realized that he was frustrated by his lack of results toward his goal. He needed to get stronger first, but felt like he was betraying his earlier resolution. How could he take his revenge on the guilds sitting in school?

That idea percolated before being swept away by his next breath out. Once his Ether Manipulation offered him a view of his internal channels, the first thing Azrael did was deconstruct what he had built up. The whirlpool slowly stopped spinning and became a calm sea with some underlying currents. On Tech Duinn, he had widened and slowed down the Ether flowing out of the pool and back into it.

His mind studied the concept of flow he had been manipu- lating inside of those channels. Creating a thinner channel wouldn't create higher velocity by itself. Subconsciously, he must have kept the volume of Ether moving through the channels the same. Instead of adjusting the size of the channels, he concentrated on one and willed more Ether to move through the loop. It had the same effect, and the flow increased, speeding up the velocity.

Theoretically, he could create the same whirlpool in this method and tried to do so. The whirlpool reformed in his center but there was a noticeable difference. The edge of the spiral was thin, almost ephemeral. The peak of the vortex was nearly triangular in its point. He approached that spot with his mind and felt a headache cut through his meditation, which caused him to pull back, like his hand had approached fire.

How was he supposed to get a channel from the tip of the vortex? It wasn't like his Ether pool, and he couldn't touch the virulent flow there. He tried his trick from the day before and pulled a strand off the middle of the whirlpool. This strand caused some discomfort today and made him realize that the thinner wall of the vortex was flowing at a much faster pace.

He touched this to the dry, driftwood-like floorboards of the room he was in and instantly felt the discomfort intensify. Instead of the room reacting tiny splinter by tiny splinter, though, he felt a few centimeters of the wood begin to brighten —then inches. This speed, while still slow, meant that he could probably revitalize a room in a few days. Was the change due to his change in the channels? Or because a room was easier to work with?

"We have to get going," Jophi said as she stood up from her own meditation a few feet away. Azrael hadn't felt her come in and felt the strand of Ether snap back into the vortex and intensify his burgeoning headache. A band felt like it was slowly compressing over his eyebrows and a debuff notification popped up.

Ether Headache

**You have badly mishandled your Ether and your brain
is now suffering a type of stress headache.
Duration: 23 hours, 59 minutes, 57 seconds.**

He groaned, not looking forward to having to deal with this uncomfortable feeling all day. How had he let Jophi *sneak* up on him this morning and out of the room the previous night? He resolved to be more careful in the future. Just because he trusted Bat to a degree he had been letting his guard down, and he truly wasn't sure how that could affect him around Jophi.

"Let's go," Azrael grumbled, when he noticed Bat was also sitting a few feet away.

I really need to pay attention to my surroundings as I meditate!

———

"Class Synergy. What is the first thing that comes to mind when you hear that term?" Professor Telerude asked the class. The professor was a bit of an oddity when compared to Maat and Darwin Faige. She lacked the stuffiness of the latter, and the intimidation of the first. If Azrael was to put his finger on it, he would have said she was unimposing and relatable.

Instead of wearing professor robes, she was wearing a casual outfit that highlighted her beauty. She held herself in a manner that suggested she was talking with equals and not students. She had short-cropped blonde hair and an athletic frame. Azrael was curious what class she possessed but failed to Analyze the woman because of the school trinket. He really needed to get himself one of those.

Jophi raised her hand beside him. The class was taking place on the grass in front of a large brown brick building. Telerude had claimed she despised classrooms and opted to host the first-year course out here instead. Azrael wouldn't complain about fresh air and sunshine as he learned. Telerude indicated Jophi and she stood up. "The first concept that comes to mind is team composition."

Azrael nodded as he agreed with that answer. Telerude smiled at the response and waited. Another hand shot up and, once called upon, this student offered, "I can't help but think about personal classes, skills, and stat allocation."

Again, Telerude nodded and so did Azrael—that was another option, certainly. Three more hands shot up. Kuhl was called on next, and he stated haughtily, "I would think it refers to the grade of classes available."

The response forced Azrael to roll his eyes. Coming from the Asgardian, it sounded like he was condemning all the others in the class. Calling their class choices subpar.

Then again, could the Asgardians have Legendary classes? Epic? Azrael looked around and studied each student in turn. How many of them possessed unique rare classes from other Planetary Gods? He hadn't seen any of their classes in the Cavern of Choices, but Revenant had clearly come from Tech Duinn.

"A perfect synergy of classes chosen as one advances through the ranks is rare. It is often said that 'diversity of class can increase the versatility of an individual, but synergy will specialize,'" Prateek said from near the front of the classroom.

"I see someone has been reading the textbook. What does that mean, though?" Professor Telerude responded with a genuine smile for the healer. The smile made her seem to shine in the sunlight and Azrael watched as a few male students adjusted their seats.

"I think it means that choosing too many varying classes will water down your effectiveness. Choosing classes that complement each other will sharpen it," Prateek responded, again seeming to quote a script.

Telerude's smile widened, and Azrael heard a few males sigh around him. She turned to the class and opened her arms to encompass all the students but somehow made the gesture bigger. The world?

"He is right, but it also isn't that simple," she began. "Let me give an example. If you choose a hunter-type class in apprentice levels—is it best to choose a hunter class in the journeyman ranks?

"A great many people would say yes. The system would continue to offer similar skills that would complement your earlier ones. This is an absolute," Telerude said, lightly closing her fist and holding it up. "In this way, you will solidify yourself and become powerful. But let me ask you another question. Why not pick a rogue or assassin-type class?"

Many of the students scratched their heads and Azrael narrowed his eyes. He could see her point clearly. If hunters were said to have a weakness, it was close range. If rogues and assassins were said to have a strength, it was melee. She opened her hand and displayed 'knife hand' from classic martial stances. "While a fist is strong, is not an open palm?"

"This class will explore the weaknesses of classes—find their counters and ask you to offset them. Remember, at Master rank you regain access to your Apprentice rank class tree," Telerude chided, as she formed a fist with one hand and an open palm with the other. "Life and death, failure or success, the choices you face in this class may set you upon the path to either fate."

The rest of the class was spent in small groups discussing the premise Telerude introduced.

Azrael stayed mostly silent; his mind was occupied with his own dilemma; was an Epic-ranked class inherently stronger than the ones below it?

Maybe he would ask Professor Telerude after class.

Unfortunately, when class ended, the line to ask *questions* of the professor was filled by every male in the class.

CHAPTER TWENTY-EIGHT

Azrael decided not to wait in the line of admirers and hoped he could ask her or another professor at a later date. Jophi was no longer around and one of the Cathodiem guildies told Azrael she had been called away for guild business. Azrael couldn't help but assume she was reporting on him again. He really wasn't sure how to feel about the whole situation. For now, all he could do was follow the adage taught to Sovereign Sons for political situations. *Turn the spy of an enemy into a source of information.*

Of course, that was taught in the espionage class and the whole class focused on creating double agents, which admittedly wouldn't work here. Or would it?

The approach of Kuhl and Magnus interrupted his internal debate, and he closed his eyes. Would these two be seeking him out after every class?

"I can't wait until the vagabond chooses a guild to join," Magnus said to Kuhl as they walked beside him. So, this was their next choice of tactics. Insult him in casual conversation. He felt like giving the two a slow clap for their ingenuity. Not using his name and discussing something near him would make him look foolish if he interjected.

Kuhl guffawed before retorting, "Everyone seems so interested in the gutter trash. You would think the shit stains on his clothes would have turned them off."

Magnus reached out a hand and put it on Kuhl's shoulder, pretending to console his lackey. "It's okay, the Asgardian guild has recognized the smell, and doesn't want it fouling up our halls."

Azrael rolled his eyes and walked away as a path turned toward the cafeteria. While the name calling didn't particularly bother him, he wasn't a glutton. These two wouldn't be caught dead eating cafeteria food was his guess, and without a chef chosen yet, admittedly, he could only hope to find Oliver back behind the counter.

Unfortunately, the Hashslinger wasn't in the kitchen. Instead, a portly chef inside claimed that the last chef was hired by a teacher at the school for her dormitory. Azrael angrily slopped the mashed potatoes onto his plate a few moments later and resolved to find a different chef at Oliver's level. The potatoes still had chunks in them, for Sovereign's sake. He moved over to join Bat, who smiled on his approach. Bat, because of his status as Azrael's butler slash servant, had been allowed to eat at any of the campus cafeterias. The fact that he was here likely meant he had been hoping to find Oliver as well…

"Thought that was you. I have been reading and meditating in the second bedroom all day. Your textbooks are really interesting. There is a large amount of information that we wouldn't have had in my home world. It's a bit slow going because it isn't the batkin's tactile writing but my excitement at new knowledge keeps me going."

That admission made Azrael jolt in his seat. It always amazed him how the Batman managed to get by even without the assists specifically designed for his race. Someone plopped a tray down next to Azrael and his scrutiny of Bat was interrupted. Jophiel shook the bench as she sat. Her face was red, and her knuckles were white on the edge of the tray.

"Everything okay?" Azrael asked her.

She shook her head and forced air out of her lungs through her nose. It sounded like a small wind tunnel, and a moment later she reversed the flow and took a deep lungful back in. Azrael looked to Bat and saw his companion shrug and continue eating. Azrael did the same but asked Bat, "You said you're reading my books, Bat. Any chance you can help me keep up with the readings too?"

Jophi's knuckles cracked as the synovial fluid popped. "That would be cheating."

"How so?" Azrael asked. His fingers moved to rub his temples as his headache flared from her tone and choice of words.

"You can't have someone else do your work for you. It is in the student handbook that you should have gotten on Freyaday."

"May I remind you, I wasn't in class on Freyaday. Also, I wasn't asking him to do my work for me!" Azrael began, his voice slightly elevated. He caught himself shortly after remembering that his headache was causing him to be grouchy. He modulated his tone to as close to normal as he could. "I'm just asking him to summarize what he reads. I have a feeling some of what will be taught will be repetitive to —" Azrael looked around but no one else was nearby. He still lowered his voice. "—the Sovereign Halls. I would rather not read a whole chapter just to find the one piece of information I need."

Jophi's eyebrows raised, and she bit her lips. After a pause, she said, "I am sorry, Azrael. I was in a terrible mood and jumped to conclusions. I kind of forgot that you have been through schooling already."

He just shrugged and rubbed his temples. She wasn't the only one in a bad mood. He turned his gaze on Bat. The Batman nodded eagerly. "Of course I will help. I also noticed how much of the flooring in the bedroom you fixed before class this morning. How did you do it?"

He scratched his head a bit more vigorously as the headache spiked. Azrael tried to come up with an answer. He had noticed the increased speed as well, but wanted to confirm if that was something to do with his experimentation or just because the interior of the house was easier than the porch. This admission confirmed that for Azrael, and he wasn't sure if he should share the secret with the two just yet.

"I tried making the channel larger, which allowed more Ether to flow into the room, but because of that I have a headache debuff, which is why I am in such a bad mood today." He gave a small smile to Jophi, who nodded in commiseration. He knew his answer was a half-truth and now he needed to worry about whether they would discover the spiral and Essence Conversion skill on their own.

He figured he would likely share that skill with Bat, if they were alone. But anything he told Jophi would inevitably end up back in Cathodiem's ears.

Both of his table mates became animated; Jophi blinked rapidly, and Bat's hands spread wide on the table as he squeaked, "I never thought of that! I am headed back now!"

Jophi looked at her plate and grimaced before standing up as well. "Azrael, we really need to find a chef. This cafeteria food is almost inedible," she stated as she too followed Bat back toward the house.

Azrael felt his stomach fall from her words. Was she now planning to live with him? Or was that his stomach complaining about the food quality?

Why does she have to be in such a hurry to sleep in a different room?

He chuckled to himself and tried to dispel the minute sense of nausea. It did make sense that she didn't want to spend more time with him. Afterall, she was only living in the house due to a guild assignment. Just like her 'marriage' to Ogma...

Azrael chose to take a walk to the school docks and check on the Cussing Parrot. He needed some time to think, anyway.

He hadn't been back to the docks in more than a week and, to be honest, he wasn't sure what the school rules were when it came to long term storage of puddle-jumper class ships.

The Cussing Parrot was still there, but to his surprise it had metal clamps on the landing gears, attaching it firmly to the pad. He scratched his head and approached the entry door. A yellow piece of paper was jammed into the door and waved in the intermittent wind. He pulled it out and read.

This ship is at risk of abandonment. It has been parked illegally for more than a week. If this is your ship, please see the docking authorities, immediately, or risk losing it.

Azrael sprinted back to the docking tower and the first-floor registration building it seemed to grow out from. He entered and immediately noticed the eerie silence that seemed off in a place of business. Moving to the front desk he found a hunched over, very small woman. Moving his head around, he could see she wore headphones that were nearly as large as her entire head, and she was currently playing some type of game on her tablet.

The game involved some very vigorous clicking and he hesitated to interrupt her, as she seemed extremely concentrated on the task. Instead he analyzed her.

Jess Weir
Master-Administrator
Level 33
Health Points: 1,100 / 1,100
Skills: Numerous

She must have noticed his shadow moving above her because she paused her game and looked up with a smile. "Sorry about that, I was trying to beat this pot smashing mini-game! Have you ever played The Recorder of Time?" Jess asked, her clear excitement easing Azrael's nerves a bit.

He shook his head but couldn't get the thought of losing the Cussing Parrot off his mind, so he held up the yellow paper. Jess had short blonde hair and faerie-like features. Azrael hadn't thought her eyes could get any bigger, but she managed it somehow. She slid her headphones down to rest on her neck and exclaimed, "You are the owner of the Cussing Parrot?"

His sullen nod provoked an unexpected laugh. "Oh, my word! I thought my friend Kota was having some fun at my expense. But a teenager..." She faded off as her laughter intensified. She exited out of the game she was playing, and speed-typed a short sentence into a chat.

Found the Cussing owner!

The top of the chat read 'Kota-private message.'

Her laughter died down to chuckling before she wiped tears from her eyes, and she looked back at him. "Out of curiosity, what in Gaia possessed you to choose that name?"

Azrael felt his cheeks flush, and he shrugged. "It wasn't my choice, actually—"

He told her the story of how the Cussing Parrot had come to be his, and after some prodding told her all about his first few days after he parked it. She grew very skeptical when he told her he was the prospective apprentice of Merlin the headmaster. "Look, the amusement this has given me alone will get you out of any fines. I will even help you get it registered and transferred to the student docks, but think before you create a lie that big."

Her tablet chimed and she glanced at it. Kota had responded, *'Poly gone but shall never be forgotten.'* Jess began laughing again and Azrael tried to figure out the humor. He reread the message and groaned—he didn't love puns. Admittedly, these types of puns seemed to have been what had gotten him out of any fines.

He smiled and forced a few chuckles out, then attempted, "I assure you my answer wasn't a parrot-y."

Jess grimaced and her laughter cut off. "Good try, but parody doesn't really work there. You aren't lying about the headmaster, though? Show me your token; I can have the ship moved to the villa in that case."

Azrael's face fell when he failed to make Jess smile with his pun. *Man, I definitely suck at these sorts of things.* Then he registered her words and tapped all of his pockets subconsciously. "I was never given a token, just sent to live in the villa. In fact, I have only seen Merlin once since the exams."

Jess gave him a very skeptical look but responded politely, "Merlin is a bit strange. How about I fly your ship over to the villa, then?"

He realized she was testing him. If he was lying, now would be the time to go back on his answer or come up with an excuse. Instead, he shrugged and said, "I hope you can find her perch with all the overgrowth over there."

Jess glared at him for attempting another pun. Or maybe it was her way of attempting to discern if he was telling the truth.

CHAPTER TWENTY-NINE

"This lock is clearly broken," Jess stated, with a stern look on her face. She had landed the Cussing Parrot in the overgrown field, where she said a helipad used to reside. When Azrael walked down the ramp, he thought he could make out some asphalt or concrete under the weeds but honestly wasn't sure. "This, combined with the state of the grounds, tells me you aren't supposed to be living here!"

He groaned and desperately searched for the envelopes that Merlin had left him. He found the yellow paper sitting on the rotting bench near the door and quickly retrieved it before handing it over. She read it and looked around at the state of the house. "You're telling me that it's your job to restore this entire place?"

He could only nod helplessly. "I don't think he expects it to be finished anytime soon…" he responded dejectedly.

"Yeah, no kidding. I can force the grounds crew to come up and have them maintain the helipad for you, but that's the best I can do—good luck," Jess said as she glanced at the rotting support beams and promptly stepped back outside. Azrael watched her descend the steps before calling back, "Oh, get an identification talisman from your prospective mentor, though. Otherwise, you will have problems in the future."

Azrael waved and slunk up the stairs to find Jophi and Bat meditating in the second bedroom. "Any increase to speed for you two?" he asked as he walked through the door.

Both smiled but neither responded. It was clear enough to his sight, not even the Ether version, that his advice was having an effect on the speed of rejuvenation. The increase, while noticeable still, wasn't anything to get too excited over; it looked like they still had two days of hard work to complete this room. He tried another question, hoping for an answer this time, "Jophi, did you get some sort of token from your mentor?"

Without opening her eyes, Jophi pulled a talisman from around her neck. Azrael could only groan and sit down to join them. This was getting ridiculous—wasn't his prospective mentor supposed to guide him? Right now, it felt like Azrael had a crazy absentee uncle in his life. Then again, he had only been a student for about half a week and Merlin wasn't his full mentor... yet. He would have to give it time.

"Anyone know of any chefs that would want to work in this dump?" Azrael asked, his voice a bit sour. Both Jophi and Bat blushed in response.

Bat was first to respond. "I found out Oliver is working in the vice-principle's dorms. Even the cook in the cafeteria laughed at me when I asked him if he was open to working here."

Jophi chimed in, "I asked a few as well, and got very similar responses."

"Can't you just ask your guild to send someone?" Azrael questioned, confused.

Jophi made a sour face and shook her head adamantly. He waited for her to elaborate but she closed her eyes and returned to her meditation. Bat shrugged and also hooded his ears. Azrael was left to wonder why the chefs from the school didn't want to work at the headmaster's villa. Was Merlin stingy on top of everything else?

Azrael began reorganizing his channels and pulled a strand from his spiral to feed the room. His area began to rejuvenate at a speed nearly ten times faster than his two companions, and he purposefully disconnected that strand, not ready to reveal this secret that Ogma had warned him of. Not to mention Merlin hinted at.

It's not like I know much about it myself. I just know that an Etherience boost from a skill is very rare.

He pulled up the skill to re-read its contents, confirming he already had a boost of ten percent.

Essence Conversion

- **You have made your body a better vessel for converting Ether to Essence. Your body's ability to act as a filter increased fractionally. Planetary Gods always need more Essence; since you stand out in this regard, you will be awarded 1% more Etherience per kill per level in this skill.**

Current Rank: Weak level 10.

He pulled a strand from one of his loops on his leg and widened it. The speed this time was more on par with the others, and he concentrated back on the spiral at his center, attempting to discover exactly what it was doing. His limited understanding led him to believe that every living organism converted Ether to Essence. The Ether Channels, Manipulation, and Essence Conversion he was currently exhibiting was just increasing the amount of Essence. Thus, his increased Etherience reward from the Essence Conversion skill. It would seem that all Planetary Gods would appreciate someone who could convert Ether to Essence at a faster rate.

If he was to compare Ether to water, then he would say that the whirlpool was somehow cleaning or aerating it. His heart began to beat rapidly and sweat broke out on his skin. He shivered away the feeling of goosebumps and slowly broke down the pattern he was holding. If a whirlpool was somehow aerating the Ether, he knew of a few things that would quite possibly increase that.

One problem; how would he maintain control of the whirlpool in his center?

What if he built the channels like joining rivers? Tributaries that continually joined together to lead back to the ocean.

He began the slow process of picturing his branches, arteries, and veins of Ether returning to his center, and flowing along a circulating river. As the river passed each channel from his head, legs, and arms, he joined them in. This increased the pressure in the river and began to create a torrent. His head began to pound as the Ether frothed and attempted to break the banks his mind was attempting to create.

Azrael had made a full circle with the river before he brought it to the center of his pool and extended it up as high above the pool as the pressure would allow. Once he reached that point, he allowed the channel to widen into a cone that led all the way back down to his pool. His head throbbed, but he watched his creation with his mind's eye.

His idea was simple: create an Ether 'waterfall.' As far as he could remember, a waterfall or a fountain were two of the best ways to aerate water. The Ether behaved in the same way as flowing water and formed something like a cascading mist, but because of the extreme pressure and the cone shape, a great deal of the Ether hugged the channel's edge as it swirled around the almost vase-like creation and down to the pool.

Azrael watched the pool as it drained away along his extremities and then refilled from his pseudo waterfall above. He touched the pool with his mind and felt that something was different in the Ether, but he didn't black out. His headache might have increased in intensity, but he wasn't sure. He pulled a channel from the pool and exchanged it with the one that was touching the flooring.

The speed increased to perhaps five times the speed of Bat and Jophi. Of course, that was a decrease in efficiency from the whirlpool strand he had pulled earlier. Azrael left this one connected and called up his stats sheet. Essence Conversion had increased by a level, but if he was to guess, this method was inferior to what he had stumbled upon on Tech Duinn. Perhaps there was some method to combine the two?

He studied the waterfall, mentally prodding at the empty spaces where Ether wasn't filling the channel. Perhaps aeration wasn't the proper approach. If his body was filtering Ether into Essence, that also fit with the skill and reward it gave. How then could you increase the filtering of a substance you couldn't control?

By the halls! Merlin asked me a question just like this. Was he hinting at something?

A spike of pain shot into his head as he traced a small drop of Ether from the top of the waterfall to the bottom. Suddenly it evaporated, seeming to almost combine with the empty space and he collapsed to the ground with a shout.

"Azrael, are you okay?" Jophi asked as she shot to her feet.

He rolled around helplessly on the floor, clutching his head. At this point, he would have preferred the unconsciousness the bottom of the whirlpool offered. The pain was similar to that of a brain freeze but increased by several degrees of magnitude.

Bat squeaked, "Look how much of the room he managed to revitalize. He was experimenting with his channels, I think."

The pain was only intensifying, and Azrael realized that his tightly controlled riverbanks near his center were eroding and beginning to run out of control. He gave a half-hearted effort to rein them in and the pressure that put on his brain sent him spiraling into unconsciousness.

———

He woke up to a bucket of cold water being dumped on his head and a raging headache. Jolting to a sitting position made his head throb.

"I told you a bucket of water was a bad idea," Bat squeaked from somewhere nearby.

"It always worked when my masters used it on others in training," Jophi said a bit too smugly. She followed it up with,

"Azrael, can you explain how you were increasing your efficiency?"

He groaned as loudly as his head would allow in response.

What, do you want some information to carry back to daddy? he grumped internally. Perhaps he should have accused her openly, but he wasn't sure his head would be able to handle an argument right now.

Azrael could hear Jophi open her mouth, as if she was going to press the issue, when suddenly the room went eerily quiet. Bat gulped audibly, and Azrael could swear Jophi stopped breathing.

Both fell to the floor. "Headmaster," they said in near unison. Were they prostrating themselves?

Azrael moved his fingers to the bridge of his nose and attempted to open his eyes. Merlin was standing in the doorway, smiling, his long white hair and beard almost seeming to rustle in an unseen wind. "So, this is where you chose to start. Need more sleeping space it would seem," Merlin crowed into the room, his voice exaggeratedly loud.

The pain this brought to Azrael's head forced him to close his eyes and apply pressure to his ears with his hands. He was practically in the fetal position from the pain. Because of his current death grip on his ears, he didn't hear Merlin approach, but did feel when the man touched the top of his head with a single finger.

The pain vanished as Azrael jerked back from the contact, expecting his head to split in two. It took him several moments to realize that Merlin somehow took away the headache and another few heartbeats to remove his hands and brave moving his head further. He glanced at the corner where his headache debuff had been. It was gone, along with whatever new debuff his experimentation had brought. Pain free, he stared wide-eyed at Merlin.

The old man chuckled and said, <It appears you are attempting to find an answer to my question. Have you shared it with these two or should we continue to talk privately?>

Azrael stared at him. His lips hadn't moved. Was Merlin communicating telepathically? <I haven't yet. I believe Jophi is a spy for Cathodiem,> Azrael thought furiously at the man.

<No need to shout. Just think normally, and I will be able to hear you,> Merlin responded sternly. <It would appear you discovered a fundamental law of Ether. Your brain couldn't quite cope with it, yet.>

<You mean when the Ether evaporated? I haven't really thought about it yet,> Azrael mumbled mentally at the man as he looked down at his wet clothing. <The whirlpool wasn't evaporating, but I got the same feeling from its point as I did from that drop that vanished from the waterfall.>

<You are starting to see. One of the laws is almost within your grasp. This house is meant to help you practice. Consider sharing this with your friends; they can help you. Oh, and have you not wondered why Jophi chose to come live here and not at her guild manor or mentor's villa?>

Azrael frowned. He had already explained that she was a spy, sent by Cathodiem. But before he could answer, Merlin literally vanished.

"Oh, come on. I didn't even get to ask for a talisman," Azrael shouted.

Bat flapped his ears. "Azrael, I don't mean to question your sanity, but you had plenty of opportunities to say something but didn't. You both just kind of stared at each other," the Batman squeaked nervously.

CHAPTER THIRTY

"Rumor has it Merlin doesn't even want to give you a talisman, even though you're the only prospective student he has that's staying at that dump of a villa!" Magnus crowed from a nearby seat after class finished on Freyaday morning.

How had he even learned that? Jophi?

Azrael turned his head to the man-child. "I haven't had the opportunity to ask him yet. Why don't you show me your talisman from Merlin? Oh, right, you don't have one either," Azrael responded heatedly. Okay, so it turned out this was a bit of a touchy subject for him.

"Actually, I do. Unlike you, my father was a real apprentice of Merlin, and even entered the first tower of Atlantis," Magnus retorted as he pulled a talisman from his pocket. "This one is my father's. Perhaps Merlin knows he will expel you by the end of the semester and doesn't want to bother getting one made!"

Getting up, Azrael didn't respond as he left the auditorium. He didn't have time for this. His dungeon group wanted to make its way to El Dorado right after class and begin preparing for a dungeon run. Magnus' laughter was joined by the people around him, and Azrael almost turned back—but he managed to walk away.

The group was waiting for him at the Cussing Parrot when he arrived, and so he rushed into the house to get his backpack. Once back outside, he noticed Jess standing with the group. "Hello Jess, what brings you out here?" Azrael asked.

"Was just checking how long you planned to be gone. I am going to have a crew start on repairing the helipad tomorrow."

"Oh, we plan to run dungeons in El Dorado for the week. We won't be back until next Freyaday at the earliest," Azrael reported.

Jess nodded and walked away. The group loaded onto the dropship once Azrael unlocked and lowered the gangplank. The chatter was lively during the quick hop to El Dorado, mostly excitement about finding treasures and the like. Oslow eyed Bat suspiciously, attempting to discern more about the Batman, but since the Canaanite Guild member was too shy to ask questions, there wasn't much to find out.

Azrael couldn't help but shake his head ruefully. Oslow would have to come out of his shell eventually, or the tank would face problems in his future. For now, it made for a slight hiccup in the group. Azrael could tell that Prateek was unsure as well, but assumed they would all warm to Bat once the man started showing his worth.

The group arrived in El Dorado and Azrael paid for the ship's dock for the nine days, before they moved to the hotel. This was paid for by Azrael again. The idea was that he would foot the bills and be compensated by the group's earnings before splitting the loot later. Of course, this was dangerous, because his group could end up not making enough crystals to cover costs. He doubted that, but just in case, he didn't splurge for extra rooms. All four men would be sleeping in a single suite and Jophi had her own bedroom off of it.

I am going to miss sleeping in a room without snoring. Or is it a room without Jophi?

Over the remaining days of classes, Azrael had grown

rather accustomed to having the beautiful woman sleeping in a bed next to his. Unfortunately, that wasn't going to last much longer either—not with the new bedroom almost finished…

"Which dungeon would be best for us to run?" Oslow asked, interrupting the group as they settled into the suite. They had had this discussion before, of course.

Right now, it was between the Delving dungeon, and the Puzzle dungeon in the city. The benefit of running the Puzzle dungeon was that they could enter it every day and stay in the hotel at night. Of course, they could also complete puzzles until they reached a safe zone and camp at night. Puzzle dungeons often didn't give escalating rewards, unless you counted the final puzzle and completion. The other upside to the Puzzle dungeon was the lack of necessity to fight.

On the other side of the coin was the Delving dungeon. In this type of instanced dungeon, getting deeper awarded better loot—so they would have to camp. Safe zones appeared every five levels, and according to the rumors, they would need to push hard to reach the second safe zone to truly feel safe. The first safe zone was an easy target for thieves and murderers from guilds and adventurers alike.

"Why don't we run two days of the Puzzle dungeon and then move over to the Delving?" Azrael suggested. "I have been thinking that's the best of both worlds for the last few days."

Oslow scratched his chin, but at Bat's nod, Prateek finally spoke up, "You don't get a say. No offense, but you aren't a student and, in my opinion, that removes your vote."

Eyes narrowing, Azrael and Jophi both stood up together and moved to stand beside Bat. Prateek's eyes widened, and he crossed his arms protectively. Oslow coughed. "Prateek, it would seem that we should give Mr. Bat a chance."

Prateek nodded and was about to apologize but Azrael cut him off. "I understand you haven't seen Bat before, and don't believe he will be useful in the dungeon, but on my word, you are wrong. In fact, I would say he is the most important member of our group."

Jophi smiled and Bat's ears flushed a deep purple color. Azrael just shrugged—it wasn't like he was making that up. Jophi chose to respond in the growing silence, "I agree with Azrael. The Puzzle dungeon may be easiest, but we can only buy the information and try it for ourselves."

"I have heard people who clear the Delving dungeon often have enough loot and resources to retire," Oslow added dreamily.

"First of all, only a few hundred people have ever *completed* the Delving dungeon. Only a few of them were lucky enough to get the drop that allowed them to *retire*," Jophi responded skeptically. "Let's be realistic, we aren't going to be able to run through all hundred floors in a week anyway."

Prateek finally found his voice again. "Okay, let's go with Azrael's plan—as long as we aren't entering the Labyrinth, I don't care. That place has been a death trap of late. The city officials are thinking about sending some people in to destroy it and buy a new core to take its place."

"Alright, let's go collect the information we need. Tonight, we will discuss strategies, and formations. With a Puzzle dungeon, it's always best to have someone who takes final say—in case the group thinks of two responses. We will nominate who that will be later. Meet back here around the ninth evening bell," Azrael commanded before standing up and joining Bat and Jophi on their way to the door.

"Thanks, Azrael," Bat mumbled.

Bat really doesn't stand up for himself at all. Would he have been a student if he was a bit more assertive?

———

The next morning, they woke up just before the ninth morning bell and began getting set for their first dungeon run as a team. Azrael was excited to be gaining Etherience again. Plus, he had figured out a way to beat the guild's bullying recruiting policies.

They approached the southern Puzzle dungeon and found

there wasn't a line for adventurers. Instead, the noble's line was huge. Azrael raised his eyebrow as his stomach began to flip over; it felt like it was tying itself into knots. He had a bad feeling about this.

They approached the guard at the front and Jophi stated, "Azrael, the prospective student of Headmaster Merlin."

The people at the front of the line made appreciative noises, but no one moved to open up a place for them. "I'm afraid the entire line is comprised of trial members from Asgard today. Since, they are the top-ranked guild—I can't force them to let you enter," the guard mumbled in response. Based on the line, with thirty-minute entrance intervals, they would be waiting outside the entire day.

"How long will this trial last?" Azrael asked, his voice sounding defeated even to his own ears.

"The entire week, I'm afraid. I don't know how it is at the other dungeons, but the Southern Puzzle has always been the most popular."

Azrael was getting a small glimpse at what Magnus could do, and he had to admit he didn't like it one bit. He opened his arms and guided his group away from the guard and the dungeon before saying, "I think this is Magnus' doing."

"You think!" Prateek retorted very sarcastically.

Azrael closed his eyes and breathed through his nose. If he punched the healer, it wouldn't be good for group morale.

"Let's go check the Delving dungeon?" Bat suggested and they all set off.

Turned out that all the dungeons were like this. Except, of course, the Labyrinth—while it had a line, it was short. Azrael's knuckles cracked as his fist clenched around his sword pommel —he needed an outlet for his current mood. "We could be in the Labyrinth in an hour or so. We can head back to the hotel, check out, and grab our stuff for overnights. We could even read up on what we need to know in line—what do you think?" Azrael suggested.

Jophi jumped at the clear anger in his voice. The group

tilted their heads before Bat offered, "Azrael and I did run the place on our own the last time."

It seemed that the two *students* couldn't let Bat *show them up.* Once Oslow and Prateek were on board, Jophi shrugged and demanded, "Only if we grab an escape rope. It's expensive, but could save our lives."

I guess that would be prudent, but if we have to use it, am I eating the loss?

———

Under an hour later, the team was standing in the front position in line for the Labyrinth. They had gone over the new information packets and something was making Azrael's mind whir. According to the reports, Ligers, Bashers, the armored Rhino and even a Wendigo had been spotted down in the depths.

For the last hour, they had gone through the contingency plans for if they ran into these monsters. He had been very quiet during these planning sessions, despite having first-hand experience with everything but the Liger—still, he had seen a Liger fight. Was this a coincidence? His body felt hot, and goosebumps were raised all over his skin, under the Ether Tech suit of armor.

"Aren't you punching above your weight class?" Magnus' supremely smug voice called from beside the guard.

Azrael's entire group twitched and turned to find the blond man standing beside the guard. The Asgardian's smile was like ice on Azrael's skin. "The Adventuring Hall hasn't even finished reclassifying this place. Why don't you just ask your little girl-friend for access to the Cathodiem dungeons?"

Jophi reacted to that barbed comment in a way Azrael hadn't expected. Instead of firing back an insult, she blushed and turned away. He blinked at her then at Magnus before snarking back, "Are you just here to boast? Or did you plan on running a dungeon today?" He felt the inadequacy of the response, but hadn't had anything else ready. He was still a bit too shaken by the coincidences of the Labyrinth and Jophi's odd reaction.

Magnus surprised the group by laughing, and responding, "I'm sorry, I actually came to apologize for the bad blood between us." Magnus walked right into Azrael's personal space and because of the larger boy's height, Azrael was forced to look up at him. Magnus' voice dropped to a whisper, "My father has asked me to apologize for the timing of our recruitment, and his inability to allow others to supersede the applicants. I just figured I would personally let you know that it was just bad timing…"

Azrael felt his hand twitch toward his sword. Magnus' tone of voice and his close proximity conveyed an entirely different message, and Azrael shoved Magnus to get him to back out of his personal bubble instead of drawing a weapon.

"If you'll notice, we are at the front of the line of a dungeon. So, no hard feelings," Azrael said, attempting to act nonchalant but failing to hide the bitterness in his voice.

"I was going to offer you my father's old mentor talisman as a gesture of sincerity, but the fact that you're going into the Labyrinth means I probably won't ever see you again," Magnus responded, as he again moved into Azrael's personal space.

This time, Azrael grabbed the hilt of his sword but before he could draw it, his teammates interposed themselves between him and Magnus. Magnus' cronies did the same and because of the close press of bodies, a great deal of shoving occurred.

Magnus was holding two warhammers, one in each hand. The things were large and for him to take out two likely meant he could confidently wield both of them simultaneously. Unless it was just posturing.

Instead of being intimidated by the sight, Azrael smiled. "I was wondering why you were so stupid. It looks like you've been putting all your points into Strength," Azrael sniped, while indicating the two hammers.

Lightning crackled and the sky darkened. Kuhl turned to Magnus and whispered something in the teenager's ear that

Azrael couldn't make out. The two hammers vanished from his hands a moment after, though, and he turned to storm away. Kuhl looked back at Azrael and gave him a smile that set off alarm bells. There wasn't an ounce of friendship in the look. Instead, Kuhl looked like a snake ready to strike.

When the press of bodies parted, half to follow Magnus and Kuhl and his team to lightly surround Azrael, something glinted off the ground. Azrael Analyzed it.

Merlin's Mark
This talisman marks the holder as an apprentice of the Headmaster Merlin.
Additional access to the first Atlantean Tower has been granted to the holder.

After the rather unpleasant encounter with Magnus, Azrael was extremely hesitant to take the mark, but since Magnus had said he was going to offer it to Azrael anyway, it wouldn't be stealing, right? Worst case, he could just turn the mark in later, so Azrael placed it in his Ring of Holding before his group took notice. Prateek returned to the matters of healing required inside the dungeon.

Bat, on the other hand, drew close to Azrael and whispered, "I think he dropped that mark intentionally. Something about this is really off, Az…"

Azrael nodded but pointed back to Prateek, who was giving them both a stern look as he detailed the procedure if they were poisoned by the Wendigo. Azrael had first-hand knowledge of the insidious blood poison of a Wendigo and knew that without treatment, any afflicted member would likely die—they needed to be paying attention.

Still, as the healer continued talking, he considered the situation. If Magnus had dropped the necklace on purpose, what was his reasoning? Inside of the Ring of Holding, no one would know Azrael had it. Not to mention that access to the Penta-climbs was a boon Azrael had dreamed of since first learning of them at the Sovereign Halls. He was reluctant to just hand the talisman back. His mind warred with his heart before he finally decided to keep it for now. He would be wary of using it for the foreseeable future, and maybe just sell it to someone offworld.

"Alright, your group's up. Hand me your waivers," the guard shouted to them, stopping Prateek's thorough line of sight discussion. The forms were essentially signing away any and all rights to compensation from the city for any damages or death in the currently unranked city dungeon. The group had all signed the document, but the extra level of warning wasn't exactly motivational.

Azrael took the familiar walk he had made two weeks earlier down to the dungeon door. He looked back at his group and received nods from everyone. "Alright, remember the first goal is to find a safe zone. If we listen to Bat, we can find the easiest route to do so. Once we have found the safe zone, we can clear out from there. According to the data package, you can retreat to the zone to drop any monster aggro as well.

"Let's do it!"

CHAPTER THIRTY-ONE

"Give Oslow a few moments to build aggro. Once he has it, the Bashers will be easy to pick off," Azrael reiterated the planned response for the bone breaking bunny rabbits.

After each one attempted a bash and phased through Oslow, the group went to work.

Azrael dispatched two of them with quick slashes infused with his Soul Strike skill. Jophi's fireballs turned two others to ash in a blinding red blast, and three more crumpled to the ground, twitching and shaking. Only five were left after the first few seconds, and Azrael reflected on the ease of this fight compared to his solo efforts on Tech Duinn. These creatures were identical to the beasts in the Pit, near as Azrael could tell.

The last five were dispatched with the same ease as they leapt around and through Oslow. The second blessing to a true dungeon run was the break they now had after the fight. No longer were they forced to conserve Ether, at least not unless they faced a large-scale battle, which Bat could likely warn them about.

Bat pointed in the direction they had been heading as soon as the fight finished, and Azrael began picking up the loot to store. "The path splits about fifty meters ahead. The right has a large, armored Goblin. The left leads to a highly trapped hallway."

Azrael stood back up and motioned for Oslow to lead the way, but asked the group, "To the right then?"

No one voiced a differing opinion, and Oslow turned right at the fork. The group fell in behind him and within another fifty meters, the hallway opened into a rather large chamber filled with numerous pillars that reached varying heights. The armored Goblin that Bat had mentioned wasn't visible. Bat pointed unerringly toward the right side of the chamber, though. "He is behind the third pillar, and just took a spear off the nearest rack," the Batman whispered into the hush.

Oslow nodded and began moving in that direction. Once the tank reached the first pillar, the group followed inside. Prateek whispered, "Don't lose line of sight, Oslow." A stiff nod was the response.

Slayers of the Goblin Village Detected
The mark of the Goblin massacre has been placed on at least one of your members. The chieftain has sworn vengeance to his god, Gleeglob, who offers aid to his champion.
Gleeglob's sneakiness added to the Goblin Chieftain.

Bat shrieked, "The armored Goblin just vanished!"

Damnit, I forgot all about that prompt from our previous run! Azrael thought internally as he shouted, "Circle up! Oslow, we can't let it have a free shot on anyone in the group."

The danger in all stealth classes was their first attack. This encounter wasn't exactly an assassin or rogue, though; it was some sort of tank that was blessed by a dungeon. Azrael realized it would likely attack him or Bat first, due to the mark they held.

He stepped away from the group and shouted, "I am still cleaning the green blood off of my sword from killing that village!" He activated his Soul Cloak and got into a ready stance. Nothing happened, no warning shot through his Soul Cloak skill to tell him of an impending attack. Maybe this thing was too stupid to understand him?

They slowly moved through the pillars, approaching the center of the room—following Bat's directions. Azrael had chosen to get back into formation after his taunt hadn't succeeded. This wasn't the time for heroics. As soon as they crossed between two pillars into a circular space, he noticed the tent, small fire, weapon racks, and rusty chest. They had reached the campsite of the Goblin Chief, but still hadn't—

His Soul Cloak screamed, and Azrael swayed as fast as his stats and armor-enhanced body would allow. The tip of a spear skittered across his armor where his ribs would have been with a screech. Azrael stared into black eyes, which spread into veins of dark purple on a green face. The chief's mouth was formed into a snarl, and its teeth were clenched so hard Azrael saw blood in the gums. Or maybe that was its last meal?

As suddenly as the chief appeared, it vanished. Azrael's return swing swished through the empty air a split second after, and dispersed a dark black smoke, but the body was gone. "Bat, are you getting anything?"

"I didn't sense him until he struck at you, then he was gone again," Bat stated in a hurried squeak.

A strange static sound was the only precursor to a spear-head appearing and targeting Azrael's knee. Acting fast, Azrael sidestepped and buckled his knee inward as he forcibly knelt on top of the wooden shaft about three inches back from the blackened steel head of the weapon. The instant his knee made contact, instead of snapping wood, he heard his knee scrape on the cave floor, and smoke puffed out from the impact point.

"It's very similar to my dodge talent. I think the creature is still there, just in another phased reality," Oslow shouted as he ran up to Azrael and swung a fist into the smoke. That strange static sound intensified and Oslow puffed out of sight as well.

"Umm—was that supposed to happen?" Azrael asked in an overly loud voice.

Screeches and static hisses began to sound from a space directly in front of Azrael. One moment an armored Goblin arm or torso would appear and then vanish. Sometimes Azrael would catch a glimpse of the dark brown hardened leather that Oslow wore, before it too would dissolve. Azrael tried to find an opening in the flickering forms to strike at the Goblin, but it seemed like Oslow was grappling with the beast, and any strike at one would likely hit the other.

"Bat, can you hit them both with a soundwave the next time they appear?" Azrael asked.

"I really don't know how that will affect them," Bat responded.

"This isn't the time to be picky," Prateek interjected. "Oslow's health is dropping fast!"

Jophi put her hand on Bat's shoulder. "I could fireball them out, but I don't see that going well," she said with false levity.

Bat nodded and the next time the two appeared, the static crack was punctuated by a very strange muffling of the air. Two bodies fell out of the smoke, the Goblin in its slightly rusted armor was latched onto Oslow, its fangs buried in the man's jugular.

Azrael instantly began stabbing at the chieftain in light thrusts, with his sword coated in his Soul Strike skill. Without the protection of the shadows, and with all of its attention on Oslow, Azrael was free to attack at will. The problem was that the Goblin wouldn't die!

"My heals can't distinguish between the two of them, they are hitting both!" Prateek shouted from the back as he began to sweat noticeably.

"Options!" Azrael commanded a question at the stunned group, as Oslow fought for his life underneath the highly armored Goblin.

A terrifying silence stretched for what felt like hours but could only have been a few seconds.

Azrael stored his Soul Blade and leaped onto the back of the Goblin, attempting to force his right arm through the small gap the Goblin's neck created. He could feel the Goblin's muscles straining against the action but with its main focus elsewhere, he eventually succeeded. He used Maat's Earthly Embrace form and continued to attempt a triangle lock under the chieftain's chin.

Once his armored elbow of his right arm passed through, Azrael heaved with all of his strength, attempting to lock in a rear choke. To add more power to the action, he placed his opposite hand on his elbow and wrapped the gauntleted right hand behind his shoulder blade. His Ether Tech armor suit began to whine as the servo motors cranked. At first, the Goblin didn't seem to notice, but as the vice tightened, Azrael heard a sickening squelch, then ragged breathing. He couldn't tell if the breathing was Oslow or the chieftain, but he kept tightening his grip.

Green fingers began flailing on his armored arm, then toward his armored head, attempting to disrupt the martial form that Maat had demonstrated earlier that week. However, a rear choke was one of the most defended positions against a humanoid opponent, if the fight was one on one. The body of the opponent protected you from most of the punishment they could deal, and they usually only weakened over time. The Goblin attempted to tuck its chin, but it was far too late. As soon as the oxygen-starved muscles of the creature weakened, Azrael was able to pull it completely off Oslow, and roll onto his back.

This exposed the creature completely and the group began to stab and beat the proffered flesh of the chieftain, until the creature went completely limp in Azrael's arms. He quickly Analyzed the back of the thing's head, just to be sure.

Goblin Chieftain
Journeyman-Shadowmancer
Level 12

Dead

Azrael pushed the bloodied green corpse off of himself and sat up. He took his helmet off and panted into the silence of the pillared cave. Oslow groaned from right beside him, as wave after wave of Prateek's healing washed over him. Azrael made a sour face. "That cannot happen again," he huffed out disappointedly in between lungfuls of air.

Jophi pointed to him and Bat. "It would have been nice if you had told us you had a debuff from this place," she accused.

"Yeah, the damn boss activated some sort of hell mode, not to mention our *blind detector* began bugging out," Prateek added, snarkily.

Bat's head fell and Azrael's gauntleted fists whined as his fists balled. He slammed one on the ground and shouted, "Enough!"

When the two others in the group fell back into silence with downcast eyes, he continued, "I didn't mean the fight itself, I meant the inaction!

"That was not and will never be considered good enough. We have five people in this party. I cannot and will not believe that we didn't have a skill that could have helped in that life-or-death struggle. I was trying to point out that the inaction of all of us nearly cost Oslow. Yet, the first thing we all do is break down and point fingers at each other.

"Take a moment to recover, and each person come up with a way they could have reacted in that fight," Azrael finished, using an exercise the teachers of the Sovereign Hall often imparted to the losers of spars.

Azrael looted the chieftain corpse, and received a locked spear. He was still upset as he stood and began approaching the tent. That was probably why he took a deep angry breath through his nose, and retched. What was left of that morning's breakfast splattered onto the stone, and he shuddered as he stepped back. The smell of the camp was a combination of rotting meat, fecal matter, and Goblin musk. Once he was clear of the odorous cloud, he caught his breath and put his helmet back on.

Each member of the group was looking at him and he shrugged helplessly. "I wouldn't suggest going over there without some sort of filtering mask. It reeks."

———

"I have a priest's blessing that is a single target and would have given Oslow heals over time. Likely would have led to less mass heals on the Goblin and its eventual death," Prateek responded sheepishly.

Azrael nodded. "That's good. Perhaps that would have made the difference," he encouraged. The point of this exercise wasn't to find a perfect solution, but to recognize the solutions that each individual could have contributed. While this was Azrael's first group dungeon run, he had been schooled for years on team building or, more specifically, disruption of a team's tactics.

He turned to Jophi. She nodded and confidently said, "I have a few frost spells that have a frostbite effect. The effect doesn't target allies and would have been quite debilitating to the chieftain."

Azrael nodded and turned to Bat. "I have several options that probably would have helped. Primary amongst them is a skill called Deaden. It would have removed a great many of the creature's senses, leaving it confused."

Finally, he turned to Oslow. "I really shouldn't have rushed in like that. This all started because I somehow crossed into the creature's shadow dimension. In the future, I will take some time to plan."

"All good answers," Azrael stated. "I think my choice was the best option for me. All of my skills would have killed both of you. In the future, let's all stay engaged, that was too close for comfort. Bat and I weren't aware that the debuff we received from killing a village of Goblins last run would hang on for this run. We couldn't have guessed—but I apologize regardless.

"Loot wise, we got the chieftain's spear; a bag of assorted gems, marks, and diamonds; and some herbs. We also got a quest item—everyone touch this totem."

Congratulations! You have completed a hidden dungeon quest.
Labyrinth Quest
Hidden Quest
Labyrinth Goblin Chieftain
By slaughtering not only a village of Goblins but a chieftain aided by the god Gleeglop, you have become a terrifying legend amongst all Goblins in the Labyrinth.
Rewards:
100,000 Etherience.
Relationship bar for all Labyrinth Goblins has become worshipped.

"Before we leave, there are two chests hidden inside this room behind false walls in pillars," Bat added, causing Azrael to smile widely. His pleased cat expression only deepened when he saw the rest of the group react as well.

Both chests were E-ranked, but they brought some Health and Ether potions, as well as some locked gear. The group took a break as everyone checked their notification, and Azrael wasn't an exception.

Congratulations! You have reached Level 4, and 5.
30,375 Etherience remaining until Level 6.

———

Congratulations! You have completed a class quest.
Demon of Gaia

Red Quest
Class Confirmation Quest
Collect a Soul
You have collected the soul of a Devout Goblin
Chieftain. Would you like to use this Soul to complete
the quest?
<Yes> | No
Time limit remaining: 2 days
Rewards:
<10,000> Etherience.
Journeyman Demon Class Confirmation
Abyssal Skill

Azrael blinked at the quest, honestly having forgotten about it. He would not have run the Puzzle dungeon first if he had been thinking straight. He had likely put it out of his mind because collecting a soul to complete a quest had seemed like such a foreign concept while attending a civilized school on a civilized planet. He considered it again now, though.

The Etherience reward seemed like it would increase based on the level of the soul he captured, which meant that he could gamble and try for a more powerful creature. Or perhaps even try to find another party down here...

Azrael wasn't much for that option. The fact that he already had it complete was a bit of a blessing, because if he failed to capture another soul in the two days, he would lose his Epic class. Failure would lead to the system forcing him into a randomized one. Plus, this quest would allow him access to the Abyssal skill, which had been a large reason for his choice of this class in the Cavern of Choices. Still, he had two more days and didn't need to take the first soul that he received.

He closed the screen and lamented the temporary loss of the Abyssal skill. Something stronger was bound to come up...

To take his mind off of the quest he checked his other class skills.

Tier 1 Skills
Ring of Fire
Creates a storm of fire around the Demon. The storm will move with the Demon, creating a devastating damage and a fiery shield against many attacks. Damage dealt is based on your wisdom and your opponent's wisdom. Costs fifty Ether to initialize and one Ether per second after.
Skill gained at 5/5, "Ring of Fire."
0/5

———

Ether Burn
Viciously burn Ether from your opponent's pool. Each point of Ether burnt will do half a point of damage to your opponent. Base cost of twenty Ether per cast, but can vary based on comparative Ether levels. Ether burnt is based on your and your opponent's Intelligence.
Skill gained at 5/5, "Ether Burn."
<5>/5

He had been going back and forth with which skill to choose since he had woken up as a Demon. He couldn't help but land on Ether Burn. Ring of Fire was a powerful skill that would likely make him a nightmare in one versus many fights. He couldn't help but remember the Fire Giant he had fought on Tech Duinn. Getting close to the creature had been like standing near a furnace.

Yet, it would only be usable in a solo environment. It had other downsides, like the fact that it would funnel him toward pure melee fighting, and he didn't like that. Ether Burn was something he hadn't even known existed. Not only did it have numerous uses, and varying ranges, but also would likely be something most opponents didn't expect.

In his mind, it was possibly more powerful in a one versus one fight and could be used strategically in dungeons as well. Ether Burn was definitely the best of both worlds.

Once he confirmed his choice, the fog of war rolled back to reveal his next tier of skills.

Tier 2 Skills
Demon Step
The Demon can phase into another person's close proximity. This skill can only be used up to fifty meters away, and can only phase into an area a meter around a living target. Using this ability, the Demon can possess that area instantaneously.
Skill gained at 5/5, "Demon Step."
0/5

————

Branded Mark
Brands an individual with the Demon's mark. This mark allows the Demon to know where the person is anywhere in the EtherVerse. This skill will only give a general direction of the target if the Demon is too far away. Brands cannot be removed easily. Each point in the skill increases the number of targets the Demon can brand.
Skill gained at 1/5, "Demon Brand."
0/5

He could theoretically take the Branding skill right away, but that didn't seem like a good choice. While it was insanely powerful in many ways, it was also only good if you had already seen the person and then lost them. Creating a large information network would likely provide the same information but also overcome the whole having to have met the person part. Demon Step was the obvious choice for Azrael, and he was excited to be able to test it out when he reached level ten.

In theory, that skill would act like a teleport, but had some limitations. Against any opponent, he could close the gap for attacking, but the problem, as he saw it, was in disengaging—unless he had an ally around—but he wouldn't be sure until he had the skill and tested it.

Regardless, Azrael looked around and saw the others all looking at him. "Sorry, I had a lot of points to distribute. First time not having to deal with stasis every five levels," Azrael said conversationally.

Everyone still saw his class as Revenant, except for Bat, who could see through his Obfuscation with ease. Had he told his companion to keep that secret? He was pretty sure he had.

Bat pointed out toward the back of the cavern. "There is a fake wall back there that leads to a hallway. The room at the end of the hall has foliage," Bat suggested.

Azrael nodded, while responding, "Let's give it a try."

As the group left, the corpse of the Goblin Chieftain sunk into the floor slowly and a strange voice spoke into Azrael's mind, <Thank you for the new meal.>

Bat twitched and turned to Azrael, staring, but the rest of the group seemed to not react. What in the halls was that? And how had Bat heard it?

Azrael shook his head minutely at Bat; they would talk later.

Why was that voice so familiar?

CHAPTER THIRTY-TWO

"Why did you react that way?" Azrael whispered as he gathered some herbs from the oasis, alongside Bat.

"Remember that connection you had after Tech Duinn? Well, it pulsed rather aggressively and got larger," Bat squeaked back, as quietly as he could. "It also seems to be leading to something nearby now, instead of a thin thread leading through the planet or up into the sky."

Azrael remembered the last time Bat had seen the thread flash, hadn't they been in the Labyrinth then too? Now this dungeon was creating monsters that he recognized from the Pit dungeon on Tech Duinn. The familiar mental voice, too.

Wait, was that Apep's voice?

"Which way is the strand leading, Bat?" Azrael asked, as neutrally as he could manage.

Bat pointed through one of the entrances to the safe zone. Then flapped his ears, open and then closed. "Wait, you aren't planning to go out alone, right?"

Azrael scratched his head. "Bat, I am going to need you to cover for me if someone notices I am gone after we fall asleep," he responded sheepishly.

Bat groaned.

———

Azrael exited the cavernous doorway that Bat had indicated. No other groups joined them in the safe zone that night, which made leaving somewhat easier. All he had to do was wait until Bat's turn on watch, and then sneak out.

And ignore Bat's quiet whines of protest, he added as he heard the Batman squeak sadly from near the small campfire.

Azrael needed to confirm his suspicion, and if he was right, the group's protection was not necessary. If this dungeon was being influenced by Apep, or what Azrael assumed Apep had become, then perhaps this new connection would be something he could use. When Apep had entered the massive vat of Essence, it had been as a ride along with Oberan. So maybe Azrael should rethink this...

He took one look back and then stepped through the door. His goal was revenge on all the guilds and people who had cannibalized the Sovereign Empire—he couldn't wimp out now, because his life was somewhat better.

As soon as his body went through the door, he was somewhere else in the dungeon. It was a very disorienting sensation, but the fact that this dungeon was now able to gate people around in its depths was another confirmation, of sorts. The portal brought him right to the room where the large, statuesque boss golem resided.

A boom shook the air as the armored Rhino collided with the crouched and ready dungeon boss. The stance of the giant reminded Azrael of a parent catching an unruly child. It was impossible not to stand in the doorway stunned by the scene of two large monsters fighting. It was nearly identical to the same experience Azrael remembered from the Pit dungeon.

Maybe that was why he jumped into action after a deep breath. Apep needed his help; didn't he? The harp was held in one of the statue's hands that was occupied in holding the

Rhino, so that at least kept the boss from using some of the skills Azrael saw last time.

Azrael charged in and used his new Ether Burn skill. He felt a burn on his own swirling pool of Ether. It wasn't a pleasant feeling, but it also wasn't uncomfortable. From his chest, a smoky black flame shot forward and struck the stone boss currently engaged with the Rhino. Azrael blinked as the creature twitched and roared at the vaulted ceiling. He checked his log and noticed that the boss had been burned for ten Health, meaning twenty Ether was burned, but the skill had cost Azrael more than that. He checked his Ether bar to see thirty points of his resource missing.

Damnit, this thing must have higher Intelligence than me. That, or it's because of its level.

He charged three stacks of his Soul Strike skill and continued rushing into the fray. He would do this the old-fashioned way. Ether Burn might be something better used against humanoid targets anyway. The only problem right now was the vast size difference between him and his gigantic opponent.

He could only reach up to its stone Achilles tendon if he stretched—maybe its knee if he leaped. It wasn't like the Rhino needed his protection though. He released the three Ether blades from about ten feet away in a vertical slash. The reciprocal saws started to screech as they collided with the back of the currently crouched statue.

Azrael didn't have much else that could damage this beast. He Analyzed it, scolding himself for not doing so sooner.

Hedamite the Serene
Master-Angelic Statue
Level 55
Health Points: 8,970 / 10,050
Skills: N/A

He didn't think that this creature was beatable. He could tell by the red color of the not applicable portion of the skills that he wasn't high enough in Analyze to see the boss's list of skills. He checked the Rhino just to be sure.

Armored Rhino
Journeyman-Battering Ram
Level 31
Health Points: 1,500 / 4,200
Skills: 13

"Apep, this isn't going to work. I can't take this thing down for you without more help," Azrael shouted into the room. A sound like a bell tolling reverberated through the room, and small holes opened around the perimeter of the sandstone walls. Like charging fluffy cavalry, herds of Bashers began bouncing into the room.

Azrael blinked at his new three-foot-tall allies. Even though there were more than twenty of the mobs, he still didn't think they had much of a chance. Regardless, he checked his own Ether bar, and charged another triple stacked Soul Strike before punching his blade forward with a thrust. This fight was going to be a zerg, it seemed, and they needed to destroy Hedamite before the Rhino fell and it got use of the harp again. More Bashers continued to pour from the holes all around them.

I need to start planning an escape. If this is all Apep has, I may die here.

That was when the Bashers plowed into the lower calves and ankles of the creature. Each strike sounded like a wooden bat striking stone, and was followed by a flash of light. The hard-headed bunnies each exploded like a fluffy water balloon on impact. Still, the blows opened up cracks on the statue.

"Apep, aim for a single leg." Azrael remembered how the Radiant Rock Eaters had defeated this boss and conveyed that to the presence he believed was Apep.

The bunnies switched targets and began popping and cracking a single leg. By the twentieth strike, the right knee of the creature was almost reduced to gravel and the boss overbalanced thanks to the combined weight of the armored Rhino.

Azrael's own strikes slid off the back of the angel as it fell sideways. His Soul Strike left large gouges across the stone where it made contact. Just as the butt of the angel hit the ground, it plucked a cord on its harp and its entire body glowed golden. A wave of light shot through the room. Azrael jumped in time to watch the wave pass under him but watched as every Basher exploded. The holes the bunnies entered from sprayed blood out, like grisly fountains, and Azrael was infinitely glad he had leaped into the air.

The boss's health had just passed the halfway mark. Wait, the Rhino was barely alive…

"Apep, I'm out of here!" Azrael shouted again, feeling his chest tighten at the scene around him.

<Help comes,> the semi familiar voice of Apep spoke into his mind.

What in the EtherVerse did that mean?

The sound of hooves on stone echoed down the hall behind Azrael and he turned to find two Minotaurs charging through the doorway. Right until their shoulders collided together, and then their exterior shoulders crashed into the arch of the door. Azrael face-palmed as he watched the two ten-foot-tall morons begin pushing each other.

Bashers began parading out of the small doorways again at least, which Azrael thought was a semi-good sign. He took a deep breath in through his nose and decided to go all out. At this point, with his *help* blocking the exit, he didn't have any other choice. He chugged a bottle of Ether Draught and charged four stacks of Soul Strike. Then he punched his sword forward in a thrust and shouted, "Release ten! Release ten!"

A powerful force exploded out of the tip of his sword; Azrael literally felt his feet slide backward on the stone floor. The air in front of the sharp tipped cone parted like Azrael split the very molecules of it. When the point touched the Angel, instead of a dull thud followed by a grinding of a drill, the first tip screeched before a second, third, fourth and so on collided right behind the first impact.

The wailing intensified as more strikes drilled and hammered into the statue's back. Each collision sounded like a jackhammer. The Rhino began to trample the downed foe and many of the Bashers struck again. The golden Retribution skill started to activate, popping the bunnies, but still Azrael's trump card skill continued to fissure the smooth stone angel.

At a quarter health, the boss plucked at its harp again and began to glow white, like a neon light bulb slowly increasing the lumens. A white glow surrounded the Minotaurs and the Rhino, and Azrael looked down at his body to find himself afflicted as well.

You have been hit with Hedamite's Curse.
Hedamite's Curse
After ten seconds, Hedamite will release Hedamite's Salvation. Anyone afflicted with both the curse and salvation will turn to stone.

Damn, that must have been the skill that the Dwarves group had silenced! Could Azrael drain enough of its Ether Pool with Ether Burn before it got the skill off? He highly doubted it. His skill continued to peel health points off of the creature, and he held his breath, hoping its health would run out before the skill completed.

The health of Hedamite continued plummeting and four seconds later, the Rhino collapsed, the golden retribution of the statue finally finishing its remaining health points. The boss only had five hundred health left, and Azrael groaned as the white glow began to hurt his eyes. He was going to end up a statue in the final boss chamber!

Two Minotaurs crashed into the fallen statue just as Azrael had to avert his gaze.

Congratulations! You have defeated the final boss Hedamite the Serene.

<Stop looking at your notifications,> Apep whispered into his mind. <Come loot this thing, then get out of the room so I can absorb it.>

Azrael closed his notifications, and the Demon class quest, now awarding one hundred thousand points for the soul of Hedamite. He moved to the boss' remains—really just a bunch of large broken stones, now. He looted the corpse and moved to open the golden chest, shoving everything inside directly into his ring. He hurried toward the doorway out of the room. "What happened to your voice, Apep?" Azrael asked as he left the room.

In response, a rather strong air current buffeted him from behind, seeming to hurry him along. "I'm going! Would you relax?" Azrael shouted at the entity. This wasn't like the Apep he had known on Tech Duinn, and Azrael started to wonder if he was mistaken. Bat had definitely confirmed the connection from Tech Duinn, but something was off. It was like a personality change, like the orb had become more demanding.

Then again, Apep did essentially become a God, and he skipped a lot of ranks in between. Could the same problem exist for him—her—it—as for all races? If history had proven anything, it was that there weren't shortcuts.

Azrael stood out in the hallway and went through the notifications he'd skipped as he chewed on his lip. What could he do if Apep was somehow in a similar situation to what Dagda had been in on Tech Duinn...?

No point dwelling on that right now. I'll know more once it talks to me.

Congratulations! You have completed a dungeon quest.
Dungeon Quest
Repeatable Quest
El Dorado Labyrinth.

Defeat Hedamite the Serene
Congratulations! You have defeated Hedamite the Serene, the final boss of the Labyrinth dungeon. This is your first time clearing the Labyrinth and your rewards are greater because of it.
Rewards:
1,000,000 Etherience
An Amulet of the Angel Hedamite

The fact that this quest was repeatable meant that his group might be able to one day farm the boss here for Etherience. Especially with Apep's help… if Apep wasn't insane.

Congratulations! You have reached 6, 7, and 8.
94,375 Etherience remaining until level 9.

He smiled. The fact that his early journeyman levels for Etherience were so low was fantastic. Essentially, the Etherience needed had reset back to the numbers needed in the Apprentice ranks multiplied by a thousand and plus ninety percent.

There always was a but, and this time it was because he was already nearing the millions needed to level, thanks in large part to his new class. That meant he would be hitting the grind even sooner as a Journeyman-ranked Demon. Then again, the stronger he was, the more powerful enemies or dungeons he could face… *Silver lining*, he told himself. Unfortunately, Journeyman grinds were completely different from Apprentice grinds, as the rank up option usually occurred near level fifty…

<1 now control this dungeon,> Apep mentally screamed into his mind, interrupting his thoughts.

Azrael jumped and turned back to the room just as he was pulling out the loot from the boss fight. He shoved it back into the ring and tried to hide his worried expression. "What do you mean, Apep?"

<We can now invade this planet and pillage its Essence!> quasi-Apep continued, coming across a bit psychotic to Azrael.

"Apep, the city outside already is planning to come down here and destroy you. This isn't like Tech Duinn; the people on this planet are all quite powerful," Azrael attempted to reason with the god-core.

<I can create an army of monsters down here, and with it destroy the world,> Apep said, and this time Azrael heard Oberan dominate the accent the core spoke with.

Oh no, has Apep become an amalgamation of consciousnesses?

What was the rest of the accent then? It sounded somewhat like Ogma, but also different, maybe more subdued and tired.

Azrael shook himself out of his inner thoughts. He could feel that this new Apep was serious about invading the city outside, but if it did, it would be destroyed. Something about that made Azrael anxious. He knew he didn't care about Apep control over this core being destroyed, so what was it?

Apep has the power to take over dungeons and build armies.

The realization hit him like an asteroid clanging off a particularly dense freighter. He could use the dungeon to assist in his revenge. Would an unstable god-core-thing be a good ally for his upcoming mission of revenge?

"Apep, listen. I know you can create powerful monsters, but I am telling you, the people on this planet would be able to snap Musth in half with a finger," Azrael tried to reason with the core.

<Not a problem. If this core dies, you can just take over another one and I can start again. This shall be a war of attrition,> Oberan's voice said fanatically.

"Wait, slow down. I took over this core for you?" Azrael dubiously asked. How had he done that?

<Well, yes and no,> the tired sounding Ogma-like voice started. <In truth, you gave us a foothold inside the dungeon. Since then, we have been able to spawn our creatures and expand our grip.>

<Crush the core into submission with our superior creatures,> Oberan's voice spat, and Azrael shivered.

He was starting to see what the problem with Apep was. If

the semi-functioning warmonger Oberan was a portion of his new personality, and Apep was another, who was the third? Azrael had watched Ogma escape the planet. But Tech Duinn was, in essence, his twin brother Dadga!

Of the three voices, Dagda seemed the most logical and sane. Apep had always been a bit over-excitable, Oberan was as likely to kill Azrael as listen, and so he tried to talk directly to that portion of the god. "Dagda, if you are in there, I need you to listen. If you continually take over dungeons and then attempt to invade the planet, either I will be discovered, dungeons will be protected, or totally annihilated. This needs to be kept secret, and used at the right time."

Dagda's voice did respond but with overtones of Apep. <We do see your point, and will discuss it with the other.>

"How big of an army of monsters could you field from this dungeon?" Azrael questioned, trying to get an idea of the strength the god-core could offer.

<Of monsters only?> Apep asked, confused.

<He doesn't know—> Dagda began.

<Destroy everything!> Oberan shouted, overriding the other two.

Azrael couldn't help but cover both of his ears. Having the three talk over each other into his head was making him feel insane. He couldn't imagine what the god-core was going through on a day-to-day basis. "One at a time!" he screamed, and luckily all three mental voices quieted.

<As I was saying,> Dagda began with his dry logic. <Azrael needs to be made aware that we can also bring people we absorbed back to life. Furthermore, we can take more than a single dungeon and create armies in all of them.>

The small headache the three caused vanished as a surge of adrenaline spiked through his blood. He could help the dungeon core capture multiple dungeons. If this was played correctly, they could kick off a simultaneous invasion from hundreds of captured dungeons. He even had an invitation to run the most powerful dungeon on Gaia. The Rainbow dungeon. A large predatory smile spread onto his face. This was the exact tool he needed to take his revenge on the guilds and people of Gaia.

"What do I need to do to capture a dungeon for you?"

<To gain a foothold, you must defeat a boss level creature. To capture the entire dungeon, you must conquer the final boss, or find the room where the core resides,> Dagda responded reasonably.

<Capture everything. Destroy everything!> Oberan shouted.

<Sorry,> Apep added.

Azrael blinked and was thinking about letting the conversation end there as his headache tried to re-emerge. Wait. "You said you can bring back people. Does that include Chef Louis from the Pit?" Azrael asked excitedly.

CHAPTER THIRTY-THREE

A ding sounded, and Louis actually walked out of a door that opened in the wall. Louis looked around stunned for quite some time before finally coming over to Azrael.

"I have no idea where we are, or how I got here," Louis the Gnome chef stated simply, his pale skin and twitching features highlighting his agitation. "Also, how come I am a level one without a class?"

Azrael scratched his head and looked at the pedestal in the middle of the room. "Apep?" he prompted.

"Sapient creatures need to start at level one, and level up. We can power level them inside the dungeons with monsters," the mixed voices of the three intoned into the room.

That wouldn't work for a non-power class like Louis. Correction, it would work, but the monsters would likely have to fall over dead on their own. Louis didn't specialize in combat, from what Azrael remembered.

Non-power classes could level through their professions though. "We will have plenty of work for Louis back at the Atlantean Academy," Azrael countered. Directing the next bit to the Gnome chef, he added, "Here are five crystals, please go up into the city of El Dorado…"

Azrael directed the chef to book a room at their hotel—he couldn't walk back to his group with a new member at level one. There would be too much explaining. Not to mention both Jophiel and Bat knew Louis. He would tell Bat the whole story, but would Jophi believe it if he said Louis escaped Tech Duinn?

Not with his current level, she wouldn't.

I will have to think of something. Maybe a class reset for something rarer?

Once Louis walked out of the exit, Azrael turned back to the podium. "Okay, I need a promise from you. First, make this dungeon the same difficulty as it used to be—maybe slightly harder. Allow divers to complete it and life to get back to normal. At the same time, begin building an army. Every second week, I will try to run a new dungeon and get you a foothold there. Does that work?"

<Conquer the world!> Oberan shrieked into Azrael's mind, like a milk drunk toddler.

<Sorry about him,> Dagda's voice countered. <I will have Apep try to manage him more. We can do that. Is there anything else?>

The reminder of Oberan brought his two guards to mind, Tyr and Yonel, but the reminder of guards instantly morphed to an all-consuming rage. Azrael shook as his teeth ground together and his body temperature increased several degrees— or at least it felt that way. "Resurrect Papi and Torin."

A ding sounded and the two guards in question walked out of the room, looking very out of sorts. Azrael wished for just a moment he hadn't completed the Demon quest with the monster soul, and had saved it for these two.

A wicked smile bloomed onto Azrael's face.

"Hello, again," Azrael whispered into the silence of the room.

———

Congratulations! You have completed a class quest.
Demon of Gaia
Red Quest
Class Confirmation Quest
Collect a Soul
You have collected the soul of Torin Tarzac. Would you
like to use this Soul to complete the quest?
<Yes> | No
Time limit remaining: 2 days
Rewards:
<100,000> Etherience.
Journeyman Demon Class Confirmation
Abyssal Skill

Azrael selected yes, taking a certain satisfaction from using Torin's soul for the quest. To his surprise, though, the next time Apep resummoned Papi, Torin was not with him. He felt slight disappointment that he wouldn't get to torture Torin more in the future, but took solace in that his soul truly seemed to have been consumed. Plus he still had Papi...

Would you like to consume the soul of Papi Vears?
<Yes> | No
Rewards:
Increased levels to Soul Blade.

This time, he didn't let his new class claim Papi's soul right away.

An hour later, Azrael felt surprisingly good. Revenge was rather therapeutic, and taking it over and over again was particularly soothing. <Are you done slaughtering things for now?> Apep's voice asked confusedly. <Did that help you level?>

Azrael just smiled sardonically and said, "They were very helpful, thank you. Can you transport me back to the room I was in with my group now please?"

<Yes. Exit through the same door you entered. It is now linked to that safe zone,> Dagda's voice stated.

"Perfect, I will contact you again when I conquer the next dungeon," Azrael said and walked through the entrance.

Raven Tide – Soul Blade
Level 5
150 / 170 Ether Pool
The Strength of Arms V
+10 Strength as long as the Blade has Ether from its pool to draw on. Unlock higher levels of your Soul Blade for more.
The Strength of Body V
+5 Stamina as long as the Blade has Ether from its pool to draw on. Unlock higher levels of your Soul Blade for more.

———

"Where did you go?" Bat hiss-whispered at him as soon as he walked back to the group's camp. Azrael debated lying to the Batman but thought better of it. He didn't think that Bat would betray him—or maybe it was more of a hope. Something from the Sovereign Halls roiled in warning at Azrael. Every lesson in the Sovereign Halls was about not trusting anyone but the other sons, and really not even them. However, that was propaganda, right?

He raised his finger to his lips in the universal language that meant quiet and whispered back, "I will tell you later. Right now, let me get some sleep. I think it's still your turn to keep watch," Azrael finished with a certain level of satisfaction when Bat's mouth drooped.

After that, Azrael slept, but dreamt of conquering Gaia with Apep's aid. It felt like this was the exact tool he had unknowingly needed to complete his revenge.

———

The next morning, when Azrael found the right time, with no one else around, he told Bat. Maybe not everything, but the vast majority of it. Bat had also been imprisoned by the guilds on Tech Duinn and the Batman, while slightly paler than usual, clenched his jaw and nodded, going as far as to promise not to tell anyone about Azrael's strange connection with Apep.

The rest of the day was spent dungeon diving with the group.

"Oslow, can you phase through that entire beast or just short burst attacks?" Azrael asked as they stared down the armored Rhino.

"As long as it doesn't stop right on top of me," Oslow responded and motioned at the creature. "I don't think that beast is stopping. Can you all deal damage through its armor?"

Azrael couldn't help but look back at Bat and smile. Now that they knew it was the same Rhino they faced in the Pit, Azrael was sure he could solo the beast, if given some time. Jophiel caught the look the two of them shared and frowned, seeming to realize she was left out of something. The look she gave made Azrael's stomach knot and he swallowed bile—he assumed it was because of the risk she might report this to Cathodiem.

She couldn't have figured it out, though. But his own reassurance didn't seem to unknot his distressed organ or remove the sick feeling he had. Yet, for some reason he wanted to tell her—and comfort her?

He shook his head, dispelling the thoughts that currently warred in his head. He really should have gotten a full night's sleep yesterday. Still, he glanced at the armored Rhino that just conveniently appeared in front of his group, guarding an S-ranked chest. The benefits of a bit of missed sleep couldn't be overlooked. Apep was lobbing them easy wins and loot.

"Alright, Oslow, let's get it," Azrael commanded, and the

group surged forward. As soon as they were in range of the beast, he analyzed it.

Armored Rhino
Journeyman-Battering Ram
Level 31
Health Points: 4,200 / 4,200
Skills: 13

Azrael amended his thought about soloing the beast. This wasn't the Apprentice rank version he had faced on Tech Duinn. This was the same creature that tanked the boss the previous night, and his group might be in for a bit of a challenge.

Azrael charged his Soul Strike skill and simultaneously readied an Ether Burn. A creature like this shouldn't have a large pool, so it was possible that after its first charge, a few well-timed burns would lock its skills out.

As Oslow reached aggro range, the group fanned out behind the tank in two groups of two. This would hopefully allow the charging beast to phase through their tank, and only veer toward one of the two groups. Or that was the strategy, anyway.

The Rhino exploded forward, shaking the cavern and raining stone dust down on them with each step. Oslow stopped and let the speed of the charge build—which wasn't the typical strategy here, but with Oslow's phase skill, it was very important that the beast moved through him fast.

As soon as the Rhino reached the midway point between Oslow and itself, it glowed yellow and accelerated further. It passed through Oslow and then careened on, its skill not having satisfied its target lock. The acceleration didn't stop and the powerful beast collided with the domed wall with an explosive crash. A crack instantly creaked its way up the wall in a snaking pattern. Stones the size of emerald marks began to pelt Azrael's

Ether Tech armor. The others didn't fare as well, and he even saw Prateek fall to the ground.

Shoot.

"Bat, check on Prateek," Azrael commanded from his side with Jophi. His head flew around to her position to find a small barrier above her deflecting the stones away. He breathed a sigh of relief before he targeted the Rhino with Ether Burn. They couldn't let it charge again, not without risking the entire room collapsing atop them.

Azrael blasted the beast as it struggled to free its horn from its entrenched sheath in the stone. When the Ether Burn struck, the Rhino began to shriek and it redoubled its effort—causing the crack to elongate and widen. When Azrael saw a red glow begin to surround the Rhino, he dumped two more Ether Burns into it in quick succession. While there would still be a small risk of its natural strength causing a collapse, Azrael felt that a skill would definitely increase the likelihood.

The red glow blinked out and he heard Jophi breathe out beside him. The Rhino tore its horn out using its rather impressive strength after another heartbeat. It didn't back up so much as drag the horn through the solid rock—like the rock was paper. Its red eyes fixed on him instead of Oslow and Azrael had a painful heartbeat to realize that he had aggro.

He didn't hesitate and rushed toward the group's tank; a heavy stomping footstep told Azrael it had become a rather terrifying foot race. "Oslow, to me," Azrael commanded and the tank, who had been ordered to stay away from both groups rushed back to meet him halfway. The thudding tempo in the room increased and stone peppered everyone's raised arms or mana shields.

This fight wasn't going to plan, and they needed to get control of it. Azrael found his Ether pool at forty percent, and he chugged an Ether Draught before activating Soul Cloak; he would need it for the next part of the plan. Oslow wouldn't gain aggro from avoiding a single strike, so Azrael was going to have to stand in there and act as the offtank while Oslow worked to regain its attention.

Azrael slid to a stop and positioned himself behind Oslow who continued running forward. Since Azrael was the current target, he slowly backed away, trying to make sure that the tank didn't get stuck phased inside the Rhino—he didn't think that would end well for Oslow.

Once he deemed the distance enough, he entered into Hermes' Dare. This stance wasn't offensive at all. In fact, the sword position, held above his head in a horizontal grip, was meant to deflect blows that Azrael couldn't dodge. Deflecting the several ton Rhino wasn't going to happen, so Azrael tried to focus on the main function of this form—dodging. His feet were spaced just past shoulder width and each foot was turned out, in almost a duck foot pattern. In this way, he could use his calf muscles in a variety of ways to spring off in a near three-hundred-and-sixty-degree range. The near was because moving forward in this stance was impossible. That was how it wasn't offensive in the least.

The sword masters claimed this stance became famous when a lesser swordsman used it to fight a master to exhaustion. Never was it used in a clean victory, however.

But this isn't a duel.

Oslow vanished *into* the Rhino and Azrael flexed his legs, waiting to see if his opponent lowered the horn to either side or straight down. The Rhino prepared to gore Azrael in his Ether Tech armor by dropping its head and tilting it to Azrael's right. He responded by leaping with all the strength his body and mechanical suit could muster—also to his right. He just needed to exit the parabolic arc of the horn and he would be entirely out of harm's way.

The Rhino's neck bulged as its head cut a diagonal path, leading the horn in the slashing pattern. Azrael was watching closely and realized it would strike his thigh and reacted instinctively by firing his core muscles in a crunch that brought the blade down. Again, this wasn't an attack, and as soon as the blade struck the horn, he isometrically flexed his arms and used his hip flexors and glutes to move his lower body away from the opponent's strike.

Unfortunately, the power of the Rhino transferred to the sword and flung Azrael away in a direction he couldn't calculate. The momentum coupled with the strength of the beast spun Azrael and he lost track of what direction he faced, before he crashed noisily into something solid. He wasn't even sure if it was the wall or floor, but when he rolled along the surface while continuing to bounce along it, he knew gravity was acting with him. Which told him he was bouncing along the floor. The armor took the brunt of the damage and red lights flashed onto his HUD.

His breath caught when he realized his armor was below fifty percent durability. It still was working though, and he stood up to find the Rhino sliding to a stop and turning his direction again. His group opened up, realizing that allowing Oslow to get the Rhino's attention wouldn't work in time.

"Aggro bounce!" Azrael shouted as Bat's sound wave attack staggered the Rhino. There was one further problem, and that was the Rhino's huge health pool. Forty-two hundred had only dropped to four thousand and the eyes of the monster were still tracking on Azrael. What he had just called for was everyone's Voskresenie attack—their ultimate skills—everything they had. Essentially, this was a clear out and dump in the entire Ether pool, one by one.

"I'll start," Bat screamed over the din of the room and held both hands up above his head. Azrael, despite his own danger, was intrigued because he hadn't seen Bat use his best attack yet. A half-sphere distorted the air around the Rhino and turned a small stagger from the beast into a complete wipe out. Oslow, who had been trying to get close to the creature, had turned and run away. The sphere was maybe ten meters in front of Azrael and moved with the sliding Rhino.

The air began to become opaque and Azrael lost sight of the distorted vision he had of the enemy. The air turned completely black, trembling in the space where Bat's attack hung. It almost looked like a speaker as it rippled continuously. Bat fell to a knee a slow count of ten seconds later, and the black bubble broke apart, seeming to dissipate in small patches as the small air currents in the room pulled it apart.

As soon as the enemy was visible, Azrael checked its health; twenty-one hundred. That one attack nearly halved the creature's pool.

"I've got next," Jophi shouted and added, "Might want to back up more, Azrael."

The Rhino was getting to its feet and just began to turn toward Bat when Jophi began, raising a hand into the air from beside her waist. Azrael could only see her out of the corner of his eye as he took her warning seriously and began to flee. He saw a circle of stone with a diameter of five meters as it began rising in time with her motion. Her other hand began to light up as a fire started to form. The flame didn't form her traditional ball and instead began to spin, forming a whirling cylinder of growing orange. Just as the intensity of the fire became like a sun, Jophi threw it forward and it entered the cylindrical-hollow stalagmite just before it connected to the roof. "Fire turbine!" Jophi shrieked with pain in her voice and liberal amounts of sweat on her face.

A whistling sound began to intensify, and Azrael searched for the source, finally finding small holes at the bottom of the rock formation. Black smoke pumped out of the top of the pillar from similar holes as the rock itself began to glow brighter in unison as the whistling volume increased. This attack was immense, and Azrael could feel the heat coming off the stone from over twenty-five meters away.

Azrael was convinced that the enemy was down, but a crash and the end of the whistling sound gave him a moment's warning as a flaming Rhino began charging toward Jophi. Luckily, Azrael had charged all of his Ether into an attack as well. The armor of the Rhino was now molten metal as it charged out of the stalagmite, and Azrael thrust forward, aiming along its path.

"Release ten! Release ten!" he whispered in unison with the attack's culmination, adding the twenty in Soul Storage to the four stacks he already had on his sword. The boss's health was at six hundred and he wasn't willing to take any chances. The jackhammer-like drill front of his skill punched into its side.

The armored Rhino weathered the first few waves of the skill but then began sliding sideways on the slick stone. The instant the beast died and its internal Ether stopped resisting, Azrael's attack punched through, leaving a gaping hole in the corpse as the attack careened out into the hallway. Jophi's attack finished as well, falling into a pile of super-heated rocks, and the group slowly walked to meet at the corpse of the beast.

"Going to have to take an hour break here," Prateek said as he assessed the group.

A quick glance told Azrael Bat couldn't even lift his head, and Azrael felt the same way. Jophi looked the worst of the group, with sunken cheeks and pale skin.

"Might need to make it two hours," Azrael suggested, and it surprised him when the group laughed in response.

He was being serious…

CHAPTER THIRTY-FOUR

Saturnday and the group's chosen end of the training week came far too quickly. The group stayed within the Labyrinth the entire time, moving between safe zones. Azrael tried to recall the exact number of encounters, traps, and chests they had, but it was useless. He truly believed that Apep was giving them a great deal of help. In fact, they were leaving a few days early because all of their storage devices and bags were stuffed full of loot.

Everyone had also gained a few levels. Bat was a single level away from making it to the Journeyman ranks, and Azrael knew from personal experience the Batman would need hundreds of millions of Etherience to accomplish that. Still, the group gained in the range of fifteen million from a week's worth of dungeon diving. If they continued like this, Bat would be ranking up relatively soon.

Azrael reached level twelve, which gave him access to view his third-tier skills, and after he placed five skill points, awarded him the Demon Step ability.

Congratulations! You have reached level 7, 8, 9, 10, 11 and 12.
4,113,243 Etherience remaining until level 13.

Azrael Finch (Sovereign) Level 12
Class: Journeyman-Soul Revenant (Demon)
Class Skills: Soul Strike (V), Soul Cloak (V), Soul
Storage (V), Bloodletter (V), Call of the Soul (V), Soul
Blade (I), Ether Burn (V), Demon Step (V)
Health Points = 410/410 Points
Ether Pool = 290/290 Points
You have 18 stat points and 2 skill points to distribute.
Stamina – 41
Strength – 45
Agility – 42
Dexterity – 42
Intelligence – 31
Wisdom – 30
Charisma – 18
Luck – 12
Skills:
Analyze – Strong 11
Butcher – Moderate 21
Combatant – Strong 35
Enchanting – Weak 5
Endurance – Strong 21
Ether Channels – Moderate 12
Ether Manipulation – Moderate 14
Essence Conversion – Weak 3
Martial Arts – Strong 46
Mediation – Moderate 18
Obfuscate – Strong 15
Sneak – Moderate 4
Stone Cutting – Moderate 11

Swordsmanship – Greater 45
Tracking – Weak 12

The unassigned stat points were finally ready to be used. Azrael planned to return to the safety of a hotel and then hit his breakthrough in both Agility and Dexterity. Breakthroughs weren't pleasant experiences to begin with, but laying on the ground writhing in a dungeon would bring unneeded danger to the members of his group.

The previous night they had camped back in the first safe zone and this morning made the quick trip back to their original entrance. They had uncovered a great deal of other exits within the Labyrinth but being aware of the layout, and knowing the nearest safe zone, had kept them from taking them.

It would seem that if exits weren't used within twenty-four hours, they would close, or move to wherever the boss the group defeated to open them respawned. Regardless, when they made it back outside, with bags heaped full of loot, there wasn't a single person in line to enter the Labyrinth. Considering it was early morning, and Azrael's previous experience, this was strange.

One of the guards jumped when they walked out of the tunnel. "What are you all doing in there? Don't you know the council has forbidden entrance to the Labyrinth until further notice?" the guard shouted as he ran toward them.

That explained why they hadn't seen another group in the depths. Still, this development wasn't ideal. Azrael looked to his group, all of whom stopped at the guard's shouts. He was trying to determine a way to relieve some of the tension that surrounded Apep's dungeon. It would be very unfortunate to his future plans if the city went in and destroyed the place.

When the guard reached them, Azrael pointed to his team members' bags and then scratched his head sheepishly. "No wonder there was so much loot and monsters to fight," Azrael began, looking back at the guard captain; the rank insignia was on his chest and distinguishable now that the captain was closer. "What day did you stop teams from entering?"

"Monentag evening. Many adventurers and guilds came out during the day claiming that dungeon monsters were fighting each other in the depths, the night before. The council is ruling how to handle the situation now," the captain responded suspiciously.

"Ahh, that explains the confusion. We were all in the dungeon two days earlier, Saturnday," Prateek began and looked like he wanted to continue, but the captain cut in.

"Wait, you were in there during the monster fights, and you didn't leave?" the captain exclaimed, seeming shocked.

"Well, we would have if we had seen it, but I can guarantee they aren't fighting each other anymore," Jophi claimed, raising an eyebrow. "Can we go on our way and sell our loot?"

The captain flushed and lost some of his earlier sternness. "Well, umm, actually, the council would probably like a report since you were in there the entire week. Plus, it would really help my command if you emphasized the fact that you were in there since Saturnday."

"Prateek, Oslow, please go and report to the council. Jophi, Bat, and I will sell the loot and get rooms at the hotel. Meet back there after you're done," Azrael commanded, trying to avoid the tedium of a council meeting.

According to Verimy and Dara, the real problem with city officials was that they were often far removed from the populace. They never started that way of course, often raising their station from amongst the same people they served, but over time they would lose that part in the politics of their position.

"I truly hate bargaining for the best price, but you guys wouldn't screw us out of our share of the loot, right?" Prateek said, his voice somewhat suspicious and somewhat joking.

Oslow looked back and forth between Prateek and Azrael, his eyebrows rising.

In response, Azrael laughed. "Trust me, you will get your shares. If you want, we can change the groups."

Prateeek looked at Oslow and shook his head. "Nah, I'd prefer to do the reporting, I think. Plus, Oslow is more fun to hang out with than you." When Prateek finished, he chortled and stuck his tongue out. Was the insult meant to be funny? Of course Oslow was more fun to hang out with, those two seemed to be close friends, while Azrael was the party leader... He added a few chuckles just in case, not wanting to insult the healer.

Prateek and Oslow handed over their knapsacks and emptied their storage devices onto a nearby cart. They truly looked happy to be given the task of reporting as they were led away by a runner.

That did make a kind of sense; it wasn't like Azrael, Bat, and Jophi had an enjoyable morning ahead of them either. The only upside to selling loot was the thrill of discovery that sometimes came with it. Considering that the group was carrying large amounts of locked gear, elixirs, ore, gems, and items, probably meant they had at least something exciting on their horizon. Azrael unloaded his ring and bag onto the cart as well, before flipping a gem mark to the captain. The customary fee to use one of the loot carts.

They each took turns pulling the rickshaw cart, making their way to the merchant district. With this amount of loot, it would be best to enter a large merchant's shop and sell in bulk. That, or going to one of the seed shops to sell to a variety of buyers through the assistant stationed there. Both options would identify the gear first, and both options had merit. The seed shops gave anonymity and only allowed the party to see the quality of the wares. However, a merchant's headquarters would offer comfort, a meal, and possible trade value if desired.

Considering the week the group spent camping in the dungeon, Azrael chose the merchant's shop. They could use some breakfast, and he wasn't terribly concerned about the gear they had looted making them targets of nefarious people. It wasn't like merchants didn't maintain a level of secrecy; it was just that the greed of the merchant sometimes trumped it.

Or so the teachers at the Halls taught. They would probably roll over in their graves to see me choosing to use a merchant.

Since Sovereign Sons were rarely on a foreign planet, unless for discreet missions, the teachers made it clear to always sell to seed shops. Azrael had no mission, and discretion was the last of his worries. He currently was the prospective apprentice of the most powerful teacher at the strongest academy in the EtherVerse. He was past the point of hiding; it was time to start playing the part of a powerful individual who could cause problems for others if they made issues. Only through some arrogance and false nobility would he warn people like Magnus off in the future.

Azrael the *braggadocios* was needed.

The merchant district in El Dorado was interesting. Instead of the buildings being carved into the sandstone like many of the structures Azrael had seen to date, this area was a combination. Large wooden frontage extended into the offshoot path they had been directed to. Each building was two stories and painted in different colors. Clearly displayed wealth was the goal of each merchant, and Azrael assessed each, trying to find out which would serve his group's purposes.

One nearer to the center of the sandstone path stood out the most with elegant pearl siding and gold inlay swirling in patterns that spoke of dragons, leviathans, and unicorns. It had even gone so far as to pull up the natural sandstone and bring in multiple different kinds of paving stones to create a beautiful patio that extended halfway into the path.

Azrael motioned toward it and the group walked to the front gates. Azrael addressed the guard behind the shining silver bars. "Tell the owner that Azrael, Merlin's prospective apprentice, Jophiel, daughter of Raguel of Cathodiem, and Bat, the Batman envoy have arrived and wish to deal."

The house guard saluted and took off into the house. Within a few minutes, attendants came out and escorted the group through the beautiful gates and deeper into the grounds. They even had a burly man with them who pulled the rickshaw cart in his group's stead. Jophi eyed this new Azrael suspiciously, and all he could do was shrug in response. She wasn't one who could talk, since she was essentially a spy.

The attendants led them to a garden courtyard, with beautiful brickwork, cushioned chairs, and a gorgeously woven red blanket. If Azrael was correct, this was the home of an Elven merchant, and this was a Choo Sentani. Of course, the custom of selling on a blanket wasn't started by the Elves, but the Elven merchants had been the first to enchant blankets to protect the customer.

This had, in many ways, given their merchants the edge in the profession, and now the majority of merchants seemed to be Elven.

Once the group sat, the attendants began sorting the gear within the cart into piles. Gems, marks, chips, and crystals in one pile; elixirs, potions and consumables in another; locked gear, weapons, and armor; and finally, a pile of random things —like a candlestick that seemed to light when you pushed a button but otherwise seemed useless.

Only after the sorting did the merchant himself come out, making a grand spectacle of his entrance.

Azrael Analyzed him but was shocked when, just like with the Atlantean teachers, his skill failed.

"Good morning, fair students, Batman, my name is Aldesair Corbranthe," the merchant introduced himself. "It is a pleasure to make your acquaintance. Are you looking for any discretion today, or will my attendants identifying your loot be sufficient?"

Smiling, Azrael considered. The introduction at the gate would not have given Aldesair the information he just revealed. It would have told him about Azrael's student status but not Jophi's, and certainly he could have assumed they were all students, but to single out Bat without the distinction meant that he had gathered information in a rather hasty manner. It was also of note that Aldesair was human and not Elven as Azrael originally thought.

The distinction was quite clear, considering that the man

had dark brown skin, brown eyes and wore a traditional toga, which was not common amongst the Elves. Azrael needed to appear confident in these dealings. "Your attendants should be sufficient, but please have them identify the gear in front of us."

"As you wish, my lord," Aldesair said with a bow and his attendants began bringing pieces of gear over one by one. Some of it was gear that the group could use, and Azrael tried to sort out those pieces as they were identified. Still, much of their haul would be better for traditional tanks or was subpar when compared to the gear he knew his party already possessed. After the piles were fully sorted, he was left with gear from some of the S-rated chests set aside for his group and a pile of very high-ranked Ether Draughts and Health Elixirs. In fact, they were likely too high, and it would be best to trade them down for lower-ranked versions.

Armored Rhino Shoulders

• These shoulders have been created from fused metal and Rhino hide. They are extremely hard to penetrate while also being more supple and easier to maneuver.

Enchantments: Movement V (Dex & Agi +5), Protection V (50%)

———

Pants of Hedamite

• Hedamite was a great healer and was immortalized in a statue thanks to her selfless dedication to others. Unfortunately, that statue fell into the Labyrinth as it formed.

Enchantments: Ancient Wisdom V (Int & Wis +5), Healer IV (+20% Healing Effectiveness), Protection I (10%)

———

Robe of Darkness
- A Labyrinth should be filled with darkness, but since champions need light, all of the darkness has been pushed into high-quality items.

Enchantments: Intellect V (Int +10), Avoidance V (50% chance to cause an attack to miss)

———

Mage Focus Bracelet
- This bracelet has been formed around a Dragon Eye Ruby, which will increase all effectiveness of spells that are cast through it.

Enchantments: Dragon Mage II (+15% Spell Damage)

There were a few other pieces of gear that the group placed off to the side of the selling pile. Mostly to fully gear out Bat as best as possible. The Batman didn't have a great deal of high-quality gear and practically everything that had intellect or wisdom was an upgrade. Actually, pretty much everything identified was an upgrade for Bat. Azrael, on the other hand, needed a repair to the Ether Tech suit more than any pieces of gear in front of him and, because of that, they hadn't found him anything new.

The gems, skins, reagents, and butchered meats were also placed in various carts based on their quality and value.

"This is quite the haul. How long did you stay down in the Labyrinth?" Aldesair asked as he supervised his attendants moving a cart onto a large stone that was clearly a scale. He himself took notes in a journal as he tallied up all the items the group had 'lucked' upon.

"Just the week," Azrael said with a confident tone. "It seems that everyone running out of the dungeon left all the loot to us! Or perhaps we are just that good." He finished with a bit of a chuckle that hopefully conveyed that he didn't really think the final bit was a joke. It was a tricky thing to get right, but Aldesair didn't glance away from the notepad, so he probably got it right.

"Well, congratulations are in order. This haul may net you upward of one-hundred crystals," Aldesair said casually, and Azrael avoided shaking his head. That was clearly a probe.

"If that's all you're offering, I think we might need to take our goods elsewhere," Azrael scoffed.

"It was just a rough estimate, my lord," Aldesair hurriedly corrected as he ducked his head and continued writing in his notebook.

The final pile that was currently in the keep section was the Ether Draughts and Health Potions.

Health Potion (Concentrated) x11

(H)Restoration

• This potion will restore 1,000 Health Points over 13 seconds, but will not stack with any other (H)Restoration Potion.

————

Ether Draught (Concentrated) x12

(E)Restoration

• This potion will restore 500 Ether to your personal pool over 25 seconds, but will not stack with any other (E)Restoration Potion.

They were just too strong to use for everyone in their group, but it might be worth it to hang onto them for later. They had found some others in lower rank chests and Azrael had already stored them in his storage ring. The non-concentrated versions gave half the amount of health and Ether, and the diluted versions gave even less. Still, these were worth quite a bit of crystals or in trade. Instead of making the decision now, he pulled them into his ring and held onto them.

After some lengthy negotiations, the group left the merchant's house with three hundred crystals profit after they deducted the escape rope price and returned it to Azrael's purse. That meant Oslow, Jophi, and Prateek would get seventy-five crystals each and Azrael would split his seventy-five with Bat. For a week of work in a dungeon, that was almost unheard of, and he was sure the others would be extremely happy for the news.

———

The hotel Azrael chose to stay at this time just happened to be the same hotel where a certain level-one chef was staying. Azrael wasn't surprised that they arrived before Prateek and Oslow; council matters were never handled quickly. They walked into the carved sandstone lobby with its red leather sitting area and restaurant in the back to find a bit of a scene.

"I have money. It's just up in my room," Louis practically shouted at what appeared to be a well-dressed manager. The manager was some sort of mixed race and the green skin made it either half-Orc or half-Goblin, whereas the larger horns on the head likely spoke of Satyr in its heritage.

"As if we would believe that a level one NPC is staying upstairs and has additional money. Please leave this establishment immediately," the Satorc said with a tone of derision so strong that Azrael was almost impressed.

"Isn't that Louis from Tech Duinn?" Jophi whispered as she scrutinized the scene. Shoot, he had been hoping to have this be a much more subtle re-introduction.

"How did he become a level one?" Azrael asked, prompting a sticky subject first before people could bring it up themselves. Bat flapped his ears open and closed, and Azrael knew from his slightly down turned lips that he would need an explanation later. Jophi, on the other hand, tilted her head at Louis.

"That is strange. I think he is the same class as he was back on Tech Duinn. Why don't we go ask him?" Jophi responded, and didn't wait for the others as she strode forward. "Louis, is that you?"

"I have been staying here at the hotel for the last five—"

Louis had begun but at his name being called turned to see who it was. "Aren't you that girl who was with—" He cut off a second time when his eyes scanned across Bat and Azrael, behind Jophi.

"It is you guys... how did you make it out of that death trap?!" he asked, barely fumbling the transition. It wasn't the best acting Azrael had ever seen, but it was better than most. "I had to reset my class just to use a rare ability to phase through a wall and get to a spaceship!"

Azrael felt his lip twitch in a half smile. Good, that was a great explanation for that anomaly. While divine intervention skills were rare, they often had exorbitant downsides associated with them.

"Excuse me, could you all please take your conversation outside?!" the Satorc said with affronted aplomb. Azrael felt his smile vanish and gave the man a withering stare before fishing out a crystal and lazily flicking it over to him.

"We'll take a table and a meal each. We also will want rooms made up for five students of the academy." Azrael began walking toward a large round table that sat eight. "We have another two who will be joining us after they finish briefing the council."

Once the four of them were all in their seats around the polished oaken table, Azrael turned back toward Louis.

"Being level one again must be quite frustrating if you've been dealing with idiots like that. I've never heard such a steep price for a divine intervention skill," Azrael mused, adding his voice to the tale Louis was telling. "As for your first question, about how we managed to get out; we were in the middle of an escape when everything started to go sideways. We *borrowed* a pirate landing ship and escaped offworld."

"Azrael, aren't we in need of a chef?" Bat said with only a tiny hint of skepticism in his voice. The Batman paired the question with leaning forward and resting his chin on folded hands.

Azrael pretended to consider that statement before nodding.

"I don't think we are going to find Oliver anytime soon. Louis, are you looking for work?"

"Wait, that's it?" Jophi began and looked pointedly at both Bat and Azrael. "You both look like a couple of thieves after a successful heist. What aren't you saying?"

Louis went pale, and Bat looked at the table. So much for their acting. "It's nothing, Jophi," Azrael began. "I think Louis isn't telling us his whole story because he was probably forced to stow away on a freighter to come here. Or something equally as criminal. It isn't like a level one would be treated well by anyone in the EtherVerse…"

"That's the way of it, Mrs. Jophi," Louis began, his voice sounding sad enough for Azrael, but the narrowing of Jophi's eyes told him that she still didn't fully accept his improvised tale. Louis saw the look and continued in a more jovial tone. "I would say the largest problem I have been having since my escape has been convincing people that I have years of experience as a cook. I would gladly take a job. What does it pay?"

Azrael squinted at the Gnome chef. Wasn't it enough that he was alive again? For appearance's sake, probably not. Then again, wouldn't Merlin be paying Louis' salary? "You would have to negotiate with my sponsor, Merlin." Azrael wasn't willing to lose any of his hard-won crystals, which he was already splitting with Bat. Louis was only here because Apep had resurrected him. How that was possible was still anyone's guess…

"Wait, *the* Merlin?" Louis asked, his voice rising in octaves and drawing every eye in the room to their table. Bat and Jophi both held fingers to their lips in the 'be silent' gesture. "Well, I will accept whatever Merlin would offer, then. The job comes with room and board, right?"

Azrael nodded and after some excited squee noises, the group then turned discussions to other things, like their recent dungeon run. After about thirty minutes, the final two group members joined them and they spent the rest of the evening chatting with each other.

When Azrael finally made it to his room, he was ready for bed, but needed to force his breakthroughs in numerous stats. He stripped off all his clothing and even splurged on a thorough cleaning of the garments by the hotel. After the attendant left, he went to the shower and removed his temporary robe that came with the room.

It was time to place his free stat points. He brought both Agility and Dexterity to fifty, by placing eight points in each. Then before he accepted, he placed the final three points in Stamina. In the next five levels or so, he would break through in Strength and Stamina as well and wanted those to also be simultaneous. He took a deep breath and sat down under the stream of the warm shower water and then accepted the allocation. Every muscle in his body clenched tight like he was having a seizure, and he even felt his jaw crack as the joints popped. The combination of the pain and clenching muscles curled him into a fetal position around his stomach and he began to shake violently. It was one thing to have people tell you that this experience was painful but another altogether to feel it. He couldn't breathe even to scream, thanks to his diaphragm and core muscles spasming so drastically.

After a time, it was finished, and he slowly uncurled as his eyes began to refocus. He threw up then, as his stomach complained about the treatment it had just been given by all the muscles in his body. Using the sides of the tub, he managed to lever himself back to a sitting position. He had just managed to grab a bar of soap when he heard someone trying to quietly walk out of the room. He turned his head to find Jophi. When his eyes landed on her, she froze and her lips peeled back from her teeth in an awkward facial expression.

"I'm sorry, I heard banging and rattling through the wall." Jophi pointed to the shower wall nearest the tub and Azrael. "I thought you were hurt. I realized after I got here what was going on, but…"

"Wasn't sure I would remain conscious through the whole thing?" Azrael finished her thought for her.

"I would have got Bat or one of the guys to come take care of you if you had. In Cathodiem, we are told to never break through without someone nearby," Jophi said helplessly as her face blushed bright red.

"Don't worry about it. I appreciate you checking on me. Have a good night, Jophi," Azrael said and was surprised to find that he meant it. His relationships with the others were going in a direction far different then what he had been taught at the Sovereign Halls, and he wasn't sure if it was a good direction.

What was the warm feeling in his chest from her admission of checking on him?

CHAPTER THIRTY-FIVE

The group checked out of the hotel just before noon on Voskrenie and made their way back to the port to board the Cussing Parrot. Everyone was in really good spirits at breakfast, the walk, and even on the flight back to the Atlantean Academy. The yard and helipad surrounding the villa was entirely transformed. Jess and whatever grounds crews the school had access to had completely fought back the encroaching nature, repaved and painted the helipad, and even given the exterior of the villa a good weeding of creeper vines.

The villa still looked like a haunted mansion about to collapse in on itself, but at least the yard and garden looked more befitting a villa of the headmaster's prospective students. As the group arrived, the first hiccup in the good mood came in the form of Louis surveying the site. "Wait, that's the villa I will be staying in? You said room and board, not rotting food and a collapsing roof!"

Oslow and Prateek's hands shot to their mouths to cover the laughter that tried to escape. Azrael groaned and allowed the ship to touch down on the circular black pad with the painted 'L.' Once he switched off the power and lowered the gangplank, he finally turned to their new chef. "Louis, we are in the process of repairing it and it is still Merlin's villa. Just no one has stayed here in quite some time."

"How is the man going to pay me if he can't even pay to keep his students' villa in good repair?"

"Prospective student," Jophi corrected with a wink and smile at Azrael. She did continue after a moment, though. "Don't worry, Louis, we should have a bedroom repaired and ready soon. Right now, Azrael and I have one, and Bat is using the one off the kitchen that will later be yours."

The laughter of Oslow and Prateek cut off and the two teenagers stared at Azrael with eyes wide. Were they shocked by something? They tilted their heads in his direction and Jophi began to blush red. What was going on?

Even Louis didn't voice more complaints and eyed Azrael with a strange half smile he usually would have associated with something sneaky. Azrael shook his head and stood up. "Bat, do you think you can take Louis with you and find the quartermaster who is in charge of stocking our kitchens?"

Azrael didn't blame Louis for his trepidation. In fact, if he wasn't nervous about the state of the villa, Azrael would have been more concerned, but luckily the name Merlin seemed to carry quite a bit of weight. Even with the tiny Gnome who had never set foot on Gaia in his life. The academy and its headmaster were legends across the entire EtherVerse, it seemed.

Despite Louis' complaints as they exited the ship, the Gnome returned from the trip with Bat in raised spirits. "Louis met with Merlin and they worked out a contract for his services. He's getting two whole crystals a week!" Bat explained.

"Wait, I can't even get Merlin to chat with me for longer than five minutes, and they negotiated a contract?"

"Well, it didn't take longer than five minutes. My guess is the salary offered kind of trumped everything else…"

"This is the room I need to sleep in? And you're telling me I can't use my new salary to have someone come repair it?!" Louis called from upstairs. Bat had pointed the Gnome in the direction of the bedroom they had been working to repair since the start of the semester.

Azrael groaned and gave a withering look to Bat. "He better be able to cook better food than what he made in the Pit dungeon on Tech Duinn. Or I am going to kick him out!"

An hour later, Azrael was forced to admit that the chef's experience trumped the levels of his new class. Louis refused to make a communal meal and had chosen to make each person their own plate. Bat was practically shoving handfuls of a grasshopper-meat ceviche into his mouth with moans of pleasure at each crunching bite. Jophi was eating what Azrael would have called mac and cheese, but the plate had a crust of breadcrumbs on top. The smells of the spices within also reminded Azrael of something foreign, maybe Martian. Azrael was staring down at a bone-in rib steak of some sort of bovine monster. The cut must have been close to thirty ounces and it was accompanied by potato spring rolls and deep sea asparagus. With each bite of his own food, he was forced to wonder who was better, Oliver or Louis.

The three of them got nothing done later that night as each lapsed into a contented food coma as soon as they were finished. Azrael realized that they barely said a word to each other at the table and wondered if that was because of the food quality.

———

On Monentag afternoon, Azrael could tell that the other students were a little taken aback by the level increases that his group displayed, and he even caught Magnus cracking his knuckles in his direction in the morning class. Azrael didn't pay the rich kid any mind and distracted himself with the thought that had been percolating since he discovered Apep could capture other dungeons. Azrael had gambled and was now owed a dungeon run of the Asgardian's, and possibly this world's, most powerful dungeon. He wasn't sure how strong the Rainbow dungeon actually was, but based on the rumors and prestige people seemed to hold for it, he assumed it was a quite powerful. The fact that there was next to no information he had been able to find in the school library or in shops made him slightly worried about the run. Due to this lack of information and its powerful reputation, he decided to run other dungeons until his group was more ready for the challenge.

After Silfa, one of Asgard's recruiters, and her cronies had been so 'kind' to Bat and him, the thought of a bit of payback brought a smile to Azrael's lips. He heard the pops of Magnus' fists behind him, which only widened his grin. Apep would hopefully be able to get a foothold within the Rainbow dungeon, and traditionally that has been all the god-core has needed.

The teacher today was discussing the Power Economy, a term that spoke to a Territory's average level and how best to raise or lower that slider to promote steady growth. It seemed like there was a job here on Gaia where you could pay high-leveled individuals to come live on your Territory for a time to raise the level of the monsters your Territory would spawn. The concept was amusing in some ways, but also extremely clever. Azrael furiously scribbled notes about the topic once he tuned back in. This wasn't something that had been taught at the Halls.

During the afternoon's combat class, Azrael continued to work on his new personal styles of martial arts, attempting to remove all the flair from his learned forms. It was then that Maat said something that snapped Azrael out of his concentration.

"There are two weeks of class remaining before midterms. At beginning of next class, I will go over what is expected of each participant who undertakes test. Ensure practice of katas is priority. Learn a single form highly. You may go."

Azrael shook his head. Only four classes total before midterms? That seemed extremely short, but once he did the math in his head, it fit. One week of classes and a free week meant that two months would have passed by the fourth class.

He was sure he had missed this rather stressful tidbit when he had missed the first Freyaday of the semester. It also hammered home the timeline for fixing the house. While initially his brain had been thinking he had four months to repair everything, he now realized he only had half that amount of time. Minus sleep time and classes, as well.

He practically sprinted the entire way back to the house after that realization.

The moment he walked through the front door, he heard someone in the kitchen and knew Louis was hard at work raising his level and cooking them dinner. Predictably, he found Bat upstairs in what was currently Louis' room but would soon be Bat's; once they finished repairing it, that was.

He took a seat beside Bat and pulled a strand from as close to the bottom of his Ether spiral as he could. The group was getting close to finishing this room, but still had a long way to go to finish the entire villa. The fact that Merlin wanted them to spend so much time on this project likely meant he was doing it wrong. Unless the headmaster wanted him to fail the other courses and focus entirely on the villa.

As he dropped into meditation, he began considering that very issue. He had discovered a way to speed up the process. Should he teach the other two about it? Merlin did tell him to share the skill with his friends... But honestly, the skill that it paired with was something incredible.

Could he tell Jophi about that skill? Telling her was akin to telling Cathodiem, which made him hesitate. Bat, on the other hand...

"Bat, we probably don't have much time before Jophi arrives. I'm going to share with you how I am still able to repair the room faster than both of you. But it needs to remain our secret. Deal?" Azrael insisted.

"Then are you going to finally explain what happened in the Labyrinth?" Bat countered, and Azrael winced. Right, he still owed that explanation to his *friend* as well.

"That one will have to wait until later, after Jophi goes to sleep…" he responded hurriedly. After that, he instructed Bat on the way to circulate his Ether and earn the Essence Conversion skill. He was a bit rushed in his rather succinct description, but Bat picked it up quickly all the same.

Jophi entered just as Azrael was relaxing back into mediation. "I thought you rushed back to begin repairing the room, but it looks like you barely started," she stated as she joined them in a comfortable sitting position on the floor.

Azrael just shrugged and fell into meditation. Teaching Bat had allowed him to think of something. If this skill somehow converted Ether to Essence and Azrael was pulling Ether from as close to the end of the process; was the house looking for Essence?

The only thing he knew about Essence was it was a higher form of energy that the planetary gods used. So why would this house want it? He understood the Essence Conversion skill and why it was given to him. If he was a better producer of something, it made sense that the systems, which were run by the planets, reward him. Right?

The more obvious question, could he use Essence?

His fainting spells were a clear indication that he couldn't even approach the semi-converted wisps of the second-tier energy. Still, could he give the energy to the house instead of the planet?

He destroyed his spiral and then began to reform it. This time, though, once he reached the point he usually stopped, the point where the Ether inside the strand vanished, he instead continued the hollow strand of Ether. He elongated it out through his palm and touched it to the rough wood beneath.

He felt something then. Almost like the floor itself grabbed his hand in one of its own. Almost like the wood was alive and sucking blood from him. His eyes flew open, and he saw that the wood had in fact wrapped itself around his hand in a strong grip. A chime sounded and a ripple began to undulate from under his palm. Not some metaphysical wave, either. A wave of wood as it bucked and pulsed out around the nucleus of his palm. He started to feel a massive headache coming on as Bat and Jophi were shot into the air.

In his interface, Azrael watched his Ether bar drain precipitously past the halfway point. His headache intensified then and he began to scream. What in the abyss was happening? He was at twenty percent when his migraine forced his vision to blacken, but just before it took him, he saw the white-bearded headmaster in the doorway.

Typical…

———

The taste of blue raspberry and someone massaging his throat was what brought him back to consciousness. Once he realized it was an Ether Draught, he greedily began to gulp more of it, as he cracked his eyelids. Merlin was standing above him looking around, but Jophi was the one bent over him feeding him a potion.

As soon as the bottle was empty, Azrael pushed it away. "What in the abyss was that, Merlin? Did you put us inside of a monster hidden as a house? Is this a mimic? I swear it tried to eat me!"

"No, dear boy. Still, this house is quite alive, and I'm afraid I haven't been feeding it enough. Next time, can I suggest you don't combine physical contact with its feeding?" Merlin said with a hint of amusement in his voice. He turned back to look at Azrael, finally. "I would say you overdid it."

Azrael looked around himself for the first time, noticing the stark difference in the state of the room. Every surface gleamed as if the wood or stone was not only new but freshly polished. The sheets looked to be of a quality that guild masters might fight over, and the paint on the walls glowed with a vibrancy usually reserved for sunrise or sunset skylines.

"What happened?" Azrael asked.

"You figured out what this house truly wants," Merlin crowed at the three of them. "But you didn't figure out my other riddle first." After those agonizingly cryptic words Merlin spun in a circle and... vanished.

"Okay, did you guys see what actually happened?" Azrael asked his two friends.

"Well yeah. That wave flung us around like ragdolls, and then the room practically undulated with changes as you screamed and passed out. I think it's time you told me the whole truth!" Jophi responded, her tone annoyed.

"First, I think it's time you told him why you came to live here, Jophi. Don't you?" Bat's quiet voice interjected.

"I already know you were meant to spy on me——" Azrael began but cut off as Jophi began shaking her head.

"Well, yes, I was supposed to spy on you, but I told my father that I wouldn't do it. He then threatened to have me removed from the school if I didn't continue..." Jophi said in a blur of syllables barely understandable. After she finished, she took a deep breath.

"I'm here because if I am staying in Merlin's villa and having opportunities to meet with the man, no one from Cathodiem would dare pull me out," she said a bit more calmly.

"So, you're not spying on us anymore?" Azrael asked skeptically before turning to Bat. "Come on, you fell for this?"

"Azrael, I——" Bat began but a full hand slap across Azrael's face and a crying Jophi interrupted him. Azrael blinked up at Jophi and transferred his gaze between Bat and the woman, his mouth hanging open.

Jophi began to cry and fled from the room. He heard her go down the hall and slam another door. It wasn't in the direction of the room they shared, and Azrael wasn't sure whether to be happy about that or disappointed.

"I think she is having a much harder time than she is letting on," Bat said quietly as he stood up. "I think I will go grab my stuff and switch rooms with Louis. Excuse me."

CHAPTER THIRTY-SIX

The rest of that week passed strangely. Azrael attended classes and saw Jophi in those classes and back at the villa, but they didn't speak. It almost felt like something was hanging in the air between them, preventing it. Jophi slept in the fourth bedroom that they began fixing up. Of course, Azrael didn't repeat his performance from Bat's newly refurbished and pristine bedroom.

Still, by the following Freyaday her room was looking passable. Of course, Freyaday brought with it the inevitable discussion of the free week and what the group would plan to do. After a Projectile Weapons class, Prateek and Oslow approached Azrael. "Did you three decide what the next plan will be?" Oslow asked.

Azrael shook his head. He glanced over to Jophi, who was looking over to the three of them but not coming to join them. "We have a bit of an issue…" Azrael said sheepishly.

"More like a lover's quarrel. Get over it already, and don't let your second brain affect the group dynamic. We were the most successful group by far last off week!" Prateek stated, with a bit of heat in his voice. Azrael was shocked not only by the tone but also by the choice of words the usually proper student chose.

Azrael sighed and moved with the group over to Jophi. "The guys are wondering if we have a plan yet for after class this afternoon?" he said as nonchalantly as possible.

"Well, I've heard the council re-opened the Labyrinth, so we could try that one again. Or any of the other dungeons in El Dorado," Jophi suggested.

"If this was just about leveling speed, I would agree," Oslow began. "But shouldn't we work on some other dungeons to better our tactics? We have entire classes on boss encounters, ambushes, and puzzle strategy. Getting some first-hand experience with some of that would certainly help…"

"So, you're voting for something new?" Azrael summarized.

"As am I." Prateek raised a hand.

Jophi shrugged and looked to Azrael. "What does our *fearless* leader want to do?" she asked, her tone making it clear she really didn't want to know.

"I'll do whatever the group wants," Azrael said. "Do you guys want to come to the villa for lunch, and we can ask Bat? Our new chef is pretty fantastic and gaining levels."

———

The group ruled in favor of something new, which was a bit troublesome to Azrael. To conquer another dungeon for Apep, he likely needed to find the final boss chamber. Since they were headed back to El Dorado, that meant they had a puzzle dungeon, a delving dungeon, or a challenge dungeon. Of those three, the only chance his group had of making it to the final encounter was the puzzle dungeon. The other dungeons scaled far too quickly. Just like the Labyrinth.

He now realized how lucky it was for Bat and him to come upon the nearly defeated Hedamite during their attempted escape. Having watched the Stone Axes conquer that boss, and the strength each member had, really put into perspective how much help Apep had given him on the second try. Could they conquer the Puzzle dungeon and make it to the final room? Or, more importantly, would they get an opportunity to run dungeons in El Dorado? Magnus could easily be up to his same old tricks.

Azrael did also have a few guilds' recruitment offers that would allow him and a group access to the guild's dungeons. If they couldn't run any of the El Dorado dungeons, that would be their backup plan. Each offer would likely only come with access to a single of the guild's Cardinal dungeons, but it was better than nothing. The group boarded the Cussing Parrot right after class that afternoon and headed straight to El Dorado. From the docks, they marched directly to the Puzzle dungeon as well. Their hope? That Magnus wouldn't have had time to enact a plan their first night. It would either work or there wasn't going to be a sudden mass recruitment push by the Asgard guild again. Regardless, they ended up being the third noble team in line. So hopefully they would only have to wait an hour.

"We can always try multiple dungeons now," Prateek suggested now that they had successfully made it into a line that wasn't long enough to snake around an entire city block.

"Shouldn't we be trying to get into a dungeon we can spend the entire week in?" Jophi said with a great deal of annoyance tingeing her words. Azrael knew she was right too, but that wouldn't serve his purposes. He was about to respond when a group of well-geared adventurers approached the guard. That in itself wasn't strange, but the fact that they were breathing hard was.

Azrael was too far away to hear what was said but the group at the front of the line made room for these newcomers. He looked at his group and saw a frown on Bat's face. "What is it, Bat?"

"I've got a sneaking suspicion that Asgard is recruiting again..." Bat whispered.

The group watched helplessly over the next hour as the line

grew longer in front of them. After they were pushed back by about eight groups, Azrael had finally had enough. "Do any of you see the point in staying here?" he asked.

The shakes of numerous heads was all the answer he needed. They began walking toward the port and the Cussing Parrot. "So, what's the strongest dungeon from the list of guilds that want to recruit you?" Oslow asked.

"Truthfully, probably the Hindu guild. They have a Tomb dungeon that sounds like it takes a few days to clear. Still, Prateek should know more," Azrael ventured.

"That is pretty accurate, but they don't let recruits run that dungeon. They will only give you access to one of the lesser ones."

Azrael nodded. That was pretty much what he was expecting. "Are any of the others worth the trip?"

"I think there is a Puzzle and a Living Maze dungeon that they allow recruits access to. I can also try to pull some strings for the Tomb dungeon, but I doubt it will work."

"Not to worry. Let's stay the night at the villa and head out at first light? Do you two want to crash at the villa?" Azrael asked the group, then Oslow and Prateek separately.

They both looked at each other before Prateek sadly shook his head. "Our guilds are getting a lot of heat from the Asgardians about grouping with you already. While your possible connection to Merlin has kept them from forbidding it, let's not push it. We will return from our dorms bright and early tomorrow."

Azrael felt his blood temperature rise, and he looked at Bat and then Jophi, hoping they would share his indignation at the lengths Magnus was going to. Jophi wouldn't meet his eyes, which cooled his temper very quickly. He was going to have to find a way to apologize to her if he wanted to keep group composition and teamwork strong.

"I understand," Azrael responded, trying to keep any hint of his anger from his voice. It wasn't Oslow and Prateek's fault that Gaia was ruled by politics.

———

They were already at the fifteenth challenge of the Hindu Puzzle dungeon, whose name was Ganapati's Obstacles. While there had been a few challenges and even a few failures that had resulted in spawned mobs rushing them from an open wall, Azrael was feeling a bit underwhelmed. The Etherience rewards were just okay, and he had only received ninety-five thousand points. That amount hadn't even moved his progress bar by a single percent.

Still, they were making progress toward his secondary goal of conquering dungeons for Apep and taking revenge on the guilds of Gaia. "I'm not alive but I grow; I don't have lungs but I need air; I don't have a mouth, but water kills me?" Azrael re-read the clue of this room out loud for the third time.

He glanced around at the others, who all looked as perplexed as he felt. Except for Jophi who was standing with her arms crossed and attempting to hide a smile. "You could just volunteer the information, Jophi," Azrael said with a hint of amusement in his voice. He had tried to apologize the previous night and while it had seemed Jophi was over it, her actions in the Puzzle dungeon made him think she still wanted to make him suffer a bit.

"Come on, it's easy. Our leader should be able to solve it…" Jophi cooed under her breath. Azrael thought about it again, then added the fact that Jophi was confident she knew the answer and it clicked.

"Fire. The answer is fire. So where are we supposed to start a fire?" Azrael looked around the room, not seeing any obvious firepit or offering bowls. A whoosh sounded behind his back and he turned to see a fireball ignite a track along the brown ornate-brick wall. Jophi was giving him a smug look.

A loud click sounded as the entrance door to the sixteenth level unlocked. It also paired nicely with a swish and click as the brick wall beside the door slid back to reveal some rewards. It wasn't anything to brag about, especially when compared to the rewards from the Labyrinth the previous week. Still, the relatively weak gear and minor potions might sell for five crystals. Seeing as the rewards scaled in strength with the levels of the dungeon, the group could hope to make fifty crystals from the run.

The real downside to installing Apep here was that Azrael wouldn't get the opportunity to reap the benefits of the dungeon's strength gain. Too bad, really. Still, if the Sovereign Halls had taught him anything, it was that the end objective was always the focus.

Oslow grabbed the loot and stored it in a large backpack before opening the next door. He stopped dead when he was greeted by a wall of water. Out of the water popped five pairs of what could only be described as very uncomfortable boots. Azrael studied the wall of water first.

It was like gravity was having no effect on it. Azrael looked at the group and then back at the perfectly straight division of water into the next room. "This looks like a water level. I've only read about them. Anyone have experience inside one?" he asked and then poked a finger through the curtain to the next room. The water was cold enough that he gave an involuntary shiver.

"I've run this one before," Prateek stated with a shrug. "Those boots force you to sink when you wear them. Last time, the pieces of the puzzle you needed were at the top of the room and you had to take the boots off and go get one before putting the boots back on..."

Bat's ears flapped. "The boots allow you to float if you're holding them, and sink if you're wearing them? That seems to break the laws of physics."

"Dungeons do that sort of thing all the time," Jophi said with a smile and gentle push to Bat's shoulder. So, it was only Azrael she was mad at?

That seems a little unfair? I mean, Bat could have told me earlier that Jophi had refused to spy on us for her father.

Azrael picked up a pair of boots and found them to be

surprisingly light despite them looking like solid metal. He sat down and pulled off his current pair of boots and stored them in the ring. Then took off the rest of his Ether Tech gear and placed it in the ring where his helmet had always been. The few fights they had gotten into were precluded by a flashing red light, giving him plenty of time to get the head piece on and sealed.

Now he didn't think he wanted to take the suit into the water. After he was in his regular clothes, he stepped through the water without waiting for the others. He felt strange after Jophi's most recent display with Bat. His best description was like someone was squeezing his heart and adding heat to his blood simultaneously. He didn't like it and figured the cold water would help.

As soon as he crossed into the room, he began to swim toward the surface. He broke free of the water and took a gentle breath of the air at the top. The room differed from the ones that came before. It was filled with fifty feet of water and the door that he entered through was around halfway between the bottom and the top.

The water was crystal clear, and he could see a large square indent at the bottom that seemed to glow from some sort of light source he couldn't make out. Above him in the open air was blackness that his eyes could only penetrate a few feet of. Someone surfaced nearby and Azrael turned to see very large ears dripping water. Bat had surfaced near enough to him that the dim light from below created a shadowed outline. Azrael was about to say something when Bat screeched, "Look out!"

Azrael sucked in a breath and ducked beneath the water. The percussive sound of something landing on top of the surface assaulted his ears, and its intensity told him just how close that had been to his head. He surfaced again and heard a conversation as his ears cleared of water.

"That splash was likely one of the puzzle pieces. It's a bit too dark up here to see it though," Prateek said clinically. "Are we supposed to just swim around until we find it?"

"It's right here. It nearly fell on top of my head. Bat gave me enough warning to avoid it, though," Azrael responded as his arm fell atop a bobbing piece of the puzzle.

"I can see the pieces as they come within twenty feet of me. Maybe we should group up so I can warn everyone if something is going to hit us. Then we can move around after a splash as well and send someone down with the piece?" Bat responded from nearby.

"I'm going to head down with the first piece now." Azrael pulled out the Ether Tech helmet and placed it on. It would seal the water out and give him a few extra breaths of air. "Wait to descend until I am back. We can trade the Ether Tech helmet between us and take turns."

Then Azrael pulled the boots from his ring and struggled on the surface to put them on. It wasn't exactly easy to maneuver them. The others continued to chat, but Azrael couldn't hear them as his head continually entered and exited the water as he fought with the boots and his feet. Finally, they both were on, and the strange effect was nearly instantaneous. He felt doubly glad for the helmet a moment later when the boots struck the floor fifty feet below him. That change in pressure was sure to cause discomfort or even pop an eardrum if he hadn't worn the thing.

The bottom was well lit, and Azrael studied the space. It was comprised of gray interlocked stones that were sealed to each other by some sort of white grout. In the center of the room, there was an indent sunk down by about half of a brick depth. He moved over to that space and noticed that the light came from the edge of this puzzle board. He called it a puzzle board because it was perfectly square and the wood he carried would likely be a perfect fit for the depth of the thing. He studied that piece now. It was a central piece, as evidenced by the inserts and no flat sides. A problem quickly arose. How was he supposed to stop this piece from floating back to the surface?

He tried pushing it down into the space, hoping for some

sort of magic or mechanism to hold it down. Nothing happened.

He was about to struggle out of the boots when a thump from behind startled him. He turned to find a large rock on the brick where there wasn't one before.

Well, that's convenient.

He moved over to it and, using his storage ring, he managed to easily maneuver it on top of the driftwood puzzle piece. The next issue was that the piece itself was just plain wood with no defining feature that he could see. It had a few knots and rings, but if those didn't line up with the next piece, this puzzle was going to be difficult to solve. His boots came off much easier thanks to the stability of being on the floor of the room.

Azrael quickly fought his way back to the surface and explained his findings to the group.

"Wait, the second splash was a stone? We've been swimming around looking for another piece," Oslow complained.

"Well, the different sound makes sense now," Bat chirped from the center of the swimmers.

"So, you think we should just wait up here and collect pieces until we find edges?" Jophi asked. "Sounds reasonable, but ducking under the water isn't going to stop a stone from falling on us…"

"Shoot." Azrael began thinking hard. "Well, if the pattern continues, every second projectile will be a stone. Do you think your Ether shield can bounce it away?"

"It kind of can. But it uses my body as a transfer for the gravitational forces. So, it will likely shove me under the water. And then a few seconds later, you will all get dunked too by the inside of the shield and that isn't going to help my Ether pool," Jophi said from nearby. It was tough to tell by just her tone how confident she was in her Ether shield saving them from the falling stone. It would be helpful if he could see her face to better gauge her current mood.

"Well, the rock would have to fall on top of us. And the

odds of that aren't one hundred percent. Let's see what happens."

The group swam around and collected three more pieces before they found an edge. The nice part about having a piece in hand was that you could rest on it and float without using as much energy to bob in place. In the five splashes that proceeded finding the edge piece, not a single puzzle piece or stone fell atop the group.

Oslow, who didn't yet have a puzzle piece floaty, volunteered to go down. Azrael handed over his helmet just as a loud splash and pop reverberated through the darkness. That would be the stone.

"Guys, I think we have a problem," Prateek said. "The time between splashes is speeding up…"

CHAPTER THIRTY-SEVEN

"By the Depths!" Bat exclaimed. "It can never be easy with dungeons, can it?"

Azrael winced at the news. How many pieces were in the puzzle down there? Should they send Oslow down with all three now, instead of holding the middle ones to float on? "Oslow, go see if you can place that piece. If you have enough air in the helmet reserves, begin moving some of the stones nearer the center. Okay?"

Oslow took the helmet that had remained held in Azrael and his hands during the rather bad news from Prateek. "Got it," Oslow said and Azrael heard the click of the helmet sealing in place. A moment later, Oslow also struggled to get his boots on in the water, if the nearby splashes and grunts were any indication.

"Is this about to get as dangerous as I think it is?" Jophi asked, her voice a bit nervous.

Azrael nodded before realizing she couldn't see it. "I think so. At a guess, we need a hundred pieces to fill that space below. So, they are going to be coming down fast as we near the final pieces. Not to mention, I don't think putting the boots on is completely safe without the helmet. The speed at which you sink to the bottom could cause pressurization problems."

"Are we sure it's only going to drop a hundred…?" Prateek added some more bad speculation, and a new, softer splash sounded shortly after. The group swam in that direction and found another middle piece. Azrael's hand was the one that brushed it and he hurriedly passed it off to Prateek so he could float as well. Of the four on the surface, Azrael was now the only one without a piece to bob on.

A slow count of twenty later, another stone cannoned into the surface close enough that Azrael felt the wave, but far enough that Bat wasn't alerted. Azrael swallowed a lump in his throat. It definitely wasn't going to be an easy puzzle to solve if pieces and rocks began falling every few seconds. Or worse yet, every second.

"Alright, I think I got it placed well," Oslow blurted as soon as he broke the surface. Azrael heard the helmet click open as the group waited for the next splash. It came nineteen seconds after the stone and the group collected another middle piece. This one was given to Oslow and Azrael continued to tread water for another thirty-five seconds. The next piece was an edge and this time Prateek was handed the helmet. Jophi and Bat both needed to stay on the surface for emergencies.

It took far longer for Prateek to maneuver the boots onto his feet than the others, but once he did, he vanished along with a stone splash. "Would our light stones even help in here?" Oslow asked into the silence.

"Doubt it. They won't illuminate further than ten feet in this darkness, and they will just sink if we let them go. I think for future dungeons, I should pick up some sort of light ball spell," Jophi suggested unhelpfully.

All the members of the group on the surface had a piece of puzzle to float with now and they made their way to the next piece to find a fifth. That meant when Prateek returned, they would have one for each of them. The splashes were now under ten seconds apart when Prateek broke the surface.

The helmet clicked open, and he took a deep breath before sighing. Azrael just knew bad news was about to come out of his mouth. "I think your estimate was a bit off, Az. Looks like we need close to two-hundred pieces. The edges don't fill as much as the middle ones."

Does this guy not talk unless it's something negative?

Azrael just groaned in response, choosing not to share his internal assessment. Finally, what was an inevitability happened. "Down!" Bat called and the group dropped off their puzzle pieces and into the water. Luckily, this was a puzzle piece and not a boulder.

They returned to the surface and found another central piece. A splash of a stone hitting the water surface came and Azrael felt the inevitability of a problem. "We are going to have to change the—" *splash* "—plan."

He heard murmurs of agreement, but no one volunteered a new plan. "Okay... What if we split up and hugged the walls?" Azrael ventured a thought into the semi-silence that was being punctuated by splashes.

"Do pieces not fall—"

"Shield!" Bat shouted, interrupting the question from Oslow. A blue dome flared around them a fraction of a second after the shout, and something immediately thunked into it. The interior of the dome hit Azrael in the top of the head just as he tried to duck under the water. Once below the surface, he watched the boulder roll down the side and slowly sink toward the bottom.

The group resurfaced, a few coughing up water they swallowed; Prateek and Bat had clearly forgotten to hold their breath and were subsequently dunked.

"I won't be able to use the shield more than twice," Jophi said hurriedly when she resurfaced.

"Okay, we are going to need to find the wall. We can still stay in a group and make quick ventures out to find puzzle pieces." Azrael made the decision for the group. It might not be the best option, but sticking with the current plan would quickly spell disaster. At least with the wall, they might save Jophi some Ether, if not avoid the falling stones or wooden pieces entirely from a lucky ricochet.

The group had just begun swimming in a direction that Bat had indicated by creating a sound beacon, when he shouted, "Shield!"

The stone struck more centrally this time on the domed blue surface, and the group was submerged again as Jophi was forced under the water. Instead of the stone rolling off the shield, the shield shattered. The stone sunk through the water between the group and caused an undertow in its wake. As the shield shattered and Azrael was spun by the current, he noticed something out of the corner of his eye. He could only see because of the fading glow of the shield and even then it wasn't much. He thought he saw Jophi grab her head and begin convulsing as air rocketed from her mouth. The strangeness of what he thought he saw came in the form of her wearing a two-piece swimsuit.

Azrael managed to get himself oriented and took a risk. He triggered Demon Step, and felt himself phase to a new point in the water. Admittedly, he had been training around the villa with the skill, but he still wasn't confident in keeping his orientation correct on the back end of the skill. He tried to stretch his arms around himself in the dark, knowing she was nearby. Instead of finding her with his hands, he felt a part of her body bump into his head. Right, the shield skill would have been above her head, so any shadow would have been below her. He prayed to the Sovereign that she hadn't passed out from her Ether exhaustion. He reached up and his arms closed around warm, smooth skin.

Damnit! Based on her limp muscles, she has passed out.

He kicked his legs as hard as he could and attempted to find her head in the darkness of the water. He managed to find the straps of what he had assumed was her swim top, but now due to the lace, realized was a bra. He followed them up to her shoulders and found her neck. As soon as he broke free of the water, he wrapped his elbow under her chin and across her chest. Once he had a good grip, he pulled her limp head out of the water using his body as a lever. He leaned back, away from her body and attempted to use his body position to continually keep her head out of the water as he dragged her in a random direction.

Splashes continued to sound all around them and he attempted to call out to the group multiple times. But the position of his body and Jophi's weight kept dunking his head under the water. He was sure he made some pretty pitiful noises, but he couldn't tell if the others were able to hear him because his ears spent more than half of the time submerged.

It was then that Azrael realized that it wasn't only Jophi's body that was forcing his head into the water. The splashes all around them were creating waves. They might have been ripples at first, but now with a splash every other second, they were growing.

Floating wood bounced off his head, shoulders, and hands as he continued to drag Jophi through the waves.

Finally, his leading hand struck stone and he braced himself as best he could on the wall before levering Jophi's head close to his ear.

She wasn't breathing.

CHAPTER THIRTY-EIGHT

Azrael could still feel her heart thudding desperately in her chest. So he assumed this was a case of water in the lungs or a blocked airway. He needed to force her body to cough.

He attempted to bang on her back with his hand, to help her cough up any water she swallowed, but every time he raised his hand to try, he would unbalance her weight and her back would submerge into the water. He quickly readjusted to prevent her head from dipping under as well, and chose to try the maneuver he had been shown for someone choking on food. He wrapped his arms around her abdomen, pushing his thumb into the soft area a few inches below her sternum. He then doubled the speed at which his legs were churning water and pulled his fist toward himself before making a motion up toward but also under her sternum.

The first pull did nothing and so he adjusted his grip slightly as his legs burned in protest. He tried again and heard a sound of vomiting followed by liquid striking the wavy surface of the water. He kept his legs churning and attempted to keep Jophi's body out of the water as she retched a few more times. Her body shivered in his arms and his legs were just about to give out when he heard her suck in a desperate lungful of air.

"Thank the Halls." Azrael slowly changed his grip on her and lowered back into the water. He returned to the leaning back position, continuing to support Jophi as she heaved in air. Splashing continued to serenade them and they were either lucky to not get struck again, or the walls were far safer than the center.

"Guys, we are over here. Jophi nearly drowned," Azrael shouted and heard a few answering calls from his party across the chamber. "Jophi, do you think you can hold your breath and help me swim back to the door to the previous room?" he asked more quietly.

He felt her bob her head up and down. "Okay, guys, I'm going to go back to the entry door and get her on solid ground to recover," he shouted before changing tone again. "Ready. Three, two, one, and hold your breath."

Together they swam lower, and Azrael pulled out a glow stone to light the wall nearest them. About halfway down, the water itself lit up enough that he could see through it more easily. They weren't on the wall with the door to the previous area. They were near a corner about half a wall away, though. He dragged Jophi as much as he could as she weakly kicked to help, and together they managed to fall through the curtain of water.

Azrael went through first and managed to catch Jophi before she collapsed to the stone floor. He carried her a short distance in, only now fully comprehending how near to naked she was. The light in this room highlighted that she was only wearing her smallclothes. A heat rose to his cheeks, aided by her close-pressed body heat. The dripping wet and cold clothing he wore didn't help either. After they were ten feet from the water curtain, Azrael gingerly put her down and pulled two blankets from his Ring of Holding. Before he could think more on her state of undress, he rolled her onto the one and covered her with the other.

She curled into a ball and Azrael figured she was likely going to be okay. "Do you need anything?" he asked as he looked back to the curtain of water. He should probably head back in there and ensure everyone made it out okay.

"I'm—" She coughed. "—okay… ank you," she mumbled from inside the blankets.

Turning around fully, he was just in time to see Prateek and Bat fall through the water. "Oslow?" Azrael asked.

"He has the helmet right now, and is further away," Bat gasped.

Azrael stepped through the curtain of water and looked around. Gazing from this point in the room was surreal. From the darkness of the water above, stones would appear and careen their way toward the bottom. Each stone streamed bubbles behind it and grew clearer as it neared the lights at the bottom of the pool. Above him was pure darkness, below him blue light with three puzzle pieces inside the central depression. It was sad to see…

Hold on. There are no other stones falling on the puzzle area. Does that mean that area is safe?

Scanning away, Azrael saw Oslow enter the more illuminated waters off to his right. Azrael watched as the tank swam toward him and once he was certain that there wasn't going to be a problem, he step-swam back through the door. Oslow fell through a heartbeat later and Azrael caught him.

"We should probably call it here and make sure we have equipment for water levels in the future," Oslow suggested as the helmet unclicked from his head.

"I think I might have a plan. Just keep an eye on Jophi and make sure she recovers." Azrael grabbed the Martian Ether Tech helmet just as Oslow pulled it off. He clicked it on and walked back through the curtain.

Once he was on the other side, he swam to the middle of the room and confirmed his earlier assumption. No stones fell onto this area. Using gravity as a counter direction he swam straight up and broke the surface above. There weren't even that many wooden puzzle pieces floating here. Azrael swept his hand around and pulled out a glow stone. His plan could work. He grabbed the nearest piece of wood and pulled the all-purpose adhesive tape from his ring. He lashed a glow stone to each side and then went back for another. After five boards, he ran out of glow stones. Each party member carried ten stones though, so if they needed more, they could rig it up.

There was now a dome of light maybe twenty to thirty feet in all directions from where Azrael swam at the center. Next was to see if he could see it from underwater. He dove back down and now he could make out four lights at the top, as well as the lighter blue outline of the puzzle area at the bottom. This could work. He swam back to the water curtain and fell through.

"How is she?" he asked first, still willing to cancel the run if Jophi needed serious attention.

"I'm fine." Jophi was sitting up and shivering a bit, but otherwise had color back in her cheeks. "Did you figure out a way through?" she asked, which answered his next question of if she could continue. The blanket slipped off a bare shoulder and he blushed before fixing his eyes above her head and explaining what he had noticed and subsequently done.

After that, the group just used the room as a staging area and made forays into the room to find pieces one at a time. They likely took longer than the day they were supposed to, but they managed to clear the puzzle after each person had taken a shift sleeping.

———

"For how much trouble the water level room was, I would have expected better loot," Oslow complained as they finished the nineteenth puzzle and received rewards that were better than that of the water stage.

Azrael shrugged, silently agreeing with the assessment, but simultaneously more concerned with how few rewards they were receiving. This dungeon had already taken them four days of work thanks to that level, and they hadn't even managed to recoup the costs. At least they were about to take on the final room.

"Is everyone ready for the final challenge?" Azrael asked, changing the subject away from the poor loot. "Prateek, do you know if it's a Sphynx?"

"No Sphynx. My parents have run this before, and they said it was an Arachne."

Well, that explained the low-level loot. Puzzle dungeons were ranked in a few different ways. They often would be classified not only by the strength of the monster, but also the final boss. A Sphynx dungeon was widely considered to be the highest. Arachne was somewhere in the middle, and somewhere near the bottom were Harpies. So this wasn't only a low age rank but also a low-quality puzzle dungeon as well.

Since no one claimed to need more time, Azrael opened the door to the final challenge. Behind it were brick stairs that climbed up into moderate gloom. At the top of the stairs, the flickering light of torches or perhaps fire burned. With a glance back at the group, he began climbing.

At the top of the stairs was a cavern, filled with webbing starting about seven feet into the air. At equal intervals on the black stone walls that were still visible, torches hung from strange, webbed sconces. Azrael scanned around looking for the Arachne, but was unable to penetrate the thick white film that was the lair web.

"Ahh, the slowpokes finally join me," a chittering voice called into the cavern, and it seemed to be coming from right above him. One strange oddity with Puzzle dungeons was that groups didn't have to fight the final boss, unless, of course, they get the riddle wrong. That was also why all the final bosses were half-humanoid, so they could communicate with travelers.

I wonder if planets with Martians have half-Martian bosses.

The rest of the group joined Azrael, and he did not bother

to respond to the slowpoke comment. They had only been slow because of the water level, and that was luck of the draw.

"Not very talkative. Pity. Here are the questions for you, then. I speak without a mouth and hear without ears. I have no body, but I come alive with wind. What am I?"

"I've heard this one before!" Oslow claimed and then looked at the group. "I think it's an echo. My parents used to say that to each other."

"I agree, that's an easy one," Jophi said while looking at Azrael. He shrugged at her and nodded to Oslow, who then confirmed his answer to the Arachne.

"What word in the Gaian English language has three consecutive letters back to back."

No one immediately spoke up, and so Azrael looked at Jophi with a raised eyebrow. She rolled her eyes and made a motion with her hand, as if to say, 'get it over with, then.'

"Bookkeeper." Azrael smiled at Jophi and crossed his arms.

"One more, then, and why don't we make it harder?" the Arachne clicked from above. "I am something people love or hate. I change people's appearances and thoughts. If a person takes care of themselves, I will grow. No matter how hard people try, I will never go down. What am I?"

Jophi looked at Azrael and crossed her arms. He just smiled wider because he knew the answer as well.

"Age."

Bat flinched as Azrael gave the final answer and turned large ears directly at him. Simultaneously, the Arachne said, "Congratulations. You can collect your rewards as you leave. However, I don't like your attitude, so if you ever come again, I will ensure you get only water puzzles. Good day…"

Azrael felt his eyebrows raise. Guess they should have pretended that the puzzles were tougher?

The group did complete a quest once the dungeon was finished. Unfortunately, it came with no Ether crystals, but did award two-hundred thousand Etherience.

Congratulations! You have completed a dungeon quest.
Dungeon Quest
Repeatable Quest
Hindu Puzzle Dungeon
Defeat Queen Aranae the Arachne
Congratulations! You have completed all twenty puzzles in the dungeon and even defeated Queen Aranae's more difficult questions.
Rewards:
200,000 Etherience
Increased Puzzle difficulty on next visit

———

3,706,243 Etherience remaining to level 13.

CHAPTER THIRTY-NINE

"Are you doing what I think you're doing?" Bat asked Azrael late one night when the two were finally left alone. It was Saturnday, and the group had just finished a third dungeon run for the week. They had chosen to stay the night and head back to school tomorrow, on Voskrenie. They were staying in an inn on the Territory of the Pagan Guild. It was a guild just outside of the top fifteen on Gaia, but had quite a bit of power on other planets. Particularly amongst the tribe races. So that of Beast-kins, Orcs, Trolls and a few others.

Just like the other guilds, Azrael and the team couldn't afford to offend them by immediately rushing back to the school and the villa. Azrael still wanted to, if for no other reason than to continue meditating in the villa, but unfortunately they would have to at least pretend to be considering the offers of recruitment.

Azrael knew what Bat wanted to talk about, but still wanted to put it off longer. "What exactly do you think I am doing?" They hadn't discussed the events of the Labyrinth, and Azrael wasn't sure how much to tell Bat. It wasn't that Azrael didn't trust him, but more that the best kept secret was always the one that was never disclosed.

"Well, somehow you are linking dungeons to Apep, or whatever that void where Tech Duinn used to be is. What's your plan? The more dungeons we tackle and defeat, the more I'm feeling it isn't going to be good."

"Well, it really depends on what side you're looking from. I'm not on the side of the Gaian guilds. So, it isn't going to be good for them. For the Empire and other races farther removed from this planet, it will likely be considered good."

"We're not at war, Azrael."

"Are you certain of that?"

"I guess not, but are you even sure that Apep can be controlled? Aren't you essentially handing over power to something that has never been seen before?"

"Do you think the power of Apep can surpass that of Gaia and all the monstrously powerful people in this world?" Azrael looked out the window, thinking about all the extremely powerful individuals this world had to contain.

"I don't have any idea, Azrael. All I'm pointing out is that you can't know either…" Bat scratched his head nervously.

Azrael nodded. It was a good point, but what was the power of four dungeons against the might of Gaia? All he needed to do was cause enough of a problem here on the planet to force the guilds to call back their forces. Then the Sovereign Empire would get a reprieve and likely even be able to re-assert some of its control.

"I see your point. Still, the only goal is to have the guilds' forward operating troops called back, and threatening their Territories will likely do that."

"Just be careful, Azrael. Apep is stronger than us," Bat said as he frowned.

Azrael's fist clenched hard at that reminder.

Not for long. Not if I can help it…

———

"So, do we have any sort of plan for next week?" Prateek asked as the group trudged up the gangplank of the Cussing Parrot.

"What if we were to skip Freyaday's classes and get into El Dorado's Labyrinth or Delving dungeon early?" Oslow suggested.

"We definitely had much better weeks when we were running the El Dorado dungeon," Jophi stated with a shrug. "How do you think we did this week, Azrael?"

"If we broke even, I would be happy. But my gut is telling me we didn't." Azrael took the captain's chair and began preparations for takeoff as the others sat down. The mood in the small dropship grew somber and the silence stretched as Azrael pressed buttons and pivoted in his chair to access the vertical thrusters.

"Well, it probably would be best if we could get back into a more established dungeon. A lot of the guilds aren't anywhere near as powerful as some of the original cities," Bat chirped from the co-pilot chair as he attempted to 'watch' Azrael perform the start up procedure. Azrael glanced at him and sighed. Was Bat's choice because he disagreed with the plan to use Apep to invade guilds? Or was his decision based solely on wanting the money to invest in Batmen piloting instruments...

Azrael looked away, choosing not to comment. The thrusters fired as he increased the throttle, and the hum and rattle of the Cussing Parrot filled the new silence with its vertical struggle. It wasn't the newest ship by any means, but it was still better than nothing. The group approached Atlantis a few minutes later, and they radioed down to inform the security that it was the Parrot, and they were landing at the villa. In response, they heard a chuckle, some mumbling in the background, and then uproarious laughter. Azrael shook his head; the security personnel still hadn't gotten over whatever jokes or puns they liked to tell.

The landing was over in a few more minutes and once the engines shut down, Azrael finally turned back to the group with his opinion. "If we can get into the Labyrinth or the Delving dungeon, then I would say let's do it. Let's skip a class and try, but as soon as Magnus finds out we have left, he is going to react. So, at what time do we leave and how do we make it less conspicuous?" Azrael pointed at the rather loud ship around them.

"We could order an AGT," Jophi suggested, referring to the Automated Gaian Taxi service.

"You can't get a ship from your guild?" Prateek asked, his voice genuinely curious.

Azrael winced and held his breath. He looked over to Bat and found him doing the same.

"Nope. Only full members can requisition a ship. Right now, since I am in school, I kind of fall into the student category." Jophi didn't look at anyone as she responded and unstrapped herself from her jump seat. Since Prateek had asked someone else, Azrael assumed his Hindu guild also couldn't get them a ship. A quick glance told Azrael Oslow was in the same boat, since he was shaking his head.

Azrael sighed out his held breath and finished shutting down the ship and lowering the gangplank. The group walked down and stopped again waiting for a final answer. "Alright, why don't we try to get into one of the El Dorado dungeons early next Freyaday? I suggest Oslow and Prateek move in here so Magnus isn't suspicious why we all head back to the villa. What do you think?"

The two looked at each other. Then they turned back to Azrael. "We would need to talk with our guilds first. I'm still not sure they will allow us to be to associated with you…"

"There isn't even a fully restored room for them yet. Unless you want to go all fainty again?" Jophi teased.

"They'd have to bunk up and maybe even help us restore the place. But if I do go all 'fainty,' you all get to meet Merlin…" Azrael teased back, hoping that the meeting Merlin part would help the two convince their guilds. The reminder that his villa mates got more time with Merlin than he did also grated on him.

———

"So, Merlin still hasn't accepted you as a full apprentice then?" Magnus sneered at Azrael from his spot on the sand of the coliseum. It was the next afternoon, Monentag. Oslow and Prateek had moved into the villa yesterday after talking with their guilds. Still, everyone except for Bat was in Maat's Monentag afternoon combat class. Azrael didn't bother responding and continued through his forms. He was trying to mesh Viper Coils with Coiling Viper; the latter being the Gaian name for the somewhat similar form from the Sovereign Halls.

"Ignore me all you want, but my father used to tell me that the number one benefit of apprenticing under Merlin was the access to the Atlantean Tower that his insignia gave. So, if you aren't getting that, you're basically just fixing his villa for him." Magnus laughed and his cronies joined in.

Azrael stopped his forms and looked at Magnus. The laughing didn't bother him in the least, but the access to the Atlantean Tower was supposed to be something that he received as a full apprentice to Merlin? That was a bit of a fireball tossed into a well. The Atlantean Towers were the four strongest dungeons that existed across the entire EtherVerse. The Prime dungeon they created was said to have one hundred floors and rewards that increased with each level. His desire to graduate from prospective student to full apprentice grew to a level he couldn't describe.

His breathing became a bit shallow, and his heart rate increased. Conquering the hundredth floor was said to grant any wish the climbers desired. Azrael wasn't a child and didn't believe the final rumor, but he did believe that a group had to conquer each tower to get access to the next and that each tower was filled with riches. So, conquering any of them would be like a dream. He also knew for a fact that each tower conquered did come with a system reward. Specifically, the ability to lock a class to your ancestors or a particular group.

That was from the lessons of the Sovereign Empire, though, and he wasn't sure how truthful they were.

So, the pendant of Merlin's that Magnus threw at him gave him access to the first tower? Magnus wouldn't have just dropped it, right? Something about him bringing it up now was very fishy, but he would still check it out if it meant he would get into the fabled Atlantean Towers. Maat noticed his inaction and the direction of his stare. The teacher followed it to Magnus and called out loudly, "Men settle things with duel. You two, center of sands. Now."

Azrael blinked but began moving; his body was used to following orders from teachers. Magnus was only a split second behind but because of his hesitation, he ended up looking like he was goaded by Azrael. By the red in Magnus' face, it didn't make him happy when he realized it. As soon as Azrael turned back around, he found the Asgardian with a hammer in hand.

"No, not like this." Maat stepped in between them both and held up hands. "Today, you will spar using only martial forms. No skills."

Placing his sword into his inventory, Azrael got into a martial stance, choosing Crane's High Guard as his starting point. Magnus adopted a more neutral posture that was closest to Highway Brigand. If his stance told Azrael anything, it was that he would favor his hands in the exchange. However, he knew better than to count only on a first impression. He took a deep breath and entered the headspace that made Magnus an opponent, changing him to a genderless lump of skin, muscles and bones.

"Begin," Maat called and the thing named Magnus shot forward. Crane Spreads its Wings answered the charge, confusing the brawler for a split second as Azrael spread his arms and took up more space while simultaneously attempting to strike out with the back of his leading hand. His opponent stuttered and rocked back onto its heels, so Azrael entered Boar's Rush, pulling his leading arm into his body and firing a side kick at its head. The forearm of his opponent deflected the blow, but he could tell that the strength of his kick still rocked the defender back. He dropped the attacking foot back to the ground and lunged forward, firing both arms in a Scorpion Pincer. The one fist aimed at his opponent's stomach while the other rocketed at its face. Most opponents over-defended the head and would fall victim to the blow aimed at the stomach.

Magnus was an exception and it blocked both blows before countering with an attempted Elephant March. This offense was aimed at stomping on feet while simultaneously blocking the opponent's footwork. Azrael answered with Harpy's Sting, a good counter to Elephant March. Harpy's Sting utilized the opponents own legs as steps and was extremely hard to defend against when strongly rooted to the ground. Its downside was the lack of power behind blows, due to poor base. So while Azrael scored two hits in quick succession on his opponents' torso and neck, they were nothing more than annoyances.

His opponent changed form and attempted Maneater Plant, a defense that lowered its body toward the ground and turned its arms into whips. Azrael received two blows and disengaged from Magnus with a backward tumble. Its blows were also small, the whip-like hands not yet having enough blood in them to turn its arms hard and dangerous. Azrael hated to admit it, but he and his opponent were relatively well matched.

Tiger Palm met Lion's Mane. Rocks Final Stand met Flowing Stream. Cross Wind met Flickering Candle. Still, Azrael began noticing that his new forms, at least the ones he had managed to work on since discovering the subtle differences between Gaian forms and those of the Sovereign Halls, were beginning to score hits. They weren't finishing blows, but they were causing mounting damage. Azrael began leaning into those forms, cycling through the eight he had adjusted. His opponent's face began to morph into something less confident. It began with a narrowing of the eyes and soon a tightness in the jaw.

Azrael had only a moment's notice as Magnus erupted in electrical current. It was like pulses of blue lightning coursed inside its arteries and veins. As an upward palm from Stormwall came toward Azrael, he triggered Demon Step and Soul Cloak simultaneously. He had learned that the addition of Soul Cloak helped him orient himself after he teleported. When he flashed into his opponent's shadow, simultaneously he began triggering his Soul Storage, ready to release ten stored Soul Strikes from point blank range.

He blinked and, instead of the ten strikes releasing into the back of Magnus, Azrael was near a wall of the coliseum class-room. His Soul Cloak hadn't warned him of someone entering his space, and from one moment to the next it was like his opponent just vanished. His ten strikes blasted into the sand and blew him backward into the nearby wall. Thankfully, his Soul Cloak cushioned his collision somewhat, but it still dazed him. He sprang back up, looking around wildly for his opponent. How had it managed to disrupt his new skill? Azrael had been practicing with Demon Step in dungeons last week, and using it to annoy his friends around the villa, but he had never moved to an area he had not intended.

Once or twice, it had moved him in front of an opponent because the individual turned, but its shadow stayed, but that was part of the learning process. Azrael knew that he had checked Magnus' shadow before using the skill. Also, the skill had to bring him into a living creature's shadow. But he was nowhere near anyone currently.

He looked back to the crowd and saw everyone watching Magnus attempt to buck off Maat, who had the Asgardian in a back mount and pinned. Jophi was splitting her attention between that spectacle and Azrael as he stumbled back to the group.

"That was exciting," she whispered as he got within ear shot. The group of students was buzzing with speculations about the fight, about the outcome, and about repercussions for breaking the rules.

Azrael opened his mouth to respond as he fully exited his combat mode, only to be interrupted. "I think that will be all for combat class today," Merlin seemed to whisper over the crowd. His voice was low but somehow carried over the din of the students. The direction it came from caused all the heads to turn up into the stands in unison. There, seated in a red and gold chair, sat Merlin. He didn't look upset, or angry. In contradiction to expectations, he looked bored, maybe even disinterested. "Magnus and Azrael shall stay behind. Everyone else, take an early lunch."

CHAPTER FORTY

"Merlin didn't even stay to dole out a punishment. By the time you all left, he was gone," Azrael explained to the group, over a bowl of Louis' food at the villa. Jophi still didn't seem to believe the story he'd concocted over the chef's arrival but they still had a chef now, and Louis did seem to be rather good at his job. He had even chosen a new, rarer cooking class he had always wanted to try.

At everyone's continued stares, Azrael relented some more. "Maat declared that I was the winner because Magnus activated his skill first. He still gave me detention for my intention to use lethal force. So for the next five days I am going to have to go to Maat's classroom after classes. The only good news is that Magnus was sent home for two weeks. He isn't allowed to participate in any school classes or dungeons until his punishment ends."

Prateek perked up at this news. "Do you think that means we will be able to get into a dungeon next week?"

"Maybe, but I think you're missing the part where I have to go to detention every *night*," Azrael said, driving home the point that he would have detention even on Freyaday. Their plan to leave after the first class had now become invalid. "You could all try to enter somewhere without me…"

"That's true," Oslow began but was punched in the arm by Jophi.

"He doesn't actually want us to go without him. Not to mention, entering a dungeon without one of our members seems like a bad idea," she explained her punch in the arm to the group.

"Oh right…" Oslow said and gave a look at Azrael. "But, like, if we did go without you, you could probably find us after, or work on repairing rooms here?"

Jophi facepalmed. "I don't think you understand the group dynamic, Oslow. Azrael is our most versatile member. Without him, we would be in a lot of trouble if a fight didn't go according to plan."

Bat nodded along, as did Prateek, but Oslow still looked unconvinced. "I get it, but if we end up running small guild dungeons again, we are likely going to lose money. I think it would be better for our long-term success to go without Azrael if it means higher Etherience and Gems." Strangely, Bat and Prateek nodded along with Oslow's point as well.

Azrael blinked, seeing the group slowly come around to Oslow's thought process. Jophi gave him a look that contained the hint of a frown and some sort of sadness before she nodded as well. He thought he heard her mumble, "Sorry, Az," but he couldn't be sure.

"So, you guys are just going to leave me behind?" Azrael asked, feeling his chest tighten at the realization that it had been decided, and so easily.

"We'll still give you a cut and your pick of some of the loot!" Bat countered. "It isn't like there aren't plenty of other things that you can be doing. You keep saying you don't have time to work on your martial forms, or that we need to spend more time on fixing the villa…"

It's true, but I also need to be getting stronger and conquering dungeons for Apep…

Azrael squinted at Bat. Was that why his friend was choosing to sideline him? "I assume you're all planning on *borrowing* the Cussing Parrot…"

"It would be helpful. And don't worry, I'll pilot," Jophi said, which caused Bat to groan.

Despite feeling like he should have a bit more loyalty from his group, he chose to let it go this time. There still wasn't a guarantee that they would get into one of the El Dorado dungeons, anyway. Plus, there was one thing that he really did want to look into… and it was walking distance from the Atlantean Academy.

———

"Go through the movements, like in a fight with Magnus. Show Maat what you do to his forms," the large muscular man said as Azrael arrived at his first detention.

Azrael paused for a moment, expecting detention to be a solemn affair where he might have had to clean weapons or write out lines on a sand tablet. That had been the way of things in the Sovereign Halls. "I've had some instruction on forms from a young age, Maat. So I am combining some of the similar ones to try to create efficiency."

"Even blind man see this. Maat does not ask this. He ask student to show him."

Azrael only hesitated a moment more before stepping into the martial forms he'd used earlier in the day. Maat walked around him, making small noises that could have been disapproval or approval, but Azrael couldn't tell. The large man was growly and gruff in the best of situations. So, these grunts weren't exactly informative. Until Azrael extended a finger strike from Mantis Sickle. The movement was late in the form, and he hadn't yet gotten around to truly thinking about how it connected to the one before or after. The grunt from Maat was deep and disapproving enough to pull Azrael out of the motions.

"You worked on this since start of semester?" Maat asked, more disapproval tinting his words.

"I prefer the sword, sensei," Azrael responded, using the honorific and hoping that he was reading the situation correctly.

"Baleed, then use sword. Show Maat what you know."

For the next hour, Azrael went through his much more practiced sword forms. His focus during his free time sessions had been to work on forms that were more practical in fighting monsters. While he did want to get to the other forms that were more prominent in competition, he knew that the large motion and more powerful swinging ones designed for combat against monsters would have a more immediate impact. Maat's grunts had become more approving, but Azrael only received a few that he could definitively say were wholehearted acknowledgement. He tried to figure out what he had done in those moments, but he honestly couldn't tell. He finished a diagonal slash and held the final position, sweating.

"That's all of them."

"Amateur at best. What monster you fight that is size of human? What monster you attacked that does not need a skill to defeat?" Maat's questions were clearly rhetorical because the answers to both were also obvious, at least to Azrael. "You focus too much compacting movements. This good. Still, not true efficiency. You look internally, should look at past fight that lose or fled. These are outcomes that warrior must change. Detention is finished. Come back tomorrow and use brain!"

Azrael watched Maat turn and leave the stadium dungeon, moving toward a small door that Azrael had never been through. A smile grew the longer he thought about the gruff advice. His 'detention' was just extra hours of practice and instruction. He would have paid good crystals to have a one-on-one tutoring session with the martial teacher.

Leaving through the main door, Azrael made his way back to the villa as the sun began dipping below the horizon. Something bumped into him, and he looked down to find Louis climbing back up from the ground.

"What's up, Louis?" Azrael asked, assuming that the chef had been sent to tell him something.

"We are going to the coliseum to conquer it," the multi-toned, never meant for a human throat, voice of Apep answered him. The voice shocked Azrael, and he immediately grabbed Louis, and hurriedly dragged him into the shadow of a nearby tree.

"Apep? You can't just take control of someone like this and roam around!" Azrael whispered with as much command as he could. "We talked about this!"

"Louis is not an army," Louis-Apep argued. "He is but one man and can go unnoticed. Oberan said, 'When overwhelming force is not an option, one must use subterfuge.'"

By the Sovereign. Any stupid decision made by Apep seemed to be under the directions of Oberan. The man was dead, but he still seemed to want to inconvenience Azrael. "Apep, right now you are at the direct center of power in all of Gaia. If you were to capture a dungeon here or be revealed, your presence on this planet would be known and immediately communicated to the entire universe."

"So?"

"So, any dungeon you currently control will be destroyed, and they will then be on the lookout for dungeons controlled by you in the future."

"They cannot destroy Apep."

"Sure, but they can destroy Azrael!"

"Why should Apep worry about that?" Apep responded, his voice only that of Oberan.

"Because right now I am your best chance to conquer the oldest and strongest planet in the EtherVerse!"

There was a long pause after Azrael's pronouncement and he breathed heavily, hoping he wouldn't have to kill Louis and begin eradicating Apep-controlled dungeons himself. There was a good chance that his small connection to Apep would go unnoticed, but unfortunately if all the dungeons that began acting up were ones he and his team had run, it would likely be too large of a coincidence to overlook.

"How did I get out here?" Louis said and Azrael sighed.

"What's the last thing you remember?"

"I was just cleaning up the kitchen and starting my own meal."

"You were acting strange a moment ago. Maybe it's a side effect of your rebirth? Let me know if it happens again?"

"You are sure I shouldn't go see a healer?"

"I'm positive."

———

"Apep can control humanoid minions outside his controlled dungeons?" Bat asked incredulously. "It's strange, because there is a connection kind of like yours that attaches to Louis."

"You didn't think to mention that earlier!" Azrael groaned in response.

"Well, Apep had never taken over your mind, plus I told you this was a horrible idea!"

"Thanks for that one, Bat." Azrael closed his eyes again and returned to meditation. He'd pulled Bat to the fourth floor and begun repairing a rather large workroom as an excuse to be alone with his friend. He had been hoping for some insight, but should have expected the 'told you so.'

After a few moments of silence, Bat responded. "I think we should be careful from now on. It doesn't seem like you can control Apep, and if you continue to expand his power on the planet, it might not end well."

Azrael nodded in response and waited.

"Do you think it's worth trying to remove his control from the four dungeons you already infected?" Bat asked the question Azrael had been considering already.

"I'm hoping I don't have to. Apep is just too good of a tool to discard. I am actually hoping to use it to give Magnus a bit of payback."

"You mean the Rainbow dungeon?" Bat concluded. "I've heard that it's far stronger than the El Dorado dungeons, and I don't think we would have defeated any of those on our own…"

"I know. That's why I am waiting until we get stronger. For now, is there any way that you can see to control that connection I have with Apep?"

"I still think attempting the Rainbow dungeon is a bad idea, and as for your question… Honestly, it seems to be made of Ether and something else I can't see. So unless you figure out what that second power is, then no, I don't think we can do anything."

"It has to be Essence." Azrael focused on the point at the end of his spiraling Ether. He was careful not to touch it, but he really needed to figure out how he could. That phantasmal energy was something that the powerful could use, and if he gained control as a Journeyman… he may just increase his odds of revenge.

CHAPTER FORTY-ONE

Azrael sat in the Spell Casting class, which he only had to take two times a week. As a damage dealer role who specialized in melee combat, his afternoon was scheduled with five combat classes. It was different for mage classes or ranged classes, who then had only two combat classes and five Spell Casting or Ranged Combat classes. Madame Marjoree stood at the front of the classroom.

The venue for this class changed every week, and would range from a cave, to a training room, to a typical tiered classroom. Madame claimed this was to help the students master spells in varying environments, without destroying the spaces themselves. Today they were in a classroom that had fifty meter long lanes with a stone statue acting as a target on the far end. The sides of the long lane were filled with glass vials and beakers. Four line-ups of students were waiting for their turn to attempt to try the exercise. Each student at the front of the line was attempting to control their ranged spells to cause maximum damage to the stone bust of a monster without destroying or disturbing any of the very fragile equipment that lined the walls.

With the thought of midterms and finals around the corner, Azrael was currently trying to think of any spell he could use in this environment to destroy the monster without destroying every piece of glass on display. He ran through his skills; Blood-letter was only good on living creatures that bled, and even then it was a damage multiplier and damage over time skill. Soul Storage was probably his most versatile, but he would need to ask another student to fill it with a skill that wasn't Soul Strike if he wanted to use it. He glanced at Jophi, who was the only option he could use for that strategy.

Keep thinking, and use her as a last resort.

Call of the Soul was similar to Bloodletter in that it would increase his damage, which in this case likely just meant more destruction of the fragile glass. Soul Cloak was purely defensive, but did help him with orienting himself after Demon Step, which currently was the only skill he could think of that gave him a chance of success in this test. Ether Burn, while precise, wasn't a particularly high damage skill, not to mention that the statue didn't possess Ether. That really only left him Demon Step combined with Soul Storage and Soul Cloak to get him out of this.

He surveyed the shadows of the lane, and saw that the statues were lit from below and above, making numerous shadows. The problem was that his Demon Step ability had an effective range of fifty meters, and the statue was at the very edge of that range. While he had still been practicing with the skill on his own around the villa and on his walks from classes, he had found that the farther he ported, the more disorienting the skill became.

The person in front of him used a wind bullet spell that took a large chunk out of the monster statue and only knocked down three glass vials due to the turbulence the projectile left in its wake. The statue sank into the ground and was slowly replaced by another as Azrael stepped to the front of his line. He took one more look at Jophi who had already finished her turn, having melted the statue without breaking a single fragile item.

He shrugged to himself; this isn't the midterm or final yet, despite Madame Marjoree hinting that it was something that would likely be included in both of the aforementioned tests. Azrael looked around himself and found only one usable shadow, the teacher's assistant with the clipboard, which instantly reminded him that he couldn't use the shadows of the statue. He raised a hand and the older student who was holding the clipboard raised an eyebrow. "Is there a problem?"

"Yes, I have two abilities that would work in this situation, but I can't use it on a statue."

"The test is the test, student…" the man faded off, clearly looking for Azrael to supply his name which he did. "Student Azrael. I'm afraid exceptions can't be made for any one student."

"Then can I have a moment to get prepared?" Azrael responded, thinking his only remaining opportunity was to have Jophi load up his Soul Storage with two skills that would work here.

Before the teacher's assistant, whose name was Arthur, could respond, Magnus shouted, "Oh, does Merlin's prospective student need help from someone to pass a simple mock test?" Laughter broke out from the nearby students and Azrael shook his head. Wasn't that the point of this particular test? Using spells or skills you possessed in an intelligent way that wouldn't cause widespread destruction.

Jophi, who must have heard Azrael's initial request, began making her way in his direction. Azrael held up a hand; this was just a mock test, and Magnus' goading had actually allowed him to think of a possibility. He was one of Merlin's prospective students, and what was the only thing Merlin was trying to teach him?

He reached into himself and began his meditation. Once he was in the right state of mind, he stopped his churning pool and pulled every drop of Ether from his channels. Then once he had all two-hundred and ninety drops, he spooled it out, creating a channel with a diameter of five feet. Azrael felt sweat drip down his brow as he pushed the channel out past his skin and down the tunnel. When he got to five meters in front of him, his brain told him he couldn't go any farther.

Clenching his jaw, he created a second wall of containment at the center of the channel, almost like a bored hole. He increased the size of this hole until he created a thin tube like the barrel of a gun. Now with his Ether less dispersed, he was able to stretch the tube another ten meters before his brain gave him the same warning. His teeth whined as he strained his jaw muscles farther and narrowed the tube from five feet to four, then three and finally stopped at two feet in diameter. Now he was able to stretch the tube forty meters, but he could feel his whole body shaking with the effort.

Deep in his meditation, he still knew that he would pass out if he held this for too long, or tried to push the construct any more. Hurriedly, he pulled out his Soul Sword and thrust it out into the Ether Tunnel he created, while mentally commanding, *<Release ten! Release ten!>* He fell back onto his butt from the recoil of the double Soul Storage release, but focused on holding the channel. He felt the skill scrape the walls as it surged down the construction in his mind. He even felt the moment that the skill, which automatically spun like a drill, began to increase in centrifugal force.

In the blink of an eye, the skill traversed the Ether Channel and exploded out the end like a ballistic bullet. Azrael heard the boom of a cannon before concrete dust bloomed from the far end of the lane. The ground under his butt shook and he watched dumbfounded as the entire lane began to collapse in on itself. The sound of every beaker and vial breaking seemed extremely loud in the silence of the students, teaching assistants, and Madame Marjoree. Azrael pulled back in his channel and found that more than half of his original pool was missing.

Jophi moved up to help Azrael to his feet. "I think you missed the point of this test… I also think you are holding out on me when it comes to those skills Merlin is trying to teach you," she whispered. Azrael found that she was smiling at him.

He grimaced but nodded to her. It was probably about time he showed her the Essence Conversion skill.

"Madame Marjoree," Arthur began from beside Azrael, where he had retreated to upon the start of the collapse. "I'm unsure how to rate that particular attempt. Would you care to offer your opinion?"

"I would prefer that students do their experimentation of new skills outside of my class, Azrael. Still, you did destroy the statue before destroying any glass vials. We will call it a D minus on this attempt. Barely a pass. I would expect more from a prospective student of Merlin's…"

Azrael let his head hang as Marjoree's words sunk in. She was right; he had let Magnus goad him into trying something before he had fully thought it through. He glanced at the tall blond boy, only to find him wearing an expression of utter shock and looking away. Azrael followed his gaze and found Merlin smiling at him. It was only for the briefest of moments before he spun and vanished.

Maybe that wasn't a total failure then?

"So, I just need to change the flow in each channel until I have a whirlpool in my Ether pool," Jophi repeated what Azrael just said.

"More or less. I originally discovered it on Tech Duinn by slowly narrowing my channels as they rejoined the pool. It's easy in theory—"

"Done," Jophi interrupted him, and he blinked. Okay, maybe it was time to admit that Bat and Jophi were both better than him at Ether Control. Azrael glanced at Bat, who was smiling widely. The Batman was overjoyed that Azrael had chosen to share this skill with Jophi, finally.

Azrael rolled his eyes at his friend and turned back to Jophi. "Can you try not to share this new skill with your guild? I'm pretty sure they might already know it, because the teachers they recruited from the academy probably have it, but…"

"I already told you I am not spying for them anymore, Azrael. I assume you don't want to tell Oslow and Prateek about this skill yet, or they would be here, right?"

"Not yet. I think this skill is the reason Merlin picked me as a prospective student. I've got a strange feeling that the upside to this skill is something that Merlin wants people to earn…"

"I know you don't trust the guilds, Azrael, but honestly, if the teachers of this academy knew this skill, they already would have shared it with the leadership," Bat said, adding his voice to the conversation.

Azrael nodded and looked around the room, recalling Merlin's question to him in the interviews and the function of this house itself. "Something tells me this skill is just the start, Bat…" he whispered in response.

———

Wodensday morning, Azrael had Dungeon Dynamics, which was a theory class. It focused so far on the types of dungeons and the strategies that were common to defeat each. Today, the teacher had discussed the variation between puzzle dungeons, trap dungeons, and maze dungeons. Specifically, how to tell them apart if you found yourself in a wild one. Azrael took notes despite already knowing most of the subject matter.

It was nearing the end of class when the teacher made an announcement. "For the midterm and final, this class will be doing group presentations. They will account for seventy percent of your grade. Twenty percent of which will come from the midterm pre-presentation, and fifty percent will come from the final portion.

"Groups and subjects are on the notices that should have just been sent to your user interface. Find your group members, and use the rest of this class to discuss what you might present on the subject you were given. If you need any help or direction, come see me or one of the teacher assistants."

Azrael found his name in group eight, and slowly stood up to look for the students that were holding up the hand signal that corresponded. It turned out that he didn't need to even look for that. Amelie, the teacher, had put numbers up at the side of each row in the auditorium. Azrael scanned the room and found four students already at the number eight. It was the fifth student that made his jaw clench.

Magnus stood speaking with group number eight, and Azrael double checked the group assignments. He sighed when he discovered no Magnus in the list. But then what was the oaf doing?

He rushed down the stairs toward his group, but didn't catch the conversation. By the time he arrived, Magnus was already turned away and walking up the stairs with a large, self-satisfied smile. The fact that Magnus didn't take the opportunity to jibe at Azrael made his stomach turn itself into knots. He hesitantly approached the group he was assigned and forced his face into a smile.

"Alright, high-level dungeons. There is a ton of information under that umbrella, what should each of us present?" Azrael asked, hoping his false cheeriness wasn't as apparent to the others.

No one responded and Azrael blinked. None of the group would meet his eyes. He analyzed each in turn, noting that not a single member wore clothing of the Asgardian guild. "Come on, guys, you have to have at least heard of a few powerful dungeons, even if you haven't been in one. I would say we focus on the clear line of delineation between dungeons that create a space using the planet and its surrounding resources, and the ones that are powerful enough to create pocket dimensions. Then another one of us could go into how that allows instancing of the—"

"We're sorry, Azrael," a tall, whip-thin teenager said as he stared at the ground. "Magnus threatened to have us removed from our guilds and expelled from the school if we didn't purposefully fail this class."

Azrael's eyes widened and he looked up the stairs in the direction Magnus had gone. The Asgardian was smiling down at him, his amusement clear. "You have to know he doesn't have that kind of power! And what does failing a course get you? Other than being expelled?"

"Well, he said he would get us all spots in Asgard if we did. He even promised to get us reinstated as first years on next year's intake..." This time it was a short female Karacy that spoke. She wore the guild colors of the Mountain Tribe and also refused to look at him.

"Really?" he called up the stairs to Magnus. "You think that Amelie will just let this happen?"

"Let what happen?" Amelie said as she looked up from another group who must have asked her for help.

"Magnus has told my group that he will get them expelled and removed from their guilds if they don't purposefully fail this class."

"Is that true, Mr. Thorson?" Amelie shouted up the stairs and disengaged her group of students with a stern expression.

"Of course not!" Magnus responded, with mock outrage. "Why would I want students to purposefully fail a class?"

Amelia frowned and approached Azrael's group. "Speak," she commanded and each of the four denied that Magnus had done anything. Azrael felt his teeth clench again.

"Azrael, I'm afraid I will need to keep you in this group, but mark you only on your own merit," Professor Amelia said with a frown. She could clearly tell something was off with his group, but without their admissions it was just Azrael's word against Magnus'.

"Pick a topic under the heading of your assigned subject. Make sure it isn't a topic someone else from this 'group' has chosen. You will be graded on your own performance."

The tall whip-thin kid glanced at Magnus and must have received some sort of sign because now the group began discussing what subjects they would cover. Azrael, who was currently trying not to unleash a Soul Strike into the four, listened, taking notes as to what each student was planning to cover.

Magnus is becoming a true nuisance...

CHAPTER FORTY-TWO

"The role of a damage dealer isn't as simple as dumping your Ether and destroying enemies. At times, a damage dealer must prevent a blow on the tank with a precise strike, or they must hold back to allow the tank time. While many places in the world will value a damage dealer in a group by his top end skill, the truly great groups will value a damage dealer for their decision making."

Azrael listened to the teacher continue his lecture and smiled. This was nearly identical to a lecture he'd received in the Sovereign Halls. Only there, this lecture was focused on the strategy to be multifaceted. To be able to fulfill any role in a group so as to better infiltrate into foreign territory. That or how to disable groups using these very tactics if you were facing them on a front line. At the Atlantean Academy, they were teaching students so they could go out into the world and succeed. At the Sovereign Halls, they were teaching students to go out into the world and be useful. Small distinction, but one that Azrael contemplated currently.

Were the Sovereign Empire and my 'father' really all that great? Is the Empire deserving of vengeance?

His answer continually returned to his desire for it. Perhaps his vengeance would help the Empire, but more than likely it would just make him feel better. The teacher began demonstrating the types of support skills that damage dealers in the group should try to cultivate, and Azrael came out of his contemplation. He had a few skills that could be used in ways to offtank or distract, but he had almost none that were precise. Perhaps that would be something he could try to obtain in the future.

Can Ether Burn be considered precise?

He glanced at the group around him, trying to determine a way that a precise skill could be beneficial. Jophi was squarely in the category of large and flashy for her high end damage, but had some precise skills as well. In fact, she was a great compliment to him, who had little in precision skill, but good survivability as an offtank. Then there was Bat, who currently was back at the villa. Bat was easily the least defended of the group, but also the most versatile. His top end damage might not be as high as Azrael or Jophi, but he had great distraction skills and also skills that were extremely precise. Since today's class wasn't at all about tanks and healers, he ignored Prateek and Oslow in his assessment. The three original group members were intriguing enough as it was. It was almost like they were perfectly paired... or maybe grew to complement each other?

Azrael raised his hand and waited for the teacher to see it.

"—some groups... Yes?" Professor Gnarck said as he faded to a stop in his tirade and caught Azrael's hand.

"I was just wondering if you could touch on the importance of established groups and growing together," Azrael said, a bit sick and tired of Gnarck going through different types of skills and theoretical ways to use them. It was such a strange concept for Azrael, that people would try to think of possible uses for their skills outside of combat. It was like holding a sword and getting told to go practice forms while picturing the weapon in a hand.

Plus, his contemplation on his own group leaving him

behind after this lecture was making him slightly aggravated. He knew he had his own things to do, but honestly maybe the teacher could change their minds—because he'd much rather be in a dungeon than attempting to gather information on the Atlantean Towers.

The teacher made some reasonable points about group longevity and even strongly advocated for trying to never split a group, but ruined it by ending on the note of when it was appropriate to do so. Azrael sighed and joined his team as they made their way up the stairs and out of the amphitheater. He waited until they were halfway back to the villa before he spoke up. "Are you guys certain you can't wait until after my detention?"

"We've been over this, Az. We might not even be able to get in. Remember, you're the prospective apprentice of Merlin and thus carry the greatest clout of any of us. Otherwise, we are counting on Prateek's Hindu guild connection," Jophi emphasized a bit morosely. The fact that she still was refusing to use her Cathodiem connections was also obvious from the tone.

His face grew a few degrees warmer as he realized that some of his dislike of them leaving him behind stemmed from her not sleeping in the same room as him anymore. Or nearby, like they would in a dungeon. It was a strange enough realization that he actually could feel himself blush a bit. It wasn't like he hadn't been able to sleep without her in the room after they'd fixed a spare and before Oslow and Prateek moved in. It was just that he'd taken a bit of time to adjust to the silence. Yeah, that was it.

Regardless, they did speak on this and Azrael already agreed. It just felt strange to be left behind by the group. To not feel needed. He must have gotten used to being the leader on Tech Duinn, or something...

Louis met them at the Cussing Parrot and had a packed lunch for everyone but Azrael. Watching the Cussing Parrot depart didn't sit well with Azrael and so he went inside the house to sit down at the kitchen island and eat his own lunch.

Of course, the rattle and whine of the engines could be heard from inside the house, and so he still felt like he was outside watching.

As the noise faded away, Louis finally re-entered the villa and then the kitchen. "Do you have any plans for your week?"

"Just one, but it shouldn't take long," Azrael responded while taking a mouthful of food. He truly didn't plan to enter the Tower yet. He was more curious why Magnus would hand him a necklace that was so incredibly powerful. It seemed like a trap, and he wanted to check it out before committing to entering. He had already asked around the school to figure out if having Merlin's Mark meant you got access to the mythical dungeons, but so far none of the staff he had asked knew the answer. Should he ask a teacher?

The issue there would be the loss of the item. Even if it didn't grant him legal access to the dungeon, he wanted to hold onto it for later. It was like if an enemy handed you a battleship with a bomb on it. They clearly hoped that their enemy would fill it with their people and use it. Then they could devastate even more people at an opportune moment. However, if the individual took it apart and used the materials and technology to build their own, it was turning a trap into an advantage. Maybe not the best metaphor, but having access to the same towers that his father had never conquered was something he wouldn't hand over willingly.

"Do you have any special requests for meals when your team is away?" Louis asked, looking up from cleaning up the space. Azrael used Analyze and was surprised to find the cook already nearing the grind of the Apprentice levels.

"Level sixteen already, huh? I mean, if you have some quests and recipes that will give you higher Etherience, I will fund the ingredients. Within reason..." Louis was now a Chef de Partie, which he'd explained as being two full rarity tiers above his old class of a common Saucier.

"I have an excellent recipe for Minotaur Steaks that would be of minimal cost since you have some of the meat already."

Azrael nodded before leaving the kitchen. He walked up two flights of stairs and moved to the fifth bedroom that the group had been working on revitalizing. It was almost finished, which would mean that he or Jophi could move out of the shared bedroom. On second thought, he climbed another level and moved to the dojo there.

A quick glance at his system time told him he had about two hours before his afternoon combat class, and so he sat down to work on the assignment from Merlin.

———

His speed of repairing the villa with Ether still far outstripped the others, and he wondered if it had anything to do with his Essence Conversion skill's level. It did seem like he was able to use a strand of his internal Ether Channels that was ever closer to the bottom of the spiral. Still, his head ached as he moved through his combat forms. Magnus' face when he realized some of the others from his group were missing almost made up for Azrael being left behind.

The entire week he had been looking forward to each 'detention' session with Maat. After that first day, the big man had become much more hands on, even going as far as to spar lightly with him at times to help him see flaws in his adjusted forms. Today was the last day, and he was hoping Maat might teach him one of his own personal forms. Through the week, it had become increasingly obvious that the powerful man was far ahead of Azrael in terms of compacting his movements and making his forms more efficient.

"No detention, Azrael. I've got important meet with school benefactor," the large man said as he stormed by Azrael outside of the coliseum.

"Wait, can I maybe meet you after class next week then for more lessons?"

"I may not be teaching. All depend on meeting result. Walk with me," the teacher responded, which made Azrael's chest tighten. What did that even mean? Instead of asking, he turned and jogged to catch up with the larger teacher.

Once they were at the same speed, which admittedly was more of a speed walk for Azrael, he turned to Maat and asked, "What do you mean?"

"School has been losing top teachers for last few years. Guilds make offers to us all. We see way wind blows and of original sixty teachers, only twenty of us remain. New teachers replace old but they are young, and only here to look for opportunities with guilds. Atlantean Academy is slowly being picked clean. If not for Merlin, it already be empty of us old teachers."

"What does Merlin offer that keeps the teachers around?"

"Same thing he teach you." Maat stopped walking, causing Azrael to stop as well. He looked around and then leaned toward him and tried to whisper. "Essence Conversion." His whisper was more like a growling bear but there wasn't anyone near them for a few hundred meters.

"It isn't that difficult to learn, though? Once you've had some direction, it's very straightforward." Azrael scratched his head, trying to understand why teachers would stay to learn that skill.

"This will be impolite, but what level is skill currently?" Maat said with little to no shame, despite the first part of the sentence. Azrael knew that asking about someone's status was somewhat impolite, but from the context he had to assume that this was to make a point.

"Weak level eighteen."

"You're really close to stagnation point of skill. Mine Poor eight." Maat began walking again and Azrael joined him as he continued. "I had multiple one on one session beside Merlin, and all growth since Weak twenty-two is because of advice and guidance."

"So, teachers were staying to be taught by Merlin? Then the skill has amazing secondary characteristics at higher levels?"

"It does that, but it's more what teachers have seen Merlin do, that kept around."

"I'm confused. Hasn't anyone reached a similar level as him in the skill?"

"No, no one he taught made it out of the Weak rank. He tried many ways to teach but each person must find own path. I think my skill reached peak, and I think time I gained support of guild to attempt own research. Cathodiem offered me place, and I going into Atlantis to meet them. Blue Dragon restaurant. They much wanting Maat, no?"

Azrael felt his eyes raise. That restaurant was spoken about heavily by the students, with reservations taking years. "How did they get a reservation?"

"Many of top guilds have reservation for room all nights. Often no use. The best chefs in EtherVerse are there, and guild not know when they need to entertain or host."

Azrael's opinion of the guilds was already quite high, at least for their combat power, tactics, and wealth. Still, to see such a casual use of wealth and privilege in their recruiting was simultaneously impressive and stomach turning. How did you compete with powers like that? "Mind if I join you on the walk, then? I was heading into Atlantis anyway."

"Not at all. I assume you ask about perfecting forms?"

"Of course. I guess the most important question I have for you is how long have you been at it?"

"As Merlin says, there is neither beginning nor end in a journey. There are just milestones along way. As you learn from me this week, I also learned from you."

The walk continued as Maat explained his philosophy on the forms. Much of what the big man said widened Azrael's eyes. Why should you use forms that others are taught? Isn't it more effective to know your opponent's moves and them to not know yours? Maat claimed that every person on the journey for improving martial forms and fighting skills had their own path to take, and the only thing he learned in his long years of teaching was that you must observe others and try both the good and the bad you find. The teacher was a firm believer in muscle memory, as hinted at by the first day of lectures.

Azrael took some of the big man's philosophy and applied it to what Merlin was doing with him. If the principal had tried to teach hundreds, maybe even thousands of students in the past, why would he stop and suddenly stay distant from Azrael? All he could think of was that it was a new method of teaching he was trying. Maybe Merlin was hoping for Azrael to pick things up on his own?

How do you hold something that you can't see? Azrael returned to the first question the teacher had asked him. The same question he had reiterated in different ways throughout their brief encounters. As he was thinking, he and Maat arrived at the Blue Dragon and the big man offered him a handshake.

"I wish well, Azrael. Even though I go Cathodiem. I hope we spar again."

"Good luck, Maat."

He watched the teacher enter the grandiose building, which had two massive glass double doors and a ton of white stone which matched the other buildings Azrael had vaguely registered as they'd walked through the city. Now he stepped back to marvel at the city around him. He stood on an interlocked road made of gray stone and outlined by a black, knee-high curb. Each building had steps from the walkway to large doors. Each building could be called a work of art. Not a single one looked like the cookie cutouts Azrael was used to from the Sovereign Halls. They each were made from white stone and glass that seemed to glow blue in the light of the setting sun. Each contour of the neighboring one flowed into the next and was clearly planned to do so.

"This place is like some sort of fairy tale." They had crossed a bridge to enter the island and looking around, he could see that every space on the island was used for a building, which meant any establishment, house, or business inside Atlantis was wealthy or long established. Probably both. He oriented himself from the center tower and the four that were in each of the cardinal directions. He marked north and then began walking the beautiful street toward the eastern tower. The east was the first of the four cardinal dungeons that climbers would have to conquer if they wished to enter the others. At least according to everything he could find on the subject.

Every few hundred feet, a new building would need to be ogled, and it was perhaps after the fifth that he realized there weren't any vehicles that he could see. Either ones in the sky above the city or ones down on the street with him. A great many people walked the large thoroughfare around him, and they were all dressed finely. Additionally, every race he had ever heard or read about was on display. It was like a mixing pot of races, languages, and cultures. It was pleasant to him, and he again began deliberating over his chosen path of revenge.

Right up until someone bumped into him from behind. He immediately scolded himself for not paying closer attention to his surroundings like he'd been taught. He turned to apologize to the individual only to be grabbed about the shoulders.

"Do you have any idea who you're bumping into?" a man in a suit made of finely woven Iron Worm silk spat in his face.

Johnadeer Furdinan
Level 24
Journeyman-Hoplite
Health Points: 315 / 315
Skills: 12

His level wasn't impressive, and Azrael pulled his Soul Sword without hesitation, aiming the one end toward the man's neck. The man immediately backed off with wide-mouthed horror. "How dare you pull a weapon in Atlantis! Guards!"

Azrael allowed his blade to sink bank into his skin and watched with his breath held as guards and pedestrians rushed toward the two of them. A moment before, he hadn't even seen guards but suddenly from behind white columns men emerged carrying laser rifles and wearing strange white body armor. There were ten in total, and they quickly cordoned off Azrael and Johnadeer.

"Who drew their weapon?" one of the ten asked, and Azrael turned to see his helmet which covered his entire face had a yellow mark on the forehead.

"That barbarian did," Johnadeer practically shrieked. Azrael narrowed his eyes at the act he was putting on. He was so overdramatic that he was shaking as if he'd just suffered a near death experience.

"Sorry, gentlemen," Azrael began and forced his Soul Blade to coalesce onto his arm but not form. "It was an instinctual reaction when he grabbed me threateningly."

"Is your blade in a storage device?"

Azrael nodded in confirmation, and he had the pleasure to see Johnadeer pale. A spacial storage device was still relatively rare to possess and could denote wealth. Perhaps the idiot was finally realizing he was playing a dangerous game. Azrael suspected he had targeted him because of his less than impressive clothing, or because someone had hired him. The captain of the guards turned to Johnadeer. "Why did you grab this man?"

"He bumped into me and threatened me. I didn't grab him."

"He grabbed the boy, I saw it," somebody in the crowd shouted, and a few others chimed in in the affirmative. Johnadeer paled further.

"I don't plan to press any charges, gentlemen. Can we go about our day since no one was hurt?"

"Well, I do plan to press charges," Johnadeer crowed, his voice taking on a victorious undertone that was impossible for Azrael to miss. "This bumpkin has not only run into me but has defamed my good character. The character of the Furdinan family!"

One of the guards pulled out a notepad and Azrael sighed. "Fine then, I would like to file charges as well…"

"Too late, he already chose not to."

"No, actually I said I planned not to, but plans change."

The guard with the notepad out turned to Azrael first. "We

will begin with the most severe of the charges. Since this man was assaulted intentionally, that means we need your statement. What's your name and position?"

Azrael looked at Johnadeer before he rolled his eyes and answered. "I was willing to let this go, but my name is Azrael. I am a student of the Atlantean Academy, and more specifically a prospective-apprentice of Merlin—"

All the guards flinched. Johnadeer flinched and began making a strangled sort of noise in his throat. "Do you have any proof of that?" Clearly, the guard was talking about Azrael's claim of being an apprentice of the headmaster.

He began to shake his head before he remembered that he technically had the mark that Magnus had thrown at him. He deliberated about using it, as it wasn't his. "Why do you need proof of that? Can't you just find out by inquiring at the school?"

Johnadeer's eyes, which had been wide and fearful a moment before, seemed to regain some sparkle as he blinked. The man's lips even twitched into a smile. "Clearly, the boy is lying. An apprentice of Merlin wouldn't be walking around here without an entourage of other students and sycophants."

"Prospective apprentice," Azrael corrected offhandedly as he continued to deliberate.

The guard ignored Johnadeer's words and even went as far as to roll his eyes at the Hoplite. "We can certainly inquire with the school, but depending on the severity of the charges that Johnadeer wishes to press, we may have to hold you in a cell until trial. It would take at least a day to hear back from the school and we couldn't release you from the cell without bail or a guarantor. Merlin's name carries quite a bit of weight in Atlantis, and his prospective apprentice would be able to remain free until the time of a trial."

Sighing deeply, Azrael shrugged. He couldn't pull out the mark that Magnus had 'given' him. He knew that Magnus had something up his sleeve or planned in regards to that particular item. Azrael wouldn't be surprised to learn that it was reported stolen.

Instead he responded, "I guess I will have to accompany you to the nearest guard station and wait for Merlin to be contacted."

"As you wish. Please follow me," the guard responded and Azrael gave Johnadeer a withering look before following after the guards as they marched both of them away from the crowd.

———

It was Voskrenie, two mornings after his arrest, and Azrael was standing at the bars to his holding cell. It was hard to sleep, as anytime he closed his eyes, memories of the Pit dungeon seemed to bubble up from his psyche.

Johnadeer had posted bail almost immediately that first night, which grated on Azrael. Johnadeer was charged with disrupting the peace of Atlantis, which was a small comfort to Azrael. Still, Azrael was also looking at a charge for Threatening Behavior with a weapon in Atlantis, which was a more severe accusation.

Maat had come by yesterday to speak on his behalf, and confirm that Azrael was a student of the academy. Despite his confirmation that Azrael was a prospective apprentice of Merlin, the guards hadn't freed Azrael. There was something deeper going on. Something political.

Magnus and the Asgardian guild were likely behind it, but Azrael was forced to endure the treatment. His only hope was that Merlin would eventually get around to responding to the guards' calls and requests. According to all his and Maat's inquiries, the guards needed to speak to the headmaster to acquire more significant proof.

His group had also visited last night and told Azrael that the same shenanigans were at work in El Dorado. His eye twitched and his mouth turned into a sneer. Three days wasted, not only for him but for everyone in his group, was infuriating.

His cell door opened and Azrael blinked before focusing his eyes on the approaching guard. "What's going on?" he asked.

"Please follow me," the guard said and led the way to a nearby room with a metal table and four uncomfortable chairs inside. On the table was Azrael's gear, which had been taken from him upon arrest. One man was already sitting at the table, and he had a manila folder in front of him. "Please have a seat," the guard who had led him here said and indicated a chair across from the seated man.

Moving around the table, Azrael studied that seated figure. He had dark black hair, and darkly tanned skin. His eyes were a light brown that seemed to glow. Azrael's scrutiny triggered Analyze.

Themis Athen
Master-Justicar
Level 41
Health Points: 4,300 / 4,300
Skills: Unknown

Azrael sat down. Themis looked him over for a moment before looking down at his folder and pulling out a few papers. On papers were pictures, and Azrael tilted his head to try to make out the object depicted. His heart began to beat erratically as he recognized it.

"Your assailant in Atlantis, one Johnadeer Furdinan, has filed a report claiming that he was attempting to recover stolen property that he saw you holding. According to his claims, you were in possession of a Mark of Merlin that he recognized as belonging to Thor Odinson. We must confirm that this isn't the case to dismiss his accusation and release you. Please empty your storage device…"

Azrael felt his jaw clench, but instead of doing as he was told, he responded, "The burden of truth lies with the accuser, does it not?"

Themis tilted his head as a small frown settled onto his face. "As you can imagine, when something is stolen from the most powerful man on Gaia, the line for the burden of truth wavers slightly."

"Even if I have a Mark of Merlin, I am one of his prospective apprentices, which Johnadeer knows..."

"Are you denying having a Mark of Merlin or having the stolen Mark of Merlin?" Themis asked as he narrowed his eyes.

Azrael kept his face impassive and refused to respond to those questions. There were a fair number of skills that could indicate truth from lie, and those skills could indicate he had the item without asking if he 'stole' the item, which was a significant problem.

Magnus and the Asgardians... Azrael sneered and clenched his jaw as he stopped speaking.

"I will warn you that this report is going to be forwarded to the Asgardian guild in twenty four hours if you don't prove it invalid. Thor has requested to be kept apprised of any lead found in the investigation of the theft."

CHAPTER FORTY-THREE

"He is my prospective apprentice, and I have given him one of my Marks. Thank you for contacting me, Lieutenant. Please tell Azrael to come back to the villa immediately. I would like to have a word." The blue holo-image of Merlin finished before he flashed off the desk of the lieutenant. They'd questioned Azrael all morning, but were forced to stop when Merlin finally contacted the head of the unit. They actually brought Azrael into the room and revealed the situation in front of the headmaster.

Azrael had held his breath but was rather surprised to hear the headmaster not only offer to pay his bail, but that his sponsor lied on his behalf.

It was painfully obvious that if he revealed it to the Atlantean guards, he would be blamed for theft. His only shot was that Merlin would listen to the whole story. Merlin was acutely aware that Azrael should not have had one of his marks. So, the fact that he had taken his side likely meant he would listen.

Azrael fought the urge to run a hand through his hair in distress as the lieutenant narrowed his eyes at him.

"Well, I guess that settles that," Azrael said as he stood up and began walking toward the door.

"I'll give you twenty-four hours before I send this report on to the Asgardian guild. Even Merlin's word might not protect you from an illegal search. Do you understand?"

Azrael looked back at the lieutenant and nodded. He did understand, or at least he thought he did. He hurried out of the barracks and back across the long, elegant bridge that separated the floating Atlantis from the Atlantean Academy.

His brain whirred with possible excuses the entire way back to the villa. As far as he could tell, there wasn't a way for him to keep the mark which would have given him access to the tower. He was planning to tell Merlin the truth either way, but he assumed his mentor would force him to hand over the necklace. Magnus hadn't had the right to give it to him, obviously.

With his fixation on the upcoming talk with Merlin, he walked by the Cussing Parrot on the way to the front door and when he opened it, he found Bat, Jophi, Prateek, and Oslow sitting in the living room meditating. Louis was clearly in the kitchen cooking, if the noises coming from behind the large, insulated door were an indicator.

"I'm assuming that there were still problems with getting into a dungeon this morning?" Azrael said in way of announcing his return.

"Asgard Guild is currently running an initiative level up through any available dungeons, worldwide. They are hoping to get more students into the academy at the end of the semester. Most of the smaller guilds are bending over backward to charter some good will," Jophi responded as she opened her eyes from the meditation.

"Is that even possible?" Azrael asked, not having heard about a mid-year recruitment for the school.

Jophi shook her head and sighed. "Not really, no. But if people fail, then those spots become open and can be filled. You should probably hear this from us first, but the initiates are all vying for your spot specifically."

Azrael laughed out of surprise. This was a childish rumor or tactic, even for Magnus. Especially after the rather well thought out plan he had just enacted. After shaking his head to clear the surprise and humor from his thoughts, he turned to look at Jophi. "Have you seen Merlin at all? He's supposed to—"

"Azrael, please come with me," the headmaster said from behind him. He turned and saw Merlin in the door, his robe billowing out behind him in a wind. Azrael hadn't remembered feeling a strong breeze on his walk. A quick glance back at his party showed that they had all stood to full attention. Each set of eyes was on the headmaster with mixed levels of awe, greed, or fear.

Azrael turned back to the man and began closing the distance to him and the front door. Merlin stepped aside and motioned toward the decrepit gazebo that looked one strong wind away from collapsing. It hadn't even been mentionable upon first view of the villa because of the long grass, but thanks to Jess at the ship pads, it was now mentionable as a safety risk.

Azrael stepped onto the boards of the structure first and the ominous creak made him pull up and stop. He turned back to Merlin, who clucked his tongue at the sound. The man waved a hand and Azrael watched in amazement as a wave washed over the wood. Just like in the house, the wood repaired itself, even the semi-fallen beams popped back up a few inches, making the roof straighten. The underside of the roof also transformed, going from decaying to just unmaintained. "It should be safe from falling on us now," Merlin said as he moved into the center of the structure. "I expect you to start speeding up on the villa's repairs…"

"You make that look so easy. That would have taken all five of us a full day of meditation," Azrael commented as he looked around himself at the semi-repaired space. If Merlin was talking about the repairs, maybe Azrael wasn't in as much trouble as he originally thought.

Merlin didn't smile and Azrael felt sweat break out on his skin when his eyes returned to the headmaster. Merlin waved his hand again and a sheen of distorted air surrounded the space. It was very noticeable because everything outside of the gazebo was suddenly blurred, as if being seen through clear water. "Tell me where you got my mark."

The story came out of Azrael's mouth as if it was poison from a wound. Merlin listened and asked clarifying questions that seemed to lead to a direct yes or no. "I hadn't thought that you'd stolen it, as the theft occurred when you were upgrading your class. Still, to think that Magnus took it and threw it away. By right of law, it is actually now your belonging, but the enchantment with access to the first tower is quite literally priceless."

"Your mark doesn't normally come with that?"

"No, Azrael, it doesn't. Once every ten years in Atlantis, a tournament is held for that privilege. Let's just say that Thor losing it won't go over well."

"You're not going to tell me to give it back?"

"If you'd taken it, I would have forced you to give it back. However, my spell has confirmed everything you've said. Magnus intentionally dropping the mark and then setting all of this up has shown he intended for you to take it. By Gaian loot laws, that does make it yours, but I don't think the Asgardian guild would see it that way. What would you like to do?"

"What if I gave it to you?"

"I'd give it back to Thor; I have no need for an enchantment to enter the first tower."

"So, you'd suggest giving it back then?"

"That is not what I said. I would give it back, but for you there is a great deal of value in that enchantment. So, I will ask again; what would you like to do?"

"Obviously I'd love to keep it, but I can't take on the Asgardian guild."

"No, you cannot, but you are also my prospective apprentice, and I could give you one of my marks. Yet my mark is usually reserved for full apprentices. So, the police report saying you have one will be slightly suspicious, especially to Thor.

However, I will gladly claim to have given you one if you would like. Most importantly, though, do you think Magnus will tell his father that he gave his mark to you?"

Azrael blinked. While Merlin was breaking it down and making it rather simplistic, it was a good point. He thought about all the complications that still would likely arise, even if Merlin did tell Thor that the necklace was not the stolen one. Most likely suspicion would be aroused and Asgard would take even greater stalling actions against Azrael.

"While you are right, it doesn't mean that Thor couldn't get me into a room and ask me a very different set of questions. If he also possesses some sort of truth detection, then all he needs to ask is if I possess his necklace."

"Good, you're thinking it through. So, are you going to give it back?" The inflection in Merlin's voice did seem to hint that there were still other options. Azrael began thinking furiously. If having the necklace on him was dangerous, he could hide it.

But then Thor can just ask if I know where the necklace is.

But what if Azrael wasn't the one to hide it. "What if I asked you to hide the necklace for me?"

Merlin smiled and stroked his beard in consideration. "You're on the right track, but I won't be able to help you in that manner. All the best." Merlin waved a hand and suddenly Azrael was alone in the gazebo. A quick look around showed him that the barrier was gone as well. On the ground where Merlin had stood was an identical necklace to the one that Magnus had thrown at him. Azrael picked it up and smiled as well.

I wonder what Thor or Asgard did to Merlin to have him react this way...

He would have to get Bat to hide the necklace and begin coming up with scripted answers for some of the other dangerous questions that could be asked. A great example would be if someone asked Azrael if he ever held Thor's necklace. His answer would have to be something along the lines of, Magnus once showed it to him. He continued to consider the problem from all angles as he walked back into the villa.

"Wait, do you think Magnus will take away access to the Rainbow dungeon over this?" Azrael mumbled to himself. Much of the grind of other dungeons was leading to that eventual dungeon dive. His gut knotted itself and he was certain that was exactly what Magnus would do.

"Guys, I think it's time to cash in that trip to the Rainbow dungeon that Magnus owes me," he stated as he walked into the kitchen.

"You know we won't be able to clear it right?" Bat said instantly, his large ears standing straight up.

"I've got a feeling that Magnus is going to go back on that bet if we don't take the opportunity tomorrow morning. That, and it doesn't seem like we have another option, anymore."

"What did you do?" Jophi asked, her tone condescending.

"Why do you assume I did anything?"

"He definitely did something," Prateek said as the others groaned or rolled their eyes.

"Listen, do you guys want to come or not?" Azrael wasn't in the mood for this, especially when he couldn't explain the situation to them. Magnus had really put him into a corner by reporting that he had Thor's Mark of Merlin.

The others eventually came around, even with Azrael refusing to say anything more. Once that happened, Azrael pulled Bat aside and handed him the Mark of Merlin with the enchantment on it. "Hide this somewhere and do not tell me where it is. Also, avoid being questioned by anyone in the Asgard Guild."

"Does this have anything to do with the rush to attack the Rainbow dungeon?" At Azrael's nod Bat continued, "Aren't I the first one people will think to interrogate after you?"

"Yes, but you're the only one who will do this without asking questions!" Azrael said pointedly.

"You really need to expand your circle of trust, Azrael. You're about to bring this group into a dungeon where they will

risk dying and you don't feel comfortable telling them why…
What happens if they send people into the dungeon after us to
kill us?"

"If we don't run the dungeon now, we probably won't get
another chance… Do you really think they would send people
in after us?"

"They didn't even know us and their 'recruiters' force fed us
a Heartworm…"

"All the more reason we should try to disrupt their strongest
dungeon." Azrael finished, his voice low and menacing.

Bat's ears drooped, but his friend let the conversation drop.

CHAPTER FORTY-FOUR

"I've got five hundred crystals that says your pitiful group won't even be able to get past the first Realm!" Magnus said. The fact that Magnus was suspended from school for two weeks and still causing both Azrael and the group problems was frustrating enough that Azrael felt his eye twitch.

Azrael ignored the bet and raised the eyebrow on the same eye that was betraying his anger "I'm just glad that you're going to hold to your earlier bet. Remember that one? Free access to the Rainbow dungeon…"

"Honestly, I've seen Master class groups fail and die in there. You seriously think you and these misfits have a chance?"

"We're not expecting to conquer the entire dungeon, Magnus," Jophi came to Azrael's defense.

"I'm just saying that there is going to be a lot of problems if you go in and die, Jophi," Magnus responded, his voice not actually concerned.

"Just get us access, please," Azrael said while crossing his arms. As far as he could tell from what little information existed outside of the Asgardian elite, the Rainbow dungeon had nine levels that were practically worlds unto themselves. To advance from one Realm to another, there were multiple options in the form of conquest, bosses, or wealth. And most of that information came from Jophi who had family members who had run the Rainbow dungeon before. Still, the more Azrael heard, the more he realized that this dungeon wasn't something typical. In fact, Jophi claimed that there were things her family member couldn't reveal and she didn't know why.

Magnus shook his head and approached the rather large man who leaned against a grounded greatsword. "Heimdall, this group would like to enter the dungeon."

"Are you going to pay for their fee?" Heimdall responded coolly. Azrael studied the muscular man. His eyes were a vibrant orange, and his skin was somewhere between tanned and black. He wore armor that looked extremely thick and heavy, but he didn't seem to mind the weight.

Heimdall Gullintani
Epic-Watcher
Level 44
Health Points: Undefined
Skills: Hidden

"I'll use my yearly allowance from the guild," Magnus mumbled and Azrael couldn't hide his smile at Magnus' tone. Heimdall seemed to notice Azrael's smug expression and his eyes twinkled with something that could have been amusement or displeasure.

"As you wish, Thorson." Heimdall hefted the sword off the ground and walked backward into a circular room. Magnus didn't follow and after a moment, Heimdall called from inside the sphere, "Enter, young ones."

The group all jumped and rushed in, leaving Magnus outside. Something about Magnus' downcast expression as Azrael walked by didn't seem natural. Was the kid smirking?

As soon as Azrael entered the sphere, he forgot all about Magnus. He felt his mouth fall open. They were standing in the center of the sphere but could see the entirety of it from the clear glasslike platform they stood upon. The inside was gold with runes carved extensively upon every surface. In the center of the room, where Heimdall stood, there was a crystal pedestal, almost a throne. The large man had grounded his sword behind the pedestal and seemed to wait on the group to approach.

As they approached, he asked, "Are you familiar with the nine Realms?" When everyone shrugged or shook their head, Heimdall continued, "The ninth Realm that you will enter first is known as Helheim. To clear the world, you will either need to defeat Garm or slay a thousand fallen dead who didn't make it to Valhalla. If you complete either of the tasks, you will be granted access to the eighth Realm, Niflheim. A world of ice and snow. The home of the Frost Giant tribes. To move to the next Realm, you will be expected to befriend a tribe of Giants or destroy one.

"After that, you enter the Realm of Muspelheim. That world is filled with magma, Fire Giants, and Demons. To defeat that Realm, you must defeat Surtr or—"

"Pardon me, Heimdall, sir, but where is the best place to fight for Etherience?" Oslow asked with only a small stutter. Azrael was a little upset that he'd interrupted the man, but this was something they needed answered anyway.

"The last three Realms have the most abundant enemies. However, if you make it to Midgard, there is a unique quest line that offers high Etherience, as well as many alternative training methods."

"What realm is Midgard?" Jophi asked hesitantly.

"The fourth Realm, or the sixth level of the Rainbow dungeon."

"So, in five days, we don't have much of a chance of getting there?"

"Due to the time dilation, you may be able to make it there, but I doubt you could complete a quest or learn the cultivation system that governs the floor."

Heimdall opened his mouth to continue, but this time Azrael raised a hand. "We'll likely just stay on the first Realm then, if that's the best place for Etherience. Do the Realms get more difficult the farther in you go?"

"Yes. The first Realm contains Apprentice to Journeyman rank threats, and each floor after increases by about half a rank. Not many have returned from the final Realms… Still, I don't think you understand how this dungeon works. You must advance to at least the Vanaheim Realm on your first trip, or you won't ever be allowed to enter the dungeon again. Vanaheim is the fourth level or Sixth Realm."

"Let's get out of here, we aren't ready to try to advance through this dungeon, Azrael," Prateek exclaimed as he began walking toward the exit. However, he stopped after two steps. The entrance they'd come through was gone.

Azrael spun along with his entire team, everyone trying to find the open part of the dome that they'd entered through. He didn't make a full spin before his eyes fell upon Heimdall's eyes. They were glowing like two eclipsed suns and even his dark skin seemed to be crackling with some sort of unseen power.

"You've already entered and cannot go back. Shall I continue with my explanation?" Heimdall asked, his voice booming over the space. Everyone stopped their search and went deadly quiet. Azrael knew that a few of them would be angry with him after this, and he could understand why. The Rainbow dungeon was one of the most powerful opportunities on the planet, and to lose access to it in the future could turn into a huge roadblock in level advancement. Still, it wasn't common to have access to it unless you were an influential member of Asgard, or if you were backed by someone with a great deal of political pull.

The silence stretched and Heimdall took that as an affirmative to continue. "The fourth level, or the sixth Realm, is Vanaheim and to advance past this floor, one must join the Vanir or defend against a Jotun attack on the Vanir. Since the start of this floor is your goal, I will leave off the explanation of the higher Realms and notify you all of the Ether contract that prevents you from speaking of most of what you see within."

A contract popped into view on Azrael's interface and vanished just as quickly.

Azrael tried to protest by raising his hand into the air; he hadn't read the contract. In an action he could barely follow, Heimdall lifted his massive sword and inserted it into the pedestal. The floor began to pulse with every visible color spectrum and probably a few that weren't. Within an eyeblink, Azrael couldn't see anything inside the room anymore. The glare of all that light soon washed out all other colors but white, and even with his eyes closed tightly against it, the glare wouldn't go away. "Wait, we didn't sign the contracts," Azrael shouted.

"Entering the dungeon constitutes agreement..." Heimdall responded, his voice seeming to come from a long tunnel.

A feeling of weightlessness hit Azrael at the same time as Heimdall's response. Azrael heard shouted exclamations of surprise from nearly everyone on his team before his feet touched down on something solid again. He could tell it wasn't the glass floor from before because his feet slid over dust or small pebbles before they met enough resistance to hold his weight. He also heard scuffs and a few more exclamations as people landed around him. By the sounds, he guessed a few didn't remain on their feet like he did.

Possibly more disturbing than the sounds of his teammates falling over were the groans that surrounded him. Perhaps if his eyes could see something, those sounds wouldn't be making his skin crawl, but with a white glare that was fading to black, his whole body was on the verge of shivering. He pulled out his sword and swore he was going to feel claws of some sort of creature at any moment.

Several tense moments went by before he was able to see outlines in the gloom around him. Gloom was the only word he could think to use for the low levels of light that seemed to be coming from a star hovering on the distant horizon. The ground he stood on was a barren place devoid of all greenery. It wasn't black either, but something closer to a muted, dusty brown.

"Is everyone okay?" Azrael croaked, realizing he should have voiced something sooner. The outline of each of his teammates were spaced out by about five feet, and like him, they all had either a spell or weapon in hand.

"Are you all not seeing the massive horde of shambling creatures just outside of this field?" Bat asked, sounding confused. Azrael facepalmed. Of course the lights wouldn't have affected the Batman.

"Bat, we're all recovering from light blindness. Are we safe where we are?" Azrael asked as he tried to find the shambling creatures that Bat was talking about.

"As far as I can tell, there is some sort of protective barrier surrounding us. So we should be safe here. Is this Helheim then?"

"It definite—" Jophi began when a loud howl broke the semi-silence. "—ly is," she continued as the howl faded away. "And that was most likely Garm."

"Is Garm a huge dog?" Prateek asked, clearly associating the howl with some type of dog-like creature.

"I'd probably call it a wolf, after that," Oslow said as he turned to face Azrael. "You know we all could lose access to this dungeon for the rest of our lives because of you!"

"Honestly, the Ether contract seems to prohibit people from speaking of that restriction, specifically," he countered, as he read the document their entrance had forced agreement upon. "I think Magnus knew, though. He's likely hoping we do get barred for life. Still, if we get to the fourth level, then we can shove it in his face, right?!"

"But how hard and dangerous is that going to be?" Prateek shouted.

"Well, that Heimdall guy did say that we could make it to Midgard in five days, so it is possible." Jophi interposed herself between Azrael and the two others that were subtly squaring their shoulders toward him.

Azrael's eyes slowly adjusted to see what Bat was talking about. A dome of shimmering blue surrounded them and outside of the strange dome, things were moving around. Still, Azrael would never have called the movement shambling. The creatures seemed to blur as they flashed into and out of his vision. The groans and scuffles never seemed to line up with their appearance either. Another howl reached his ears and from the pitch and tone, he could tell that it was identical to the last—so it wasn't from an answering wolf.

He scratched his head and studied the area they were ported to. It contained tents and cots, and even had a few vending-type machines that seemed to display food items. If this was a safe or rest area, then what was outside of the dome? Everyone was now studying the blurs and space like Azrael. His silence had likely sparked the others to join him in his assessment.

"By Vishnu's fourth arm, how are we supposed to fight against things we can't even track with our eyes?" Prateek asked under his breath.

"Bat, didn't you say they were shambling corpses?" Azrael asked, trying to understand how the blurring speed could be classified by his astute friend so poorly.

"At first, I thought they were moving very fast as well, but after a while I realized that the way the creatures move couldn't provide power for the speed my ears were tracking. I think this dome and safe zone is in a different time dilation."

Azrael tried to track a blur with his eyes to understand Bat's assessment of their situation but failed. To him, it just looked like a body-shaped shadow flashed into an area and then sped away again. "Are you certain?"

Bat held up a clump of muted brown earth and threw it through the air. As soon as it crossed the dome, it either disintegrated or sped up so drastically that it vanished. "Unless this dungeon is meant to kill people who leave this safe zone...?"

Azrael smiled and looked at the others who all were staring at the place in the dome that the dirt vanished from. "I think it's pretty safe to assume Bat is right. Also, that the time Heimdall was mentioning to clear to the Midgard Realm was something that we could do if we don't take rests in safe zones."

Another howl pierced the dome and Azrael took that as a sign of the day turning over on the other side of the barrier.

"Are you suggesting we take rests out there with the monsters? You know that safe zones in dungeons are usually created for a reason, right?" Oslow said.

In response, Azrael shrugged and began walking toward the shimmering dome. Jophi and Bat both opened their mouths before shutting them again and following. "We aren't going to talk about this then?" Prateek asked as the three passed.

"I don't know about the rest of you, but I think a time-dilated area is exactly what I was wanting for my training!" Azrael retorted, and kept walking. Prateek's eyes widened before he tilted his head in a minor movement that Azrael took as acknowledgement. Oslow also shrugged and double-stepped to catch up and even overtake the group.

"It's the tank's job to lead the way, you know," he said.

Azrael allowed a corner of his mouth to turn up at the semi-apology.

Oslow led the way as they strode confidently into the swirling blue dome.

CHAPTER FORTY-FIVE

Moving through the barrier Azrael felt strange. It was painful, like someone was attempting to stretch his bones. It lasted for a period he would classify as a conundrum. Like his arms and leg that went through first felt like they'd experienced the pain for hours, becoming achy, while the back of his body after his head felt like it had been stung by a low-level insect. The constant hum of groaning also changed, becoming a beat instead of a buzz. Now a groan would sound every few moments but as he listened, he could still hear a far more distant humming groan. He turned to find Bat but didn't find his friend beside him.

He looked back and got to witness Bat's dark-blue hand enter the air from the shimmering field. At first only his well-manicured fingernails poked through and then, as if he was defrosting from inside an iceberg, the rest of him slowly entered. As soon as his head passed through the field, Bat seemed to physically be vomited out by it, going from a slow exit to something like a speedster coming to a stop. In his peripherals, he saw Prateek and Jophi go through the same experience at the same time, but he couldn't watch everyone.

"So weird," Oslow, who had been the first through,

commented beside Azrael as Bat's ears bounced off of his cheeks. "It's my first time seeing a time dilation field. It must be a very powerful dungeon to maintain something of this level."

"It kind of has a similar feel to a dungeon Jophi, Azrael, and I were in before," Bat stated extremely casually. Azrael looked at Bat and saw his friend give a slight nod of his head.

"Really, that dungeon was a strong one. I guess we should just be glad that both scale challenges, right?"

"What dungeon is he talking about?" Oslow asked, his voice excited. "I'd love to know where it is so we can run it and level quickly!"

"Unfortunately, it was destroyed along with the planet owned by the Tuatha."

"Wait, you guys said before you were on that planet but refuse to talk about it. How did the Tuatha have a dungeon this powerful on a brand new, unstable planet?"

Prateek must have exited the field in time to hear the final question because he asked, "Wait, what are you talking about? Do they know where a dungeon comparable to this is?" He sounded partially affronted and also extremely excited.

"We don't know where another dungeon like this is. And clearly, we have no idea what the Tuatha have, or how they managed to have it. All Bat is saying is that the scope of this dungeon seems to fit with the one we were in, right Bat?"

"Correct. I would add that the other dungeon was terrifying and left a lasting connection to fear in my head. So, I was just commenting on it trying to sever that feeling." Again, there seemed to be more said by Bat to Azrael. Was he suggesting that his connection to Apep was somehow severed here?

That would not be good at all. Azrael had somewhat been counting on that connection, in case the Asgardians did send people in here after them.

"Okay, did anyone else see the quest we just got?" Jophi asked, interrupting the conversation and steering it back on track.

You have a new quest.
Ninth Realm – Warrior or Saint
Gold Quest
Aesir Generated
Clean up the Wandering Dead
Many warriors weren't strong enough to defeat Garm
and climb their way through Valhalla. These souls are
trapped within Helheim and will not get a chance to
be reborn unless they are released. Help the Aesir
dungeon release these souls.
Kill 1000 shambling dead to help their souls
reincarnate.
Or defeat Garm to prove your strength.
Best of luck!
Rewards:
Etherience
Access to the Eighth Realm

"Is it asking us to choose a path, or repeating what Heimdall said?" Prateek asked after reading it. "I thought Heimdall said either works?"

"The quest seems to imply that we will be choosing a direction if we do one or the other. Doesn't it?" Bat said.

"We could always do both…" Azrael suggested. "Maybe there are bonuses to the quest?"

"Let's find a shambling corpse first and see how strong our enemies are." Bat pointed to the nearest source of occasional groans and Azrael followed his finger. After a moment, he nodded and tapped Oslow to lead the way. No point taking a risk, even though he guessed these mobs on the first level would be Apprentice rank.

Marty Roestan
Apprentice-Shambling Undead
Level 18
Health Points: 90 / 90

Skills: 0

After seeing the rank and health points, Azrael felt his head fall. This wasn't going to be a challenging quest because of the strength of the enemy. No, this was going to be difficult for another reason. Only one undead creature was in sight from the top of their current position, and by the deep groans, the next nearest was about fifty meters.

"This is going to be more about finding a thousand of these things quickly," Azrael muttered and heard murmurs of agreement.

"Boys and their complaining," Jophi growled and lobbed a small ball of fire at the Shambling Undead. The thing burst into flame like a candle dipped in an accelerant. It managed a single step in their direction before it fell to the ground, dead.

Azrael groaned even more when he saw that his quest log didn't update. "Did only Jophi get credit for that kill?" he asked the group, already knowing the answer.

This time even Jophi groaned, going back on her original complaint. They needed five-thousand undead in total to pass what Azrael assumed was the Saint path.

A howl came again from the distance and Azrael pointed in the direction he believed it originated from. "Let's head in the direction of Garm while we release some souls."

"Just so you know, I now have a twenty-four-hour timer," Jophi interjected, bringing the group up short.

"To kill a thousand?" Azrael asked.

"Well, it isn't specific. It says I have twenty-four hours to get off this floor, or I will remain here forever. However, it has only ticked down two-seconds, despite it being about twenty-seconds since that thing died."

"Oh God... What if it turns you into one of the undead if you don't kill enough?" Oslow asked, his voice beginning to go manic.

Azrael rushed over and grabbed both of his shoulders, giving him a short shake. "Now is not the time for that. We will funnel all kills to Jophi first. That way no one else gets the debuff until she has a thousand kills. Then we can—"

The howl interrupted him and Azrael blinked and looked in the direction of its origin. "Does the howling still seem too fast to be natural to anyone?"

"It slowed down a bit." Bat shrugged as he pointed in almost the same direction as Azrael. "My guess is there might be more time dilation if we go further. That's why the howl is so frequent. Not to mention the ever-present buzz."

The group set off and walked for what felt like an hour but was only considered six minutes by Jophi's quest timer. She killed another hundred and fifty low level undead before they reached another huge shimmering blue field. Again, just like before, the other side was filled with blurring shapes and it was clear the howls and buzz were emanating from the other side.

"If this area is approximately ten times faster, will the other side of this field be a hundred times?" Prateek asked, holding a hand up just before the field. Azrael shrugged, not really interested in the question. The answer would become apparent soon enough, anyway.

"Oslow, lead the way." Azrael began walking toward the field and let Oslow sprint a bit to get in front of him.

The same painful and strange feeling occurred as the last time dilation field, and Azrael got to watch the rest of his group come through in slow motion. They had to wait a full minute and a half before Prateek followed. Azrael guessed that he'd only hesitated on the other side for a few seconds, but on this side, it translated to a lot longer. It was strange to think about, but his musing was quickly interrupted by a new debuff on his bar.

"Warm body. You have a warm body that will attract the attention of all nearby undead. Good luck," Azrael read aloud as the rest of his group also glanced up and left to their own status interfaces. Groans sounded from all around them, and Azrael drew his sword. It would seem the rules changed in this second zone.

Azrael looked around and felt his eyes widen. What he'd mistaken for the ground a moment before was undulating toward their group. What was Jophi's timer for then? He wondered as he began charging his sword edge with a single stack of his Soul Blade. "Guys, I think we are going to have to abandon the one at a time rule."

CHAPTER FORTY-SIX

Azrael killed fifty each time he released a Soul Blade, but the wall of flesh was still coming. He peeked at his quest counter and found he was already over four hundred souls. "How many released is everyone at?" he called over his shoulder.

"Six hundred and fifty-one," Jophi shouted back.

"Two hundred and twelve," Prateek responded. "I'd be higher if you allowed more to enter the consecrated ground of my spell."

"Seven-hundred and eighty-one," Bat practically whispered. His sonic attacks covered the widest area of any of the group's Area of Effect spells.

"Twenty-two," Oslow mumbled with enough volume to be heard. On the other side of the coin was the group's tank, who relied heavily on the rest of the group to deal the damage while he held enemy attention. "Also, I don't know what Jophi is talking about with the quest timer... mine seems to be moving faster than normal."

Azrael looked up to his timer and found his not moving. Only five seconds had ticked away, and the massacre had been going on for just under ten minutes. "Mine's moving extremely slowly?" he responded and turned it into a question for the group with his tone of voice.

Everyone agreed with him, and Oslow scratched his head as he used his sword to strike down another corpse. Oslow was also the only one who was fighting from melee distance, and his latest strike added blood and viscera to his already disgusting appearance. "Mine just sped up again!" he called after the kill.

"Pull back and see if you have any new debuffs," Azrael said as he charged another Soul Blade and released it, his Ether pool dropping below half. "Let's use Ether Draughts now. This doesn't seem to be letting up."

"There isn't an end to them," Bat answered a question Azrael hadn't asked.

"By the Martian's red armor!" Oslow swore. "It's the damn blood. If you touch it, the timer speeds up. Mine has sped up by two-hundred times. One sec, I'm going to try to phase it off me." A pool of blood seemed to suddenly splash to the ground, followed by a few audible splashes as viscera landed inside of the macabre puddle. "Okay, that's better, the timer is barely moving now. On the note of using consumables, I could toss some explosives into the throng so I can get to a thousand souls freed faster."

"Something about the ease of releasing a thousand souls is making me very nervous," Azrael responded to Oslow and conveyed his gut instinct to the group. It felt like something was terribly wrong with the strategy. The timer, the debuff that sped up the timer, everything seemed like it was designed to make it harder to reach Garm, which set off alarm bells. "I think we need to fight our way through this horde and defeat the boss of this Realm," Azrael concluded.

"Heimdall said that we can advance floors in either way, though?" Prateek called.

"I've got the same feeling," Jophi added. "It's almost like the first objective is a trap."

"Okay, let's say you're right. How do we get through the horde of undead without getting covered in blood and guts? We can't all just phase through it like Oslow," Prateek countered.

"Jophi's attacks burn the corpses and blood away, and Bat's don't leave a mark on them. I say we use them to clear a central path, and the rest of us focus on widening it. After we find Garm, we can ensure everyone is at a thousand souls released."

Prateek nodded and pulled out an Ether Draught. Azrael followed suit and chugged down the sweet tasting blue liquid. "Oslow, toss the explosives we purchased to up your kill count. My guess is that Garm is behind the next time dilation field." The group was still hearing howls with a frequency that suggested the wolf making the noise was far too actively to be in their current flow of time.

Once everyone was bunched back together, Bat nodded to Azrael. "We ready?"

He nodded once, which signaled Jophi and Bat to unleash their spells in near unison. Jophi sent out a Fire Tornado that began sucking the nearby undead into itself. Bat's attack was far harder to see, but a line of undead collapsed just outside of the tornado's range without a mark on them.

The tornado began moving away from the group, toward the origin of the howls, and Oslow led the way behind it. Azrael fired off a Soul Blade at the closing sides of the pathway whenever the undead seemed to begin filling it in. On the other side, Prateek used some sort of holy spell that burned the corpses that Bat left behind. Any undead who attempted to walk through the flames died very quickly.

Oslow helped thin Azrael's side further with a lobbed grenade or Molotov whenever he saw a large enough group gathering together. The tornado was a bit of a bottleneck because it took some time to pull the undead into its burning red center. Azrael assumed Jophi couldn't just send it through the group at full speed. Azrael kept expecting to see her stumble or have to release the spell, but only saw her sweat and consume two more Ether Draughts.

"How are you managing to hold the tornado so long?" Azrael asked, as he saw the next blue field in the distance. He estimated that they were halfway there.

"I'm just channeling the lowest level of it. The undead don't have a ton of health, so I don't need to pump my Ether into it for damage and am instead just maintaining the channeling cost with my regen."

Azrael was impressed. Jophi had already been strong, but to see her and Bat tear through these enemies like they were paper made him feel even more confident that they could make it to the fourth level. A howl sounded nearby, and Azrael recognized the tonal difference between this howl and the other howl they'd been hearing since the beginning.

He turned to see a massive, twenty-five-foot-tall wolf scattering corpses and charging toward them from the side. A quick Analyze made him freeze.

Garm
Journeyman-Spawn of Fenrir
Level 44
Health Points: 2,315 / 2,515
Skills: 14

"Incoming!" Azrael shouted in warning, but it seemed like his notice wasn't necessary. Everyone was staring at the incoming wolf, and so Azrael looked around him. The complication in this fight was going to be the horde of undead, which they had unknowingly put themselves in the center of. Luckily, the boss was only a Journeyman in rank, even though its level was rather high.

The wolf sped toward them and its eyes began glowing red. Each footfall seemed to pulse a red undulating wave through the ground and up into the Shambling Undead. Azrael analyzed one of the glowing red creatures.

Jeffrey Monsera

Apprentice-Shambling Corpse
Level 31
Health Points: 1,000 / 90
Skills: 1

"By the Council—they have a skill and enhanced hit points now!" Jophi shouted, probably having realized at the same time he had.

"Kill the boss first, it should remove any buff effect!" Azrael called, making a logical choice.

Oslow ran forward to meet Garm, and the wolf lowered down, tilting its head sideways to snap the tank in half with its massive jaw. Oslow phased through the mouth and Garm's whole body as the wolf seemed to tumble ass over teakettle to a stop a dozen feet from the group. It stood back up growling and attempting to stomp Oslow into the dirt. Garm rose up on its hind legs and fell down, using its two front paws like a pancaking device. Of course, both paws also phased through their target and with the second attack now complete, the group unloaded held spells with abandon. The horde of undead closed in even as Prateek's Consecrate spell set them alight in holy fire.

The health of the boss dropped down precipitously, crossing to fifty percent in an eye blink. Then as Azrael watched, it filled back to full. "What just happened?!" he shouted in confusion.

"It consumed a nearby red glow from two zombies to heal itself!" Bat responded, and Azrael looked over to see his friend not attacking. "Should we keep attacking?"

"One more time. Let's see if it has a cooldown!" Azrael ordered and released another Soul Blade. The boss got hit by three spells and healed itself to full again by consuming three nearby zombies. "By Erebus' beard!"

Azrael looked around, trying to figure out a strategy that would work against this boss. The mob of undead were ten feet from the group and less than three feet from Oslow and Garm.

Teeth clenching in frustration, Azrael watched as new undead collected the red glow from either the undead near them or the proximity to Garm. So they couldn't kill all the undead with the glow. Should they try to exhaust its Ether?

His scanning eyes crossed the blue field of the time dilation to the next zone. An idea came to mind, and he shouted, "Train the boss through the time dilation field! Jophi, we'll need a stronger version of that tornado." The distant mobs likely still had low health, but all the ones near them now had too much to die instantly. Thus the tornado and its ability to clear the path due to its strong winds.

"Everyone else try to keep them off of Oslow and Jophi. Move!" Azrael continued as the group jumped to obey his order without questioning his plan. Either they trusted him, or the intention was obvious. Either way, they began slowly training the massive wolf and strange procession of glowing red undead.

Oslow drank Ether Draughts whenever he saw an opportunity between attacks from Garm, and the rest of the group did their best to keep the undead five feet away from him. Many of the corpses got smashed by Garm's hind legs as it essentially raced around and through Oslow. Azrael was sweating from Ether Exhaustion by the time he heard Jophi wheeze, "We're here!"

"Okay, to make this work the DPS needs to pass through first!" Azrael shouted. "Prateek, stay with Oslow and pass through at the same time." Prateek nodded while Bat and Jophi both lined up beside Azrael with their backs to the field. "On the count of three," Azrael commanded.

"One."

Garm rushed by Oslow and attempted to tackle, or flop on the tank. It crushed about two hundred undead in the ensuing slide and roll.

"Two."

Garm got back up and pumped its legs through corpses and dirt as it tried to close back in with Oslow.

"Three." Azrael stepped back and felt his leg explode with pain just like the previous two fields. His back and head followed and suddenly he was standing on the far side of the time dilation. A few of the zombies were falling through the portal beside them, and a few had already gotten back to their feet and began hobbling toward them. They still had the red glow from Garm.

"Kill any undead on this side. Conserve Ether and be ready to unload on Garm when it comes through." On this side with the increased perception of time, it was easy to watch and time an attack to easily decapitate or critically strike an undead as it fell through the blue field. Bat and Jophi took care of the ones who'd already fallen through, and luckily no additional creatures began swarming from this side. It took ten minutes or so before Oslow reached the field and another minute for him to step through.

Azrael continued slaughtering undead as he held his breath in anticipation. Just as Prateek and Oslow popped onto their side of the time dilation field, a paw from Garm appeared. It inched out of the ethereal divide like it was forcing itself through rock. Its open maw and sharp teeth followed and before its whole head emerged. Azrael shouted, "Now!"

Every point of Ether the group had left rocketed into the open mouth of Garm and its health went from full to zero without a single heal going through. The wolf's snout exploded and gore rained down on the five people standing on this side. Then the rest of the corpse and their spells were ejected into the space on the other side of the barrier. The rest of the boss's corpse exploded in slow motion on the other side. To call the scene gory would be a huge understatement. Azrael felt his knees try to buckle as his Ether Exhaustion weakened his body and brought on a headache. But he couldn't let himself fall like some of the others in his group. Undead were still falling through the field even as the red glow on them faded.

Azrael had dumped everything he had in his Soul Storage

as well, which meant he currently had very few options to defend against stronger enemies.

"Who still needs to kill more of these?" Azrael asked, his voice a hoarse whisper as he tried to predict where the next Shambling Undead would exit from.

CHAPTER FORTY-SEVEN

The Shambling Undead lost interest in the group after the death of Garm. It took a full minute or more for the corpses to stop falling through the barrier. Azrael, who already had a thousand released souls, moved away and let Oslow kill the creatures. While Azrael sat to recover, he read over the quest.

You have a completed a quest.
Ninth Realm – Warrior or Saint
Gold Quest
Aesir Generated
Clean up the Wandering Dead
You have helped Fenrir keep his Realm tidy and have earned both the Warrior and the Saint achievements.
Congratulations.
Rewards:
1,000,000 Etherience
Access to the Eighth Realm
Move to the Eighth Realm
<Yes> | No

"Don't click accept just yet," Azrael said, thinking of their current time displacement and the opportunity to recover resources. If the next Realm acted like this one, then they would enter a safe zone without increased time, which would slow down the group. "Let's recover here since we don't seem to be attracting—"

A howl warbled the very air and Azrael felt his heart shudder with it. Since entering the new zone, Azrael had been focused on the field to the prior zone and the undead that slid through it. For the first time, he scanned the surroundings more intently. He already knew no enemies were nearby but that howl certainly made it seem like there was a massive wolf right above them. This zone was lightly permeated with a white mist that rose from the ground. It allowed relatively good visibility for fifty feet in any direction but created a pure white wall any farther than that.

That effect combined with the howl could mean that something rather huge was just out of sight from him. He turned to Bat and found the blue-skinned Batman shaking.

"What is it?" Azrael asked, feeling his heart quicken with panic.

Bat didn't answer but pointed up. Azrael tilted his head up and saw only white, similar to the mist in every other direction. Wait, was the white mist moving—that was when Azrael realized he was looking at the underside of something hairy. The hair was white and looking in either direction, Azrael couldn't see anything but more hair until it faded into the fog. His scrutiny triggered Analyze.

Fenrir
Epic-Mythical Wolf
Level 58
Health Points: 45,180 / 45,180
Skills: Hidden

"How many more kills do you need, Oslow?" Azrael whispered without looking away from the huge creature above him.

"Just about ten," Oslow said from somewhere closer to the blue field, his volume entirely inappropriate for the situation.

"Okay, well let's loot Garm and get out of here..." Azrael whispered urgently, hoping to convey the situation without screaming it.

A glance away told him that Prateek and Jophi had also noticed the creature above them. Oslow was still killing a final few of the Shambling Undead, as they hobbled around aimlessly on this side of the field.

"I thought you wanted to rest here," Oslow answered in what might have been a normal tone but set off another huge rumbling howl. "Wow, the howling in this zone sure is creepy. Alright, and done!"

"Everyone complete the quest now," Azrael shouted as the fur shifted further. It might have been his imagination, but he swore he could see two terrible yellow eyes deep in the mist above him. Oslow followed his gaze and Azrael watched his Adam's apple bob up and down. The two yellow orbs rushed down and Azrael mentally slammed the yes option of the quest.

———

Azrael flinched and began to cover his head with an arm just as his vision of two approaching eyes changed to the blue and white ceiling of a cave. He blinked and scanned the cave, seeing both stalactites and dripping icicles hanging from the roof. There was also a magical fire burning to his right. He knew it was magical because of the lack of both smoke and any fuel. Still, without a fire he assumed this cave would be hovering near the freezing mark, but he would estimate that it was currently sitting at just above his body temp.

All the others were standing in the cave as well, and it was Jophi who spoke first. "What in the hell was that Epic-ranked creature doing on the first floor of the dungeon?!"

"I was there long enough to see its teeth. I swear a single tooth in its muzzle was as big as this cave!" Oslow said, his voice shaky.

You have a new quest.
Eighth Realm – Ally or Enemy
Gold Quest
Aesir Generated
Make Allies or Enemies
Defeat or befriend a tribe of Frost Jotun. Since you're both a Warrior and a Saint you still have both options to advance to the next stage. You also have access to all of your skills.
Rewards:
Etherience
Access to the Seventh Realm

———

901,111 Etherience remaining to level 13.

"Access to all of our skills?" Prateek read the quest aloud. He was clearly, like Azrael, also choosing to ignore the final moments on the last floor. "Do you think if we had only completed a single version of the quest, we would lose access to attack or healing spells?"

Azrael shrugged. "No idea, but it certainly sounds something like that. Does that mean we should try to complete both objectives again?"

"Probably," Prateek stated. "That first Realm took us about three hours to complete, according to the clock. It felt closer to half a day though, so I think we could likely rest here in the non-time-dilated safe zone. What do you think?"

"I'd say let's go see what this floor looks like first, then we can still come back."

Jophi, Bat, and Oslow had stopped their awed conversation

about the beast on the last floor to follow the plan, and that was the real goal of Azrael's loud and overly enthused answers. Sometimes people fixated on things they couldn't control and allowed it to fester and affect the present. Right now, they just needed to be careful not to enter too deeply into any of these Realms.

Azrael walked toward the blue shine that emanated from the cave entrance. The other side of this barrier was not intimidating for the same reason as the previous floor. Last floor, it had appeared that numerous fast-moving enemies were just outside. On this floor, it seemed like there wasn't anything but snow for miles in any direction. Azrael scratched his head. "Guess we should take the thermal regulation potions..."

Everyone pulled out the orange cocktail and uncorked it. The thickness of this particular potion was more similar to congealed fat than liquid and as he tilted it back into his mouth, he felt an involuntary gag as the potion entered his mouth. The taste was something like cinnamon and created a hot sensation on his tongue and down his throat as he swallowed. When he was done, he couldn't help the few coughs that escaped.

"That's disgusting," Jophi wheezed beside him. He glanced at her to find her doubled over with her hands on knees and half of her bottle still full.

"It's not going to get any better," he said quietly, hoping to coach her into finishing the rest. He didn't keep watching though, choosing to give her some privacy in case she or he was truly sick. "Just be glad we bought the standard dungeon-diving kits after the water level of that puzzle dungeon. Now, I'll go first," he announced as he put on the Ether Tech suit he hadn't worn on the previous floor. In retrospect, saving it from accumulated damage from low level mobs was probably a bad choice. He shivered, thinking about Fenrir and its teeth that were bigger than him.

He stepped through the shimmering field and despite the mechanical suit felt the same stretching-stinging pain. As soon as he was ejected out of the other side, he watched the Ether Tech monitoring HUD begin dropping the external temperature. He moved away from the field and the numbers went below freezing and continued to fall. The suit's warning lights quickly came on, followed by a timer indicating how long the suit could operate in the terrifyingly cold weather. Twenty-five minutes, and that wasn't counting down at a slower rate because of the time dilation.

His teammates came through the barrier wearing every piece of gear they had and still immediately crossed their arms and began to shiver. "Are those disgusting potions even working?" Jophi asked, sounding slightly heated but also concerned as her breath fogged out in front of her.

"They were only rated for sixty below freezing, and this place is hovering just below that. My suit can't even operate for more than twenty minutes. Let's see if we can find somewhere out of this wind."

Bat walked up beside him, looking the least affected by the cold of the other four group members. "Your connection to Apep came back for a moment just as we escaped the previous Realm, but it's gone again now. I actually think that this dungeon is taking us to other planets…"

Azrael didn't respond right away, and instead looked around himself at the frigid expanse. The last floor was a barren wasteland covered in a perpetual gray cloud cover and lit by something above it. Could that have been a planet? "How could a planet maintain time dilation spells?"

"I only caught glimpses of it, but the enchantments were carved into the planet, or floor beneath our feet. Some sort of power was flowing along in the channels, but it wasn't Ether. It's the same in this 'Realm.'"

"Does it being a world or something inside a dungeon change anything?"

"I don't think so, but I've got a feeling this dungeon is on the same level as Apep, or a Planetary God…"

"What... are... two... planning." Prateek shivered from his place a few feet behind them, reminding Azrael and Bat that their conversation wasn't anywhere near as important as finding shelter.

"Sorry, Bat was just theorizing that we aren't inside of a dungeon right now. It feels more like a planet," Azrael responded quickly and then checked his suit's timer. Under twenty minutes left. "Sorry, I got distracted. I will go scout in front since I have the suit."

He sped off, slightly embarrassed that he let himself get distracted because of the lack of enemies around him. In this situation, the very environment was an enemy and needed to be treated as such. He reached a relatively large hill and moved to the leeward side, out of the chilling wind. The temperature bumped up above the safe zone for the potion, which meant this was at least a step in the right direction. What he hadn't seen or expected was the drop away into a carved pit. The snow of the surface was carved out, but because it was the same white as everything else, it was hard to see it unless you were almost right atop it.

Stairs that were easily as tall as he was in the suit of armor fell away into a pit that continued to descend. He peered down the crevasse, trying to find the creatures that created it. They were clearly intelligent enough to dig themselves a place out of the wind, but if the stairs were an indication of size, then they were at least three or four times as large as a human. Instead of venturing inside, Azrael moved back to signal his group. Everyone jogged the rest of the way to the leeward side of the hill before stopping and staring down the same steps he had found.

"Do you think these are those Frost Giants that Heimdall and the quest mentioned?" Oslow asked as he rubbed his arms furiously. At least no one seemed to be shivering now.

"I had assumed it was Frost Giants the size of the Fire Giant race, but this would seem to indicate that they are far larger than that," Azrael responded, his suit still counting down its remaining time. It would likely be warmer down in the crevasse, but he wasn't willing to venture down there without a plan.

"Well, since this is the first group we've met, should we try a diplomatic approach?" Jophi asked, her shivering still somewhat audible in her speech.

Azrael nodded and removed his suit of armor before it could lose the final ten minutes of functionality. If they did decide on the friendly approach, it wouldn't do to go in looking like he was an invader, anyway.

"Bat, can you tell how many there are down there?" he asked, trying to get an idea of how dangerous trying the diplomatic approach would be.

"There looks to be only two," Prateek responded instead as he hunched over the stairs. "There are two sizes of footprints here and that's all."

Bat shrugged, conveying that he couldn't give a better answer than that. Either the cold was affecting Bat's sonar ability, or the snow couldn't convey sound the same way as deep caves.

An unspoken agreement was reached, and the group began climbing down the stairs. It was strange as the drop down from each step was either a large jump or a hang and drop, bringing the sheer discrepancy in size between these Frost Giants and the group into the forefront of Azrael's mind.

As they descended, he couldn't help but think that this was a similar situation to the first Realm. They could likely fight the two below and finish the quest to wipe out a tribe of Frost Giants, or befriend them and finish the quest that way, but these Realms seemed to offer an easy option to advance, which rang metaphorical alarm bells in Azrael's head.

He would have to see what happened below before he decided, but he was relatively sure that taking an easy route through the Realms was a trap. They continued down into the snow, and while the natural light darkened, blotches of blue emanation that splattered the wall kept both the stairs and the walls mostly visible. It was almost like something was glowing under the ice, or the very snow itself was. Azrael approached one of the splatter marks and saw that some of the snow was melted and fused with something blue. He touched it with a finger and found it to be thick and viscous. It smelled like the first snowfall of the year, and he wiped it back off his finger into a flask, after he considered tasting it. He decided not to taste the thick liquid because it could be poisonous to humans and while he was curious about its origin, he didn't need the answer right away.

After ten minutes of descent, Azrael saw the bottom, but no enemies. The amount of blue illuminating liquid increased the deeper they trekked, and Azrael had to assume that someone was spreading it deliberately. The bottom was a round clearing maybe a hundred feet in diameter, and a casual glance up showed that they were at the bottom of a very deep hole. The walls were perfectly sheer without any patterns or handholds for climbing out, which made their current situation extremely odd. In the very center of the clearing was a blue teepee made of a cone of snow. Some splotches of blue glowing liquid were on the extremely large cone, but the entire cone glowed from a massive light source within.

The silence of the hole was like a crypt, and Azrael had to wonder if this was perhaps a burial site. "Could this be a burial site, and someone is going to start filling in this hole?" Azrael asked, looking for another way out of the deep cylinder they had just climbed into.

"There is no other way out," Bat responded, obviously noticing his head movements. "There are two living—"

"Who is there?!" an extremely loud question reverberated through the pit. Azrael could tell it was even muffled slightly by the snow tent. To his surprise, though, no movement accompanied the shout.

"Something is terribly off about all this..." Prateek murmured, trying not to respond to the question but also convey his thoughts to the group. Azrael looked around at each person in turn. Jophiel was wide-eyed and staring back at him, her knuckles were white on her staff but she hadn't yet cast a spell. Bat had his head tilted and was kneeling with a single hand on the compact snow beneath their feet. Oslow had his sword up, ready to defend if required, but Azrael could tell he was waiting for a decision. Prateek shrugged when he returned his gaze back to him. Everyone was waiting on his decision.

"We are travelers and came down to get out of the wind and cold. We don't mean any harm," Azrael responded, raising his voice to ensure it was heard through the glowing teepee walls.

"Cold?" A grating noise sounded in front of Azrael and a triangular opening grew until it was a tall as he was. At first Azrael thought that might be an invitation to come into the tent, but two blue eyes peaked out of the space and narrowed when they fell on them. "What are you tiny creatures?" the voice boomed, all the louder without the separation of the wall.

The interior of the tent was covered in the blue liquid and glowed brightly. The arms and hands that supported the speaker were also covered up to the elbows in it. Long, even more brightly glowing lines decorated the arms and face. The liquid seemed to leak from those lines.

"Are you injured?!" Prateek shouted, recognizing the lines as cuts and gashes first. Azrael blinked, seeing the whole situation very differently now. He looked back up the huge stairs and his eyes widened. Was all that glowing blue splatter blood? If so, they were very injured and likely on death's door.

Azrael spun back around as he heard the same soft grating of the triangle door moving. This time it was closing. "Wait! We can help!" he shouted, making a split-second decision. This was likely one of the easiest kills they could get, which made him even more skeptical about the tactic of finishing a quest by killing these two.

The opening stopped closing and even opened back up to the size of the Giant's head. "How can tiny ones help? Jord, my sister, has already passed out from blood loss, and I am light-headed. We have dug our grave and will soon return to the ice."

Azrael turned to Prateek. "Cast a healing spell on him."

"What?!" Prateek protested.

"Just trust me. I think this is the solution for this Realm," Azrael encouraged, and Prateek raised both of his eyebrows for a slow count of three before he sighed.

"Fine," he said and began glowing.

"You try to trick Baugi. I will not allow it!" The door began closing but Prateek's glow began surrounding Baugi, or who Azrael assumed was named Baugi. The triangle stopped closing and a deep grunt echoed from within. "What is this? I feel my wounds beginning to close." The door opened larger, and continued to grow until it was likely as large as the Giants were tall. "Come in! Help Jord before it's too late!"

These Giants were clearly used to ordering others around, but Azrael held up a hand to stop Prateek. "You come out of there first. I will not enter an enclosed space with possible enemies," Azrael ordered back. "Prateek, heal him again when he exits," he continued in a side whisper.

The sound of someone getting to their feet came from within and a massive blue-skinned monster limped out of the cave. The glow that surrounded Prateek didn't transfer to the creature and Azrael had to elbow the healer as he studied the twenty-foot-tall Giant. Its head, while shaped like a human's, was easily as tall and wide as one of the steps they had climbed down. The thing's eyes were black with blue glowing irises; it had two massive, clear fangs that protruded from the bottom of its mouth, as well as two clear horns that sprouted from its head and curled around its ears. The legs were bare until about mid-thigh but then the creature seemed to have either packed snow around its upper thighs and privates or had very thick white hair there. Its chest was again bare, and its arms as well.

Prateek's second healing spell went off and this time the Giant growled. "Do not waste more on me! Help Jord!"

"Move to the side and he will!" Azrael ordered back again, trying to make it clear that this wasn't a situation that Baugi oversaw. The Giant hurriedly complied; his limp less noticeable.

Azrael nodded to Prateek and together they moved forward. A few feet from the doorway, they caught sight of Jord, and both gasped. She was infinitely worse off than Baugi was.

"I don't know if I can heal this…" Prateek mumbled as he began glowing.

CHAPTER FORTY-EIGHT

The next thirty minutes were a bit of a blur as the group attempted to help Prateek in any way he directed. Jophi was by far the most helpful as she could cauterize wounds, but Bat was also able to help by locating internal bleeding that needed more attention. Azrael and Oslow, on the other hand, just fed the Giantess healing potions while the other massaged her massive neck attempting to get her to swallow the liquid. Each member of the group was soon covered in glowing blue blood and sweat, but they did manage to stabilize Jord.

At first, Baugi continually tried to get closer but after the first ten minutes of being told to move further away, he sat down and just watched the progress. He still gasped and twitched violently whenever Jophi cauterized a wound but as some of the Giantess' blue coloring returned he seemed to relax —slightly.

Once they all fell onto their butts, he sprang up and began to rush to Jord's side. Prateek shouted, "Do not jostle her! Some of the wounds are barely closed... I will continue to cast more widespread heals after I recover some Ether."

Baugi seemed to be torn between going to the Giantess and

following Prateek's order. Eventually, he sat back down and regarded all of them. Jophi and Oslow began shivering since the temperature at the bottom of this pit was still below zero and they were covered in sweat and blood. Azrael assumed the elixirs were likely still more than capable of keeping everyone from freezing down here, but the added dampness was uncomfortable.

"Why do you tiny things shiver? It is quite warm down here…" the Giant asked, seeming genuinely curious.

"We are not made for these temperatures, Baugi," Azrael answered. "We are from a world with very little snow."

Baugi narrowed his eyes but then made a motion with his hand. A ceiling slid into place above them, and a wall rose in front of the stairs, closing off the pit. "Will this help?" he asked, looking back at Azrael, his eyes still skeptical.

The temperature in the large space was still cold, but Azrael felt the change in the air once the pit was sealed off from outside. He peeked at his two shivering friends and saw the shaking lessen. "Yes, it has. Thank you. May we ask how you two became like this?"

The Giant sneered and faced down to the ground, as a massive grinding sound louder than the moving snow emanated from him. After a moment, Azrael realized Baugi was grinding his massive, clear teeth. "We were part of the Icicle Clan in the second ring. We are both the children of the previous clan leader, Alvaldi, but Thrym has risen and taken over the clan. We fought hard but could not stop him.

"I thought it was mine and Jord's time to die, but now I'm unsure what to do."

Azrael felt his plans begin to unravel. These two weren't a clan anymore, and that was probably why they hadn't yet received a completion for either part of the quest. "So you two aren't part of any clan anymore then?"

"That isn't true. Thrym will rename the Icicle Clan and any survivors who still stand with Alvaldi will inherit the clan. They will come find the leader, which will be me or Jord. Thrym will likely not kill Alvaldi right away, and instead choose to consume his blood and grow in strength."

Oslow held up a hand. "Wait, consume his blood and grow in strength? New clan?" Oslow had stopped shivering but couldn't contain a small tremor as he clearly considered the act of drinking blood.

"This is the way." Baugi waved away the question, clearly nonplussed with the consumption of blood. "Alvaldi was nicknamed the all-powerful one because his blood is the strongest. Everyone who joined the Icicle Clan was given a single cup, which drastically increased their strength. If Alvaldi wasn't currently asleep after his fight with Odin, then Thrym would not have been able to defeat him!" Baugi was practically shouting in outrage as he gave voice to more of the story.

"Could you and your sister retake the clan with the ones who find you after Thrym creates his clan?" Azrael prompted.

"We were not able to stop their rebellion and would have no chance of beating them after they solidify their power."

"And what if you had help?" Azrael continued, knowing that Baugi would answer in the negative.

Baugi narrowed his eyes and studied the group. "What can ants do to help?"

Prateek stood up and began casting healing spells on Jord and Baugi again, and slowly Baugi's eyes widened. "Can all of you do this?"

Clearly, the Giant wasn't the sharpest wit around, but Azrael shrugged and said, "We can't all heal, but we all have areas that we excel at…"

Jord coughed violently and levered herself to a sitting position so that she could see the group and Baugi. "What is going on, Baugi? And who are these tiny people?"

"They are the ones who saved our lives, and now offer to help us recover Father!"

Jord managed to sit up and studied everyone, her eyes resting longest on Baugi. "Yes, and I am Hella the Undying. Stop making jokes, Baugi, and tell me how we survived."

It took a while, and a few more healing spells from Prateek, before Jord was convinced by Baugi. When she stood to her full height, she was clearly smaller in all dimensions than Jord, and didn't have any tusks or horns. However, if her snow attire was anything to go off of, she was much better with the ice magic than Baugi. Another reason Azrael believed her stronger in that aspect was that she immediately changed the space into something more livable, with tables, chairs, and an actual front door. She even was able to gather the blood from the snow and turn the pools and splotches into lights around the space.

Everyone in the group had questioned Azrael, asking him if he was sure about befriending these two and attempting to take on another clan until the quest was updated.

You have a new quest.
Eighth Realm – Ally or Enemy
Gold Quest
Aesir Generated
Make Allies or Enemies
You have successfully befriended the Icicle Clan of the Frost Giants. A new quest has been created, Defeat the Bloody Thrym Clan.
Rewards:
1,000,000 Etherience
Would you like to access the 7th Realm?
<Yes> | No

You have a new quest.
Defeat the Bloody Thrym Clan
Realm Quest
Help Jord and Baugi retake their clan and save their father Alvaldi.

Rewards:
Etherience
Weapon of Frost

After the next quest appeared, Azrael was far more confident in his decision, and the others seemed more convinced that he was onto something. The Realms were meant to be conquered by completing both quests that were offered.

Shortly after the quest arrived, other Frost Giants began arriving one after the other. These other Giants didn't seem to be keen on conversing or asking questions, but instead just sat down and waited for Baugi or Jord to give them orders. After they were told to cook food, or melt snow for water, they complied but before that they seemed almost lifeless. Azrael had to assume that this Realm was created with only a few intelligent creatures and then a large group of what he would call mobs in any other dungeon, but in this case were something like quest mobs.

Once there were ten of the mindless Frost Giants, Baugi stood up and exclaimed, "We have everyone in our clan. Let's rest up for the night, and attack in the morning!"

Azrael looked around, trying to understand how Baugi knew this was everyone, but only met the confused eyes of his group. He stood up and approached Jord. "How do you know that this is everyone?"

"Baugi was chosen as the leader, so he can feel the others out there. Most Frost Giants communicate in their heads with only the chief. They have all accepted you as allies and are keen to retake the clan."

Blinking, Azrael tried to take in the situation. Was this true or just a convenient story the Rainbow dungeon created to cover the mindless Frost Giants? He shook off the useless thoughts and asked a follow up. "Could you create a small house for me and my friends to sleep in tonight?"

"Certainly," Jord said and waved a hand nonchalantly. A door that was still twice the size of Azrael carved itself into a nearby wall and he motioned his group to follow him as he thanked Jord and moved toward it.

Azrael tried to study the exquisite ice cottage that Jord carved into the wall, but as soon as they entered the common area of the place, Jophi put a hand on his arm. "How did you know that we'd get another quest?"

"I've had this strange feeling since the last floor. It's like there is an easy way to advance and a more difficult way. Something about the easy way seems *too* easy. Plus, there was that warning about losing access to skills... Do you know what I mean?"

"I thought we were in a rush to get to the sixth Realm, though?" Prateek added his confusion to the conversation.

"I think that's a trap," Azrael began and moved to a couch made of snow before choosing not to sit down. "I have a feeling that each decision we make on a level of this dungeon affects the next one. For example, if we had only done a single portion of the previous floor quest and completed the Saint achievement; I think we would have been offered a different quest here. Likely with only a single option to complete it. Or perhaps we would have been prohibited from attacking creatures on this floor. I can't say what the consequences would have been, but I have a gut feeling that says this floor would have been harder if we took the easy route on the previous."

"I agree that we've stumbled into a situation for more Etherience, thanks to healing these Frost Giants, but we only have five days left, Azrael. Are you sure we should stay on this floor longer? What if the next floor is harder to complete?" Oslow added his opinion to the conversation.

Azrael shrugged. He was going off a gut feeling, but truly believed in it. "I don't think we will find a safer place to sleep that is already in a time-dilated area, and the attack tomorrow should take place in the second, more time-dilated space. So I would say it makes no sense to rush to the next floor right now. If we spend eight hours here, it will only equate to about an hour."

"Forty-eight minutes, actually," Prateek corrected with a smile.

"You've calculated the speed of the time dilation?" Jophi asked, sounding a bit shocked.

"I believe it's an increase of ten times whenever we pass through the barrier," Prateek responded, having come up with the same number Azrael had estimated earlier.

"So does everyone agree then?" Azrael asked. Everyone nodded, but he heard Jophi and Prateek grumble about sleeping on beds of ice. "Just put your sleeping gear on top of the snow beds and stop complaining," he added and then chuckled as they both glared at him. Maybe that wasn't the right thing to say in this situation?

CHAPTER FORTY-NINE

Azrael peeked over the top of a windblown hill of snow. He was looking down on what could only be described as a city of snow mansions, at least from a human perspective. "Jord, how many Giants are down there?" he whispered to the huge Frost Giantess who was sprawled on the ground beside him. Her head was still nearly as tall as he was, and she was far more conspicuous because she had to put a good three feet of that head above the hill to clear her eyes.

"There should only be three-tens or so. They killed half of the clan in the uprising, and we fought back, killing many of them."

Considering that their troops amounted to nineteen meant they were fighting from a disadvantage. Though to somewhat balance that number was that a great deal of the thirty against them would be mindless Frost Giants, who Analyzed as low-level Journeymen. "How many on the other side are prominent members of the clan?" Azrael asked, trying to get a picture of how many high-level Journeymen they might be facing. That was also assuming that they would take after Jord and Baugi.

"Only Thrym. He is the only council member left below, but his son should also be down there."

Azrael looked behind him at Baugi, who was at the bottom of the hill with the other Giants, and then back to Jord. These were likely sons and daughters of a council member, which meant that there was one high-level Journeyman below and one Frost Giant who was even stronger. Maybe even a Master. Azrael motioned for Jord to retreat as he turned and walked back to his group.

"There are likely thirty Frost Giants in the clan on the other side. Two of those will be as strong or stronger than Baugi and Jord. What do you guys think?"

"Do you think Thrym will be as strong as Fenrir?" Oslow asked, his voice just a little squeaky. Azrael gulped, understanding the sentiment. If Thrym was a high-rank Epic class, they would be slaughtered here.

Baugi must have overheard Oslow because he paled and looked around himself. After confirming that they were safely still alone at the bottom of the hill, Baugi said, "Do not mention the son of Loki here, unless you want his attention! Vánagandr would swallow the entire village in a single bite."

Azrael raised a shaky hand toward Baugi. "See, no crazy powerful opponents here." He turned to Jophi and Bat after that announcement and continued, "I think you two should help the Icicle Clan even the field with your AoE spells. Oslow, Prateek, and myself will attempt to engage Thrym or his son when we see them. As long as our group isn't overwhelmed by numbers, we should be able to gang up on Thrym at the end."

Everyone nodded and as a group they walked over to Baugi, who was staring at his twelve Frost Giants silently. His glassy blue eyes seemed to almost glow as he scanned over each member. Maybe the telepathic communication was real, and he was giving a rousing speech? However, as soon as Azrael approached, Baugi looked at him and asked, "Is your group ready?"

At Azrael's nod, all the Giants stood and began climbing the hill, their steps eerily in sync, almost like a military march. At the top of the hill, Baugi shouted, "Thrym, we have come to take back what is ours. Prepare yourself!"

So, much for the advantage of surprise. Azrael would have liked to have attacked before the enemy formed into lines but instead watched doors swing open and Frost Giant after Frost Giant begin forming up at the bottom of the hill. He Analyzed each one and didn't find a single member who was a stronger level then their own lower-leveled mobs.

"My father is busy!" a new voice boomed back, as a towering Giant even taller than Baugi split the forming line and shouldered a massive spiked-ice-club.

Tyrüm
Journeyman-Frost Berserker
Level 44
Health Points: 10,000 / 10,000
Skills: 14
Boss

This was going to be a staged encounter. "New plan," Azrael shouted over the rising shouts and war cries from both sides. "We need to keep as many of our side alive for the next stage. Oslow and Prateek, keep Tyrüm busy, and the rest of us will take out the adds."

Without warning, Baugi began a charge down the slope, which Azrael thought was tactically the wrong choice but considering that the encounter was likely staged for each group, he and his group were forced to rush after. The other side counter-charged, which again was stupid and illogical if this was a real war. As the Giants closed the gap, weapons of ice and storms of snow were conjured from thin air. Azrael put on his Ether Tech helmet in response and glanced at the timer. He had just over twenty minutes to end this battle.

The approaching wall of snow was going to impede his vision in a moment, so he used Demon Step to flash behind one of the opposing Giants and used a single charge of Soul Blade layered onto his sword to hamstring the monster. The creature's skin was tough and he needed to increase the charge to three before his sword finally cut through. As this Giant crumpled to the ground, it pinwheeled its arms and took out two others that ran beside it. Azrael Demon Stepped to two others, managing to crumple about a third of the line of charging enemies as they raced uphill. That should give his side the advantage at first contact, which in combat was something every general should look for. At least, that was what his lessons in the Sovereign Hall taught.

A multitude of crashes and booms shook the air, and Azrael turned back to the recovering Giants that he'd downed already and chugged an Ether Draught to recover his pool. He avoided using another Demon Step to conserve Ether and instead released a triple stack of Soul Blade, launching the phantasmal version at the first group of three as two of them got back to their feet and the third kneeled. The blades hit two of the monsters and began cutting through skin, but the third managed to conjure an ice vambrace on its arm and raise it in defense.

Azrael chugged another Ether Draught, clenching his teeth and looking for another couple of easy targets. He felt the snow crunch a few feet beside him and his eyes widened. The flying snow was concealing an approaching enemy. He leaped to the side and tucked into a roll as a club crashed down into the place he'd just vacated. Out of the snowstorm, Tryüm's head, shoulders, and then legs appeared as it heaved its massive club back onto a shoulder.

"Boss here!" Azrael shouted, using the Ether Tech suit's volume amplifier to hopefully be heard over the combat.

"What sort of gnat did those traitors bring with them?!" Tyrüm shouted as it closed the gap with ground-shaking steps. Azrael peeked at his pool and then used Demon Step to phase into the shadow of the only other Frost Giant nearby. He used the move just before Tyrüm's massive club crunched into the snow again.

The Giant that was nearby was the one who had managed to fend off his Soul Blade and it was leaning into the attack, still holding it back. The two beside it were dead already, which was a nice surprise. Azrael had hoped that his phase would not be noticed by Tyrüm, but the Frost Giant's eyes tracked him somehow and it changed direction, charging directly at its own clanmate.

To Azrael's surprise, it used its club to obliterate the still-fighting member, which released Azrael's Soul Blade. He was forced to duck under the leading horizontal edge of his own attack as Tyrüm returned its club from its own horizontal swipe up above its head. Azrael sprinted forward, pushing the Ether Tech suit and his muscles as hard as he could. He dove between the boss's legs as it crunched down and pulverized the snow once again.

"Oslow!" Azrael shouted again, hoping that the tank who was much more suited to this would show up. That was when the wind and snow began to abate and he heard it. It was like a group of lumberjacks hitting a bunch of trees, or maybe a musician on a percussion instrument. It thudded in Azrael's ears, and he chanced a glance away from Tyrüm as he turned toward the sound. At least eight Frost Giants circled around a spot, thumping their clubs into the snow. Azrael felt his breath catch; there was only one reason the Giants would be acting that way. Oslow was phased in the center of that group.

Tyrüm turned awkwardly as it simultaneously attempted to find its target. Azrael began charging his blade as he drank another draught, hoping he could pull the frenzied opposing Frost Giants from Oslow, but his Ether wasn't climbing fast enough. He sucked back in the Soul Blade and instead chose to use Demon Step to phase to the far side of the circle. Tyrüm crowed, "Found you!" and Azrael hoped it had calculated correctly.

The boss charged the circle of thundering Giants and

swiped its club through them, again without a care that they were its allies. From the center of the group, Oslow said, "I'm sorry, those snow storms were conjured spells and when I used phase to avoid a strike from one of them, I ended up aggroing all of them by phasing through the snow 'attack.'"

Azrael backed away as Tyrüm continued obliterating its own troops. Once Oslow had a reprieve, he chugged two Ether Draughts and then intentionally stepped in the way of Tyrüm, who attempted to kick him. The foot phased through Oslow and the tank swiped his sword at the heel, causing Tyrüm to look down. It turned back to Azrael and tried to stomp Oslow as it continued to chase his first annoyance. When the second attack phased through and Oslow stung its foot with his sword again, Tyrüm finally changed its mind.

Free of the boss, Azrael scanned the battlefield to find that Jophi and Bat had everything well in hand. Only eight enemy Frost Giants remained, as evidenced by the yellow snow they wore instead of the white from the Icicle Clan. Azrael had to wonder if the color choice was intentionally disgusting or just the dungeon differentiating the sides.

Instead of joining that battle, Azrael turned back to see Tyrüm's club begin glowing blue. Oslow chose to dodge the skill-infused strike and good thing, because the area that was struck became a massive pyramid of ice. "Hold still. Damn ice ant!" Tyrüm shouted as it released its club and raised its hands in the air.

Azrael backed away as both of its hands began to glow the same blue its club had just done. Oslow took off running as well, just before Tyrüm finished casting and shouted, "Ice Meteors!" High up in the air, massive balls of ice easily as large as a Frost Giant began forming.

As if on cue, the white-clad Frost Giants, Azrael's allies, charged at Tyrüm. Azrael could see what was going to happen and he shouted, "Oslow, get out of there!" as he himself ran toward Jord and Baugi's figures still nearer the top of the hill.

A massive crash sounded behind him and Jord fell to her

knees as Baugi began shaking in rage. It had been obvious because of Tyrüm's lack of care for its own allies, but the far too powerful attack had been the second clue. Once Azrael and his team had cleared enough of the opposing Giants, all the remaining brainless mobs needed to be wiped out. The class at Atlantis had called these 'phases of a boss fight,' and if Azrael was correct, the fight against Tyrüm was about to begin in earnest.

"Tyrüm, you killed your allies along with ours. Some of those had to be your friends!" Baugi shouted, spittle flying from his mouth.

"Friends! The strong don't need any friends…"

The scripted scene continued to play out as Oslow, Prateek, Jophi, and Bat formed up around Azrael. He looked over his group and nodded to each one as they stood staring at the cloud of snow that was beginning to settle.

"That was likely phase one of the fight. I think this floor is highly scripted by the dungeon," Azrael said as he watched the still monologuing head of Tyrüm exit the falling cloud of snow. "Get ready, this speech sounds like it's coming to an end."

As if on cue, Tyrüm shouted, "Let's see who's stronger between you and I, Baugi!"

The two Giants charged each other, and snowy white armor began forming around Baugi as his sister Jord wove her hands. Azrael rolled his eyes and turned to his group once more. "This is definitely not the final fight. Conserve Ether as best you can. My guess is that Thrym will appear once we defeat its son. Oslow, don't bother tanking Tyrüm, as it appears Baugi is meant to do that. Just be ready to intercept if it charges one of our casters."

The group spread out as the two Giants collided and began laying into each other. Azrael waited to allow his Ether to refill in slow ticks as his team slowly began damaging Tyrüm. Azrael watched its health slowly descend and just before it crossed the seventy five percent mark, Jord shot out a massive ice spike that collided with Tyrüm's shoulder, skewering through the chest muscle and out the back.

"Father, they are ganging up on me!" Tyrüm cried as its health dropped into the mid sixty percent.

"Who dares attack the Bloody Thrym?!" a new voice bellowed, and Azrael watched as a house that was easily forty-feet tall exploded near the center of the ice hut town. What Azrael wasn't expecting was to see a head appear at the very top of the cloud that was forming. If that was the height of Thrym, the Giant was easily forty feet in height. The new Giant stormed through the other huts and made its way to the bottom of the hill.

Azrael stared in horror, feeling the presence of this new foe wash over him.

Thrym
Epic-Blood King
Level 44
Health Points: 100,000 / 100,000
Skills: Hidden
Boss
Cursed

"Fall back," Azrael called as he took an involuntary step in that direction himself. This creature was nearly on par with Fenris from the first floor. His team gathered around him, and Azrael opened his quest, ready to take the portal to the next floor if needed. "Be prepared to finish our quest and leave. We cannot fight that monster."

The team watched as Thrym surveyed the scene. It pointed a massive, clawed hand at Jord and ordered, "This is a one on one duel. If anyone interferes, I will personally crush them." Both Baugi and Jord looked up at the massive Thrym with wide eyes.

"How much blood did you consume?!" Jord asked, her voice shaky but filled with heat.

Thrym began to laugh and the mirth reverberated through the snow, shaking the loose surface and causing pieces to fly back into the air. "Alvaldi still has a few pints left. I was interrupted before I could drain him dry. Son, hurry up and finish these two! Prove to me that I haven't wasted that pint by giving it to you."

Tyrüm smiled and pulled the large icicle lance from his shoulder. Without responding, it charged back at Baugi, who was still looking up at Thrym with a horror-filled expression. Baugi managed to raise his own club but his feet weren't set properly, so the collision of the two weapons sent him sprawling. Azrael wasn't sure if this was part of the script anymore. If they helped Baugi in any way, then Thrym would kill them with a wave of its hand.

"What do you all think? I thought this was a scripted event, but I'm not sure anymore..." he asked in a low whisper.

"I think we are either meant to help Baugi or let him die to trigger the next phase, but we can't beat Thrym," Bat whispered back. The rest of the group shrugged, not seeing an answer. Tyrüm raised its club and struck down at the fallen Baugi, connecting with his ice club which was held across his body with both hands. Cracks began to form and Azrael knew they needed to make a decision. Bat decided for them, though.

Tyrüm stumbled and went to a knee even though it seemed like no attack hit him. Azrael knew better as he saw the skin of the Giant ripple with unseen sound waves.

"Get up, boy!" Thrym shouted, not noticing Bat's attack. Azrael smiled; that was the answer. They were supposed to help covertly. The rest of the group had no way of helping in that way, though, so they relied on Bat's sonic attack.

Baugi saw the opportunity presented and swung his club from his back, battering Tyrüm in the side of the face and causing it to sprawl onto the ground. Bat stopped his attack as Baugi leaped atop Tyrüm and began pummeling with fists and club. Just as the health of Tyrüm neared zero, a huge foot, which came from Thrym, crushed Baugi and Tyrüm from above. Azrael blinked as Jord cried out.

So much for no interference…

"My son!" Another booming voice echoed over the snow from the village, and it was Thrym's turn to look back, his jaw clenched and his eyes wild.

CHAPTER FIFTY

No explosion of one of the snow houses followed the statement, but something stood up. The figure, while over forty feet tall, didn't look like a typical Frost Giant. In fact, it was closer to a skeleton with sagging skin hanging off it than it was a muscular Giant. The figure encased the tops of massive houses with thin fingers as it hobbled in the group's direction.

"Alvaldi!" Thrym sneered at the approaching figure and even went as far as to lift its foot, which had been crushing Baugi and Tyrüm, to turn and face the tall, thin Giant. Azrael kept his quest open, ready to port to the next floor at a moment's notice.

Azrael glanced down and found that Baugi was still alive, and so as discreetly as he could manage, he nudged Prateek and motioned at the unconscious body.

Prateek glowed for a moment before his eyes widened and he turned back to Azrael. "I can't heal him for some reason…" he whispered quietly.

Alvaldi exited the houses and surveyed the scene in front of him; his face was sunken and there were even small crystals of ice frozen to his body in numerous places that seemed to depict that the sickly Giant had been sweating.

Alvaldi
Epic-Ice Mage
Level 99
Health Points: 99,999 / 1,000,000
Skills: Hidden
Weakened-Chieftain
~~Cursed~~

"Thrym, what have you done?!" the chieftain asked, his voice hoarse and raw.

"I have taken control of your pathetic clan, and now am about to finish off the final two members," Thrym responded, its voice matching its wild eyes and clenched fists.

"You can have this clan, Thrym, just let me and my children go," Alvaldi whispered so quietly that it sounded like a gust of wind over the ice plains.

"Go? Why would I let my source of power leave?" Thrym scooped up Baugi in one hand and held the twenty-foot-tall Giant out toward Alvaldi. "If you go back to your resting area and swear on your blood, I will let your son and daughter leave this circle and return alive."

"Father, no!" Jord spoke up for the first time.

"Silence, girl!" Thrym barked. "What is your answer?"

Alvaldi looked at his daughter and then his son before scanning over Azrael's group. His eyes looked sad, almost pleading. Alvaldi raised a hand and his son's armor which had been grown for him by Jord began to grow and turn to ice. Thrym's hand attempted to crush down, but the growing ice fought back against it. Alvaldi fell to a knee and coughed up blue blood that glowed far brighter than the blood Azrael had seen until now. "Please, strangers, help me," he croaked out.

A quick Analyze told Azrael that Baugi's health was falling by a point a second and it had already been low to begin with, at a thousand points. The group looked to Azrael for a decision. There was no way that they could tear through one hundred thousand hit points on an Epic level Frost Giant though. He turned to Jord, who began forming an ice spear in both hands. "Unleash everything?" he asked the group.

"Just be ready to accept the port to the next floor if it doesn't work," Jophi added with a large smile. Azrael nodded, and each member of the group began casting their strongest spell. Oslow, who was the only one without a large attack spell, pulled out a bandolier of grenades and began tying them together.

"On my signal," Azrael said as he finished his ninth charge of Soul Blade into his sword. He held up his hand and lowered one finger at a time. Jord threw her spears first and they shattered against the armor Thrym wore, but Azrael kept his countdown pace. When he hit zero, he mentally commanded both stored Soul Blades from his Soul Storage and the nine in his sword to release in a thrust that slid him backward on the snow thanks to its counter force.

Bat's attack struck first, and the cracks in the armor grew wider as the ice they were made of vibrated. Jophi's flaming tornado formed next, starting from the Giant's feet and quickly encasing the monster in a whoosh. Prateek's light spear and Azrael's layered Soul Blade swished through the fire tornado and crashed home, but thanks to the tornado spell, no one could tell what happened.

Something dropped out of the tornado a moment later, and Azrael thought he saw Baugi's body encased head to toe in the ice Alvaldi conjured. Jophi fell to her knee a slow count of two seconds later, and the tornado receded in the opposite direction that it formed in. With the tornado's disappearance, the sound from inside of it returned and he finally heard Thrym laughing maniacally. He swallowed a lump that formed in his throat as the form of the forty-foot Giant resolved itself out of the shimmering heat haze.

Azrael's strike had pierced through him, but the wound

looked no bigger than a human arm, and it was high on the massive boss's shoulder. Beside Azrael's strike, a small chip of flesh was missing and bleeding as well, likely from Prateek's light spear attack. The armor Thrym had worn was entirely gone, but other than those minor injuries and approximately five thousand health points missing, Azrael's team hadn't managed to do more than aggravate the boss.

It began to turn toward them when Alvaldi began to laugh, in a gravelly start and stop that sounded almost like coughing. "How much of my blood did you drink, brother?"

Everything in the valley went quiet, and Azrael scanned back to the wounds that were leaking a black blood that didn't seem to glow at all. He and his entire group held their breath as they waited for what Alvaldi and Thrym would do next. Thrym turned to his brother and resumed his laughing as well. "Enough to finally become stronger than you!"

Alvaldi's face cracked into a large smile. "Yes, you have finally taken from me the source of my power, dear brother." Alvaldi held up a hand from his kneeling position and the two wounds began gushing blood as if there were pumps inside Thrym. The blood began forming two balls in the air between the two boss Giants. One was black and roiling while the other was blue and glowing like a small sun god.

In front of their eyes, the group watched Thrym collapse to a knee and become sunken and sickly like Alvaldi. The orbs kept growing and for a moment Azrael thought that Thrym would die.

Did we only have to injure him, then?

Then the two orbs formed and Alvaldi raised his other hand and gestured the black ball back toward Thrym. The black rushed back into Thrym and seemed to repair the sunken, mummy-like body to some degree. "You forget, dear brother, that I was cursed by the All-Father. He forced upon me his Odin sleep so he could continue to fight his bloody wars, but you took it willingly!" Alvaldi ran an ice finger over the palm of one of his hands and the blue blood began soaking into him.

"The curse that could only be removed by Odin himself or taken willingly is now yours, and you are right that if you sleep long enough, you will become stronger than me, but you are a century too soon, fool!"

It might have been Azrael's imagination, but he thought he felt Apep's presence for a heartbeat. Bat jerked his direction and then stared back at the two disappearing balls of blood, his face scrunched up and his ears opened fully.

The two orbs of blood both finished absorbing simultaneously and Thrym collapsed onto his back while Alvaldi stood up, looking much healthier. With a snap of his fingers, the ice encasing Baugi cracked and split, spewing his son onto the snow. Jord ran to her brother, and checked his pulse, but Azrael only needed an Analyze to see that he still lived. That was when their newest quest completed, along with the second portion of the Realm quest.

Alvaldi, who had seemed so powerful a moment before, stumbled and fell through a nearby ice hut. Jord looked between her father and her brother, seeming torn for who to approach first but then she looked back to Prateek. "Can you heal them?" she asked, her voice pleading. Prateek glowed again, but the spell still didn't seem to want to work. Then the seated Alvaldi surveyed the situation.

"They won't be able to heal us anymore, Jord. Since the curse is nearby, all healing spells will automatically fail, but do not worry, your brother and I will be fine." He turned to the five of them and continued, "Thank you for your help today. Who is the leader of your group?"

Azrael was shoved from behind by a hand that felt small and feminine. He glanced back to see Jophi shrugging but also smiling behind him. Clearly, she believed that they were out of harm's way now. He faced forward and nodded to Alvaldi in response instead of verbalizing it.

"I'm afraid I must ask you for more help, despite you already doing so much for my family. The Icicle Clan has no members anymore, and without members, we cannot be a clan by the rules of this Realm. Please go and gather ten Ice Cores from the Frost Wolves in the third ring and bring them back to me..."

Azrael sighed as the quest popped up in front of him. Should his group take the time to run some quests on this floor for Etherience or move on to the next floor?

You have a completed a quest.
Eighth Realm – Ally or Enemy
Gold Quest
Aesir Generated
Make Allies or Enemies
You have successfully befriended the Icicle Clan of the Frost Giants and defeated the Bloody Thrym Clan.
Rewards:
1,000,000 Etherience
Would you like to access the 7ᵗʰ Realm?
<Yes> | No

——

You have completed a quest.
Defeat the Bloody Thrym Clan
Realm Quest
With the help of Alvaldi and Thrym's stupidity, you were able to conquer his new clan.
Rewards:
1,000,000 Etherience
Sword of Frost
Accept the rewards?
<Yes> | No

CHAPTER FIFTY-ONE

The group stayed back for a full day of real time to finish side quests and gain Etherience. The majority of the quests were hunting Frost Wolves, or trading with other Frost Giant clans for materials. Yet, the most interesting quest was when the newly resurrected Icicle Clan moved into the third time dilation barrier.

Azrael stood in the new village, surveying the fifty or so Frost Giants that differed greatly from the original ones that were part of the Realm's scenario. These Giants each possessed a name and spoke out loud to each other.

"Something about them each having a personality now seems off, don't you think?" Bat commented as he joined Azrael.

Without turning around, Azrael responded, "Well, you did say that my connection to Apep is gone right now, right? So, it must be a normal part of the Realm, right?"

Bat shrugged and made an oscillating motion with one hand, clearly indicating Azrael's thoughts on the matter were not complete. "I've seen the connection flare back up, but I think it's because of the time dilation that it's stretched very thin. So, perhaps this is normal, but I'm willing to bet that Apep has something to do with it."

Azrael scratched his head. "I sure hope so. Perhaps, if the mobs are stronger on the lower Realms it will protect us from pursuit in some ways…"

"I think we will be relatively safe until the Sixth Realm. Remember, people aren't allowed back in until they make it to that space, so if they are coming back into the dungeon, they might be waiting for us there."

Bat's thought process made a type of sense but simultaneously had a few holes in it. The problem they were facing was a lack of information on the Rainbow dungeon. "There is no way to know for sure," Azrael responded and used Analyze to check on Bat's level. Seeing it still at twenty-four, he continued, "All we can do is keep our guard up. How much more Etherience until you're at level twenty-five and ready to rank up?"

"I'm under the five million mark. So, once we turn in the two quests to advance to the next Realm, I will only have about three million remaining."

Azrael nodded and checked his own progress.

Congratulations! You have reached Level 13.
13,312,111 Etherience remaining until Level 14.

This dungeon certainly lived up to its reputation of being one of the strongest on Gaia. The group had all managed to level or significantly increase Etherience in the day they had quested within Niflheim. Still, the time to move to the next level of the dungeon was coming up fast, and Azrael could only hope that the next Realm would possess similar opportunities.

"Let's go wake everyone up, and head to the next level," Azrael said, in response to how close Bat was to level twenty-five. "Let's try to get you to Journeyman rank!"

Azrael was sweating as he looked around the Seventh Realm, or the third level, of the Rainbow dungeon. The difference in climate couldn't be more pronounced between the two floors and even though they were inside of a cave that didn't seem to have any source of heat, the temperature was sweltering.

The blue portal that led out of the cave was tinged with orange from the other side, and Azrael had to assume that Muspelheim was a fire-based Realm. Just as he opened his mouth to chat with the group about a course of action, the floor quest populated.

You have a new quest.
Seventh Realm – Fire Giants or Demons
Gold Quest
Aesir Generated
Choose a Side
Since you have befriended and helped a race of the Jotun, you have been given the option to choose a side in this Realm's ongoing violence. Slay ten Fire Giants and bring their cores to a Demon, or slay ten Greater Demons and bring their cores to a Giant.
Rewards:
Etherience
Access to the Next Quest of the Realm

"Does anyone have a preference?" Azrael asked as he hurriedly began removing layers of clothing. His sweat had already soaked through his undergarments, and he was hoping to avoid more. Unfortunately, the discarded clothing didn't help.

"I wonder if the Elixirs of Frost Blood we got from Jord's Frost Wolf quest on the previous floor would help with the heat?" Bat asked instead of answering Azrael's question. Wiping the sweat from his brow, Azrael had to admit that was probably the more pressing dilemma for the group. The non-stop pace of the dungeon and the sudden climate change made his mind feel sluggish.

I hope that's why I didn't think of the Elixir first! he internalized as he pulled out the light blue bottle from his ring. A quick swirl made the elixir glow, and he couldn't help the flashback of Frost Giant blood on the previous floor. Glancing at his party, he found he was the only one who hadn't uncorked and drank the elixir, so he Analyzed it, just to be certain it wasn't blood.

Elixir of Frost Blood
Adds Frost damage to all attacks but reduces core
temperature by thirty degrees.
Effects last 24 hours.

Well, that's inconclusive…

Taking a deep, dry lungful of stifling air, he chugged it down. The taste was minty, almost like a designer toothpaste. Goosebumps rose on his skin, and he shivered as his core temperature dropped. The heat that a moment ago had felt oppressive now felt like a warm fireplace after spending hours out in the cold. He sighed in relief and smiled at his party, who all appeared to be in the same state of bliss.

"Let's see what we find first," Jophi responded to Azrael's earlier question and began walking toward the blue time dilation portal. Azrael followed, also feeling excited to see what opportunities this floor had for them. His level had increased on the two previous floors and he was hopeful this floor would be the same. There was a nagging suspicion in his mind that reminded him Heimdall had claimed the first level offered the most Etherience, which meant they missed a great deal there.

The group walked through the portal and the feeling of being close to a relaxing fire turned into the extremely uncomfortable feeling of standing too close to a burning building. The air was so dry that Azrael thought he felt his lips crack almost immediately. He pulled out the helmet of the Ether Tech suit, hoping that it might offer some protection, but found heat warnings in the HUD almost as soon as he put it on. He took it off with a sigh and looked around.

The portal led to a larger underground cave system with magma rivers undulating alongside a wide path of raised basalt stone. The slow creep of the magma was accompanied by an ever-present crackling hiss that reminded Azrael of a large insect. The top of the large cave system contained small holes that almost seemed to poop the magma down in strange blobs or bursts depending on the pressure that was obviously contained within the channels Azrael couldn't see. There weren't any enemies in sight, and so Azrael made a motion to take the only path available.

Ten steps in, something erupted out of the magma. Azrael Analyzed it as it climbed onto the basalt walkway.

Lesser Demonic Lizard
Journeyman-Lava Newt
Level 41
Health: 8,000 / 8,000
Skills: 1

Red hot magma still dripped off the beast, so with quick hand motions, Azrael motioned for the group to slowly retreat to give the dangerous substance time to fall off the creature's scaly hide. Oslow stayed put while the rest of the party moved ten paces away. Like a large dog, the Lizard shook itself and slithered its tongue out of its mouth.

As if the tongue sensed something, the head of the beast turned in their direction. Once its eyes alighted on the group, it raised itself into a strangely high position on its four somewhat bowed legs and charged toward Oslow. A few more hand motions had the rest of the team retreat a bit farther. Azrael hadn't expected the speed from a creature that lived in liquid rock and had hugged the ground so closely. He clearly was wrong.

The beast barreled through Oslow, snapping jaws first, and not feeling a human-sized treat in its mouth, it hit the brakes and began skidding over the basalt floor as it scrabbled with long sharp claws for additional purchase. White scrapes formed under its claws, but it managed to stop and turn back around mere feet from the rest of the group. Oslow officially had its attention now, but the rest of the group waited for Azrael's signal to attack. He let the beast pass through Oslow another time before issuing the attack signal.

The group began unleashing spells in a slow and steady way, like their classes had taught, not trying to dump damage into the beast and accidentally pull its attention. Azrael closed in from Oslow's back, in a line that was rehearsed numerous times with the rest of the team. Since Bat's spells didn't travel to the enemy and instead formed at the creatures, it was more Jophi who avoided sending her ice shards on the melee fighters' line of approach.

Azrael stayed cautious because this was the first time he wouldn't be able to wear his Ether Tech suit into a group combat scenario. The suit provided a layer of protection against stray spells and accidental phase throughs that wouldn't be present on this floor. He charged three stacks of Soul Blade as he closed and smiled to see a blue tint added from the Elixir of Frost Blood. He timed his arrival with the Lizard planting its feet and beginning to snap and claw at Oslow's phasing form.

His first strike created a line of frost on the black scales of the beast and drained all of his Soul Charges from the blade but failed to cut through the Ether-infused hide that could withstand magma. He clenched his jaw and checked on the health of the creature. Only down about five hundred hit points. A glance down its body showed no signs of damage from Jophi's spells, and Azrael realized that the only damage so far was coming from Bat and his skills that bypassed the strong scales.

From this close, the back and head shimmered like onyx, but as the sheen descended the legs, it became dull and pale. Azrael charged his sword back up and attempted to strike at its back leg, low enough to avoid the shining scales. The triple charge cut through the scales, and he yelled, "The legs are the weak point in the scales," making sure Jophi noticed what he hadn't seen from a distance.

Soon, the closest legs had collapsed under the onslaught, and so Azrael and Jophi began circling around to keep layering damage on the other side of the beast. The basalt walkway wasn't extremely wide, which forced them to pass within ten feet of the Lizard's head.

Just as Azrael rounded behind Oslow, something whipped out and struck at his head. Azrael managed to duck the leading point of the blow but felt the widening tail scrape against his shoulder as it continued past him. Jophi screamed from behind him, and he acted on instinct, charging his Soul Blade with everything he could. He pivoted and slashed downward with all the strength he could muster. The blow severed the tail where the scales were small and dull, but his turn told him he was a moment too late as Jophi had the tail spike through her shoulder. Azrael dove toward her and managed to catch her before she stumbled back and off the ledge.

Her face was pale but once the surprise faded, her lips twitched up at the corners. "That's the second time you've saved me," she whispered.

"It can't be that bad if you're smiling," Azrael stated before taking a grip of the protruding tail. "Ready?!" he asked but pulled the tail out before she could respond, not wanting her to think about the upcoming pain in the middle of battle. Almost in unison with the removal, a healing spell from Prateek enveloped her. Her smirk morphed into a glare at Azrael and he shrugged.

Both of their attention was called back to the fight when multiple trumpets sounded from the Lava Newt. Along with the trumpeting, the creature glowed yellow and promptly collapsed, dead.

"What was that?" Oslow asked as he poked the corpse of the giant Lizard.

Bat pointed to the magma. "Incoming!"

The lava exploded with five of the massive Lizards and

Azrael felt his breath catch as they began climbing the sides of the walkway. "Top up on Ether if you can!" he shouted but checked his own debuff bar. Unfortunately, a single stack of Acidic Blood was already there, which meant he had been overusing the elixirs on the previous floor.

"Already at eight stacks of Acidic Blood," Oslow mentioned, but he drank down an Ether Draught despite his notice. Others were all higher than Azrael, and it became clear that they would need to take a break. Should they retreat through the barrier? The problem with that plan was it was the wrong direction. The beasts would come through the barrier at speed if they followed.

Still, the cave entrance should be a bottleneck, and rushing through this dungeon does us no good if we're dead.

"Retreat!" Azrael commanded and allowed the casters to move first. He helped Jophi to her feet and gave her a light push toward the cave entrance to give her a head start.

The group was halfway through the shimmering field when the huge Lizards finally stopped fighting each other with snaps and hisses and turned their way.

Azrael was the second last to back through the portal and immediately scanned behind him to see the first three scrambling away from the field to create some space to fight. Oslow came through almost on top of Azrael. Both scanned the field furiously, looking for fast-moving shadows that would signify a Lava Newt. Thirty tense seconds passed, and a glance told Azrael the group continued to hold ready for combat.

Oslow and he looked at each other and then slowly backed away. Once they reached the middle of the room, Oslow sheepishly asked, "Are we forgetting that Heimdall said this was a safe area?"

Azrael nodded, feeling his face flushing furiously. "Oh," was all he could muster as he unsummoned his blade and blinked stupidly. It had been what felt like several days of high-intensity fighting and his mind felt almost foggy. "Right. I don't think we can take those things on in groups of more than two. Unless someone has a plan to get through those scales."

"How do we expect to take on Greater Demons if we are struggling to take on Lesser ones?" Prateek asked, voicing something that Azrael was currently thinking about already.

"They seem to be specialized in defense with very little offensive power," Bat pointed out helpfully.

Azrael thought about it and still felt that foggy feeling impairing him. "I think we should all think about this and then decide after we manage to get some sleep. When we wake up and have had breakfast, we should be able to figure this floor out."

"Aren't we in a bit of a rush to get through floors?" Oslow asked.

"I think it's okay if we stop rushing now and begin taking this dungeon more seriously on this floor. We just struggled to fight against a common mob, and probably shouldn't have. The rush likely put us in that situation. So let's slow it down." Azrael turned away from the group after that, and began setting up his sleeping tent, not bothering with any of the extra layers of insulation meant to add heat. It was hot enough in here already.

Everyone seemed to understand his desire to think alone and sleep, so they moved off to do the same. All except Jophi, who surprised him with a kiss on the cheek. "I didn't get to thank you for saving my life again. So, thank you, Azrael," she said quietly and turned away as her cheeks reddened.

Well, that's new...

CHAPTER FIFTY-TWO

The next 'morning' was a slow start as everyone needed some time to clear their heads. It was almost as if Azrael's sleep from the other floors hadn't helped his recovery at all. That or something on this floor was causing him to feel like his head was stuffed with wool. The fact that everyone else appeared to be struggling with the same problem forced him to consider that option more seriously. He pulled out his Ether Tech helmet again and placed it on his head.

There it was. The entire HUD was red with warning notices, which was likely why he missed it the first time, but in the bottom right corner, there was a low oxygen warning. "I think I just figured out why my brain is so foggy. Is everyone else feeling the same way?" Azrael said as he took the helmet back off.

Everyone nodded as they mechanically ate breakfast, except for Bat. Bat turned his large ears back and forth, 'watching' the rest of the party nod before he responded. "I feel fine. What is the problem?"

Azrael blinked a few times before he responded. "There are low levels of oxygen in the air down here."

The rest of the group seemed to perk up slightly now that they had a reason, but Azrael still felt the foggy slowness of thought.

Bat nodded, though, and took a deep breath. "Now that you say so, I can definitely tell that this air is much closer to what we have on my home planet. It is higher in nitrogen and carbon dioxide. It's why these caves make me feel at home. Didn't we buy the air converters after the water temple?"

"You think they will help?" Jophi asked sluggishly. "They were made for water more than oxygen-low air. Wait, weren't they?"

It took a moment for Azrael to find them in the group backpacks, but as soon as he did, he placed the rubber mouth-piece between his teeth. He needed to slightly clench his jaw to hold the metal contraption the mouthpiece was attached to upright while he tied a strap up over the back of his head and one down to the back of his neck. He breathed through the air converter but didn't notice a difference. He opened his mouth to ask the others if they felt better and ended up mumbling into the mouthpiece. Bat heard his mumbles and held up a hand before he removed the contraption from his head. "Give it a minute. Let's just use me as the touchstone for now, and assume anything you four are thinking is slightly off. Okay?"

At everyone's nod, he continued. "We all slept in a low oxygen environment, and since your bodies aren't used to the low levels, I have a feeling your bodies are playing catch up as they start taking in higher levels. I can't be sure if the air converters are able to break the carbon dioxide into oxygen and increase your blood oxygen levels, but if we wait five minutes breathing through the mouth pieces, we can find out."

The group sat in a circle, all breathing through the obnoxiously loud converters and feeling sheepish, but after a few minutes, Azrael did notice a difference. After five minutes, he felt his mind begin to clear enough that he began to understand just how dangerous of a situation this was. After fifteen minutes, he had a headache that could be called catastrophic, but he was still able to think underneath it all.

That was when the shivering hit the group and Azrael's body, despite being in a sweltering cave, began raising the core temperature back to a more acceptable level. It was also when he felt his heart for the first time he could remember this morning. It began thudding more rapidly as it forced blood through the lungs that finally had oxygen to impart. His heartbeat must have been slowed from nitrous poison, he realized, and the sweat on his skin turned cold.

"I know that this break was already time we couldn't spare, but I am going to suggest we spend a few hours here to make sure we all recover," Bat said and now that Azrael could think properly, he nodded vigorously, not daring to take the device from his mouth. Instead, he pointed at Bat and made a hand motion to say 'you will be on top of the party.' He couldn't think of a way to hand signal 'you should lead the party.'

"I agree. I am going to take over as party lead for this floor since everyone else should keep the mouthpiece in. Take it out only sparingly, got it? I'm going to go grab some water from the back of this cave, and I want you all to drink and eat between breaths for now. Once you are feeling like yourselves again, come tap me on the shoulder. Good?"

Everyone nodded as Azrael watched, and he could tell by the paleness of their faces that they likely felt the same fear he did. They had been extremely close to passing out and likely never waking up again. This was the most insidious trap he had ever heard of in a dungeon. The group began eating and drinking bottles of water as they slowly recovered from the trap. Unfortunately, they didn't feel normal again for another eight hours based on the clock.

The break for sleeping turned into the loss of almost twenty-hours total by the time they felt ready to leave, which meant they had already wasted another whole day. The news got worse when Bat ordered, "Everyone is to sleep again." Azrael groaned and Bat snapped his head and ears around to him. "No protesting. That's an order. All of your bodies just went through something horrible and need to recover. I will wake up hourly and check on everyone to ensure the mouthpieces stay firmly in place. Now go!"

They hadn't packed up their sleeping gear that morning and even though Azrael laid down thinking it was unnecessary, he was asleep almost instantly.

———

Azrael woke up twelve hours later and sprang out of his cleaning gel sleeping bag, startled by the loss of an additional half a day. He immediately exited the tent and looked around to only find Bat and Jophi awake. Jophi regarded him as Bat continued with whatever they had been talking about, "…if that skill of the Demon Lizards is somatic, I can silence it and we shouldn't have to fight a group of them again. Otherwise, we will have to see what the Fire Giants or Greater Demons can do before we decide how best to conquer this floor. Glad to see you looking better, Azrael," Bat finished without turning his head away from Jophi.

Taking a deep breath, Azrael removed his mouthpiece for a moment. "We only have a day and a half left after this break, Bat. Don't you think we should get moving?"

Bat waved a hand toward another flat-topped stalagmite and waited for Azrael to sit. Azrael replaced his oxygen converter and began breathing normally before he sat down. "Once we cross through that first barrier, one and a half days becomes closer to fifteen days. And now that we are all thinking clearly, I think we should be able to handle the Lava Newts much better."

Azrael wanted nothing more than to protest, but the time dilation was in the group's favor as long as they didn't have to retreat to the safe zone again.

"Plus, there was a limited number of mobs in that first cave if the Newts call brought all of them. So, if we clear out that cave, we have a new safe area to rest."

They waited another two hours before Prateek, the last member to wake back up, emerged from his tent. Bat outlined the silencing plan to each member as they awoke, and even covered the initial part that Azrael had missed. "If we manage to remove the tail and Oslow turns the beast's back to us, we should all be safe and able to attack the wound created there. You all probably didn't notice, but when Azrael severed the tail to save Jophi, the wound closed quickly but was still completely without defense compared to the scaly hide surrounding it. I think the final skill it used was just a rallying cry, and if that skill…" Bat continued explaining the final somatic theory with Prateek.

Bat's strategy was flawless and for the next few hours they cleared the Lava Newts one at a time as they advanced down the basalt path toward the exit from the first room. It was strange just how much of a difference the oxygen made, and Azrael felt almost sheepish about struggling with such a straightforward and simple beast. No one in the group even needed to consume a Health or Ether potion this time.

Azrael peeked through the opening into the next room, looking for enemies or changes in geography. Bat could only 'see' the Lava Newts when they were moving in the magma and even then, he could only assume they would be Lesser Demons until they exited it. This next room had no magma though, and instead possessed massive ruby stalactites and stalagmites, creating line of sight issues for everyone. "I'm no better than you guys in this next room. Whatever those protrusions are, they refract sound in very strange ways, making it very hard to sense around them. Let's proceed cautiously with tank and offtank leading," Bat suggested, and the group got into forma-tion. His leadership so far was impeccable, and again Azrael had to think about his luck in having the Batman around in dungeons.

Azrael used his Soul Cloak now that he was acting as an

offtank. Hopefully the barrier would warn him of any surprise attacks and help him avoid them as well.

At Bat's command, the group entered the next room and began to navigate through the cave toward one of two openings in the stalagmites jutting up from the floor. They were so closely packed together and combined with ones from the ceiling that only two larger paths existed. The only sounds were from the breathers they all wore and the scuff of their shoes on the floor. They were about to pass through the leftmost opening when Azrael raised a hand and leaned in to study the ruby formation more closely. Something looked to be moving inside, but it was hard to tell. It could have been the group's movement causing the swirling patterns of light. Now that the group was standing still, he was certain that something was moving in the ruby.

That, or it was hollow. He reached up with a fist and knocked on the surface. The responding thuds confirmed the formations were hollow. What was the swirling orange and white inside of them? He took out his mouthpiece and pointed. "Something is inside these. Do you think it's more traps?" he asked then replaced his breather.

The rest of the party shrugged, and Bat moved forward to the same stalagmite and placed his hand on it. "Oh. Retreat to the door, now!"

The group double-timed it back to the door, and Bat pointed back into the room. "Inside those stalagmites and stalactites are some sort of elemental…"

Azrael turned back with wide eyes, trying to count the ruby spikes he could see. Was each one an enemy?

"I'm going to try to use a sonic attack against the nearest one. Let's see what happens." Bat held up both hands after his announcement, but waited for everyone in the group to nod before he did something. Or at least Azrael assumed he waited, because the ruby-like structure didn't start cracking until they all nodded.

An extremely large flame burst forth but didn't dissipate. The ruby pieces pinged off other hanging and rising ruby cones and small cracks began forming in them as well. Azrael was too transfixed by the flame forming into a bulbous Flame Elemental with two arms and deep red eyes. Those eyes were fixed on the group and it opened its mouth and hissed at them, like a campfire burning wet wood, only louder and sharper.

Fire Demon
Journeyman-Elemental
Level 35
Health Points: 4,000 / 4,000
Skills: 12

The cracks in the other ruby structures grew wider as the single elemental charged forward. Azrael had a feeling that this room was intended to trap the group in the center as the Fire Elementals broke free. As the creature charged, it raised both hands and began emitting a five-foot stream of fire in front of it.

Oslow shook his head at the group, indicating his tanking abilities weren't going to be effective against an attack that could damage him in both phases.

Bat made the call. "Unload all of your Ether, and prepare to fall back. Target the clearing and use Area of Effect. These things seem to be the opposite of the Newts, in that they have little defense and high offense."

A frost tornado immediately began to form, and Azrael mentally commanded his Soul Storage to unleash ten stacks of Soul Blade into the multiplying Fire Demons. He used a horizontal slash and started it as close to the ground as he could to try to keep his phantasmal blades in contact with the creatures for as long as possible.

It was impossible to tell how large this room was, but Bat had given up on fighting these creatures one at a time with the last order. If the first room was about overcoming a single foe with high defense, this room appeared to be about overwhelming large groups of foes with no defense.

Azrael watched as the leading flame-throwing Elemental

was segmented into ten separate pieces before the next was sliced into nine. Then his blades began crashing through ruby crystals in explosions of fire and red, glowing rocks. The cavern started to look like one chain reaction just before the frost tornado occluded it from sight.

Jophi's tornado dropped the temperature of the air by twenty degrees almost instantly, and Azrael watched on as the Flame Elementals began wisping out toward it. After the spell consumed ten to twenty forming and charging beasts, the ice had changed states twice and was now steam. The tornado released the mist and it floated up to the ceiling to form clouds as Jophi let go of the spell, took out her breather, and drank an Ether Draught. Azrael nodded and waited for the vision of the room to clear again. When it did, he felt his mouth go dry. The floor, walls and ceilings were carpeted in Fire Elementals.

There was a large area in front of the group which was clear, but hundreds—if not thousands—of enemies stared back at them with angry red eyes. The hiss of an exploding geyser echoed from within, and the carpet moved in unison, charging toward the entrance. "Hold until they get close!" Bat commanded and the group obeyed, waiting to unleash the next wave of spells. "Jophi take right. Azrael use nine stacks of a thrust down the center. I will take left. Prateek and Oslow, be ready to pick up anything that gets through."

Bat counted down for them and then closed his fist, signaling them to unleash. Azrael's lance-like thrust punched nine expanding holes through the forms of the central line of Fire Demons. The ones on the left seemed to waver like candles in the wind as they slowly shrank and puffed out of existence. The ones on the right were sucked into two ice tornadoes that were both half the size of the previous one Jophi cast.

Azrael used his final Soul Storage to punch a thrust through the ceiling Elementals as well. The attacks killed hundreds of the creatures. But each one that puffed out, collapsed, or wisped into a tornado was replaced by another.

"Retreat and recover!" Bat ordered and the group slowly

backed away from the entrance. The spells being held by Jophi and Bat dropped, and Fire Elementals surged into the gaps left by them.

The group turned and fled, ending back in the safe room. Bat was first to speak once they were through the gap. "We managed to get a large portion of them. Let's top up our Ether here and then head back out."

They needed to perform two more strategic retreats before they cleared the room of Fire Elementals, but because of the time dilation, Bat gave them some bad news once they did. "Unfortunately, I think that's the last time we can use that strategy, because we have respawned Newts in the magma."

CHAPTER FIFTY-THREE

Azrael listened to Bat debate out loud about clearing out the respawns behind them and he eventually made the choice to do it. Now that they would hopefully stay in the time-dilated field, the respawns wouldn't occur as quickly, or at least that was the hope.

The clearing went quickly and the group moved through the ruby stalagmite room and down a spiral staircase which had been in the middle. "Maybe we were supposed to navigate through that prior room without killing all the Fire Elementals?" Bat wondered out loud as they peered into the blackness of the descending stairs.

Azrael rolled his eyes, realizing that Bat was feeling uncomfortable in the role of leader. Probably more so because no one was going to be able to easily question his decisions. He lit a torch and moved to Bat's back, wanting to offer him a word of encouragement but settling for an awkward pat on the shoulder. Bat looked startled but nodded at Azrael after a moment of hesitation.

Azrael let Oslow take the lead into the stairs, handing the torch to him as he passed and pulling out another to hand to each member as they passed him. He took the rear, ensuring that if they were attacked from either side on the stairs there would be a tank as the first line of defense. After approximately three flights of normal building stairs, the group came to an awkward stop and Bat called, "Clear the exit so we can all see what you're staring at!"

It turned out that Oslow had good reason to stop and stare. The stairwell ended in a long hallway that glowed with an orangey-reddish hue from an opening about a hundred meters away. The sounds of flame throwers, screeching newts, and baritone bellows were constantly steaming down the hall. There was an oppressive feeling to the hallway, like the air was heavy. It could also have been the heat, because the temperature was rising with each step closer Azrael got to the exit.

Stepping out onto a rectangle of basalt that was lined by a railing, Azrael joined the others at the edge. He felt his muscles clench harder on the breather apparatus. A hundred feet below them, a war raged. The real heart-stoppers of the battle were separated by about a kilometer of space on either end of the monstrous cavern they looked down on. Both of the creatures' heads reached to the height of the balcony and they glared at each other with red eyes that spoke of a hate Azrael couldn't comprehend. He analyzed the red-skinned creature, which had onyx horns jutting from its head, first.

Velcanius
Epic-Demon Lord
Level 72
Health Points: 100,000 / 120,000
Skills: Hidden

The ranks in front of him all looked like Lava Newts coated in a layer of fire, and identified as Greater Demons. Azrael slowly turned his head to the other massive figure on the other side of the battle.

Sutr
Epic-Calamity
Level 74
Health Points: 235,000 / 360,000
Skills: Hidden

On that side of the battle, forty much smaller Giants laid into the Greater Demons with massive swords that looked to be made of basalt. "We need to kill those creatures?" Bat asked, his voice sounding incredulous as he watched the battle of titanic beasts rage. Azrael agreed with his sentiment, but took the question posed as a challenge as he studied the field. Was there a way to peel a single fighter from either side? The balcony had two sets of stairs descending to the pockmarked stone of the battleground below. One side would place his group ten feet from a Fire Giant, and the other direction a Greater Demon.

Removing his mouthpiece, Azrael suggested, "We could try fighting one of them from the stairs. Does anyone else feel like the last two rooms have pushed us to fight the Demons, since the Greater Demons appear to be a combination of what came before?"

Bat walked to the staircase that descended to the Demon side of the battle as Azrael replaced his mouthguard. The rest of the group watched transfixed as a Giant broke his blade on the scales of a Demon beast. Azrael thought that would be the end of that particular Giant, but he raised a clawed hand, palm up, in the direction of the now-lunging beast and a spike from the ground catapulted the beast back into its own ranks.

The Giant then grabbed the spike and a layer of black dust fell from it, revealing a new sword. Azrael scratched his head. So far they hadn't seen a member of either side of the fight die, except at the hands of the two leaders.

Every so often, a spell of darkness would lash out from Velcanius and bring a Giant to his knees. When the Giant was visible again, he was bleeding from numerous cuts and only had one health point remaining. Then a race would occur as another Giant from the backline attempted to replace the injured creature before the Demons got to him.

In response, Sutr would swing his two-hundred-foot gleaming metal sword and cleave one of the Greater Demons in half. That Demon died instantly, but with a scowl, Velcanius would summon another from thin air. This was at a cost of the Demon Lord's health it seemed, and on the other side, Sutr would lose health healing the nearly dead Fire Giant back to half of its original hit points.

"The other option is to pick off the Fire Giant that Velcanius hits with his orb spell…" Prateek suggested, removing and then replacing his breather. Azrael nodded at that suggestion. That might be the easiest option, but something was telling him it wasn't the right one. Despite his class of Demon, fighting on that side of this battle seemed to go against what the dungeon intended. The previous two rooms were almost like a hint to groups that came to this Realm. Of course, that was only if every party experienced the same fights, but Azrael had to believe that was the case. This was a dungeon, after all, and as intelligent as they could be, many of them liked scenarios that brought more parties into their depths.

There wasn't a wrong option here, but there seemed to be an intended option and an easy option, just like the previous floors. Bat seemed to agree because he said, "I think we are meant to take the side of the Giants here. There is just too much that points in that direction. However, we are effectively fighting without a suitable tank because of the fire coating the Lizard's skins. Oslow, what do you think?"

Oslow rubbed his biceps and looked at the floor, which was a kind of answer. Still, after a moment he looked up with his eyes challenging anyone who met them. "I think I can do it. It will just be more healing intensive. Are you okay with that, Prateek?" Oslow asked, just moving his mouthpiece to the side and somewhat mumbling the words. That choice ruined the confident effect he probably had been going for.

Prateek nodded in response, and Oslow moved to the stairs.

Jophi looked to Azrael, her eyes wide. He made a hand gesture that said, 'let's see how it goes,' and added a shrug. The problem with Oslow's class was that he avoided damage almost entirely, and as such he didn't train in the traditional way a tank did. Meaning he might not be able to handle the pain a high Stamina and armored tank could. Yet, there was only one way to find out.

The group followed behind Oslow as he mumbled into his mouthpiece, probably psyching himself up for what was about to happen. At the final stair, he pulled out a small laser pistol and fired at the nearest Demon. Azrael, who hadn't seen the pistol before, raised an eyebrow—it certainly was an easier way to pull individual enemies from a distance. He guessed that he hadn't seen it until now because most enemies charged them first.

Azrael could tell the pistol was a cheap version, because the first few shots didn't do anything against the hard scales of the beast. Oslow adjusted his target to the eyes of the Demon after watching the beam splash harmlessly over the Demon's hide. The shots at the eyes had the desired effect and the beast bellowed a draconic-like roar before it turned and charged the tank.

Azrael watched it with trepidation from about midway up the steps, and Bat gave some quick orders to the other two standing there with them. "Wait until he turns it, like with the Lava Newts. Oslow, try to get its back facing us, if you can!"

The first strike phased through Oslow, and beside Azrael, Prateek winced as he began casting a heal. Azrael checked the health bar of their tank to find that it had dropped twenty-five percent. Oslow fell to one knee as he walked out of the back of the beast. Azrael went to step forward and help, but Oslow held up a hand and levered himself back to standing with his sword. The heal hit him a split second after and his red, blistering skin seemed to reverse as the blisters sunk back into the surface. His limp also vanished, and he managed to position himself as the

Greater Demon leaped off the wall and first couple stairs back at him.

Bat allowed two more strikes before he ordered the attack. The group unleashed the spells they prepared, right after Azrael cleaved off the tail. Azrael slowly layered damage after his initial attack, keeping one eye on the wound and one on Oslow.

Oslow let claws and teeth phase through him but the Greater Demon also possessed some skills that it unleashed. A flame breath was neatly sidestepped, but a surprise fireball in the middle of the attack exploded and forced Oslow to phase through the ensuing shrapnel and flames.

"Ether at half," Prateek shouted, and Azrael checked the health of the Greater Demon. It was also at half. They were keeping pace, but needed to be in front on this race. Azrael began using more Ether and by the intensity of Jophi's spells, she had done the same.

The health pool of the beast dipped, but then it unleashed three skills. One was a whip of fire that could have been its tongue. It came out of its mouth and began waving back and forth like a scythe in a wheat field. It simultaneously began chain-casting fireballs and flaring up the fire surrounding its body as it continued to try to claw Oslow to pieces.

The tank screamed in pain and Azrael unleashed a Soul Blade from his storage in response, thrusting the ten stacks directly into the wound at the base of the Greater Demon's tail. The creature died shortly after as Jophi and Bat's spells combined to whittle down any remaining health.

Oslow was on his back, his skin past blistering and black in places. Prateek shot a few healing spells, which reversed the black to red angry blisters, but Azrael could tell that the healer now had an Ether headache. Oslow was still below half health, and everyone else in the party was sweating profusely.

Azrael ran a quick check of his own stores and found his Ether at forty percent and only one stored ten stack of Soul Blade waiting for use. He checked if this dungeon-born beast had loot before shouldering Oslow and moving back to the top of the stairs. Once they were at the balcony, the tank drank a healing potion and the group sat in silence. That had been a close one.

"Once Oslow has aggro, we should expend our Ether faster," Bat said. "No point holding onto it for the next fight. We will just kill one at a time and come up here—"

"Move!" Jophi screamed as she dived back into the hallway. Prateek, Bat, and Oslow were slow to respond, so Azrael grabbed Oslow—who was closest and laying down—before throwing him into the exit. Bat and Prateek managed to get their wits and were right beside him as he began his sprint to avoid whatever Jophi had seen.

A ball of blackness began expanding on the balcony and Azrael, Prateek, and Bat were all grazed by it as they dived for the doorway. Pain exploded along Azrael's calves as he rolled into the darkness. The contrast from the room to the hallway was too much, so he pulled back out and lit his torch to stare in horror at his heavily lacerated calves and feet. The shoes and pants he had been wearing were gone entirely and his health was dropping from fifty percent as he bled from numerous gashes.

If that was a graze, any one of us would be instantly dead if we took it full on!

The other two were even lower on health than he was. He quickly drank a Health potion before crawling to Bat and forcing the shaking Batman to drink one as well. Prateek took one himself, and the group just lay in silence, each one breathing even heavier through the oxygen conversion mask and feeling cold sweat trickle down their back despite the oppressive heat.

"I think it's safe to say we should kill one of the Demons and then retreat all the way back to the hallway each time," Bat said, sounding like he was trying to be flippant but his already high voice cracked in places.

Azrael swallowed and peeked back into the room to find Velcanius glaring up at the balcony. A massive flash of silver sparkled through the air, and a boom shortly followed. The Demon Lord transferred its hateful glare back to Sutr. "Yeah, I think that's a good plan. It seems he targets the side of whoever killed his last minion. I assume his spell range can't reach Sutr, which is why he usually targets the Giants," Azrael observed from his position at the entrance to the cavern.

CHAPTER FIFTY-FOUR

"There is no longer a way to pull the Greater Demons one at a time!" Bat shouted as the group was forced to retreat into the hallway after three Greater Demons charged the stairs, in an attempt to slaughter the nuisance the group had become. They had managed to kill four more after the first one, but when they returned to the large cavern, they found that Velcanius had summoned back the slaughtered minions and the five positions the group had killed and respawned were now watching the stairs, instead of the enemy Giants.

With the shift in the Demons' defense, the Giants were slowly starting to move the front line of the battle closer to Velcanius, but his sphere attack was still stopping a full rout. The problem, as Azrael saw it, was that they were punching above their weight class in an unstable environment. Each Greater Demon could be considered a boss fight for the group, based on level disparity and match up against their tank.

The Greater Demons abandoned the chase at some point during the group's retreat. Azrael wasn't positive about the timing, but he saw the three returning to their spots at the bottom of the stairs. He left the doorway and returned to the group as he removed his mouthpiece. "We could try to assist the front line of the Giants from the top of the balcony," he suggested.

"Will that register the kills as ours though?" Bat responded while scratching his head sheepishly.

"No clue, but if we manage to advance the Giants' front line far enough, the five watching the stairs will be forced to engage, and we can likely go back to fighting them one at a time," Azrael surmised with a shrug.

"I'll keep an eye on Velcanius, in case he targets us with that sphere attack," Oslow mumbled around his mouthpiece. Prateek nodded and pointed at Oslow, suggesting he would do the same. Azrael nodded; the other three were the ranged fighters anyway, so that should work out for the best.

The three of them gathered at the railing, looking down on the frontline of the battle. The Giants were working in pairs now against a semi-depleted front line of flaming Lizards. It appeared that the fire attacks of the Greater Demons had little to no effect on the Giants, and most of the attacks from the Giants in retaliation were being kept to melee sword fighting. It showed that the Giants were winning in the intelligence and wisdom stat, if nothing else. The Lizards didn't seem to under- stand and kept blasting fire-based skills at their opponents, but the Giants didn't waste their Ether on useless attacks. Not a huge victory, but something that would possibly have an effect as the battle waged on.

"Target the six in front and ignore the second line that is casting the fireballs into the Giants. We don't want them to turn their attacks this way; we aren't fireproof like the Giants..." Bat suggested.

That severely limited Azrael's damage. His Soul Blade skill, which was one of his few long range skills, instantly spread out. The more charges he added, the worse it would be. Unless he went with the single target thrust attack, but even that grew the farther it traveled. He weighed both options, and chose to try a single charge, directed across the entire front line. He didn't expect it to do much damage, but if it distracted the Demons long enough, the Giants would be able to batter them to death.

Bat counted down from three once Jophi and Azrael nodded that they were ready. The air above the Lizards rippled as soon as Bat hit zero. The ground below the Demons also began to emit a dense white fog that hissed against the fire that surrounded the monsters. Azrael's skill took a few seconds to reach the front line, but it crashed down atop the backs, necks, and legs of the Greater Demons with a grinding shriek. The power of his skill combined with the other's skills drove the Demons to their bellies and the Fire Giants' blows hammered the now-flattened foes further. Azrael felt his hair begin to stand on end just as Oslow shouted, "Retreat!"

The group didn't hesitate and sprinted back to the hallway as the ball of darkness formed, engulfing the railing they had just stood at. The group watched from safety as the sphere dissipated, leaving the railing intact but with numerous serrated cuts on every surface. "How is everyone's Ether?" Bat asked.

"Enough of this, Sutr," Velcanius shouted from down below. A new cold sweat broke out on Azrael's neck. That had been what was missing, this whole time. While the combat was loud and constant, the two boss creatures never spoke to their troops or each other. He had assumed that this was a war scenario meant for a group to capitalize on. Before he could consider further, Velcanius continued, "You, the pride of your race, rely on the miniscule Vanir and Aesir to defeat me? Then I will no longer hold my allies back—Dark Elves, attack!"

The room below, which had already been loud, had a new sound added to the cacophony. The sound of army horns, and troops marching in step. Azrael chanced a peek out at the balcony on the far side of the room. It had no stairs down, and instead ran for the entire kilometer of the field below. The Dark Elves lined up only on the Demon's side, layering themselves five deep with bows strung but not pulled. Azrael scanned the battle below to see the Giants step back from the gap they just opened with his group's help. Instead of pressing into that gap, they backed up and formed black obsidian shields from the basalt floor.

At an unheard command, the Dark Elves drew and loosed. To Azrael's surprise, many arrows were aimed at him and his group, who had followed him out onto the balcony. Jophi waved her hand and an icy wind blew many of them off course, and the remaining ten to fifteen that stayed true caught fire when they drew within fifty feet of Prateek.

"I didn't call for any aid, fool. Those tiny creatures attack you of their own volition. However, it seemed like you were always prepared to call the Dark Elves for aid. Or would you have me believe that battalion was just passing by?" Sutr said, his voice more amused than worried. "Funny you should mention the Aesir and Vanir, because the lower Realms have been contacting me. Fenrir, Alvaldi, prove you're serious about challenging the Aesir, and join me to destroy the Fire Demons!"

Azrael felt the presence of the monstrous wolf but couldn't see the creature. Alvaldi appeared below the balcony on the far side of the cavern, a fair distance from the Fire Giants. Azrael still felt Fenrir's presence from that side of the room, and he scanned the area again to find a knee-height wolf beside Alvaldi. Azrael's blood froze in his veins. He could feel waves of pure menace radiating off the wolf. It was like unemotional destruction, unfeeling murder, it was like the mountaintop that the Sovereign Halls wanted its students to reach. It was like Fenrir's blood itself was so cold and unemotional, that a single drop left to its nature would consume the world or try to.

To Azrael's further shock, Alvaldi was different as well. He radiated a power that furthered the goosebumps on Azrael's arms. It was odd, because he had just seen this Frost Giant in the previous Realm, but somehow this Alvaldi felt alive instead of scripted.

"We are here, Sutr, but you must prove that you can defeat Velcanius without help if you want to join our Ragnarok clan!" Alvaldi made a motion as he spoke and the ranks of Elves froze on the balcony, ice climbing them from foot to the roof. "Still, this is a one-on-one fight—" Alvaldi looked up at Azrael and his eyes practically glowed with familiarity.

Bat whispered what Azrael was thinking before he could get it out, "Apep..."

To Azrael's surprise, Sutr laughed at the Frost Giant before every inch of his body, armor, and sword whooshed to life. Azrael felt the ground shudder under him on the balcony. Bat turned to Azrael, both ears facing him, before following a line in the air. This time, Azrael thought he felt it. A tube that felt like a line of static in the air connected from above his head and traveled toward Sutr. It felt so much like that strange source of Essence at the end of Azrael's Ether spiral that he entered the mental space that he did when meditating.

Alvaldi and Fenrir contained beautiful, compact, and swirling Ether spirals in their cores. Azrael watched as Sutr began forming one. The spiral began spinning, but at the bottom of the spiral, Sutr, or maybe Apep, took the thread and looped back up to a place above the swirling mass before the thread vanished. Something about the direction of that thread tugged at Azrael's mind.

Is Apep sending the Essence back to himself? he wondered as he watched the change overtake Sutr. Nothing was more obvious than the eyes of the Fire Giant boss. Like Alvaldi, they grew more and more intelligent. A shudder ran down Azrael's spine —this was a fight that his group had no business in. Watching Sutr change, Azrael could tell that this fight was about to grow out of hand.

"I am unsure what is happening, but I would suggest you all leave the dungeon now," the voice of Heimdall spoke from beside Azrael. He turned to find his entire group staring at the orange-eyed, powerfully built man.

"But if we don't advance to the next level, we won't be able to enter again," Azrael asked, removing his mouthpiece.

"You haven't seen what happened on the previous floors. Let me just say that you don't want to be here when the entire landscape changes... additionally, the dungeon informs me that this will be counted as a victory. The Rainbow dungeon is very happy for something you did for it."

"Azrael, I think it's more important for us to live, especially if this will be counted as us making it anyway!" Jophi stated.

"There are other dungeons!" Bat added.

Azrael blinked before nodding at his group and then Heimdall in turn.

"Exit!" Heimdall said right away, and the area lit up in the same multitude of colors that blinded Azrael the first time.

———

The white blindness slowly faded, allowing Azrael to see the still-spinning room of the dungeon entrance and Heimdall removing his sword from the altar. "Now that we are in a place of safety, I need to ask you a few questions. Do you have any idea why the floors you defeated began changing right after you left?"

Azrael looked to Bat and then glanced at the rest of his group, before returning to Heimdall. Shaking his head, Azrael fought to keep his face neutral.

Heimdall glowered back at him for a long moment. "There is something you are hiding from me. Something that I couldn't see in the dungeon, and I can't see now. What is it?"

"Azrael's heritage is a secret—" Bat began but was cut off.

"I can see his lineage, Batman, but around three of you, a darkness hovers, and when my eyes try to pierce it—I see only more darkness. Do you know what it is?"

Azrael shook his head again, along with Bat before they both turned to stare at Jophi. She raised an eyebrow before following along and shaking her head. Heimdall's orange eyes narrowed before he shrugged and pointed behind the group. "Out there, you will have to face Thor, Merlin, Loki, and even Freya. Are you sure there is nothing you want to tell me?"

The group all paled. The names invoked in that sentence were easily four of the highest-level individuals on Gaia, if not in the entire EtherVerse. Azrael coughed. "So you're blaming us for what's occurred in the Rainbow dungeon?"

Heimdall laughed, his stony demeanor breaking so suddenly that Azrael felt whiplash. "I am the dungeon keeper, and I can tell you with certainty that what has happened inside is only raising the level of the dungeon. So, blame—if there was to be any—wouldn't be a bad or good thing. However, outside of this room, those particular people are waiting because you have something that doesn't belong to you..."

"The reports from Atlantis were released then?" Azrael whispered and his group looked at him with confusion. He waved their concern away and shrugged. "Heimdall, from what you said earlier, you probably can tell I am not lying when I say I didn't steal it."

"Ahh, but you see, there is something hidden about you. How can I be sure?" Heimdall answered with a shake of his head. Without waiting for a response, he waved a hand and the sphere rotated to create an opening to the bridge that led to the city of Asgard.

From this angle, the city itself seemed to be so majestic and magical that Azrael's breath caught. At the end of the multi-hued bridge from which the dungeon derived its name stood Merlin, his back to the dungeon. Ringing the older man were three well-dressed figures, their arms crossed. Even from here, Azrael could feel the auras of those three. It was like Alvaldi, Sutr, and Fenrir were children's toys in comparison. Somehow though, Merlin stood in front of the three figures and didn't appear to even flinch.

Azrael studied each of the figures in turn as the group approached. Loki had vibrant red hair that contrasted his bluish skin. He easily stood eight feet tall, and had two horns that protruded from his forehead, almost looking like a crown.

Freya actually wore a golden circlet on her head and two white wings sprouting from the headband helped frame the wildness of her blonde hair that streamed out from behind the golden band. She had high cheekbones and a pale complexion that matched the man standing beside her.

Thor's hair reached midway down his neck and had some of the wildness of Freya's, but his hair seemed to plait itself in a pattern that appeared styled, even if it might not have been. His face was similar to that of Magnus', but also sterner, stronger, and more commanding. His blue eyes bored into Merlin in a way that told Azrael that if it wasn't Merlin in front of the imposing man—he would have already had his way.

They came into Azrael's hearing range just as Freya finished saying something. "…for you to request the report not be given for twenty-four hours suggests collusion, Merlin!"

"Freya, my dear student, you and the council must remember that guilt cannot be so easily measured. Not to mention that you wanted to send in your mercenaries to kill and capture the students immediately. You have not even confirmed their guilt?"

"Surely you jest, old man. You haven't taken the boy as a full apprentice yet, so why would he legitimately have your mark?" Thor crowed.

"Ahh, so you doubt my word now, former apprentice?"

Thor ignored Merlin and glared at Azrael's group instead. "Did one of you steal my necklace?"

"I have seen your necklace Thor, but I did not steal it…" Azrael responded, softly. His vocal cords felt tight and strained.

"How can you have seen it and not stolen it?!" Loki responded, his voice sounding loud and filled with an emotion that neither Freya nor Merlin's had possessed.

"Easy, brother," Thor said as he reached up to place a hand on Loki's shoulder. "Merlin, do you truly believe he has seen my necklace but not stolen it?"

"I do, Thor. Your level of Truth Seeker may not be as high as mine, but I am sure you can see he is telling the truth. Also, please recall where you keep the necklace in question, and then recall when Azrael would have had access to it?"

Thor pursed his lips as Azrael arrived beside Merlin. The

old man turned and smiled at Azrael, seeming to not be surprised in the least by his sudden appearance beside him.

Loki pulled out two very menacing knives that clearly weren't designed for combat. Azrael examined the thin blades and surmised they must have been torture implements. "I can make him talk, brother," Loki said.

Freya didn't object and nodded her head above crossed arms, as if to agree with Loki.

Jophi cupped her hand and whispered in Azrael's ear, "What do they think you stole?"

Instead of responding only to her, Azrael spoke to everyone. "I told Merlin, like I am telling everyone now, that I did not steal Thor's Mark of Merlin."

Thor ran his fingers over the rough stubble on his face. "But you admit you have seen it?" he asked, seeming genuinely confused by the tack of the conversation.

"I do not deny having seen the item, but, again, I did not steal it."

"Tell us who did it then?!" Loki shouted, seeming to grow angrier because his opportunity to torture was being denied.

"I believe Thor would prefer that the thief remain unnamed," Merlin suggested, winking at Azrael's group and then turning back to Thor. "Don't you, my dear former apprentice?"

Thor's eyes grew large before he turned and looked behind him toward the massive skyscraper-like castle behind him. "I will take my teacher's advice on this, but I am afraid I must insist that Azrael return the item to me…"

"I do not have the item, so I cannot return it. However, I have no issue revealing who the thief is. In fact, he has been causing me and my group nothing but issues," Azrael responded, seeing an opportunity.

Thor glared at Azrael and the aura of the man caused every muscle in his body to tense in fear. He couldn't have said more if he wanted to. Thor's eyes practically sparked out lightning bolts, but after a time, the man said, "I can assure you that the problems will lessen, now. However, I think you are *mistaken* as to who you believe the thief to be…"

Azrael looked at Merlin, who was looking at Thor. "Do not worry, my former apprentice. There is a tournament at the end of next semester to earn the same enchantment your mark possessed…"

"Wait, you get access to the Atlantean Towers through a school tournament?" Azrael asked.

"The tournament hasn't been held for quite a long while, but the teachers believe that reinstituting it will return some of Atlantean Academy's glory," Merlin responded. "Now, if you fine Asgardians will excuse me, I must get this group back to the academy. Cheerio!"

Azrael didn't even blink, but it sure felt like he had. One moment he was outside with the sun shining off a massive Asgardian city, and the next he was in the dining room of the villa. Even more surprising was that the whole group was there but not Merlin. Azrael coughed before asking, "What about the Cussing Parrot?"

"It's already on the helipad…" Bat whispered, his voice filled with an awe that Azrael couldn't place.

"Did Merlin just teleport us back to school?" Prateek asked, his voice cracking and clearly excited. "By the Ether, I need to call my parents!" Oslow joined in as Prateek and he made a dash for the door. Azrael wouldn't say they were shrieking with excitement, but they weren't far off.

Jophi and Bat just looked at him. "Can we talk about what just happened?" Bat asked and Jophi nodded.

"Yeah, we should. Let's go upstairs."

CHAPTER FIFTY-FIVE

"Azrael, I think it's time you tell Jophi," Bat began, his ears standing straight up as he made the plea. "I'm worried that what you're doing is beyond your control at this point."

Azrael sighed. He had come upstairs to the dojo to meditate and test out the new Ether Manipulation pattern that Apep had unwittingly shown him. So, when Bat brought up telling Jophi about something, his mind went immediately to Apep and the five dungeons he had helped the strange amalgamation capture.

Jophi was looking at him, her eyes neutral but something about the gaze was vulnerable in a way he didn't usually associate with the woman.

"Alright," he began. He turned toward her and gave up on meditating for now. "Remember what happened on Tech Duinn?"

"It's pretty hard to forget, Azrael," Jophi retorted with some mild amusement tinting her voice.

"It's more the little things that have happened after that you probably need to recall," Azrael countered, allowing a bit of amusement into his own voice. "Like Bat mentioning that connection I had to the big hole in space…"

"Yeah, I remember that, but he said it was shrinking the farther we got from it."

"Right, well, it turns out that Apep can use that to take over dungeons, as long as a boss or scenario is completed inside."

Jophi blinked and then started to smile as she looked at Bat. When she saw his serious expression and looked back to Azrael, who was also wearing a serious look, she blinked again. "Wait, you're serious?"

"Dead serious. Still, that's only a piece of the story..."

Azrael went on to explain the entirety of the discovery, including why the Labyrinth dungeon had increased in difficulty, and what he expected to have occurred in the Rainbow dungeon. When he admitted to Louis being reborn inside the Labyrinth dungeon, Jophi stopped him with a stern look. "You're telling me that not only can Apep bring to life humanoid mobs, but also take control of them outside of the dungeon?"

"Yes, the person returns at level one, which was the real reason Louis lost his original levels."

"The person can rechoose their Apprentice rank class as well?" Jophi asked, the concern still evident in her voice.

"Seems so."

"Can these reborn individuals take control of dungeons for Apep?" Jophi asked and Azrael finally saw the direction of her thoughts. Entire teams of adventurers had died inside of the Labyrinth dungeon, and even more high-leveled fighters had perished on Tech Duinn. Could Apep return all of those people and level them up in the dungeon?

"This is why I was originally concerned about Azrael," Bat added his voice to the conversation.

"Theoretically, that is quite possible, but I don't see that as a bad thing. I just told you my goal is to disrupt the guilds, and having other groups acting to that end on the planet isn't a bad thing..."

"Azrael, if you were more powerful than Apep or in control of him, that would be true. However, I don't think you're taking into account the escalation that will occur. Do you think Apep will stop at the guilds?"

Azrael shrugged. "So what? I don't really care if Apep takes control of every dungeon on the planet. That will just cause more problems for the guilds, and they will have to recall their fleets."

"Azrael, please just listen to me on this one. You're blind to the greater picture here. If we give Apep a large enough hold on the planet through the dungeons, it is very possible that he will never be removed. It would be like an infestation. You can come in and rain fire down upon it, but all it takes is missing a single egg and that infestation will come right back. Can we at least agree not to capture any more dungeons until we know more?"

"I agree with Jophi, Azrael. I think the five dungeons Apep already holds are enough. If he takes control of the Rainbow dungeon fully, that alone is a major shift in power. Since you managed to gain us access to the El Dorado dungeons again— let's keep to the Labyrinth in the second half of this semester."

Azrael thought about it, and admitted to himself that it wouldn't hurt to focus on increasing his own strength for now. "Okay, I can agree to that for now. Let's focus on our group and build some wealth for now."

"Since that's taken care of, I am going to go rank up to Journeyman," Bat said.

Azrael Analyzed his friend. He had finally reached level twenty-five. "Congratulations, Bat. I will make sure Louis has a feast ready for when you're finished. Just so you know, if you end up in the Cavern of Choices, make sure you ask a lot of questions, and point out all the skills you have. I think they matter."

Bat raised one ear high while the other stayed neutral, but Azrael shrugged, not really one-hundred percent sure what or who had interceded on his behalf. He didn't think he could convince Merlin to do so on Bat's behalf if it was the headmaster.

Bat left after a hug with Jophi and a nod at Azrael.

Azrael chose to sit down and finally get to the meditation he intended when he came up here. To his relief, Jophi sat down as well and closed her eyes. He already realized some of the dangers that Apep could pose. Still, when going up against the strength of the Gaian guilds, a more powerful ally was exactly what you wanted.

Putting those thoughts out of his head to consider later, Azrael entered his meditative state. He studied his Ether channels and found that his maintenance over the first half of this semester had truly done him well. His channels flowed seamlessly even though he hadn't meditated while in the Rainbow dungeon. Smiling softly, he deconstructed his current spiral and watched the spinning Ether slow down.

When it was back to its more pool-like state, he began to create the sphere he had seen inside of Fenrir, Alvaldi, and Sutr. He used his earlier trick of continuing the channels into his pool and soon was left with a hollow sphere of interwoven Ether channels. He merged new channels and adjusted the speed of each to create a virulent flow that sped up the closer to the bottom of the sphere the Ether travelled. Once the Ether reached the bottom of the sphere, he created a final channel that looped up and back into the top of the sphere, draining into the hollow center.

Hurriedly he tied off his strands as his head began to thump in time with his heartbeat. At first, he thought nothing had happened, but then a notification popped up.

Congratulations! You have increased Essence Conversion to Moderate.

Essence Conversion

• **You have made your body a better vessel for converting Ether to Essence. Your body's ability to act as a filter increased fractionally. Planetary Gods always need more Essence; since you stand out in this regard, you will be awarded 25% more Etherience per kill per level in this skill.**

- **You gain increased mental fortitude when dealing with Ether Fatigue and mental direction of Essence by 2% per level in the Moderate rank. Some laws of Ether will no longer apply to the individual the stronger they get in this skill.**
Current Rank: Moderate Level 1.

He sat there stunned by the increase in skill, and tried to find a place to tap off of this new spiral. Clearly, he was onto something with the new formation or the system wouldn't award him with an increased rank, but what exactly would that rank do to help him?

Azrael was just starting to pull off a strand near the bottom of the sphere to attach to the house when he felt what he could only describe as a reverberation, akin to a heartbeat. It was like the sphere filled up with something that was pressurized. It held for just a moment before it bulged out and released whatever the substance was through the cracks in the sphere. He felt his eyebrows raise slightly as he considered this new development. Had that been Essence?

He spent the next forty-five minutes attempting to contain this new unseen force. He even went as far as rebuilding his sphere with an increasing thickness of a single sheet like Ether Channel. However, when the pressure built, it shattered the construct and added to his ever-increasing headache.

After forty-five minutes of no progress, he gave up and joined a thread to the floor. The wood itself rippled and Azrael watched it slowly go from old and rotten to a few years from new in front of his eyes. The ring of repaired wood expanded rapidly and after only about an hour, the room was finished. Jophi opened her eyes when she sensed that her meditation was no longer doing anything. "Okay! That was far too fast for this room. What did you figure out?" she asked, blinking as she took in the completed space.

Azrael explained the new sphere-like creation to Jophi and after another hour, she too had advanced her Essence Conversion skill to the Moderate ranks. Once Bat was finished with his class ascension, Azrael would share this with him, and they would finally complete Merlin's task of repairing the villa.

Jophi and Azrael went down to the kitchen for some food in a great mood.

"Azrael, what exactly was Merlin talking about with his mark and access to the Atlantean Towers?" Jophi asked after they informed Louis that they wanted to eat.

"I'm not sure what the tournament that grants the access is, but Thor's Mark of Merlin possesses an enchantment that gives him access to the Atlantean Towers." At Jophi's raised eyebrow Azrael further explained. "I saw the mark when Magnus dropped it on the ground. He probably intended for me to pick it up, so he could frame me with the theft. Luckily, he isn't a great actor," Azrael explained.

He didn't like lying to Jophi, as she had, to all appearances, taken his side over that of her father's and the guild. Still, the less people that knew about a thing, the less chance of someone accidentally finding out.

"If this tournament has been held at the school before, I bet we can find out more information in the library. Since we are all spending next off week at school studying for midterms, maybe we can try to research the tournament as well?"

"The more we know, the better prepared we will be," Azrael exclaimed, and added that to his list of things to do.

"How do you feel about Maat's replacement?" Jophi asked, changing the subject. Her smile told Azrael she knew how much he had liked the big combat professor. Her look turned introspective when she likely recalled what guild had recruited him away.

Azrael smiled to let her know that he didn't take any offense. "Honestly, he is just okay. He teaches forms like he expects the student to become a robot and follow each minutiae that he over-explains…"

CHAPTER FIFTY-SIX

The week of classes turned into midterm prep, in all classes but the two Azrael had multiple days of. In combat class, the teacher went through forms with everyone and refused to teach new information or allow practice of higher level forms. He didn't even allow Azrael to demonstrate his mastery of the beginner katas. He would have been frustrated, but in some ways this allowed him to study the intricacies of the nine beginner katas and see their gradual progressions. The flow from stance to stance, as well as the intended lines that they were meant to form.

Each kata and form should have that kind of intention...

Azrael was currently in the library with Jophi, Bat, Prateek, and Oslow, studying for exams that he felt confident in already. Bat had only needed two days to rank up and the Batman had been able to access a rare class known as an Echo. Bat claimed that this class was highly sought after, and a perfect fit for his Journeyman ranks. They all couldn't wait to get back out to El Dorado and see what Bat could do.

Almost all of these first few months of classes were just repetition for Azrael. The Atlantean Academy was just teaching a slightly modified version of what the Sovereign Halls had taught him, or making small additions to it. This meant that Azrael was just fitting final puzzle pieces or adjusting his prior understanding of a subject.

"How does the Ether life expectancy remove humanity's morals?" Jophi asked, looking between two books. This was a question the philosophy teacher Darwin Faige had posed to the class.

"That is a hypothesis that has been put forward by certain religious sects, the Coalition of Dragons primary among them. It simply states that certain aspects of life would be governed by natural genetics and biology if Ether users didn't live for hundreds of years. The groups theorize that if system users had shorter lifespans that there would be an imperative on creating offspring, or on protecting human life. The theory states that because of longer life expectancies, people are able to put aside some of those base instincts and act immorally more often. They go as far as to claim that death is so widely accepted by system users because of some of the spells the system gives users access to. There is an entire chapter on Resurrection or Rebirth spells in the book, and the back half covers how spells like that have convinced the entire EtherVerse that killing is just a temporary thing. That the soul is reborn over and over again..."

Azrael faded off, remembering his class's ability to capture and consume souls. He felt his mental connection to his Soul Blade, which the souls of Torin and Papi had been fed to. Jophi flipped to the chapter Azrael had mentioned and began reading the theology and philosophy it contained, while he introspected on his responsibilities.

Oslow and Prateek were near one of the counters that contained librarians and students requesting some reading materials for their Healing and Primary Tanking classes. Bat nudged Azrael, which refocused not only his mind from the rabbit hole he was down but also his eyes that were gazing at the two teammates. He still hadn't taught them the Essence

Conversion skill and somehow the introspection he had just undergone had led him to that consideration.

"They're talking about an offer that lackey of Magnus' made. Something about leaving our group and getting multiple runs through high level dungeons while they are in school. It seems that their guilds are pressuring them to take the offer, but they are both refusing to."

Azrael clenched his jaw. While the Asgardian guild was now going to stay out of the politics around Azrael, it didn't mean that Magnus couldn't make his life harder in other ways. Still, they hadn't taken the offer yet. Did that mean they should be considered friends, or were they only sticking around because of Merlin?

The librarian handed over a stack of books and the two began checking what each one was.

"Honestly, I'm not sure if they're staying with us because of our ties to powerful people or if they're our—" Azrael cut off as the two grew excited and rushed back to the table.

"Look at this!" Oslow whispered excitedly as he plopped down the one book he had brought.

Prateek dropped a stack of nine others on the table's edge and spared a glance of frustration for his friend who had left them all to him. "It seems like there are specific roles tested in that tournament Merlin mentioned," Prateek said as he used a now-free hand to point at the title of the book Oslow rushed over.

Atlantean Tournament Tanks and Healers of Legend.

Azrael read the cover and felt heat surge down his limbs. So far the group had found many mentions of the tournament, and even a rule book. Still, they hadn't been able to find a single mention of what events or trials to expect.

"Well, that's some new information at least," Azrael mused, as he flipped open the book to just find a huge list of prior participants, and champions for each year. After many consecutive years of the tournament being hosted, it got moved to once every five years, until it lapsed to a decade. By the last pages of the book, there seemed to be starts and stops of returning to a five year schedule before not hosting the tournament for two or three decades. The final entry in the book was dated nearly fifty years earlier and then the remaining pages were blank. "Look at that. I wonder if fifty years ago was the tournament Thor won…"

Unfortunately, this book only listed the healer and tank that had won that tournament and gained access to the first Atlantean Tower. Azrael wondered if Hercules or Żiewe had managed to conquer the first tower or not. He flipped backward and wondered if they could find a book for other class roles; maybe even his father Eribus was in one of them.

He shook his head and checked the time. They had been in the library for the last four hours, and it was time for lunch and some meditation back at the villa. He made a motion over his books and they vanished into his storage ring. Jophi, who had a storage device with sufficient space, did the same, but Oslow and Prateek were forced to carry their books instead. Azrael had suggested they empty the adventuring gear while at school, but neither of the boys had done so. Or perhaps they had, and were carrying around other things. There was no way for Azrael to know.

The walk from the library to the villa was a good twenty minutes over the beautiful school grounds, and Azrael relished the smell of the changing season. The sun high up in the sky wasn't carrying the same intensity of the fall season. It still was warm enough during the day to forgo an extra layer, but now at night people were wearing sweaters or jackets while they traveled. This season was called winter in the far north and south, but traditionally got branded Renewal by the people in the center of the continent. Only rarely did the people who lived closer to the equator see snow, and even then it would melt on contact with the ground.

Azrael saw the villa's run down exterior in the distance and smiled. The interior was nearly completely fixed now, and the group was completing the final rooms before they chose to move on to the exterior structures. Azrael was proud of the near completion a full half-semester before Merlin wanted it to be done. It made him think they were more intelligent than the other students who came before them. This villa had remained run down and broken for a long time all because people hadn't been willing to live there when they had offers from other sponsors with fully furnished dorms.

When they opened the front door of the villa, the smells of multiple dishes tickled Azrael's nose.

Bat groaned in pleasure beside him. "I think I smell Krondisarian Larval Worms. I have only eaten them once in my life," he whispered and rushed from the entryway toward the kitchen. The others followed to find Louis putting out individually prepared plates on the dining room table. To his surprise, Azrael found Sovereign Steak with caramelized onions, mushrooms, and man eating potatoes set at the head of the table. That had always been his favorite as a student of the Empire. How had Louis known? He had only told Jophi…

Jophi was smiling at him and he couldn't help but smile back. So, she had told Louis his favorite dish. A warm feeling in his chest warred with a jolt of static electricity from his brain. Would she reveal anything else he had told her?

No, Jophi would never do that. It's not like your favorite food is a secret that can be used against you…

CHAPTER FIFTY-SEVEN

"I can't wait until the final exams, so I don't have to put up with all this trash at the school," Magnus loudly exclaimed from his spot waiting on Darwin Faige to give the students access to the classroom. His cronies were all looking at Azrael, making it very clear who Magnus was referring too.

Azrael just chuckled. Magnus' suspension had ended last night, and this was their first time running into each other. Azrael had expected threats or ultimatums from the young man, thinking he would be desperate to get the necklace returned to him, but it would seem that the petty child was just going to return to his normal antics. "I've heard there is still an opportunity to drop your classes after you get your midterm results, Magnus. You might want to set up a meeting with an academic advisor. Maybe not, though. I've heard you're pretty good at dropping things…"

Azrael faded off as a chill swept over the early morning gathering of students. The stare Magnus delivered in his direction could have killed, or perhaps should have. A few small chuckles died almost instantly thanks to the shift in mood of the students. Azrael even thought he could see lightning crackling around Magnus' meaty fist.

Guess we know who got under whose skin... Azrael thought while smiling in return to the glare. Magnus, while powerful, would be far less dangerous without the Asgardian guild behind him, and Azrael had never been afraid of the braggart. In fact, Azrael was pretty sure that his group would be able to run the Labyrinth dungeon every off week without any problems. Considering that would average them each around fifty crystals, and loads of Etherience thanks to Apep, Azrael was sure he would soon out-level the son of Thor.

"Alright, all studying material must go away now, and all students are to take a seat. If you have a storage device, it must be placed on the green jade on the desk. If you attempt to pull something from the storage device after you have placed it there, the jade will break and you will receive zero for the exam. Does everyone understand?" Darwin Faige opened the door and stepped out into the hall to deliver his pre-exam speech. When everyone was silent he continued, "Good, let's get the midterm finished then!"

———

Azrael went over his cue cards in his interface, reviewing the information for his 'group' presentation. He had chosen Boss Sequencing and had even drawn inspiration and a few diagrams from Musth, the dungeon elephant encounter. The other four in his group were huddled near the computer that would put their images and diagrams on a large screen near the front of the classroom. His images and slides were on his own interface and he would throw them up after they were finished, but what was taking so long?

The first student, Brodie, stepped to the front of the stage and made a large motion to the screen behind him. "As you can see, I will be presenting on Boss Sequencing..." Azrael blinked as Brodie continued talking. He looked at Professor Amelie, who was nodding along. Behind her, he caught a glimpse of blond hair. He scanned up to find Magnus smiling broadly at him.

Azrael felt his heart drop. Professor Amelie had made it very clear that only one person could present on a topic at a time. Surely, she would understand this situation, though, right? Brodie had claimed he was presenting on Mob Aggro Rules. Perhaps Azrael could change to that topic?

His blood felt like it was on fire as the fourth member of his 'group' chose to present on two topics as well. The four had planned this well, leaving Azrael no topics from the list they created. He listened with half an ear and debated just repeating the presentation on Boss Sequencing; his presentation was far stronger than Brodie's had been anyway. Still, that broad smile from Magnus made him consider a different route. Could he discuss Time Dilation? The events inside of the Rainbow dungeon couldn't be discussed without breaking the Ether Contract, but would an effect of the dungeon not be discussable? Time Dilation was something that many high level dungeons could supposedly do, but it was still exceptionally rare to find a real case of.

Some scholars even considered it to be a myth...

The final boy finished and Azrael stepped up to the front of the stage. He put his original slides up on the screen and heard the confused hush take over the room. Into that silence he said, "As you can see, I had planned to present on Boss Sequencing, but since Brodie has already butchered that topic..." Azrael faded off with a look at the offending boy. After the glance, he turned to Magnus in the audience and continued, "So, instead of boring everyone with a second presentation on that subject, I would like to discuss Time Dilation and its effects, using a dungeon I recently visited... I must thank Magnus for the bet he made with me earlier in the year."

It turned out he couldn't name the specific dungeon, but the murmurs that broke out from the crowd confirmed that everyone got his less than subtle nudge. The smile left Magnus' face in the crowd as Azrael's smile grew.

Fifteen minutes later, the crowd cheered as Azrael took a small bow. There had been a few stumbling points as Azrael attempted to circumvent the Ether Contract, but for the most part he was able to use the group's experience in the dungeon and convey all the information he could think of on Time Dilation and how they had used it to their advantage. He even added a second topic to his presentation, Safe Zones and Their Strategic Use.

Another group slowly made their way to the stage amidst the restless students murmuring, while Professor Amelie approached Azrael. "If you are able to discuss this topic more, I would love to offer to help you publish a book on it. I can guarantee that it will be extremely well-received by the scholarly community. You could make thousands of crystals..." she said, her excitement at an all-time high, at least from what Azrael had seen.

"I only picked the topic because Magnus had clearly coerced the other students to ruin my prepared presentation—"

"I realize that, but the fact that you have the ability to discuss the events that occurred inside the Rainbow dungeon, even if it is limited, means that we could even release a dungeon information guide on the subject. There hasn't been real information on that dungeon on the market. Ever. I can guarantee you an A+ in this class, and renown if you are willing to work with me."

Azrael sighed and looked at Magnus, who was already in a corner of the classroom, talking with someone through his interface's phone. If that book wouldn't affect the entire Asgardian guild, he might have done it, but he had just managed to get away from their meddling. "I'm going to have to think about it, Amelie. The Asgardians clearly wouldn't like that information out in the public, or they would have written it themselves..."

Professor Amelie sighed, looked up at Magnus as well, then nodded her head. "Just let me know if you change your mind. Actual proof of time dilation is worth a few ruffled feathers..."

———

"Are we waiting until exams are finished or starting on the exterior of the house?" Prateek asked as the group sat at the table eating delicious lunches prepared by Louis.

Azrael's mouth was full of food, so he held up a finger to indicate that he would answer in a moment. The steak was just too juicy to try to talk with a bite in his mouth. He would likely end up drooling the blood down his chin or something. To his surprise, a quiet voice answered from the kitchen.

"Oh, I wouldn't get started on the outside of the house when you haven't even finished the interior…" The door swung open to reveal Merlin holding a heaping plate of nachos. "Thanks so much for the food, Louis, I can't wait to dig in," Merlin added to an unseen person who could only have been Louis still cleaning up the kitchen.

Azrael forgot to chew as he tilted his head and looked around the house. They finished everything inside. He remembered his food and hurriedly masticated and swallowed. "What do you mean? Every room is repaired!" he responded heatedly.

"Nacho?" Merlin said as he held the plate of chips, cheese, beef, and diced toppings out toward Jophi. She took one hesitantly and crunched loudly into the crispy chip. Azrael felt his eyes widen from being ignored, but just before he repeated his earlier assertion, Merlin continued. "Do you want to make a trip to Bat's bedroom?"

Azrael narrowed his eyes as Prateek and Oslow also took a nacho from Merlin. Bat even went as far as to stand up and get one for himself. Merlin looked over the group and smiled. "I see three of you have the qualifications to become my prospective students as well. Bat, I think you should reapply next semester," he said as he held the plate out to the Batman.

Bat turned to Azrael and smiled broadly; his sharp teeth evident but no longer menacing to Azrael. Azrael allowed a small smile onto his lips before he returned a flat stare to

Merlin. "That's great, Merlin, but why would going to Bat's bedroom matter?"

"Surely you have noticed the shiny wood, extra comfortable bed, and delectable smell of new wood inside that room?" Merlin retorted while chuckling.

Azrael looked at Bat, whose cheeks had gone a bit purple. "You never claimed your bed was better than any of the others in the house..." Azrael began but realized that his friend hadn't wanted to lose the best spot in the place. He turned back to Merlin. "So you're saying every room in the villa needs to get to that state to complete your requirements?"

"No, I am not saying anything like that. This place is already in a far better state than it has been in years. You won't get expelled, and can consider the task complete. I'm just wondering if you noticed the difference..."

Azrael breathed out through his nose. Of course he had noticed the difference. "Do you remember that I passed out after repairing that room?" Azrael retorted huffily.

"Have you found out how to create a container that can hold something you can't see yet?" Merlin asked, before winking and vanishing on the spot, with his plate of nachos.

"Hold something you can't see?" Jophi asked while touching her chest and Azrael shook his head slightly.

He still needed to decide whether he should share the skill, and subsequent breakthroughs, with Oslow and Prateek. Their eyes had narrowed suspiciously ever since Merlin claimed that three of the group were eligible to become prospective students.

Azrael took a bite of his steak and considered the current situation. He had arrived on Tech Duinn with two teachers, and left the planet with one teacher and two people he now considered friends. Could he include two more in that circle of trust?

ABOUT RYAN DEBRUYN

Ryan has always been a dream chaser. His first career was as a professional athlete, which taught him the dedication and perseverance needed to chase fantastic goals. A devastating injury removed Ryan from this world before his prime, and taught him the value of an education.

His first book began as a hobby project while he attended Georgian College. Using his hard fought lessons, in motivation, discipline and hard work Ryan published his first book in February 2019.

He is a recent graduate in the field of Electrical Engineering and a full-time author.

Here's hoping you enjoy the worlds he creates as much as he does!

Connect with Ryan:
Facebook.com/RyanDeBruyn
Patreon.com/RyanDeBruyn
Instagram.com/AuthorRyanDeBruyn

ABOUT MOUNTAINDALE PRESS

Dakota and Danielle Krout, a husband and wife team, strive to create as well as publish excellent fantasy and science fiction novels. Self-publishing *The Divine Dungeon: Dungeon Born* in 2016 transformed their careers from Dakota's military and programming background and Danielle's Ph.D. in pharmacology to President and CEO, respectively, of a small press. Their goal is to share their success with other authors and provide captivating fiction to readers with the purpose of solidifying Mountaindale Press as the place 'Where Fantasy Transforms Reality.'

Connect with Mountaindale Press:
MountaindalePress.com
Facebook.com/MountaindalePress
Twitter.com/_Mountaindale
Instagram.com/MountaindalePress

MOUNTAINDALE PRESS TITLES
GameLit and LitRPG

The Completionist Chronicles,
The Divine Dungeon, and
Full Murderhobo by Dakota Krout

Arcana Unlocked by Gregory Blackburn

A Touch of Power by Jay Boyce

Red Mage and
Farming Livia by Xander Boyce

Space Seasons by Dawn Chapman

Ether Collapse and
Ether Flows by Ryan DeBruyn

Bloodgames by Christian J. Gilliland

Threads of Fate by Michael Head

Lion's Lineage by Rohan Hublikar and Dakota Krout

Wolfman Warlock by James Hunter and Dakota Krout

Axe Druid,
Mephisto's Magic Online, and
High Table Hijinks by Christopher Johns

Skeleton in Space by Andries Louws

Chronicles of Ethan by John L. Monk

Pixel Dust and
Necrotic Apocalypse by David Petrie

Henchman by Carl Stubblefield

Artorian's Archives by Dennis Vanderkerken and Dakota Krout

www.ingramcontent.com/pod-product-compliance
Lightning Source LLC
Chambersburg PA
CBHW030925020726
47498CB00001B/120